No Dukes Allowed

KELLY BOWEN
GRACE BURROWES
ANNA HARRINGTON

TABLE OF CONTENTS

Architect of my Dreams by Grace Burrowes   5

Pursuit of Honor by Kelly Bowen   126

The Double Duchess by Anna Harrington   201

Architect of My Dreams

Grace Burrowes

To those who dream big dreams

CHAPTER ONE

"How I envy you those new neighbors," Lady Alice said, smiling archly behind her tea cup. "All that masculine pulchritude parading before your very doorstep. You must promise to have more at-homes, Your Grace."

"One a week is quite enough." Given Eugenia's distaste for gossip, one at-home a week was more than enough. "Masculine pulchritude pales compared to the pleasures of a good night's sleep."

Lady Alice set down her tea cup. "Did you mean that the way it sounded? I know His Grace wasn't the most congenial of husbands, but one manages."

A fourth hammer—or fifth—joined the din coming from the property across the street. Men shouted back and forth amid the noise, and the jingle of harnesses sang a descant over the cacophony. Not fashionable coaches, of course. One delivery of lumber, stone, and nails after another, and all of it beginning before dawn and ending after sunset.

"One manages best with adequate rest," Eugenia replied. "What sort of barbarian disturbs his neighbors' slumber day after day, night after night?"

Lady Alice helped herself to another cinnamon biscuit. She was doubtless increasing again, else she'd stop at two. "He is a barbarian, you know."

"Who is?"

The noise grew louder, counterpointing the pounding in Eugenia's temples. This was the third week of incessant racket from the construction across the street, the third week of being roused scant hours after her head hit the pillow. The approaching full moon would doubtless result in noise round the clock.

"Your new neighbor is Adam Morecambe." Lady Alice talked around a mouthful of biscuit. "Francis says they call him More-coin in the better clubs."

Name-calling being the hallmark of adult gentlemen, of course. "Mr. Morecambe is taking up residence on my street?"

Eugenia lived in a corner of Mayfair that was more exclusive than fashionable. The families around her had been original investors on this square, and her town house was one of the ducal dower properties.

"Oh my, no. Morecambe isn't building himself a palace over there. He's converting the Campbell mansion into a gentlemen's club. Francis calls it the Blackball Club, because they're admitting only commoners, or that's the rumor."

A great crash sounded from across the street as a load of stone cascaded from the back of a wagon onto what had once been a tidily swept walkway. Mr. Morecambe had apparently devised some mechanism for tilting the bed of the wagon such that the contents, aided by gravity and accompanied by a horrific racket, delivered themselves to the ground.

"That's it," Eugenia said. "Even a duchess has limits. You are welcome to the rest of the biscuits, Alice. I have a barbarian to instruct."

"I want the recipe," Lady Alice said, swiping another treat from the tray as she rose. "I'm coming with you. Morecambe isn't a gentleman, and Francis says—"

"Enough of what Francis says, for God's sake. I am the Dowager Duchess of Tindale, and on my doorstep, what I say should matter."

* * *

"Works a treat, every time," Rosenbarker said as the mason's apprentices began piling the stones onto the lifts. "Wish you'd thought of this tipping business ten years ago."

As the apprentice turned the crank, the wagon bed slowly returned to level, a sight that always gave Adam Morecambe pleasure. The mechanism was essentially a large screw with a shallow thread angle, rotated by a long handle. Thanks to Mr. Maudsley's screw-cutting lathe, an invention a mere two decades old, Adam was making other wagons like it.

"The gears sound like they need oiling," he said, "and the whole purpose of the tipper wagon is so work can proceed more efficiently, not so you can stand around admiring the results."

The bed settled, the apprentice threw the brace securing the crank handle, and the driver gave the horses the signal to trot off.

"I do hope you've built rest for the horses into the schedule," Rosenbarker said. "Nobody designed them any fancy mechanisms to ease their work, and when the stones were unloaded by hand, the horses got a half hour's respite."

"They need half an hour's rest for every load? That much?"

Rosenbarker took off his glasses and used a wrinkled handkerchief to clean them. Building was dusty work.

"You needn't allow the horses their rest, Morecambe. You can simply work them until they drop. Then the seasoned teams wear out faster, the nervous youngsters are put to in greater quantity, and we have more coaches galloping off across more village greens on market day. The choice is yours."

Solomon Rosenbarker's memory was one of his finest qualities—usually. "That was one team, three years ago, and I still contend a wasp was involved."

Rosenbarker widened his stance and stuffed his glasses in one pocket, his handkerchief in the other. "Two and a half years, and the cost in damages ate up twenty percent of—you have trouble, sir. The kind that wears bonnets."

Rosenbarker sidled away to supervise the sorting of the rocks, which needed no supervision. The old rascal was staying close enough to overhear the coming confrontation, but far enough away so that no stray verbal bullets would threaten him.

Trouble was a fetching pair of women in fashionable day dresses. The taller of the two wore the gaudier bonnet—two birds and an entire bouquet of silk roses. She also carried a lot of pink lace on a stick that was probably intended to resemble a parasol.

The smaller woman walked slightly ahead of her companion. Her bonnet was plain straw, her parasol unpretentious. Adam had no interest in women's fashions, or in most women, but he knew an angry swish of skirts from a flirtatious swish of skirts, and the small woman had no flirtation on her mind.

"You are Mr. Morecambe," she said, marching directly up to Adam.

"And you are angry."

She was also pretty, though quietly so. Brown eyes framed with brows heavier than was fashionable, regular features, and a full mouth pinched with ire. Her hair was dark brown, what he could see of it, and she eschewed cosmetics.

The lady's companion, then, charging forth at the behest of her more genteel associate. Somewhere on this street lived a dowager duchess, giving the neighborhood a dash of titled cachet. Had the street been burdened with a ducal residence, Adam would never have bought the Campbell property.

"I am not angry, Mr. Morecambe, I am exhausted and tormented by noise the livelong day. I refuse to suffer in silence any longer."

He knew better than to apply logic to an annoyed woman, and yet, he asked the obvious question. "How can one suffer in silence if the noise is incessant?"

She looked down her nose at him, quite a feat considering she was nearly a foot shorter than he.

"Be obtuse if your intellect is truly that limited, sir, but save your disrespect for those to whom such a slight would matter. I demand some quiet."

Rosenbarker was studying the pile of rocks. The other woman was pretending to be fascinated with the work site. Typical of London's upper class, she was allowing her minion to do the figurative heavy lifting.

"Then I suggest you go somewhere quieter," Adam said. "Nobody's stopping you."

"The common law of this great land says that you are the party who needs to go elsewhere," Plain Bonnet retorted. "A woman is entitled to the quiet enjoyment of her domicile, as are my neighbors. That is the law. You will either accommodate the law, or deal with the consequences."

Frilly Parasol was looking amused. Rosenbarker was blatantly staring.

Keep the lawyers out of sight was the first rule of sound business.

That was Adam's last thought before somebody three floors up called out, "'Ware bucket!" in a thick Lancastrian accent.

Adam reacted instinctively, grabbing the woman and snatching her six feet farther from the street as a deluge of mud rained down from the scaffolding. Rosenbarker commenced swearing at the offending mason's apprentice. Lady Frilly Parasol was laughing outright, and Adam was holding a small, curvaceous bundle of female closer than he'd held a woman in months.

"Let me go," she said in a low, furious voice. "By the father of all mischief, if that is your idea of a joke, I will set fire to your benighted boys club during the four hours each night when none of your fiends are at work upon it. I will tear down every brick and stone and turn loose a plague of rodents upon your foundations. I will implore the heavens to stop your work with forty days and nights of rain. I will take my crusade to the journalists, who are ever mindful that widows in the throes of plights sell broadsheets."

Adam turned her loose. "I'm a plight?" He wasn't sure how he felt about being a plight, though the woman's creativity was impressive.

"We are airing our differences on the street, or I'd be more blunt. Suffice it to say that your project is a plight, a plague, and a pestilence upon the peace of my home."

If there was a second commandment in Adam's business bible, it was to keep the journalists farther away from all projects than the lawyers, and trailing behind those two eternal verities was some nonsense about not arguing with a lady.

Adam had always thought that prohibition disrespectful of the ladies. In his experience, they were more than capable of holding their own in a verbal sparring match. Arguing with *this* lady was downright invigorating.

"Renovations are noisy undertakings," Adam said. "Fortunately for you, our schedule will have us finished up by the end of the summer." He smiled, because antagonizing the neighbors was stupid. "A few more months, and you'll have an elegant façade where the Campbell's crumbling abode once stood. Your street will gain consequence, and—"

"Stop it," she snapped.

The hod carriers and masons weren't due for their afternoon break for another hour, and yet, work from the scaffolding above had gone oddly quiet.

"Stop what?"

"You have offended a lady. The proper response is to apologize, not to explain the obvious in overly simplistic terms. If I had somehow arrived to the age of eight and twenty in ignorance of the fact that renovations are noisy, the past ten weeks would have proved the point handily. I care not one crumbled brick what your schedule says. The schedule of every decent beast on the planet calls for adequate and regular periods of rest and quiet."

She'd jabbed his chest on the final three words: "rest"—*jab*—"and"—

jab—"quiet"—*jab-jab*.

How could one small finger cause such a sharp pain? "We don't work at night."

"Mr. Morecambe, at this time of year, London enjoys almost eighteen hours of daylight, and that means your workers are already making a racket some two or three hours after polite society has gone to bed."

"Why should I care about polite society?"

She stepped back, her gaze assessing. "Why shouldn't you? Polite society will be your neighbors and, I assume, the membership of your little establishment, if not its investors. Do you really want the ladies on all sides up in arms against you before you open your doors?"

Adam was not much skilled at dealing with ladies. He shot a glance at Rosenbarker, whose expression conveyed foreboding.

"No," Adam said, "but neither do I want my investors up in arms if the project falls behind schedule. If we're not finished with the exterior by the end of September, we'll have to halt until spring, and that will be costly."

He cast a scowl at the crew now shamelessly goggling from their perches on the floors above. They grinned at him. One fellow saluted with his hammer. Another bowed over his bucket of mortar.

"If you do not allow me and my neighbors some rest," the lady said, "we will seek redress from the courts and enjoin you from working more than ten hours a day."

She spoke as if a judge stood ready to do her bidding, but then, spinsters—she was eight-and-twenty and loose on her own recognizance— were a particularly eccentric class of female.

"What exactly are you asking of me, madam?"

"I am departing from Town on Monday. I would like to begin my journey refreshed and rested. For the next three days, you will not allow your crews to start until nine of the clock."

Lose three hours of labor per day per man on a thirty-man crew? Fall back two hundred and seventy hours *in three days*?

"What you ask is impossible."

"Very well. Best call for the ratter, because you leave me no choice but to take matters into my own hands."

She looked as if she relished that prospect. "I cannot lose hundreds of hours of labor when the weather is fair and deliveries have already been scheduled."

"Then send your deliveries around back, for heaven's sake."

The other woman opened her lacy parasol and twirled it over her shoulder. "You seem to have the situation well in hand, my dear. I'll just be going." She kissed the shorter woman on the cheek, sent Adam a pitying look, and swanned off. Across the street, a footman opened the door to a fancy landau.

"She leaves you to fight this battle alone?"

"This is *my* battle, sir."

Adam's neighbor had faint shadows under her eyes, and her dress was of the pale gray usually worn in second mourning. No jewelry, not even a brooch, adorned her attire. Rosenbarker's warning about the draft teams wearing out faster if they weren't rested enough came to mind.

"You are the only person to complain of the noise," he said, "and you are soon to leave Town."

"Everybody is soon to leave Town, and then you can use the full moon to renovate through the night. I wish you the joy of that undertaking, but not until next week, please."

Long ago, Adam had danced attendance on a proper lady. He'd haunted Mayfair's ballrooms in hopes of a waltz with her, attended every Venetian breakfast and musicale in a vain effort to spend more time at her side.

He'd ended up numb with exhaustion and despair, which was probably the only reason he hadn't finished the Season by delivering a challenge to a certain duke. Not that His Grace would have met Adam on the field of honor. Peers did not accept the challenges of commoners, which worked very nicely for the peer and not at all for the wronged commoner.

"I can have the deliveries sent around back for the next three days. I'll tell the men not to start hammering until eight a.m."

"Thank you, and please do exhort them to use less colorful language."

She could exhort them to that end, and they'd probably listen. This small woman had presence, and she would be Adam's neighbor. He could afford to accommodate her wishes on this one occasion—he hoped.

"I'll make that request of the crews and wish you a pleasant respite in the country."

She offered her hand. At first, he thought she wanted to shake hands with him, as if solemnizing the beginning of a pugilists' match. He bowed over her hand after a moment of consternation.

She wished him good day and sashayed back from whence she'd

come—a modest, tidy dwelling across the street.

"Get to work," Rosenbarker called to the crews. "Back to work, ye bloody dunderwhelps, or I'll know the reason why."

On her doorstep, the lady turned, her expression pained.

"Language, Rosenbarker," Adam muttered.

"What the hell's wrong with my bloody bedamned—? Oh." He swiped off his hat. "Beg pardon, missus," he called across the street.

She slipped into the house, and within seconds, somebody was pounding away with a hammer. A second and third hammer joined in, a hod carrier started singing about Barbara Allen, and one of the Welshmen glazing windows added harmony.

"We do make quite a racket, don't we?" Adam mused.

"That's the sound of progress," Rosenbarker said.

Noisy progress. The lady hadn't been wrong. Thank goodness Adam was also traveling away from Town, because some peace and quiet by the seaside would be much appreciated.

CHAPTER TWO

Because the seaside was the last place Lord Dunstable would look for Genie, to Brighton she did go. Then too, Diana and Belinda were joining her there, and the company of friends was a much-missed comfort.

"The scent here is always the same," Belinda said, linking arms with Genie.

"I've never been able to determine if that stink is gossip or rotten eggs," Genie replied, matching her steps to her taller friend. "Or court intrigue. Thank heavens the king's entire coterie has not yet arrived."

Neither had Diana, though she was expected that afternoon. Belinda and Genie were taking the air, one of the most popular activities in Brighton.

"How is Tindale?" Belinda asked.

Two gentlemen tipped their hats, though Genie recognized neither one. "His Grace thrives in the company of his duchess. I do believe they were a love match."

She managed that observation without sounding too envious. Genie and the previous duke had not been a love match. Charles had considered himself a decent husband, meaning he'd never taken his mistresses to the theater when Genie attended, and he'd never openly chastised her for failing to produce an heir.

The rhythm of the surf was punctuated by the cries of gulls overhead, and Genie finally began to relax. Brighton had been her haven, her respite from all things London. She'd come here to escape from the relentless burden of having married far above her station and to heal from the miscarriage. Tindale had left her alone in Brighton, one of the truest acts of consideration he'd shown her.

"You're quiet," Belinda said. "Was the trip down from Town tiring?"

"I'm a trifle fatig—merciful powers, he's here."

A gentleman approached, a lady on his arm. He was exquisitely turned out and so, of course, was she.

Belinda marched along, though Genie wanted to dodge behind the nearest hedge. Why, oh why, did Isambard Bentley, Marquess of Dunstable, have to be in Brighton now?

"Duchess!" he called, tipping his hat. "And Duchess." He bowed to Belinda and then to Genie, the dukedom of Winchester standing higher in precedence than the dukedom of Tindale. "What a pleasant surprise. I'm sure you're acquainted with Lady Naughton."

Lady Naughton was a sylphlike blonde who was no better than she should be, though she avoided outright impropriety. Genie silently commended the woman on organizing her life around who and what she wanted, though why anybody would enjoy having a parcel of randy men sniffing around her skirts was a mystery.

The ladies curtseyed, and Genie gave Belinda's arm a discreet tug. "We'll let you be on your way on this fine day," Genie said. "One must enjoy the sea air while the weather remains obliging."

Belinda, confound her, remained fixed to the walkway like a lamppost. "What brings you to the seaside, my lord?"

"The beauty," he said, treating both duchesses to calf-eyed mooning. "The excellent company, the healthful pastimes."

A ducal heir's notions about healthful pastimes did not include sea bathing and likely did include gambling, horse racing, and large quantities of liquor.

Genie tried another tug on Belinda's arm. "Taking the air is a pleasure on a day such as this, and I do so enjoy my constitutional."

"Oh, but the sun," Lady Naughton said, twirling her parasol. "One must have a care for one's complexion, particularly later in life."

God spare me. "With that in mind," Genie replied, "I won't ask you to tarry any longer." She hauled Belinda forward before her ladyship could observe that exercise was beneficial for the elderly.

"What an insecure, jealous cat," Belinda said before they'd gone far enough to be out of earshot.

"I find her impressive, insulting two duchesses at one go, but then,

Perhaps you'd like to have a tour of the premises? The whole dwelling is lovely."

An offer of tea with two duchesses had produced only a scowl. The chance to inspect the house had Mr. Morecambe opening the gate.

"Most kind of you, though you needn't bother with the tea."

How refreshingly honest. Genie linked arms with him. "We're duchesses. We always bother with the tea."

He hesitated on the front step. "*Both* of you are duchesses?"

Hadn't they just boldly introduced themselves as such two minutes ago?

"Dowager duchesses," Belinda said, as if that was the most unremarkable status a woman could hold. Belinda was, in fact, the famed Double Duchess, having a second duke panting about her heels. She detested the nickname. Genie suspected Belinda detested her ducal suitor as well.

"We put out a hearty tray," Genie said, "and you will find the arrangement of the pantries ingenious."

The allure of the pantry layout appeared to intrigue him. He paused to study the knocker—a rampant gryphon rendered in brass—then followed the ladies into the house.

* * *

Adam had no use for duchesses.

They were merely a blight upon the social landscape, however, while dukes merited his unending ire. A duke had a legal right to consult with the sovereign, could not be arrested for civil wrongs, and any criminal charges against him were tried in the House of Lords—the original exclusive gentlemen's club.

Worst of all, dukes could not be jailed for unpaid debts.

Duchesses, however, were technically commoners and thus earned a vague resentment from Adam rather than unrelenting disdain.

Resenting these two ladies would be difficult. Her Grace of Winchester was lovely, with expressive green eyes, a flawless complexion, and a voice that conveyed equal parts refinement and gracious warmth.

She was, in other words, exactly as a fairy-tale duchess ought to be.

Her Grace of Tindale, however, was in need of some renovation if she sought to present herself as the former helpmeet of a duke. She wore the same plain bonnet she'd had on last week, her dress was several years out of date and loose about the bodice, and across her nose and cheeks appeared a smattering of freckles.

Adam liked those freckles. They put him in mind of goose girls and tavern maids, women who did honest work and didn't put on airs. Her Grace's eyes were brown, friendly, and intelligent, and what she lacked in stature, she made up for in unpretentiousness.

"What brings you to Brighton?" she asked.

Adam accepted his tea in a porcelain cup adorned with pink roses and gold trim. "Business."

Both ladies gazed at him expectantly. Making conversation with proper women felt like taking a sledgehammer to a plaster wall—sheer effort and slow going.

"I'm looking over some residential properties," he added. "For possible purchase."

"You're shopping," the Duchess of Tindale said. "I haven't the knack for shopping."

Adam set down his tea cup carefully. He'd smashed more than one porcelain delicacy by accident.

"Choosing real estate to invest in isn't the same as picking out a new pair of slippers."

"Oh yes, it is," Her Grace of Tindale replied. "You examine all the possibilities, consult your budget, consider the priorities controlling your decision, then make a choice and hope for the best."

Her Grace of Winchester nodded. "Shopping, in a nutshell. Would anybody like more tea?"

Adam wanted to bolt from the tufted sofa and take his quizzing glass to the scrollwork running in two vertical columns above the mantel. The elaborate carvings framed a space occupied by a picture of a small boy standing beside a seated mastiff.

At the ceiling, the carving branched out into molding, which echoed a pattern of grapes and leaves interspersed with flowers. The transition from wooden carving to plaster molding was nearly invisible and exactly matched by smaller carvings on the underside of the mantel. The leaves appeared to be oak, the symbol for bravery, while the flowers—

"Mr. Morecambe?"

The duchesses were looking a trifle perplexed.

"Beg pardon?"

"I asked," said Her Grace of Tindale, "if you were in the market for any particular sort of property."

He was searching for a bargain, an overlooked jewel that wanted only a little care and appreciation to make it shine.

"I'm building a gentlemen's club in London, as you know. It has been suggested that we obtain smaller properties in Brighton, Bath, and Bristol for the convenience of our members."

"You'll want a residential property, then," Her Grace of Tindale said. "Close to the Pavilion and the beach, but not so close as to be prohibitively expensive."

"Recently refurbished," Her Other Grace added. "Not too recently. New construction is out of the question—a house newly built might start to leak or shift at any time—but those poky little medieval houses won't do either. The stairways in them are not to be borne."

The ladies commenced tossing back and forth the qualities of various streets—this one was near the market, that one had lovely neighbors—and Adam tried to listen, but it was no use. The scrollwork called to him, the mechanism for latching the windows wasn't one he'd seen before, and a vent at floor level along one wall intrigued him.

"If you'll excuse me," the Duchess of Winchester said, rising. "I've still some unpacking to tend to. Mr. Morecambe, a pleasure."

Then he was alone with the Duchess of Tindale and a house that cried out to be explored.

"I promised you a tour of the premises," she said. "Shall we start in the attics?"

"Always a fine plan." For the proof was in the roof, as one of Adam's master masons liked to say. If a house had been poorly constructed, the inferior materials, uneven foundation, and cut corners first took a toll on how the structure and roof joined. Water soon made an unwelcome appearance where water didn't belong—in chimneys, walls, attics, and so forth—and then the whole building was jeopardized.

"You will not find a water stain, if that's what has your gaze fixed to the ceilings," the duchess said as she led him into a dormitory under the eaves. "The present owner is my godmother, and she stewards her resources carefully."

The dormitory was both dry and airy, a comfortable place for the maids to sleep, with windows to let in light.

"Building properly is always the better bargain," Adam said, running his hand down the plaster wall. No subtle dampness, no unevenness better perceived by touch than sight. "Practice too many economies, take too many liberties, and you invite cracks, leaks, shifts, and poor workmanship."

"Rather like falsehoods in a relationship," Her Grace said, trailing a finger over the mantel. "An omission becomes a white lie, which becomes a well-meant untruth, that over time becomes a breach of trust."

She dusted her fingers together, rubbing away a fine smudge. Whatever had brought such a farfetched analogy to her mind had also chased the warmth from her eyes.

"Shall we inspect the attic?" Adam asked.

"Of course. I doubt there's much stored on the premises. Godmama mostly lends the house to friends or stays for only short periods herself."

The duchess spoke knowledgeably about each piece of art on the walls, each sideboard and reading chair. The dwelling was lovely, and the library a masterpiece in miniature. For those carvings, Adam did take out his quizzing glass to admire work so delicate, the hand of a master was obvious.

"These have to be Grinling Gibbons's work," he said. "Certainly from his workshop, but I'd be surprised if they weren't original to him." Personal woodcarver to both Charles II and James II, Gibbons had created works of genius for many a great house. His lintels of flowers were said to be so lifelike, a passing coach would cause them to bob in the breeze.

The duchess stuck her finger into a bouquet of daisies in a bowl of Delftware. The bird-pine-flower design suggested the vase was at least a hundred years old.

Her Grace shook droplets of water from her finger. "You've seen Petworth, I take it?"

"I've been marched through the long gallery once, by a housekeeper who clearly feared I'd be filching the valuables."

"That does sound like Mrs. Bryce. I can take you back there any time you please, and I can assure you, Mrs. Bryce will be more accommodating. What is the point of having such beautiful homes if they are admired and enjoyed by only a few? As an architect, you should have been welcomed."

The duchess used a pitcher from the sideboard to give the daisies a drink.

"You do know what the vase is worth?" When the Chinese had closed their porcelain export business in the early seventeenth century, the Dutch potters had created designs to compensate for the lack of imports. The work was exquisite, but when the Chinese resumed trading their wares, the Dutch had moved on to other inspirations. The container holding the mundane bouquet was a rare and beautiful antique.

"The vase is pretty enough to merit a spot in the window," she said, "so passersby can enjoy the lovely flowers too."

She was like no kind of duchess Adam had imagined, and as she'd led him all throughout this jewel of a house—the pantries were ingenious, the parlors exquisite, the bedrooms delightful—he'd admired everything, from the appointments, to the architecture, to the craftsmanship.

He'd admired *her* architecture, too, from trim ankles, to rounded hips, to hands that were both graceful and competent. She was not overly endowed in the bosom, but Adam had always preferred modest perfection to ample mediocrity.

He mentally dropped a hammer on his foot at that ungentlemanly thought.

"Would you like to sketch that scrollery?" she asked, crossing to the desk. "You've been staring a hole in it."

"Sketch it?" He would dearly, dearly love to make a drawing of the woodwork and to make enough notes to recall the layout of the whole dwelling. "If that wouldn't be too great an imposition."

She set paper, pencils, a penknife, and standish on the blotter. "I'll leave you to it. The bell-pull will summon the housekeeper, and I'll have the kitchen send you up a proper tray. Tea cakes and gunpowder will hardly be adequate for a man of your robust proportions."

Her gaze was frankly appraising. Not flirtatious, simply a hostess taking the measure of a guest and pronouncing him hungry.

Which Adam was—for food, but also to capture this house on paper. "Your hospitality is much appreciated."

"We're to be neighbors," she said, beaming at him as if being neighbors was the most enjoyable mischief known to humankind. "Make yourself at home, and I'll look in on you later."

She left the room after one more quick perusal of the accoutrements on the blotter, and Adam took a seat at the desk. The pencils were sharp, so he could set immediately memorializing what he'd seen. The carvings, the floor plans, the window latches, the ingenious vent that let heat from the kitchen rise to the family parlor.

The image that took shape on the page was a homage to lovely architecture: gracious, pleasing, and—where was the harm in a quick portrait?—sporting freckles across her cheeks.

CHAPTER THREE

Genie sat in the family parlor and tried to ignore the fact that a man occupied the library only a few yards away. An attractive, intelligent man.

Mr. Morecambe had accepted the tray from the kitchen more than an hour ago, and Genie had spent the intervening time staring at the pages of Sir Walter Scott's *Ivanhoe*. The story was too much about brave knights hiding who they really were, getting wounded and killed, and acting like complete gudgeons. The ladies merely looked pretty and endured propositions, except for Rebecca the healer.

She possessed courage and lifesaving skills and doubtless had had wonderful adventures in far-off Granada.

"I am no Rebecca," Genie informed the marmalade cat. "I am merely a dowager duchess without offspring." The most pathetic creature in all of Debrett's.

One of few appointments in Godmama's house that Genie disliked was a stuffed nightingale arranged in a gilded cage amid silk roses. The little bird stared at her out of glass eyes, until Genie wanted to fling *Ivanhoe* at the wall.

Mr. Morecambe's interest in the house had been passionate. He'd traced the woodwork with his bare fingers, sniffed the dried herbal sachets—lavender for the library, rose for the parlor, jasmine for Genie's sitting room—and rapped on any number of walls. He'd engaged with the house more purposefully than some men engaged with their partners for the waltz.

"What could he be doing over there?"

He'd merely peered into her bedroom, an airy, high-ceilinged retreat featuring a bed large enough to hold most of Genie's six brothers. She'd been seized with an impulse to lock the door and fling herself into Mr. Morecambe's arms.

"There will be none of that," she muttered, rising. "Dunstable is underfoot, and any breath of scandal will reach his ears, and then where will I be?"

The one consolation left to Genie, was that she was invited everywhere, had friends of varying degrees in most fashionable neighborhoods, and came and went as she pleased. She had worked long and hard and paid a very high price to be worthy of polite society's acceptance. Should Dunstable make good on his threat to drag her name through the sewer, even those comforts would be gone.

"But nothing says I must forgo an outing with a prospective neighbor," she murmured, hand on the door latch. "I am a widow and have earned my freedom up to a point."

She crossed the corridor and paused outside the library long enough to rap softly on the paneled door.

No response. Mr. Morecambe was likely absorbed in his sketching. What would it be like for him to focus on her? She had known one moment in his arms back in London, and those arms had been strong and sheltering.

"I'd likely need a roof and shutters before he took any special notice of me."

She pushed open the library door to find her guest seated at the desk, boots propped on the corner, arms folded, chin on his chest. A gentle snore wafted across the room, and as the cat stropped himself across Genie's ankles, she feasted on the sight of Adam Morecambe in shirt-sleeves, fast asleep.

* * *

A sharp rap on the door startled Adam from dreams of wooden flowers and freckled geese. His boots dropped to the floor, nearly clobbering an indignant orange cat.

"Where did you come from?"

The cat squinted, and the knock sounded again on the door, more firmly.

"Come in."

The Duchess of Tindale presented herself, looking as feminine and pleasing as she had in Adam's dreams, but wearing a good deal more clothing. He rose from behind the desk, holding his sketches in a manner intended to hide the evidence of his wayward imagination.

"Mr. Morecambe." She popped a brisk curtsey. "I'm looking in on you, as a hostess ought to. Do you have all you need?"

"I apparently needed a nap," he said. *And a thorough dousing in the frigid Channel surf.* "That is a diabolically comfortable chair." He shrugged into his coat as casually as he could, though Her Grace had been married. A man in dishabille would hardly shock her.

"I have remarked the same on the occasion of tending to my ledgers," she said. "The combination of accounting and that chair induces sleep even first thing in the morning. I've sent off a note to Petworth House."

Petworth was the finest collection of interior woodcarving in all of England, possibly in all the world.

"I beg your pardon?"

"I hope Friday suits. Godmama's gardener vows the weather will hold fair for the rest of the week. We can make a picnic of the outing."

She was inviting him on a tour of Petworth. Also, a picnic.

With her.

On the occasion of Adam's first encounter with the duchess, he'd swept her into his arms to spare her a soaking. The contact had startled him. He'd not held a woman closely for ages, hadn't wanted to. His every spare moment and thought went to building his business, and he liked it that way. Her Grace had tolerated the embrace for exactly two instants before she'd righted herself and shaken her skirts, but they had been lovely instants.

She was sturdy, lively, and friendly. None of which explained why Adam wanted to kiss her.

"I trust Lord and Lady Egremont will not be in residence?" he asked.

"Off to Paris. We'll have the place to ourselves."

To themselves and an army of servants. "Friday, you say?" Adam mentally rearranged lunch with friends as well as four other appointments to see properties for sale.

"Have you a conveyance?" she asked. "We can take my traveling carriage or the landau if the weather's fine."

"I'll drive," Adam said, lest he find himself plodding through the countryside when the time could be better spent marveling at the wonders of Petworth. "Shall we leave around eight in the morning?"

"Earlier than that," she replied, rolling up his sketches and handing them to him. "We have the long hours of daylight, we might as well use them. Leave the picnic basket to me and plan on a lovely day."

"The crack of dawn, then," he said, bowing over her hand as best he could with his sketches tucked under his arm. "I'll look forward to it."

The prospect of a day bouncing along the lanes of Sussex had her beaming at him, and her pleasure turned an unremarkable countenance luminous. Her eyes lit with such benevolence, that Adam held on to her hand longer than was strictly proper. She had a subtle beauty, not the boring, cameo-perfect appearance of the typical titled lady, but a personal loveliness that would make the hours until Friday morning long.

And busy.

She saw Adam to the front door, where no servant sat in attendance collecting gossip and spying on the walkway.

"Do you know," Adam said, "I do believe you are my favorite duchess in the entire world."

"How many duchesses do you know, Mr. Morecambe?"

"Two." Not strictly true. As a youth, he'd once been introduced to the Duchess of Seymouth, who'd regarded him as so much dung clinging to her slipper.

"You are my favorite architect."

"How many do you know?"

She went up on her toes and brushed a kiss to his cheek. "One, and I am looking forward to getting to know him better."

Adam tapped his hat onto his head, accepted his walking stick from her, and left the house without even taking the time to examine the fine Palladian window above the lintel.

* * *

The hamper was packed—a hamper, not a mere basket—and Genie had dressed in her most fashionable carriage ensemble. The early hour was not a reflection of her enthusiasm for stately country houses, but rather, her need to leave Brighton unobserved.

Mr. Morecambe's chaise pulled up in front of the house before the sun had topped the horizon, while the world was still in that sweet, quiet, predawn gloom. Rather than make him come into the house, Genie met him on the walk.

"Good morning, Mr. Morecambe. You are punctual."

He bowed over her hand. "Are you running away from home, Duchess?

That looks more like a wicker trunk than a picnic basket."

Genie had longed to run away, back home to Derbyshire, which guilty thought had her climbing into the vehicle unassisted.

"The day could be long, and who knows what fare will be available at the posting inns? Is this fine fellow yours?" The horse was a handsome bay, easily seventeen hands, no white on him anywhere.

"Caliban will eat my oats and pretend he's doing me a favor," Mr. Morecambe said, setting the basket behind the seat and taking the place beside Genie. "We can leave him at the first change, let him rest all day, and pick him up on our way home. Move, horse."

With a flick of a dark tail, the gelding trotted on.

Dunstable might have stayed at the Seymouth family property in Brighton, except his mama the duchess complained to all and sundry that the house was uninhabitable, a musty hovel built by an incompetent scoundrel.

Having no family residence at his command, Dunstable was thus biding with his friend, Viscount Luddington, heir to the earl of the same title. Genie had made it her business to know that the viscount's house lay on the opposite side of the Steyne from Godmama's. No telling from whose bed Dunstable might be stumbling home at daybreak, though, so Genie tied her straw hat with a scarf, securing it to her head like a brimmed bonnet.

"I should tell you that I am not highly regarded among some titled families," Mr. Morecambe said.

Interesting place to start a conversation. "Neither am I. I failed to produce a baby duke. What was your transgression?"

He glanced over at her as the horse gained the fields at the edge of town. They'd drive mostly north, toward the Downs, and being away from even the genteel streets of Brighton helped Genie breathe more easily.

"I am a commoner with airs above my station," Mr. Morecambe said. "How long were you married?"

"Five long years. You will think me awful, but becoming a duchess was not a pleasant adjustment. I was a gentry heiress—copper mining proved a very wise investment several generations back—and thus I was bound to marry a man with an impoverished title. My father was determined to see his progeny rise in the world, and I was determined to make my papa happy."

"That sounds like a fine ambition, to make your family happy. What does your father say now?"

"Not a word. We laid him to rest three years ago. This is such a beautiful time of day." Genie had forgotten how cheering, how fragrant with hope dawn was. She'd never quite lost the sense of having disappointed not only Charles, but also Papa, and to have this conversation so early in the day was especially painful.

"Do you miss your husband?"

The question was personal, also one Genie had considered many times. "Yes, and no. Charles was not a bad man, but he was an indifferent husband. He needed a duchess, a gracious, poised woman who could produce multiple sons in quick succession while making no demands of him that couldn't be met from her pin money. I was a disappointment, and it took me some while to realize just how egregious my shortcomings were. I exasperated him, he bewildered me. I wanted a marriage, he wanted a secure succession."

The sun crested the surrounding hills as Caliban trotted through the first crossroads, and Mr. Morecambe steered the chaise smoothly onto the northward turning.

"What could you miss about such a union?" he asked.

"Charles was not much older than I, and in odd moments, I'd see the man he could become. He could be funny, he was generous with his friends, and would never insult me or upbraid me publicly. In his way, he was honorable. He simply expected the world to do as he bade and hadn't much experience with frustration. Had there been a child, perhaps in time..."

"Your story confirms my conclusion that dukes are a blight upon society, and we'd be better off without them."

Mr. Morecambe's driving was deft and tactful, his opinion on dukes quite firmly stated. "You consign the entire senior branch of the peerage to perdition, Mr. Morecambe? Isn't that a bit harsh?"

The wind whipped the end of Genie's scarf behind her, and the sun warmed her cheeks. Why had she gone to Brighton instead of home to Derbyshire?

"I'd keep Wellington, and a few others, but a duke ruined my father. I haven't much patience for the lot of them."

He leaned closer to make that admission, bringing with him the scent of lavender. He favored clean linen, then, and made conscientious use of soap and water. Fine qualities in a man.

"Is there a scandal I should know about?" Genie asked, though any warning he offered was coming at least two miles too late, if that was the case.

"A quiet scandal, the worst kind, because then nobody champions the outcast. He's left to slink away, hoping the rumors die down along with his fortunes. Papa built a fine dwelling just as Brighton was becoming truly popular, and the duke not only refused to pay, he claimed Papa had done shoddy work. Papa was old-fashioned. He never built a house he wouldn't be proud to live in, and the work was anything but shoddy."

"But the damage was done," Genie said. "His reputation in tatters, and then nobody else felt compelled to pay him or to hire him. That is a dreadful tale, Mr. Morecambe."

"A tale you believe."

"Oh yes. When a man is seldom told no, or not now, or not at that price, he develops little patience or understanding. Such a man can either be grateful for the privileges of his station, or he can be a complete donkey's arse. Your papa's client doubtless had solicitors, barristers, and even judges in his pocket, while your father had a family to feed. I'm sorry your father ran afoul of a donkey's arse. Tell me how you came to build your gentlemen's club."

By degrees and questions, Genie drew him out, until it was time for the first change. She heard a tale of hard work, determination, sound investment, and more hard work, as well as several panegyrics to houses that had enthralled Mr. Morecambe.

"How can a house enthrall?" Genie asked as they trotted away from the posting inn. "A house is a place to get out of the wet, to take meals, or to sleep. A fine idea, but not... not enthralling."

He clucked to the horse, a gray this time. "Consider that vent in your parlor, the one that lets warm air waft up from the kitchen. That is genius, Your Grace. The bane of every soul in Britain the livelong winter is cold feet, and some mason, architect, or apprentice noticed that if a gap was allowed just so in a wall and a vent placed thus, the people in that one parlor in all of England would have warm feet, and without roasting their boots by the fire. I'm enthralled by such ingenuity."

And when he was enthralled, Mr. Morecambe became animated, charming even.

"Might I ask for a slight innovation where our dealings are concerned, sir?"

"You may ask."

Caution was usually a virtue, but Genie wasn't feeling cautious. She was feeling like herself for the first time in years.

"Will you call me Genie when we are private? This business of your-gracing and her-gracing, when I'm really not much more than a farmer's daughter, has long struck me as ridiculous. I'm Genie to my friends, and I hope we are to become friends."

He drove along in silence, and once again, Genie feared she'd blundered and failed to grasp soon enough the extent of her error.

"You truly do not like being a duchess, do you?" he asked.

"If I answer honestly, I'm the most ungrateful fool in the realm. Every little girl aspires to be a duchess."

"You are not a little girl, which fact gives me significant joy. My name is Adam, and I invite you to use it, Genie."

* * *

"You look like the tomcat who got into the cream pot, Dunstable." Jeremy, Viscount Luddington, moved the teapot to his house guest's elbow.

Dunstable had come to the breakfast parlor from the front door rather than down the steps. His cravat was wrinkled, and his hair was styled *a la mare's nest*. One button of his falls was loose, and the chain of his watch fob had come undone from its buttonhole to flap about his waist.

"I need coffee." He ran a hand through his hair, creating further disorder. "You see before you a survivor of Lady Naughty's worst excesses."

Luddington motioned for the footman to pour the marquess a cup of coffee. "One doesn't romp and tell, Dunstable, particularly not with a married lady."

Dunstable slurped his salvation with all the delicacy of a thirsty coach horse. "If she's romping, she's not a lady, is she?"

"If you're telling, you're not a gentleman. Would you like some eggs?"

Another slurp. "Let's start with toast." Dunstable reached for the rack. "Some hair of the dog would likely serve a medicinal purpose as well."

Luddington passed over his flask, which held a fine Madeira. Dunstable was getting old to be sowing wild oats, particularly when he'd started on the project shortly after birth. The marquess's hand shook slightly as he buttered his toast, and he got a spot of jam on the tablecloth.

"When the hell is the rest of George's set coming down from London?"

he asked. "The place livens up considerably when his toadies are in town."

"I honestly prefer Brighton when our dear sovereign is elsewhere. I did notice that the Double Duchess is among those enjoying the seaside."

Her Grace ought to be a double duchess because she was as gracious as she was good-natured, but the woman had married one duke and was rumored to be the intended of another. Luddington felt sorry for her—duke number two was hardly a prize—but she gave no sign of feeling sorry for herself.

Dunstable bit off a corner of toast. "That one. Doubly difficult. She's due for a comeuppance, I say. Did you know she's biding with Her Grace of Timid-dale?"

Luddington had never learned to appreciate the harsh charms of coffee. He poured himself another cup of tea and cursed Eton for the crop of inconvenient friendships it had produced.

"Her Grace of Tindale was kind to both of my sisters upon their come outs, and they are a provokingly shy pair of young ladies. I doubt they would have taken without the duchess's aid. You insult her at your peril."

Dunstable laughed, getting toast crumbs all over his cravat. "When did you become such a bishop, Luddy? If we didn't talk about who we've swived, who we'd like to swive, and who'd like to swive us, what conversation would remain?"

A note to Mama was in order. Both of Luddington's sisters were happily married, but Mama was quite the hostess. Her guest list needed to become shorter by one name. Luddington caught the footman's eye, and that good fellow took up the almost empty teapot and departed on a bow.

"Dunstable, allow me to presume on our long and amiable association. You are nearly penniless, which I gather is something of a family tradition. Not your fault, but there it is. Unless you want to be refused my hospitality effective immediately, you will cease to slander every woman who has granted you a waltz. We are no longer boys, trying to impress each other in the public school dormitories."

Luddington meant the rebuke kindly. There had been talk in the clubs of Dunstable playing too deeply and taking too long to make good on his vowels. His most recent mistress had left him for the company of a mere cloth merchant, and nobody had seen Dunstable's high-perch phaeton since April.

The marquess stirred sugar into his coffee. "No need to get up in the bows, Luddy. I'm still a bit cup-shot, not at my best." Dunstable smiled by way of further apology, and such was his inherent charm, that Luddington felt an iota of relenting.

"We're none of us at our best after a night of carousing, and if you're not inclined to sea bathing, Brighton can be a challenge."

Dunstable shuddered. "Sea bathing. Tried it once. My stones were the size of raisins by the time the ordeal concluded. Never again."

Which raised a puzzle: If Dunstable wasn't in Brighton to enjoy the sea, and the Carlton House set wasn't present in any great numbers, what was the marquess doing here, and when would he be finished doing it?

"I find a dip in the ocean invigorating. Have some more toast. When are you off to the family seat? The countryside is ever a pleasant respite in the summer."

Dunstable finished his coffee and refilled his cup. "I dare not show my face at the ancestral pile, lest visiting heiresses pop out of linen closets at me. My parents think I'm in Brighton to refurbish the sole asset deeded to me on my twenty-first birthday. That abysmal excuse for an abode is not four streets from the Pavilion, but a sorrier dwelling you never did see."

Only a ducal heir could complain about owning such a prestigious address. "Have you inspected the property?"

"Had to. The solicitors would tattle otherwise. It's an awful place, all dusty and gloomy. Not a stick of furniture, not a potted salvia to be seen. Pater says the roof leaks, the cellars let in the damp, and the parlors are drafty. Not exactly what you call a bachelor establishment for one of my station."

"That was his idea of a birthday gift?" No wonder Dunstable was in the doldrums.

"For which I'm to be grateful," he said, rising. "You defend Her Grace of Tindale as the wife of our late friend, but Luddy, I could tell you a tale in confidence that would tarnish your regard for her considerably."

"If you told such a tale," Luddington said, "my regard for you would be tarnished as well. When you've finished breaking your fast, I suggest you have a bath and a nap. I'm off to call upon my aunt." He patted his lips with his table napkin and rose.

"It's easy for you," Dunstable said, brushing toast crumbs from his cravat onto the carpet. "Your papa doesn't meddle. Your properties send cash flowing into your coffers. You haven't got four sisters beggaring the family exchequer while you try to make a pittance serve as a quarterly allowance. There's nothing I can *do*, Luddy. I'm not to have a profession, Papa doesn't want me mucking about with ducal properties, I haven't a head for academics, and yet, I'm to appear charming, well informed, and gracious at all times."

Was that such a burden? But then, Luddington had spent an occasional school holiday at the Seymouth family seat and did not envy Dunstable his parents. They were an arrogant, unsentimental pair who had high expectations of their son and little sympathy for his situation—or anybody else's.

"You bear up wonderfully under these hardships," Luddington said, "most of the time. Have that nap, and your outlook will be brighter for it." Luddington spoke to his four-year-old nephew in the same tone.

"I suppose I shall, and I'm working on a means of making everything come right. I intend to have a conversation with a certain dowager duchess, and then I'll not need to impose on your hospitality."

That did not bode well for the duchess. "If you need a small loan, Dunstable, you know you can count on me."

Dunstable waved a hand. "Small loans ceased to make a difference months ago, but thank you for the gesture. I'm for my bath and a bottle of that fine Madeira."

He sauntered from the room, his gait a bit unsteady, and Luddington sent up a prayer for his friend—and for any duchess upon whom that friend sought to call.

CHAPTER FOUR

"I am inebriated," Adam said, turning his chaise down the Petworth drive. "Drunk on the abundance of art and craftsmanship under one roof."

"Petworth has an enormous roof," Genie replied. "Would you like me to drive?"

He surprised her by passing over the reins. "A squire's daughter is likely more proficient at the ribbons than I am."

The horse in the traces was an inelegant piebald cob from one of the posting inns. A few adjustments with the reins revealed a surprisingly soft mouth and clockwork gaits. A duchess would never be seen driving such a lowly beast, which was silly.

"This is the best horse we've had all day," she said. "Not much to look at, but her trot is smooth and tireless. She has excellent conformation for the job she's doing, and that means she'll stay sound long after the flashier animals are in the knacker's yard."

"Shall I buy her for you?"

He wasn't joking. Adam Morecambe almost never joked, as far as Genie could tell. Never flirted either, drat the luck.

"Thank you, no. I'd rather buy her for myself." Her friends would consider the purchase eccentric, despite the mare's spanking pace in harness.

"Tindale doesn't manage your funds, does he?"

"My father negotiated the settlements, and I'm well provided for. If you think the current duke would meddle with my money, you don't know him."

"I don't," Adam said, bracing a boot on the fender. "Given the damage done to my father's reputation, I'm not likely to. You are a very skilled driver."

Something Genie herself had forgotten. "Thank you. What did you like best about Petworth?"

He was silent for a long time, while the harness jingled in rhythm with the mare's trot. "I can't choose a single item, but do you know the legend of the peapod where Gibbons's work is concerned?"

Genie had seen more fruit, flowers, fish, and game carved from wood that day than she would have seen offered fresh at most country markets, but she hadn't noticed any peapods.

"Enlighten me."

"He'd carve a closed peapod early on in a project and not carve it open until he was paid. Anybody observing the carving knew if the artist had been compensated for his labors. I like that Gibbons held his patrons accountable. I also like that so much of his work remains. I do not like that I must accord aristocratic families the compliment of having been the ones to commission and preserve it."

"They doubtless preserved his art because nobody else has matched it. The formal gardens of a bygone age were simple to rip out, when rebuilding them would take only time and money. Art can't be so easily reproduced."

"Good architecture is art," Adam said, sitting forward. "It takes into account everything from the local soil and flora, to drainage patterns, available materials, the owner's aesthetics, and, of course, budget."

He was off, expounding on the challenges of building a gentlemen's club in London. Done right, his current project would function as a restaurant, coffee house, subscription library, gentlemen's lodging house, and gaming hell. The club had to be both spacious and efficient, unpretentious and elegant, dignified and distinctive.

"You see it as chess game," she said, when they'd traded the piebald mare for a rawboned chestnut. "Sacrifice a pair of pawns for a rook, stay out of check, while pressing ever forward."

The sun was low across the fields, and fatigue put a soft edge on the day. Genie spent many evenings talking among acquaintances in polite society at card parties, musicales, or balls, but she didn't *converse*. Those ladies and gentlemen did not argue that if London was to progress, then decent housing had to be erected for those who had only their labor to sell. They never stopped halfway down a corridor to stare at a ceiling while rhapsodizing about Michelangelo and Brunelleschi.

They chattered and gossiped and drove Genie nigh to bedlam.

Adam took the reins from her in a maneuver they'd perfected over the miles. His hands around hers, left and right, then she eased her grip on the ribbons, while the horse trotted placidly along.

"After the lunch Mrs. Bryce set for us," he said, "I thought I'd never be hungry again, but even that feast has become but a memory. Shall we investigate your hamper?"

The hamper was still mostly full, the Petworth housekeeper having insisted on feeding a visiting duchess and her escort. The meal had been lovely, but so too had been having an intelligent male companion with whom to share it.

"I did promise you a picnic, didn't I?"

"We're making good time. We can afford a short respite."

A longer respite would suit Genie. She wouldn't mind returning home as gathering shadows afforded privacy. The chaise's hood remained down, meaning anybody might note that she'd driven out with Mr. Morecambe.

"Let's make the last change," he said, "and then find a quiet spot for a quick meal."

"Would you like to see the Pavilion?" Genie did not want the day to end, though it must. The next best thing would be another day with Adam. If the weather held fair, King George would likely be out and about during the day, and thus Lord Dunstable would have no reason to haunt the Pavilion.

"Everybody wants to see the Pavilion," Adam replied. "That's the whole point of the place, from what I understand—to be seen, to make an impression. The roof is rumored to leak, and other rumors claim George is soon to pull down Carlton House altogether."

Their conversation became desultory as they traded the chestnut for Caliban at the last coaching inn. The sun was touching the horizon, and Genie was famished when Adam gestured with his chin to a grassy stream bank shaded by leafy oaks.

"How about over there? Caliban can have a drink, and if we spread the blanket on the far side of the oaks, we'll have privacy."

Genie saw to the hamper while Adam released the check rein and tethered the horse. She chose a spot along the stream out of sight of the road and spread two blankets over a bed of soft clover. The water babbled quietly, an evening zephyr carried the scent of scythed fields, and Caliban added to the bucolic peace by steadily munching the grass.

Why can't life be like this? Why couldn't life be peaceful and pretty, calm and relaxed? Why did life have to be stealing pleasures like a truant schoolgirl, hoping Dunstable or some other gossip wasn't watching?

"What has put the sadness in your eyes?" Adam asked, standing before her.

He did this—noticed what was around him. Observed and remembered. "I've been going about this duchessing business all wrong."

"You are my favorite duchess. How could you be doing anything wrong?"

"I'm not in a cottage in Derbyshire, watching the lambs frolic while the sun sets. As a girl, that's how I saw my dotage, and it was a happy picture."

He took her hand to assist her to the blankets, then came down beside her. "Sounds lonely."

The notion that even *he* saw Genie as already in her dotage provoked her nearly to tears.

"That cottage in Derbyshire is not as lonely as being a duchess. The first year of my marriage, I was so homesick, I wrote to a different brother each day of the week, then started the rotation all over again the next week."

"Did they write back?"

"They're brothers. Of course not."

Adam put an arm around Genie's waist, she let her head rest on his shoulder, and some of the sadness slid away.

While the determination to change, to take charge of her life remained.

* * *

All day, for every moment of this damned, wonderful, unexpected, unforgettable, grueling day, Adam had been torn between the marvels of a spectacular country house and the marvels of his companion. The Duchess of Tindale was so quiet about her accomplishments, they almost eluded his notice.

She knew her art, knew how to drive a fractious coaching hack so the horse was happy to do her job. She knew how to eat a sandwich without getting a single crumb anywhere, and she knew how to keep silent while Adam was moved beyond words by the woodcarving of a man long dead.

Genie didn't mock his passion for architecture, didn't grow bored when he waxed effusive about capitals and astragals, finials and stringcourses.

She also touched him. Casually wound her hand around his elbow, patted his arm, stroked his lapel as if to smooth a wrinkle. Her caresses soothed a restlessness Adam had long been ignoring, and they enflamed a desire as surprising as it was inconvenient.

She was a duchess. He could never move in her circles. His Grace of Seymouth had made that plain. Adam had approached the duke about unpaid bills at the time of Papa's death and had been escorted from the ducal town house under permanent threat of unending litigation.

"I don't want to climb back into that chaise." Genie put the cork in the bottle of lemonade and set it back in the hamper.

"Because the bench isn't sufficiently padded?"

"Because this has been a lovely day, Adam Morecambe, in lovely company. I don't want this outing to end." She leaned over on all fours and kissed him, and the moment became gilded with possibilities.

Rather than sit back on her haunches, she stayed where she was, her palm cradling Adam's cheek.

An invitation? She probably thought herself very bold. Adam thought her overture wonderfully understated. He kissed her back, smoothed her hair from her brow, and then she was on him, pushing him to the blanket, turning a polite kiss into a plundering of his mouth and wits.

"Your Grace, you needn't—"

She got him by the hair. "No more your-gracing."

"Genie, we have—"

He'd meant to say, *We have time to discuss this*, but the rest of his thought flew from his head as Genie loomed over him.

"I am inebriated too, Adam Morecambe. Drunk with the pleasure of a simple day spent in company I chose for myself. Do you know how long it's been since I was permitted to drive my own gig?"

Rather than let him answer, she kissed him again: *Too long. It has been much, much too long.*

She broke off the kiss and remained crouched over him. "Do you know how long it has been since I was permitted—permitted!—to climb in and out of a carriage without some man handling me as if I were a doddering granny?"

She wrestled her skirts—Adam helped—until she was straddling him. "Do you know how long it has been since I could *stay home* for three days in a row, no callers, no compulsory entertainments, no matchmaking mamas currying my favor, no *fortune hunters* complimenting my *fair gaze*?"

Her gaze was furious and determined, much as it had been when she'd scolded Adam into modifying his construction schedule.

"Genie, there is nobody here to tell you what to do. There's only me. Tell me what you want."

The ire went out of her like a balloon losing loft. "Hold me, Adam."

He rather was. He tucked her against his chest, wallowing in soft linen and softer curves. "What would make it better?"

"I can't think about that at the moment, though I *shall* think about it, now that I've engaged in strong hysterics."

Her hair remained in a neat bun despite miles and miles of driving. He set about freeing her braid.

"You merely expressed your frustration and shared a few delightful kisses with me."

She was sharing her weight as well, settling agreeably close to a part of Adam that was feeling interest and frustration.

"I can't even dress myself," she muttered against his throat, "without two maids interfering with my attempts to put a button through a buttonhole. I'd like to undress myself now."

Holy cavorting cherubs. Adam and his duchess were on a blanket on the outskirts of Lesser Cowclap, Sussex, and she wanted to undress.

But why shouldn't she? Why shouldn't Genie... Adam didn't even know her family name, though duchesses all but lost a family name... Why shouldn't she take a little joy for herself?

"Nobody is stopping you, Genie. If you want to dance naked under the rising moon, you're free to do that."

Her fingers went to the top button of her bodice. "You'll think me daft."

"I think you desirable." Also dear, and in the grip of some thorny issue Adam couldn't parse at the moment when every particle of him was longing to see the duchess unbuttoned.

He'd apparently said the right words, because Genie smiled at him with all the lovely mischief any man had ever longed to behold in a lover. She was still smiling eleven buttons later, and he was smiling too.

* * *

Genie hadn't admitted to herself that morning that she'd set out to tryst with Adam Morecambe, but she had chosen front-lacing jumps instead of stays and a carriage dress that unbuttoned down the front. She wasn't wearing drawers—not all ladies did in warm weather—and in an astonishingly short time, she was sitting on a blanket under a darkening sky in her shift, boots, and stockings.

"These..." Adam said, scowling at her boots. "I can't nibble your toes if you're intent on keeping these on."

Nibble my toes. She shivered, not from cold. "Far be it from me to frustrate your appetite in any regard."

He started on her boot laces. "When you talk like that, all prim and tidy, I want to muss you."

"I want to be mussed." The desire—the need—to be wild and wicked had erupted of a sudden, driven by frustration and discontent Genie had been ignoring for most of her widowhood, if not most of her adulthood.

"I want to be naked," Adam said, setting her boots on the edge of the blanket. "I haven't the patience."

He undid his cravat, sleeve buttons, and watch, then peeled both shirt and waistcoat straight over his head. They joined the heap of linen Genie had started on one corner of the blanket.

His hands went to his falls, and Genie put her palm on his chest. "Might you pause for a moment? I'd like to admire the Creator's craftsmanship." He was no pale, pampered duke. He was closer to the heroic marble on such abundant display in the Petworth staterooms.

"I *like* manual labor," he said. "I like wrestling with stone and brick, I like digging foundations so I know they're level. I like.... I like *that* a lot."

She'd traced the muscles of his chest, then down the midline of his torso. Dark hair dusted the terrain, and he was everywhere warm. He watched her in the gathering gloom, watched her gently cup him through his clothes.

"Genie..."

"So serious." And so ready to indulge her on this adventure. Desire blended with something more complicated, not quite anxiety, but a sense of leaving the familiar forever behind.

"For a moment," he said, "I must be serious. Consequences can follow from what we're contemplating."

She shook her head. "In five years of marriage, I never bore a child, and Charles was diligent in exercising his marital rights."

They were kneeling on the blanket, face-to-face. Adam gathered her in his arms and lay back so she was tucked against his side.

"I'm sorry. Sorry you were denied the motherhood you sought, sorry your husband offered you mere diligence."

Adam had put his finger on some of Genie's frustration. Charles was the only man with whom she'd been intimate, but she'd heard enough frank talk among the ladies, caught enough muttered asides, to know that his efforts as a lover had been minimal.

"He'd come to my room after the candles were out, climb under the covers, lift my nightclothes, and fumble between my legs. He'd poke and heave and make odd noises, then flop upon me like a marionette whose strings had been cut. Sometimes he'd kiss my cheek."

This was not disloyalty to a deceased spouse, but rather, grief for a marriage mired in silence and duty.

"He was probably trying to be considerate."

"Do you think so?" Genie pondered that hypothesis, though pondering anything except the bulge in Adam's trousers was hard—difficult, rather. "I never felt so empty as when he was inside me."

Adam swore softly, while Genie undid the buttons of his falls. Then she was on her back, a blanket of warm lover over her.

He was in the mood to dawdle, while Genie was frantic, and that was a wonderful combination. Adam's deliberate caresses left her free to be wild. When he cupped her breast, she could arch and writhe into his hand. When he settled his weight on her, she could move against him with blatant yearning.

As desire escalated to craving, pity wended through all the other feelings Genie wrestled—pity for the late duke who'd owned assets beyond imagining, but had been impoverished for cash, and for courage and imagination regarding his marriage.

As Genie had also been impoverished.

Chasing that pity was a determination that she never again make the same mistake. She'd learn from this interlude with Adam, learn to take hold of courage and imagination with the hands of a skilled whip, and send her life in the directions she chose, on her terms.

She wedged a hand between her body and her lover's, got him in a firm grip, and showed him exactly where she wanted him.

Adam went still, dropping his forehead to her shoulder. "If you deny me some patience now, the pleasure will be too soon over."

His voice had acquired a growl, and his embrace enveloped her with the immutable strength of a masculine edifice.

"If you deny me the full measure of passion now—"

He moved, and words failed. Genie got one hand wrapped around his biceps, the other on his backside. She locked her ankles around his waist and endured such a thorough, relentless joining that the pleasure bordered on unbearable. She caught a glimpse of the night sky over Adam's shoulder, the stars emerging from their velvet darkness into a diamond-sharp illumination.

Then he gathered her impossibly close, and all the beauty and tenderness of the night sky filled her from within.

CHAPTER FIVE

Genie lay on her side, her cheek pillowed against Adam's belly. Her braid had come undone—not merely unpinned from its coronet—and a hairpin poked him in the ribs.

He was too well pleased to care. Withdrawing had been a near thing, but he wasn't about to take unnecessary chances with the lady's future. His mind was like Caliban, munching on this grassy patch, then wandering to a clump of clover—all was lovely and delectable, in no particular order.

Genie's thighs were wonderfully muscular. She must enjoy frequent vigorous walks and good long gallops.

Her scent up close was like the jasmine of her bedroom. Subtle and spicy. Adam took a whiff of a lock of her hair and brushed it across his lips.

He wanted to taste her intimately, and she'd probably let him.

She patted his cock, then held his balls in a loose grip, which sent a buzz of anticipation in all directions.

"If you start that conversation," Adam said, "we'll be here until dawn." And what a night that would be.

"My friends would worry."

Being a fundamentally considerate woman, she would not give her friends cause to worry.

"And your reputation might suffer." Adam's too, though among the titled set, he had only the merest beginnings of good standing, and then mostly among the younger men whom Seymouth did not know well.

Genie let go of him and sat up. "My friends should be having adventures of their own. Moonlight does you credit, Mr. Morecambe."

An arc of shadowy gold had just crested the Downs to the east. Adam drew Genie into his lap, and together, they watched the moonrise.

"I've never done this before," he said, though he hadn't planned on saying anything. Genie's hair tickled his chin. Her weight on his lap tickled his desire.

"Watched the moon come up?"

That either. "Not with a lover." Certainly not with a duchess. "Navigating the way back to town will be easy with all that moonshine."

Leaving their blankets would be difficult. Adam's peace was perfect— the grazing horse, the whisper of water over stones, and the lovely sense of having stumbled upon a lady in whom intimate trust could be safely reposed.

Genie kissed him, as if she sensed his thoughts, and then she climbed off his lap. She made dressing a cooperative undertaking, doing up Adam's sleeve buttons and allowing him to lace her jumps. She saw to her own buttons, and Adam tended to his, but she allowed him to assist her with her boots.

He did not trust himself to put her hair to rights, so he instead fetched the horse while Genie managed a swift braid and a tidy bun. They folded the blankets together—an excuse to share a few kisses—and then they were back on the road.

As Caliban trotted toward Brighton, the silence went from comfortable, to thoughtful, to… strained.

"You offered an invitation to tour the Pavilion," Adam said. "Were you merely being polite?"

"I'm through with merely being polite. I'd like to see the Pavilion with you, for you doubtless will notice what others miss."

Her tone was brusque rather than complimentary. "Are you cold?"

"I am quite comfortable."

Genie was also back to being the duchess. The proper, polite, unremarkable woman easily overlooked when among others of her rank. Adam missed his companion, missed the demanding lover.

The lights of Brighton glimmered on the horizon, and the air changed subtly, growing more humid and cooler with a tang of the sea.

"I won't soon forget this day, Genie."

She tied her bonnet down with a silk scarf, and thus her face was obscured by her hat brim. Adam had envisioned putting that scarf to other purposes, though perhaps his ambitions in that regard weren't shared by the lady.

"Petworth is impressive," she said.

What in the name of every marble saint was amiss with her? "Were we at Petworth? I must have missed it, so much did I enjoy our picnic."

She fussed with her skirts. "Truly, you did? You don't think me forward?"

Adam mentally whacked himself with a carpenter's mallet. He'd not given her the words, the flirtation, the reassurances, more fool he.

"Genie, I find you lovely, passionate, brave, and infernally distracting when I'm trying to think only decent thoughts and comport myself as a gentleman. How to be both lover and proper escort is a new challenge, though one I relish."

She edged closer on the bench, adding a hint of jasmine to the soft summer night. "Precisely. A new challenge. How to be a duchess and daring. I must think on this."

Adam was a builder, little more than an ambitious mason in good tailoring. Genie was a duchess. Of course, she'd regard him as only a partner for a dalliance, and he ought to be flattered to have that much of her consideration.

And yet, he was disappointed too. She was happy to build a folly with him, while he'd been dreaming of a permanent structure, complete with furniture, carvings, and clever vents—also a fine big bed in the master apartment. His disappointment grew when, instead of offering him a peck on the cheek at her door, Genie was content to let him bow over her hand before she slipped into the house.

What had he expected? She was gracious and lovely and all that other, but she was still, above all, a duchess.

* * *

Genie went about her days with two objectives in mind: First, to avoid the Marquess of Dunstable, and second, to cross paths with Mr. Morecambe. In all the hours she'd spent with Adam on the outing to Petworth, she had failed to get his direction.

And he had not offered it to her.

Brighton boasted rooming houses and hotels by the score, and even Mr. Morecambe doubtless had friends with whom he could bide. Subtle questions to Genie's callers yielded no word of a large, taciturn architect down from Town. Diana and Belinda both made inquiries, but Mr. Morecambe had little use for the idle and titled, and his whereabouts weren't likely to interest them either.

"So much for embarking on a life of daring adventure," Genie muttered to the cat.

Rather than pause in his ablutions, he adopted a pose unbefitting of a lady's feline.

"I will keep to my plans nonetheless," Genie said, "for adventure won't find me if all I do is sit about and read Mr. Scott's works of fiction." Or stare at them without turning a single page.

She put on her bonnet and cloak, found a parasol, and waved off the footman who typically escorted the ladies of the house on their shopping expeditions. A proper widow could walk the streets of Brighton in broad daylight by herself.

Not that Genie ever had.

She nonetheless found her solicitor's office—her Brighton solicitor, not to be confused with her London solicitors (plural), or her Derby solicitor (only the one, but he was prodigiously long-winded), or her Paris solicitor (an outrageous old flirt).

Her request took some time to explain, while Mr. Vernon scribbled copious notes and promised to look into the matter straightaway. Genie took her leave without answering the question Mr. Vernon was too polite to ask: The Dowager Duchess of Tindale couldn't possibly be strolling a distance of three streets without a retinue, could she?

In fact, she was, and Genie was equal parts pleased with herself and anxious that she might run into Dunstable.

Derbyshire is looking better and better.

Though she had no lover in Derbyshire. Perhaps she had no lover in Brighton. What sort of man made passionate love and stirring declarations beneath the rising moon, then sent no word for days?

A wall of well-dressed male muscle interrupted her musing. "I do beg your—Your Grace."

"Mr. Morecambe. A pleasure." *Mostly. To some extent.*

Genie was blushing and trying not to smile. She offered her hand as he tipped his hat, then dropped her hand when he reached for her fingers.

"I was on my way to pay a call on you," Mr. Morecambe said, taking her hand in his. "Shall I walk you to your door?"

His grip was firm and steadying, as was the look in his eyes. He wasn't smiling, but his gaze said he was pleased to see her.

"An escort would be appreciated. I wondered if you'd returned to London."

He tucked her fingers around his arm, placing himself on the street side of the walkway. "I did, in fact. My master mason and builder got into a spat, and nothing would serve but I must mediate between them. I've missed you."

When had anybody ever missed Genie? Oh, her brothers occasionally dashed off a line or two at the bottom of a note sent by their wives. *Hope you're keeping well!* Or, *Come home when next you can—the children want spoiling!*

Those sentiments were casual gestures of affection from people whose lives had separated from Genie's years ago.

"Did I speak too boldly, Your Grace? Should I not have admitted to missing you?"

"You honor me with your honesty. I've missed you too."

They paused at a corner. "I'd thought to write," he said, "to send a note informing you of my travel, but does a widowed duchess receive correspondence from a single gentleman? Does this widowed duchess? Dithering is foreign to my nature, so I chose to pay a call upon my return."

"You've only just returned?" How lovely that he had come directly to see her—and told her he'd done so.

"I want that visit to the Pavilion," he said, leaning closer. "You did promise."

Was he teasing her? "I keep my word, Mr. Morecambe, but tell me, where are you biding on your visit to Brighton?"

"With friends who won't mind my coming and going at all hours. This time of year, many properties are to let, and others are under renovation."

"But you're looking to purchase, aren't you?"

He expounded on the benefits of owning over renting, and Genie realized he might be making a subtle point about the difference between a courtship and a dalliance.

"One has the security of a commitment," he said. "The building is wholly entrusted to the owner, the owner knows he'd best treasure the asset in his keeping. Renters break leases, landlords neglect maintenance. The more permanent arrangement seems the better bargain, if one can make the initial investment."

They crossed the street arm in arm. "True, if one chooses wisely and is a responsible property owner. If the choice was unfortunate, the owner is stuck with an ongoing liability, or the building with a negligent caretaker." And Genie did not care for any analogy that cast her in the role of property.

A permanent arrangement, however, was all too appealing.

The closer they journeyed to Genie's doorstep, the quieter the neighborhood became.

"Was your duke so awful as all that, Genie? Did he put you off speaking vows ever again?"

That Mr. Morecambe would admit to missing her, that he'd come straight to see her, warmed her heart. That he'd think to ask this question earned her respect.

"Ladies are to desire the married state above all things," she said. "Marriage to a duke is the best married state there is, supposedly, but I was lonely and often bored, despite being run off my feet with obligations. I'm only now realizing my late husband was likely in the same situation—lonely, bored, run off his feet with obligations. He was expected to marry profitably, and he accepted that duty, but failed to get all the consideration promised in the bargain."

To have some sympathy for Charles was a great and welcome relief.

"One doesn't think of dukes as merely mortal," Mr. Morecambe said. "But they are, I suppose. You've dodged my question."

His question about marriage. *Well.* "I am considering my answer and pleased that you'd put such a conundrum to me. How does your search for a property come along?"

"Slowly. Brighton is a busy market, in terms of properties changing hands, but merely because I have coin and know well how to care for a building doesn't mean I'm a suitable buyer in the eyes of many."

His London club was nicknamed the Blackball Club for a reason, apparently. "Use an intermediary," Genie said. She was about to offer her solicitor's services—hadn't she come from asking Mr. Vernon to look for a suitable property in Derbyshire?—but remained silent as Mr. Morecambe touched his hat to a pair of beldames daundering toward them.

"What day would suit for a visit to the Pavilion?" she asked, when she was sure she could not be overheard.

"Friday. I haven't any other appointments then, and you'll give me something to look forward to."

He was flirting. He was definitely, subtly, wonderfully flirting, and they were nearly to the gate. How on earth was she to flirt back?

"Could I tempt you into a cup of tea, Mr. Morecambe?"

"Yes."

"Splendid."

"I've also been plagued by a few questions regarding the wallpaper in your sitting room. I cannot recall the exact pattern, but think something like it would go well in the cardroom at the club. Perhaps you'd be good enough to allow me another peek?"

He held the garden gate for her, and Genie preceded him up the walk. "You may have more than a peek, Mr. Morecambe."

The housekeeper took Genie's cloak and bonnet, and Mr. Morecambe's hat and walking stick. Genie led him to the steps, and they got as far as her sitting room before she pinned her guest against the closed parlor door and kissed him witless.

* * *

Adam had had a revelation on his London trip.

Journeying to Brighton previously, he'd resented the need to leave the London work site. The ring of hammers was music to him. A load of gravel or stone crashing onto the walkway was akin to the tolling of a steeple bell, summoning the faithful for the opening hymn. He loved being in the middle of a building in progress, loved the sweat and cursing, the gradual blossoming of a stately edifice where all had been disorder and noise.

Now, he loved Genie, Duchess of Tindale, and that was a problem.

In the normal course, he would have allowed his master mason and his builder to argue and discuss, and sit down over several pints to debate the need to switch plasterers. This time, he had given them fifteen minutes each to state a case and then chosen the plasterer who was available soonest. That his choice was more expensive than the alternative should have given Adam nightmares.

Instead, his dreams had been filled with images of Genie, curled on a blanket, moonlight gilding her smile. Genie, waiting patiently for him to finish sketching some pile of Mr. Gibbons's carved musical instruments. Genie, licking her fingers after finishing an apple, the core of which she'd fed to the lowly piebald mare.

And now, here he was, all but asking permission to court the woman.

And here she was, all but unbuttoning his shirt.

"The door..." he muttered against her mouth. "I'll not have your reputation put at risk—"

She smiled. "Diana and Belinda are away from home. Look to your own reputation, Mr. Morecambe."

He picked her up and carried her to the bedroom, and she kept her arms around his neck when he settled her on the bed, drawing him over her.

The rest was a blur of loosened clothing, soft laughter, and pleasure every bit as intoxicating as he'd recalled. Genie lay on the bed, her legs over the side, her skirts frothed about her waist. Adam remained standing, and the fit was perfect. He wanted to linger and admire—he wanted to use his mouth on her—but she got her legs around his waist, and her urgency overcame his restraint.

Almost. He withdrew and spent into a handkerchief, while Genie lay panting with repletion beneath him.

He crouched over her, confounded by what had passed between them. He was an architect, a man of plans and diagrams, schedules and budgets. A boring fellow, but accomplished in his humble way. How much more pleasurable to be the lover of a duchess who all but dragged him into her boudoir and had her lovely way with him.

"I'm falling asleep," she murmured, fingers trailing through his hair. "You will think very ill of me, indeed."

"I think you serve a luscious cup of tea."

She laughed, her belly bouncing beneath him, and Adam smiled against her neck.

"Will you believe me if I tell you I honestly did want to see the wallpaper?"

Not until he'd been following her up the steps, her derriere at his eye level, had his wayward thoughts crested into the beginning of arousal. Until then, he'd merely been daydreaming.

"Will you believe me," she countered, "if I tell you that you're the first man I've kissed since my husband died?"

Adam straightened, took one last admiring look at the duchess in dishabille, then twitched her skirts over her knees and assisted her to sit up.

"Why would I have cause to doubt you?" Though a part of him did. She was attractive, widowed, had means, and moved much in high society. Aristocratic men were accustomed to having who and what they wanted. As a widow, Genie should have been having who and what she wanted too.

"Because polite society isn't always so polite," she said, hands in her lap. "The London newspapers would expire for lack of tattle if that wasn't the case."

He sat beside her, and the glow of the encounter faded. "I'll not be tattling, Genie. I'd rather be proposing."

She tucked her hands under her arms as if cold. "You hardly know me."

Lately, Adam hardly knew himself. "Every couple becomes better acquainted after the vows are spoken. I realize I am presuming to raise such a topic, but I cannot countenance sneaking about alleys or hiring some cottage in Kent for clandestine trysts. My intentions are honorable."

Are yours?

Adam had worked too hard to rebuild his father's business for anybody to cast his good name away on the basis of rumor—or fact. The other consideration was that he had fallen in love, and if his sentiments were unrequited, then he'd given a duchess the power to break his heart—a heart he would have said had been quarried of good English granite. Bad enough a duke had brought Papa's standing so low. A duchess dallying with Adam then tossing him aside wasn't to be contemplated.

"I had not taken you for an impetuous man," she said. "I like your boldness, but you must understand that I have never been impetuous."

She rose from the bed and stood by the window. Her hair remained tidily pinned, but for one lock curling over her neck. Adam sat on the bed while she repinned that errant curl in exactly the place it belonged.

"Never been impetuous?" he asked softly.

The smile she aimed over her shoulder was chagrined. "Before I met you. The common perception is that titled women produce heirs and then set about taking lovers. I never produced the heirs, I never saw a man who took my fancy, and I'd promised Charles both loyalty and fidelity. Then too, given my experiences as a married woman, why on earth would I—?"

A blush crept up her neck. She untied the curtain cord and retied it to exactly match its twin on the other curtain. Then she squeezed the sachets hanging from the cords, sending a hint of jasmine into the air.

Poor Charles had been an idiot. "Shall I speak to the present duke, Genie?"

"What has Augustus to do with this?"

"He's the head of your family." Also a complete stranger to Adam, who'd likely not spare an upstart architect so much as a nod in the churchyard. "If I seek to court you, then I should at least make his acquaintance." Distasteful though the prospect was.

"I leave Augustus and his new wife as much in peace as I can. A dowager duchess trying to hoard consequence she no longer has by hovering about the ducal successor is pathetic."

An architect proposing to a duchess might be as well, and yet, Genie's regard for him seemed genuine.

"I have been precipitous," he said, rising. "I apologize."

"You have been honest. I treasure your honesty, but you've also surprised me. For five years, I've been all but invisible, except to my friends. I encourage the nervous debutantes, intervene when I see a bad match in the making, and dance with the shyest of the bachelors. The old Genie, the one who sits smiling among the potted palms night after night, is not a confident creature."

A glimmer of understanding pierced Adam's disappointment. "You would like to be wooed?"

He could do that. More outings to bucolic locations, more strolls about town—*more picnics.*

"Charles and I never courted. His papa's solicitors met with my papa's solicitors. Charles and I were permitted to dawdle about the lime park on several occasions while at least three aunts all but followed us with spyglasses. Some wooing would be lovely, but you must tell me: How do I woo you?"

He did not dare join her at the window, for there was no telling who might glance up from the alley or garden and see a man side by side with the duchess in her very bedroom. Instead, he held the door for her.

"Wooing doesn't work like that. The gentleman does the escorting and paying calls and reading to his lady in the garden." Of that much, Adam was confident.

"We're discussing *my* wooing," Genie said, as they gained the corridor, "and I'm done sitting in the parlor with a book, waiting for the gentleman to run matters to his exclusive satisfaction."

He paused with her at the top of the steps, glanced about, then stole a kiss to her cheek. "I hope the lady was satisfied with our inspection of the wallpaper?"

"You are awful. I was not satisfied for more than two minutes. I want you naked in my bed, and I want to do wanton things with you."

"What manner of wanton things?"

She started down the steps, and she was blushing again. "I don't know. I've never done them before, and Charles declared certain shelves in the library unfit for a lady's delicate sensibilities. I do believe there are places a gentleman likes to be kissed other than on his lips."

"This gentleman does." As best Adam could recall when his mind was a muddled hash of desire, amusement, and hope.

Genie paused on the landing and turned a serious gaze on him. "You are concerned for your reputation, and I respect that. I have no wish to see my personal business bruited about, and you are every bit as private as I am. But I ask myself: What would make your situation right?"

The afternoon sunshine beamed through the window, bringing out her freckles. He wanted to kiss them—them too.

"My situation is enviable," he said, "in the eyes of many. I have means, an education, a thriving business, and a favorite duchess."

She fluffed the lace of his cravat. "Enviable, yes, and likely to grow more so, but you are also discontent—over that business with your father. What would lay that matter to rest for you?"

Adam offered his arm and accompanied her down to the family parlor, which looked out over the garden. All the while, he considered her question.

"You aren't asking about revenge."

She tugged a bell-pull and took a seat in a reading chair. "I might be. That's for you to say. I'm asking about how to untangle yourself from the harm done to you and your family. Putting an old enemy in his place might be part of that."

Her question seemed to have significance beyond the obvious. "I cannot call out a duke, Genie. For one thing, the scoundrel did his damage almost fifteen years ago. For another, he's an old man, and he could ruin me with a curl of his lip."

"So the damage he did echoes to this day."

It did. Adam was having trouble even making appointments to see certain properties. Though the various agents and solicitors were polite, they were also subtly unwilling to do business with him. Perhaps they were unwilling to do business with any commoner. He had no way of knowing.

"To answer your question, what I'd seek in an ideal world is vindication—for the truth to be known. My father would never cheat a client, and the duke lied when he claimed otherwise."

Adam hadn't put that together for himself, that what he wanted was simply for the truth to be known—not such a radical outcome.

"The truth can be problematic," Genie said. "I agree in principle: Better to be judged honestly than pilloried by rumor and gossip."

As Adam swilled tea and inhaled sandwiches, he wondered idly if some aspect of the past still bothered the duchess. She seemed to have made her peace regarding her late husband, but she'd also spoken honestly: Adam did not know her well, not yet, and everybody had regrets.

Perhaps he'd learn some of hers when they spent an afternoon exploring the Pavilion, and perhaps he'd kiss her someplace other than on her lovely lips.

CHAPTER SIX

Genie was on excellent terms with the staff at the Pavilion, having lent her domestics to King George on any number of occasions when His Majesty was hosting some lavish entertainment. She knew her way around the building, or thought she did, and had already chosen several linen closets, dressing rooms, and stairways where she might have stolen a kiss.

Mr. Morecambe refused to oblige her.

If Carlton House was King George's personal art gallery, the Pavilion was his architectural peacock. Minarets and onion domes topped a palace both thoroughly modern—the kitchen was a marvel in itself—and luxurious beyond imagining.

"I do wonder about that roof," Adam said, taking one last look at the ornate ceiling doming the banqueting hall. "But I have reached the limit of what my sensibilities can absorb here. Shall I walk you home, Your Grace?"

The house steward stood by, having courteously escorted them from room to room—and closet to closet—answering Adam's endless questions.

"Thank you, yes," Genie replied. "One doesn't appreciate the size of this edifice until one traverses every corridor and stair."

Adam repeated his thanks to the steward and confirmed an appointment to tour the equally lavish stable the next morning.

"Will you come with me tomorrow?" he asked when they were strolling arm in arm along the walkway.

"I think not," Genie said. "My interest in a certain architect remains undiminished. My interest in ventilation, drainage, bearing walls, and supporting beams has been sated."

He patted her hand, a slow stroke of glove over glove. "My interest in those subjects is what keeps the roof over my own head, though I suspect even were my means abundant, I'd still be an architect. If you were not a duchess, what would you be?"

Happy. That reply would not do, not even for Adam's ears. "I would certainly bide in London much less than I do. I'd make more effort to see my family, rather than exerting myself to launch the daughters and nieces of every woman to claim an acquaintance with me. I would knit, and raise my own sheep, and spend more time by the sea and in the countryside."

"You enjoy Brighton?"

They wandered back to the house, with Genie expounding on the advantages of a simpler life, where gossip wasn't a constant threat to one's peace and expenses were reduced.

Adam held the garden gate for her. They'd come up the alley, in part because Genie preferred the quieter approach, but also because Dunstable was still in Brighton, doubtless up to no good.

"Does Tindale begrudge you your portion?" Adam asked.

"He would not dare," Genie said. "Augustus did not expect to inherit and couldn't care less what I do with my money. He was a mere cousin to the ducal line, and Charles was young and in good health when he died. Then Charles's younger brother got into that awful accident, and Augustus was left with the title. I am quite well fixed, but one doesn't speak of that openly."

Adam's gaze was serious—more serious than usual. "You are circumspect about your wealth because of the fortune hunters. I'm not after your money, madam. I can provide comfortably for a wife and children."

"The fortune hunters are a constant plague." As was a certain marquess, who any day now would once again insinuate his hand into Genie's coffers. "Do you return to London soon, Mr. Morecambe?" For if Dunstable remained kicking his heels in Brighton, Genie would return to Town.

"I'm a failure as a suitor, aren't I? Shall we sit?" He gestured to a marble bench before a circular fountain with a swan eternally gliding at the center.

Genie let him assist her onto the bench—another lingering touch of gloved hands—and realized what all the holding doors, taking her arm, and standing near her the livelong afternoon had been about.

"You are a very attentive suitor. I am a failure as a blushing damsel. All I could think about was accosting you in a linen closet, while you were doing the pretty."

He took off his hat and set it on the bench. "The linen closet under the servant's stair? The one scented with jasmine and lavender? I nearly pushed you inside and closed the door in the poor steward's face. The scent of jasmine has become an aphrodisiac."

Why should—? "Because I use jasmine in my bedroom?"

"And in the morning, the fragrance clings to your person when you rise from your slumbers. Very clever, Your Grace. Maddening, even."

Maddening was lovely. "For me, the scent of fresh clover has become enticing. Puts me in mind of summer evenings and bucolic splendors."

They enjoyed a moment, not touching, but very much courting, while a pair of sparrows splashed in the shallows of the fountain then fluttered away.

"I depart for London on Wednesday," Adam said. "Locating a suitable property for purchase in Brighton will require, as you suggest, intermediaries. The houses that are fine enough for my purposes are not available to me, and I haven't time to undertake new construction."

"You mean the blue bloods won't take your money." The same members of polite society who would have cut a bumpkin like Genie without mercy, but for her husband's title.

"A gentlemen's club can attract enterprises of a less respectable nature. In London, that's tolerated or even expected, because of the influence of the gentlemen attending the clubs. The titled gentleman's convenience matters more than his neighbor's refined sensibilities, and nobody says a word. For a club catering to the untitled, different expectations attach. I was slow to grasp what was going unsaid."

He referred to the brothels that cluttered the streets of Mayfair, side by side with fine residences, respectable businesses, and venerable clubs.

"Do you mean to tell me Brighton has no such common nuisances?"

"Brighton has a history of promoting health rather than vice, despite His Majesty's efforts to the contrary. His court is aging along with him, and the town's residents look askance at any unknown quantity."

No, they did not. If that quantity sported a title, they looked at her graciously, even fawningly.

"I must ponder this," Genie said, "and you must accept an invitation to share a cup of tea with me in my sitting room. If I cannot at least kiss you, I will next be seen marching about the beach, ranting at the sea."

He picked up his hat and rose, extending a hand to Genie. "A cup of tea after our tour of the Pavilion would suit nicely. Would you march about the beach in bare feet?"

He'd seen her bare feet. Grasped them in his warm hands, caressed them. Pleasurable heat rose from Genie's middle.

"I'd remove both shoes and stockings," she said, taking his arm, "and even lift my hems a few inches to avoid the encroaching waves. Then I'd come home and bathe thoroughly to get the sand and sea salt off my person."

He paused before the back door, his gaze fixed on the brass knocker, a gull with wings spread. "Bathe with jasmine soap?"

Genie used her parasol to shade them from view, then whispered in his ear, "I'd use that jasmine soap *everywhere*." Oh, this was marvelous fun. "We stock gunpowder tea scented with jasmine. Do you fancy a cup?"

He held the door for her, and as she swept past, he spoke very softly. "I fancy the whole, hot, delicious pot, with sweet honey drizzled into each steaming cup."

She needed to catch her balance on the sideboard after that remark. Adam presumed to take her parasol and close it for her, while she untied her bonnet ribbons.

"Allow me," he said, unfastening the frogs of her cloak.

This too was flirtation, for his fingers grazed her chin and throat, and when he drew the cloak from her, his palms stroked over her shoulders. Ye gods, she had not been done justice by her poor duke, and he had doubtless not been done justice by his copper heiress.

Genie would have stolen a kiss right there in the corridor, except that voices floated forth from the formal parlor at the front of the house.

"Guests," she said. "Belinda and Diana would use the family parlor if they were alone. We could simply duck up the back steps to my sitting room." *Please, please, please.*

"I leave that decision in your hands."

His expression had lost any hint of flirtation, and Genie recalled his words about skulking through back alleys and renting a cottage in some obscure village.

"One cup," she said, "and then I will find a way to extricate us from the clutches of strict propriety."

He kissed her in the deserted corridor, and that only made Genie's yearning worse. "You tease me, you fiend. I will have my revenge, and you may expect a few bars of scented soap delivered to your abode by this time tomorrow. I like cedar and cinnamon, though not at the same time. Do I look adequately composed?" Though she still didn't know his specific direction.

A masculine voice punctuated Diana's dulcet speech. Not friends, then, for Diana spoke freely with the few she considered friends and used that soft, amused tone only with bothersome bachelors.

"You look utterly demure, confound you."

Genie smoothed her skirts, taking a moment to savor the joy of having a suitor. She swept into the parlor, trailing streams of glee and smiling on all creation.

Only to see Lord Dunstable rising from the sofa like a spider crawling forward to greet the newest victim entrapped in its web.

* * *

If there was one person Adam loathed more than he loathed the Duke of Seymouth, it was Seymouth's heir and only son, Lord Dunstable. That disgrace to manhood bowed over Genie's hand, and she curtseyed prettily.

"My lord, a pleasure," she said, with every evidence of sincerity. "May I make known to you Mr. Adam Morecambe, and Mr. Morecambe, I present to you Isambard, Marquess of Dunstable."

Adam managed a bow, while Dunstable wrinkled his nose and barely inclined his handsome head.

"I've made Mr. Morecambe's acquaintance, though I can't recall where." His lordship resumed his seat next to a lovely blonde, while a third woman, with auburn hair and green eyes, poured out for the marquess. Genie had introduced Adam to her. She was the other duchess—Warminster, Winchelsea, Wrexham. Some damned W or other.

"I don't believe I've been introduced to all of the ladies," Adam said. Nor was there anywhere for him to sit. The sofa held the marquess and the blonde, the auburn-haired duchess occupied one wing chair, Genie the other.

"I beg your pardon," Genie said, introducing Adam to Mrs. Diana Thompson. "And I'll have the footman bring us another chair."

"No need," Adam replied. "I'll be on my way. Ladies, your lordship, good day." Even that much civility directed at Dunstable was a tribulation, but he seemed to be on good terms with the women, and Adam would not embarrass Genie with poor manners.

"Not even one cup of tea?" the blonde, Mrs. Thompson, asked.

"The press of business calls me."

Dunstable saluted with his tea cup. "Don't let us keep you. Those who labor for their bread can't be expected to savor the company of their betters when coin of the realm calls."

Adam expected Genie to issue her guest a blunt set-down. She instead aimed a pained smile at the tea tray.

"I'll see you out," Mrs. Thompson said, springing from the sofa. She took Adam by the arm and all but dragged him from the room. "Count yourself fortunate, Mr. Morecambe, for his lordship has been swilling tea and decimating the tea cakes this past half hour."

"You don't care for him?"

She led Adam to the front door. "He's not the worst of his kind, but he's a trial, and Her Grace cannot abide him. She is too polite for her own good sometimes. Do call again, please, and I mean that."

Had she meant Her Grace of Tindale? If so, Adam had no call to doubt her, but then, here he was at the door, while Genie had chosen to remain in the company of a man she did not like.

"Thank you, Mrs. Thompson, and please give Her Grace of Tindale my special thanks for an enjoyable day."

"Might I ask how that day was spent?"

"Avoiding the near occasion of linen closets. Good day."

All the way back to his quarters, Adam wrestled with the possibility that Genie had been ashamed to be seen with him. Not ashamed before her friends, but ashamed before Dunstable. He was in line for a dukedom, well favored, smooth-spoken, moved in the highest circles...

"In short," Adam muttered, letting himself in the door, "he's everything I'm not."

"I beg your pardon, sir?" The butler was a dignified old relic named Fawcett. He put Adam in mind of erudite headmasters and advanced Latin tutors, and when Adam bided here, he always felt as if he did so at Fawcett's sufferance.

Adam handed over his hat and walking stick. "I'm lecturing myself. Will Cook have an apoplexy if I ask for a tray in the library?"

"Doubtless, sir. Her third of the week by my count. You have received a deal of correspondence, including an express from Town."

The day had taken a sour turn when Adam had beheld Dunstable in Genie's parlor, now sour threatened to turn rotten.

"Please ask Cook to send up a pot of jasmine gunpowder, if any we have. Otherwise, China black will do."

Fawcett bowed and disappeared down the steps. The third stair always creaked when Adam dared trespass upon the kitchen, but Fawcett's descent was silent.

Adam saved the express—from his builder in London—for last, because at this hour of the day, he wasn't about to start a journey north, no matter what emergency had befallen the work site. He instead plowed through bills, progress reports, membership applications, and offers of employment on other projects before slitting open the express.

"Damn, blast, and to perdition with the lot of them."

Fawcett paused at the door, a tray in hand. "Having a bit of an apoplexy yourself, sir?"

"My head mason has apparently quit, my builder is threatening to do likewise, and nobody has seen our tipper wagon since the day before yesterday."

"Shall I have the livery alerted that you'll need a horse?"

Adam would normally have bolted for the door, ridden through the night, and been at the work site before the sun came up.

"I'll depart for London tomorrow, after I've toured the royal stables at the Pavilion and paid a call on a certain duchess."

"Very good, sir. I regret to report that we have no jasmine-scented tea."

The scent of plain China black wafted up from the tray Fawcett set on the desk. A plate of sandwiches accompanied the tea, though abruptly, Adam wasn't hungry.

"My thanks for the tray."

Fawcett withdrew on a bow, and Adam turned to the remaining half-dozen items of correspondence. Each one was a polite note from some man of business or solicitor with offices in Brighton. They all thanked Adam for his interest in a very attractive property, then explained that circumstances—a recent offer to purchase, schedule conflicts, the owner reconsidering the decision to sell—made showing Adam the property regrettably impossible.

They wished him best of luck on his search, etcetera and so forth, but did not foresee the property becoming available for inspection in the immediate future.

And what a coincidence that Lord Dunstable should be in town, just as door after door was closing in Adam's face.

* * *

Diana and Belinda had apparently been entertaining Dunstable for a good half hour before Genie had returned home. They had their revenge by all but abandoning her with him shortly after Adam had decamped.

And thus did a lovely day turn to mud.

To horse droppings, even.

"Duchess, let us sit for a moment in your lovely garden," Dunstable said, rising. "Old friends deserve privacy for the occasional chat about bygone times."

Dunstable had never been her friend. He'd been one of the countless toadies orbiting about Charles, most of them waiting to inherit a title, a fortune, or both. Charles had been patient with them, while Genie had dreaded the "intimate dinners" for thirty that came around at least once a month.

"I'll need a shawl," she said. "Enjoy the fresh air for a moment in solitude, my lord."

She scooted from the parlor and went in search of Diana or Belinda, anybody, who could ensure she wasn't left alone with Dunstable for more than a moment. Neither lady was to be found, and the kitchen staff was busy with dinner preparations.

Well, drat. Genie grabbed a shawl and found her guest helping himself to a pink rosebud from Godmama's bushes.

"If you have something to say to me, my lord, then best get to the point. We are observed from the house, and my lingering here with you will be remarked."

He threaded the rosebud into the buttonhole on his lapel. "You are a dowager duchess, my dear. Your conduct will be remarked regardless of how you behave, but none dare chide you for it... yet."

Genie waited, because she needed to know exactly what he was threatening. She could weather a little unkind talk, she could part with a bit of coin. She'd already paid Dunstable off twice, once with a diamond bracelet she'd inherited from her mother, once with a gold snuffbox passed down from her father. Even Augustus would notice substantial sums going missing from her funds.

"I adore a woman who can hold her tongue," Dunstable said. "Such a woman would make an admirable Duchess of Seymouth, particularly when she has already learned to wear a tiara."

Genie wrapped her shawl more tightly around her. "You are overcome with a violent passion for me, my lord? Perhaps you confuse me with my exchequer."

His rosebud was drooping at an odd angle. He attempted to reposition it. "And droll wit—I am ever amused by droll wit. I've done some investigating, dear duchess."

"Prying and gossiping?"

The rosebud hung all but upside down from his lordship's buttonhole. He took it out and swung it by the stem.

"We needn't be vulgar, Your Grace. Your late papa left you quite well to do, and he did a lovely job of protecting your inheritance in the marriage settlements. But then, you were bequeathed such an enormous pile of money that Tindale could have his portion and leave plenty for me."

Genie sank to the bench before the fountain, her knees going unsteady. In her wildest nightmares, she could not have foreseen Dunstable proposing to her.

"You needn't marry me, my lord. I'll give you the money. Just leave me alone."

He came down beside her uninvited. "Were you very upset when Cousin Augustus married his current duchess? That was bad of him, if you were still pining for his favors. He was supposed to marry you, wasn't he?"

"I will tell you this one last time, my lord: What you saw was an innocent embrace. Augustus is family, and I value his affection dearly. At no time did he, or have I, entertained untoward thoughts. I honored my vows."

Dunstable sniffed the rosebud. "I'm sure you did, but I'm also certain I saw you nestled quite close in the embrace of a man other than your husband. Within weeks, your husband was dead and that man had moved one giant step closer to inheriting the title. All quite distressing. If the wrong people learned of what I saw, then you and the current duke would be in enormous trouble. Your best option is to marry a man who can keep you safe from gossip and innuendo, and that man would be sitting beside you."

Looking so innocent, while impersonating the serpent in the garden. "Take the damned money," Genie said. "All I need—all I want—is a cottage in Derbyshire and my own sheep. I never wanted to be a duchess, much less a duchess twice over."

Poor Belinda faced that ordeal.

Dunstable's laughter was warm and friendly. "A cottage in Derbyshire and your own sheep? Will you give them names? Will you hire a handsome shepherd to keep you and your sheep warm on those bitter Derbyshire winter nights?"

He smacked her lightly on the back of the hand with the rosebud. "You have brightened my day, Duchess, so I'll brighten yours. Present me with two sons—no, three, for we must be cautious, must we not?—and I'll allow you to retire to your cottage in Derbyshire each summer when I do my duty by the house parties. A fair bargain, if I do say so myself."

No sort of bargain at all, considering that many house parties were little more than discreet, rural orgies. All Dunstable sought was to pursue his debauches without a pesky duchess at his side.

"Why now?" Genie asked. "Why wait for years after Charles's death to wreak your mischief? Most would consider eight and twenty too old to be anybody's duchess, and I never bore Charles any children."

The money must be very important to Dunstable, and the supply of heiresses rapidly dwindling.

"I have a parcel of dreadful cousins who can see to the succession if needs must," Dunstable said, tossing the rose in the air and catching it. "But I will be diligent in attempting to fill our nursery. Make no mistake on that score."

The tea Genie had managed to choke down threatened to rebel. "What explanation will you offer for waiting years to spread these accusations? Nobody would have believed them at the time of Charles's death, and they won't believe you now."

He twirled the battered rosebud by the stem. "Ah, but your beloved Augustus became duke only earlier this year, and his good fortune brought to my mind the liberties he'd taken with you—a heated embrace, a passionate kiss, under poor Charles's roof!—and my conscience has troubled me sorely."

Augustus had kissed Genie on the forehead. "Your creditors have been dunning you sorely."

"We needn't belabor the obvious. A ducal heir must maintain a certain standard, which your settlements will allow me to do." He stood, looking quite, quite smug. "Don't spend too much time with your pet stone mason while I'm paying you my addresses. A little pity for the less fortunate is all well and good—was he your escort to Petworth?—but Morecambe is not good *ton*, according to no less authority than my own dear mother."

He tossed the rose skyward, and Genie snatched the beleaguered flower out of the air. "If you think to make this farce of an offer believable, you will court me *at length*, my lord. You will show me every courtesy, you will dote, you will pine, you will flirt with me and flatter me. No dowager duchess has any need of matrimony, with its attendant risks and obligations. Only after you have convinced the whole of polite society that the sun rises and sets in my eyes will you think of approaching Augustus to ask for my hand, or he will laugh you to scorn."

By which time, Genie would have a strategy for avoiding another tiara, even if it meant emigrating to darkest Peru.

Dunstable braced his walking stick against his shoulder. "You want to enjoy a dalliance with the stone mason, is that it? I could ruin him with a whisper, my dear, so please don't think to cuckold your intended with Morecambe's bastard."

"Once again, you quite mistake a matter of which you have very little understanding. It's time you left, my lord. You have a long and thorough courtship to plan."

He laughed again—Genie already hated his laugh—and bowed over her hand. "So I do, so I do. What a delightful prospect."

He was entirely too pleased with himself, and Genie was too distraught. "You will keep this scheme to yourself if you hope to see us wed, sir. I take a dim view of any suitor whose discretion cannot be trusted, and so will the rest of Society."

Dunstable tipped his hat to a jaunty angle with the handle of his walking stick. "Said the woman caught groping her husband's cousin on the stair."

"What does your mother think of your plan to make a widowed copper heiress your duchess?"

Dunstable's stick hit the paving stone. "We'll leave dear Mama out of this for the nonce. She knows the occasional heiress has kept many a titled family tree thriving."

Her Grace of Seymouth was an obnoxious old besom. Even Charles had had little patience with her, and for Genie, she'd served as an example of how not to be a duchess.

"Go plan our courtship," Genie said, gently placing the rosebud on the edge of the fountain, stem trailing in the water. "And do a thorough job of it."

Dunstable went chortling on his way, while Genie returned to the bench and contemplated a series of unfortunate choices. One certainty emerged: She could involve neither Adam nor Augustus in this tangled web. The one would be ruined, the other embroiled in scandal short months after inheriting his title.

"But I cannot marry that grasping, greedy idiot," Genie informed the swan at the center of the fountain. "One duke was more than enough, and two would be a penance I do not deserve. I hope there are some sheep farms for sale in Peru."

CHAPTER SEVEN

"Duchess Eugenia is from home," Mrs. Thompson said. "She departed three-quarters of an hour ago, unescorted, no word of her plans. I had hoped she was meeting you for a constitutional."

Adam held his cup of jasmine gunpowder under his nose. "She knew I had plans this morning. She did not know when I would call upon her." The tea was soothing and fragrant. He wanted to smash the cup against the wall.

"Shall I convey a message to her, Mr. Morecambe? She will be very sorry she missed you."

Is Dunstable bothering her? Tell her I love her. How much courting is enough? Adam could say none of that.

"Tell her the press of business sends me to London once again, posthaste. I will return to Brighton at the earliest opportunity."

He set down his tea cup and rose before he blurted out his frustrations. Where was Genie, what was Dunstable to her, and why couldn't one work site function smoothly for even a week at a time?

"Mr. Morecambe, the press of business seems to vex you greatly. Is there anything I can do to help? I consider Her Grace a dear friend, and I'm sure she considers you in the same light."

I do not want to be merely her friend. "Can you spare me a few spoonfuls of tea from the caddy?"

Mrs. Thompson peered into the little silver cannister. "We have plenty. Have you a handkerchief?"

Adam spread out his handkerchief—monogrammed initials, no coat of arms—and Mrs. Thompson spooned dry tea onto the linen. She tied it up in a knot and passed it to him.

"Safe travels, Mr. Morecambe. I'll tell your duchess you were very cast down to miss her."

Adam stashed the tea in an inner pocket. "I am not cast down. I am determined, and she is not my duchess—yet."

Mrs. Thompson stood and smiled, and such was her beauty that Adam, to whom aesthetics had long been a priority, should have goggled at her for a full minute. He offered her a hasty bow and nearly ran for the door, grabbing his hat and walking stick from a dismayed housekeeper.

Every two miles on the journey to London, Adam took a whiff of the tea sachet and schooled himself to patience. He should have left a note. He should send an express at the next change of horses. He should turn the damned coach around and let the work site sort itself out.

Except it wouldn't. Work sites never did.

Nonetheless, the situation had improved by the time Adam arrived. Rosenbarker and the head mason had turned up, though the wagon had been stolen.

"They wanted to study the tipper," Rosenbarker said, pacing Adam's small office as if a child had been kidnapped rather than a piece of equipment. "Held us at gunpoint, directed us to drive a good fifteen miles past the quarry, and if a friendly farmer hadn't happened along, we'd still be hiking home from Berkshire."

"They used deadly force to steal a damned wagon?" Adam asked.

"They both had pistols," the head mason said, his words bearing a thick Welsh accent. "Big, ugly pistols, the use of which I trow they grasped far more easily than they did the mechanism that works the tipper."

None of the tipper's various gears, screws, or levers had been stamped with a point of origin for this very reason. Adam could bear to lose a wagon, and he wasn't much concerned that others would learn how to use the mechanical advantage of a screw to raise one end of a wagon bed. Manufacturing that wagon involved a team that included carpenters, machinists, artificers, wheelwrights, and joiners, none of whom knew the identities of the others.

Until the patent on the wagon was approved, Adam would continue to exercise caution.

"You've both had an ordeal," he said. "Take the rest of the day off, and I'll hire a guard to... We don't have the damned tipper to guard."

"The first lot of new wagons are supposed to be ready by the end of the week," Rosenbarker replied. "We can unload the old-fashioned way until then."

Which would impact the schedule, and the payroll, and the dealings with the subcontractors.

"Do the best you can. I'll revise the schedule, hire guards for the site, and notify the authorities that my wagon has gone missing."

Though they would do little enough besides condole Adam on the loss. Doubtless the tipper was already in pieces in some barn or warehouse, never to be functional again.

"The blackguards also took a team of horses, guv," the head mason said. "That's a hanging offense too."

Forcing Adam to leave Brighton without offering Genie a farewell should be a hanging offense. Consigning him to spending the evening on schedules and budgets should be a hanging offense.

"Where do we get our tea?" Adam asked Rosenbarker when the head mason had departed for the nearest pub.

"Twinings on the Strand, because it's close and they don't adulterate the product with everything from grass clippings to hedge weeds."

"How late are they open?"

"Damned if I know. Where are you off to?"

Adam grabbed his hat and walking stick. "I'll be back within the hour. I'm off to report a crime." And buy some jasmine-scented tea.

* * *

Genie had spent three days traipsing the length and breadth of Brighton, Mr. Vernon at her side. One property was too small, another had creeping damp freshly painted over in the basement, a third was going soggy about the cupola, a fourth was perfect but too far from a livery and lacked space to add a stable.

No wonder Adam had been frustrated.

Genie was growing frustrated. Dunstable had called on her twice and all but sat himself in her lap, he'd been so fawningly devoted. He'd sent flowers after the last call, a gaudy profusion of irises sure to be remarked by anybody who'd seen the delivery boy pounding on the *front* door before the housekeeper had shooed him around to the back.

Dunstable had proposed an afternoon constitutional for tomorrow, and Genie was thus praying for rain, and for Adam's safe return.

"I did hear of one other property," Mr. Vernon said.

The cat sat at the solicitor's feet, wearing an expression that suggested a pounce would follow when Mr. Vernon was least prepared to host a cat on his lap.

"I am interested in anything remotely suitable." Genie was also interested in one architect, to the exclusion of all dukes, titles, or fortune hunters. Instinct prodded her to follow her heart, but Dunstable was circling like a vulture and threatening the two men whom Genie esteemed most highly in all the world.

"Bit of old scandal attached to this property," Mr. Vernon said. "I happened to dine last night with my former partner, Mr. Bacchus Dingle, and informed him of Your Grace's present quest. Dingle's memory goes back to before Brighton became fashionable, for he was raised here. He told me that the Duke of Seymouth had a residence built not far from the Pavilion, because our then-Regent's interest in Brighton was well established. Lovely property, according to Dingle."

None of the inquiries Genie had made—and she had made dozens—had mentioned anything about a ducal residence being for sale.

"Go on."

"The duke took it into his head that the builder had been skimping on materials, cutting corners, and overcharging. His Grace refused to pay for the property, and the builder retired in debt and disgrace. The property has stood empty all these years, though the ducal heir became the owner on the occasion of his majority. What sort of papa deeds over a rattletrap establishment to his firstborn, I ask you?"

An instant of foreboding settled over Genie before recollections turned her foreboding to dread.

Adam's father had suffered a nasty turn at the hands of a duke.

Seymouth was a duke whose firstborn had come of age in recent years.

Dunstable imposed on friends when he visited Brighton, suggesting any residence he owned was not regularly staffed.

Oh dear. Oh damn. Of all the dukes in all the peerages in all the world…

"If the property was poorly constructed, Mr. Vernon, shouldn't fifteen years of neglect have resulted in its disintegration?"

The cat decided to be civil and stropped himself against Vernon's boots. The solicitor picked the beast up and scratched his hairy chin.

"Your Grace, as usual, makes a practical observation. If the property was poorly constructed, then it would be riddled with damp. The sea air is unforgiving of shoddy work and hard on even a solid edifice. Would you like to see the house?"

"Above all things, and without alerting the present owner."

Vernon and the cat turned the same impatient expression on her. "Your Grace does not contemplate housebreaking, I hope?"

"Of course not. A duchess merely indulges in harmless, discreet curiosity. On no account is anybody to learn of my interest in the place. If I do make an offer, I want the owner to regard the sum tendered as a windfall from somebody ignorant of the building's tarnished pedigree."

Vernon set the cat down and rose. "I am your servant in all things, Your Grace. Will you at least comfort my conscience by assuring me that His Grace of Tindale will approve the expenditure before you saddle yourself with an uninhabitable abode?"

Genie got to her feet. "Who employs you, Mr. Vernon?"

"You do, Your Grace."

"Then as your employer, I encourage you to refrain from dragging any unnecessary dukes into my affairs. I'm available tomorrow at any hour to view this property."

She accompanied Mr. Vernon to the foyer and passed him his hat and walking stick. He was approaching his prime, no longer a boy, his wisdom beginning to catch up to the abundance of a young man's animal spirits. He was a fine solicitor, but England was full of fine solicitors, and Genie could not afford to be sentimental.

"We'll use the servants' entrance," he said. "Dress accordingly, for the place hasn't any staff in residence. I'll come by for you in the alley in a closed coach and return you by the same means."

Genie beamed at him. "You've done this before. I'm impressed, Mr. Vernon."

"Don't be impressed, Your Grace. Be very, very discreet. Good day."

She closed the door behind him and allowed herself a moment of hope. She'd spent years being discreet, and what had that earned her but Dunstable yapping at her heels and filching her heirlooms? Now he wanted to filch her future and get children on her, three boys, at least, with no guarantee that he'd keep his word to cease threatening Augustus—or Adam.

* * *

A smartly turned-out gentleman climbed into an equally smart town coach, which rolled away from Genie's doorstep at a smart pace. Adam had paused only long enough to wash the dust of the road from his person and wasn't feeling smart in any regard.

The gentleman might have been calling on one of the other ladies. He might have been an old friend, or a garden-variety fortune hunter. Adam resented him on general principles, though, because he'd been crisp and attractive and full of energy.

"Mr. Morecambe, a pleasant surprise," Genie said, ushering him into the formal parlor—not her private sitting room.

The leavings of a tea tray sat on the low table, and the cat, balancing on its back legs, was making designs on the cream pot.

"I was called to London again. Did Mrs. Thompson tell you?"

"She did. Shall we go upstairs? I've had about as much tea as I can tolerate for one day, but I will never tire of good company."

Genie's words should have reassured Adam, but her manner was merely friendly, and she looked tired. He followed her up the steps, long hours in the saddle making even that slight exertion an effort.

She left the door open and settled on the sofa. "How goes the work in London?"

Adam remained standing. "Somebody is trying to steal my tipper-wagon design. They won't get far without knowing how I put the thing together. Screws have been around for millennia. Might I sit?"

"Of course. I gather the tipper wagon is very clever?"

Adam took the place beside her on the sofa. "Very valuable, because it saves time and labor." *Who was that man?* "I've missed you."

She rose and took the wing chair when Adam had hoped she might instead close and lock the door.

"I've missed you as well, but in your absence, my situation has become complicated."

"In what regard?"

She tried for a smile and ended up studying the carpet, a fine Dutch weave of flowers and leaves in red, green, blue, and gold.

"Another suitor has presented himself, a most unexpected and ardent admirer."

Adam knew all about competing bids, and they didn't intimidate him. "Your expression suggests that admiration is not mutual."

"Admiration can take many forms."

He would have bet his tipper-wagon patent that Genie had not admired this rival in the privacy of her bed or on any picnic blankets.

"Are you showing me the door, Your Grace?" Part of him accepted that possibility as inevitable. His version of courting had been to drag her all over the backstairs of two large houses between disappearances to London. Not very impressive.

But his heart—his purely human heart—ached to think she'd give up on him so easily.

"I am not showing you the door, but if in the coming weeks, I am less available to you, or you see me in company that you cannot condone, then you must not take it amiss."

Adam rose, for he refused to take such a reversal of his dreams sitting down. "This is called letting me go gently. My spirits will soon be level with the pavement, but nobody will be troubled by a loud, impolite crash. I am to pretend your announcement has not devastated me, pretend my affections were only superficially engaged. That is what an almighty duke or a marquess or an earl—"

She'd flinched at the word *marquess*.

Dunstable, then, the pestilential spawn of a posing, prancing, lying old scoundrel of a duke.

"You fancy to become like your friend," Adam asked, "the Double Duchess? I read the papers, Your Grace. Has ducal consequence once again exerted itself to crush the aspirations of the lowly Morecambes?"

Say no. Say of course not. Say anything honest.

She shook her head. "Mr. Morecambe, I consider you a dear friend. I am not at liberty to say more, but please believe that my regard for you is genuine. I simply need time…" Her breathing caught, an odd hitch that she tried to cover by rising. "I simply have a few complications to sort out. I hope that one day soon, I might again be able to welcome your attentions."

She was tossing him out on his ear, ejecting him like a tavern regular who'd overimbibed.

Adam's pride demanded that he make a dignified exit, before overimbibing in truth. He was exhausted, furious, minus his tipper wagon, and soon to be minus his intended. Minus the woman who'd sat for hours while he'd sketched woodwork at Petworth.

Minus the lady who'd cheerfully driven through miles of countryside so he could spend a day admiring parts of Petworth he'd never be admitted to without her.

Minus the high-born friend who'd earned him a peek at every royal pantry in Brighton.

Minus his lover.

Minus his favorite duchess, whose first marriage had been bewildering, grueling, and, above all, *lonely.*

She was staring out the window, a pillar of unshared confidences and private woes. How stubborn she was, and how he loved her.

His father had slunk away from the prospect of holding a duke accountable. That course—bitter retreat—was unthinkable for Adam.

"Do you know," he said, "how strong a man becomes when he spends his youth wrestling good English stone? Do you know how determined that man learns to be when turning stone into art?"

"You should go. For your own sake, Adam, you should go."

She confirmed his suspicions with that warning, bless her proud, obstinate heart.

"I'm not going anywhere until you put aside your tiara long enough to tell the man who loves you which varlet has set himself against us and why he has you so frightened."

Genie didn't take a seat on the sofa, but rather, she deflated, from a proud duchess to a woman overwhelmed.

"I hate tiaras," she said. "My tiaras are heavy and old, and they give me awful headaches. I'm frightened—you're right—but I'm also bitterly, mortally angry."

Adam shifted to the sofa and put an arm around her shoulders. "Angry is good. With a little anger and a trusty sledgehammer, you can bring down almost any edifice. Now tell me where I need to swing my hammer and why."

CHAPTER EIGHT

The parlor door was open, and Genie did not care. She cared only that Adam had his arm around her and wasn't put off by a rival suitor.

Not by anything.

She could make another attempt to dissemble, to persuade him to give her time to deal with Dunstable on her own, but she'd been dealing with Dunstable, and her efforts had only made the cad bolder.

"I have been dissembling since the day I became betrothed to a duke," Genie said. "Wearing a tiara forged of lies. I'm a sheep farmer's daughter, and I am proud of that."

Adam kissed her hand. "No tiaras, I promise, but you have to tell me the rest of it."

A tiara of truths, then. "You cannot swing your hammer at a ducal family," she said. "Seymouth takes his consequence seriously, and though he might not respect his son, he'll take any affront to Dunstable as a slight to himself."

"As he should. An affront to my father, even fifteen years ago, offends me still." Adam scooped Genie into his lap, an exceedingly comfortable perch. "An affront to my intended will see me laying about with any tool I can grasp."

His intended. Not his duchess, thank the kind powers.

"Dunstable wants my money," Genie said. "I've rather a lot of it, and I gather his debts are enormous. He can't afford to open the house your father built here in Brighton, which has been deeded to Dunstable. I've seen the interior, Adam. It's a jewel of modern convenience and excellent taste, worthy of a ducal family trying to discreetly rival the sovereign."

Adam's hand on her back went still. "You've seen my father's house?"

She withdrew the pin from his cravat and snuggled closer. "Toured it from top to bottom. Dunstable's man of business attempted obstinance, but duchesses have reserves of stubbornness mere lawyers cannot hope to achieve. I found no hint of damp, not a whiff of subsidence, not so much as a stuck window. Seymouth would have known that if he'd bothered to inspect his own premises."

Which dukes rarely did. They relied on stewards, men of business, solicitors, and an overworked duchess to keep all running smoothly. Augustus would not be such a duke, but Seymouth exercised every privilege of his station.

"Thank you," Adam said, kissing her temple. "I knew my father would not cheat a customer, but I haven't been able to prove it. Your eyewitness testimony erases my last doubt."

She sat up to peer at him. "You would doubt your own papa?"

"Not his integrity, but the best architect can be hoodwinked by a dishonest builder, the best builder can be taken advantage of by a lazy master mason, and the best mason can be cheated by the quarry. Constant vigilance is impossible when an architect's practice is going well."

"You sound like a duke." Adam smelled like himself, though, mostly cedar with hints of linseed oil and sawdust in the far corners of his fragrance. Genie loved the scent of him, loved the feel of his arms around her.

Loved him for telling her to put her tiara aside.

"I have not the resources of a duke," Adam said, "but I have the ability to take a bare patch of ground, and from nothing more than a sketched elevation, I can build an edifice that will last for centuries. Tell me why you haven't laughed in Dunstable's face on the dance floor at Almack's."

Delicious thought. "He has threatened me, which would be of no moment, but he's also threatened Augustus, and—lest that not be sufficient—he's thrown a few vague aspersions in your direction as well."

Adam kissed her cheek. "He's promised to ruin me."

"Promised with a casual cheer that makes me uneasy."

Adam was quiet for a moment, his hand resuming a soothing rhythm on Genie's back. "Do you esteem the present Duke of Tindale?"

"Augustus? I adore him. He danced with me at my presentation ball, a great, growling brute of a man whom nobody dared cut, but nobody wanted to acknowledge. He was the cousin they had to invite and wished to never see. He told me not to let a parcel of prancing ninnyhammers send me to bedlam. He also told me we were to be family, and I was entitled to his unquestioning loyalty for the rest of my days."

"I like him already, but you are a woman of great sense, and you feel you have to protect Augustus from Dunstable. What is the rest of the story, Genie?"

Genie wiggled from his grasp and rose, an undignified undertaking. Adam made no move to thwart her and had sense enough to remain on the sofa.

"I betrayed my husband in one sense and in one sense only."

"You failed to conceive a child, which is hardly your fault."

Any other man would have dodged that topic, brushed it aside with platitudes about the will of God, the futility of dwelling on the past. Adam started his enterprises from bare ground, though, and planted his foundations securely on truth.

"That is not quite accurate. I did conceive. I'm almost sure of it." Even now, Genie had to leave herself a reprieve, a hope that her sorrow had been unfounded. "The early signs were there, the very early signs, that is. I hadn't said a word to Charles, on the advice of the midwife. She suggested I wait at least another two months to be certain. I was counting the days, my hope nearly eclipsed by my anxiety."

The hope had been excruciating, and the sorrow proportional.

"You lost the child."

"If a child there was. We were having a dinner party, and I told myself the discomfort I was experiencing was from the wine, the candle smoke, anything. When I found a moment to use the retiring room, I learned my courses had started. Augustus came across me sitting on the stair, unable to speak, unable to return to my guests. I could not cry—duchesses don't cry in the middle of their own entertainments—and the tale came out. I never told Charles, but I hoped desperately to conceive again."

The weight of that hope had dragged at every moment of her marriage, added to her grief, and still threatened to overwhelm her. She braced herself on the mantel, and then Adam's arms were around her and she was sobbing against his shoulder.

She cried not simply for a barren marriage, but for a happy Derbyshire girl who'd come to London with stars in her eyes and been handed a cold, heavy parure. She cried for all the girls and all the busy, self-important men casually crushing their spirits because those men had never been taught better. She cried for her widowed self, looking after those young women and spreading graciousness in all directions, while longing for the rural splendor of the north.

"I told Augustus," she said, her voice made low from tears, "and he has kept my secret to this day. Dunstable saw me in Augustus's arms, saw Augustus kiss my forehead, and has made a great salacious interlude out of it. Nobody would have cared if I discreetly dallied with my husband's cousin—though I ought by rights to have produced sons first—but now that cousin has the title, and Dunstable has debts."

Adam walked her to the sofa, came down beside her, and tucked her close. "So Dunstable must threaten a woman who has done him no wrong rather than take up an honest profession or tell his father he's in dun territory. If he'd stolen from the poor or turned the elderly out of their homes, I might not hold him in greater contempt."

"He's threatened you and Augustus. He sought to marry me, but he can ruin you and make false accusations to the authorities regarding Augustus. Augustus is not a typical duke."

"For which we must commend him. I need to think."

While Genie needed to be quiet, recover her composure, and for once let somebody else consider her situation while she dozed against his side and dreamed of chubby lambs and lush meadows.

* * *

"Luddy," Dunstable said, taking a seat at the luncheon table, "you see before you a man in anticipation of matrimonial joy. Pass the wine."

The earl obliged, though he took the precaution of pouring for himself first. Dunstable started his serious drinking with the midday meal, and Luddington had no reason to believe today would be an exception.

"Has the young lady accepted your addresses?"

Dunstable filled his glass to the brim. "She's not young, but her fortune compensates for a host of shortcomings. I do fancy a hearty merlot, though not usually so early in the day."

"Jones," Luddington said to the footman at the sideboard, "please serve his lordship some of the soup, and then you may be excused." Not that Dunstable would bother with excellent beef and barley stew when he could instead be swilling wine. "What does your papa think of your choice of bride?"

More to the point, what would the Duchess of Seymouth think?

Dunstable's dame could make any young woman's life merry hell on a good day, and bachelors regarded time in her company as durance vile.

"Haven't told Papa yet, but he's been after me for years to 'start conducting my affairs like an adult.' To hear him tell it, he was meeting with his stewards before he was breeched, and Mama was stitching prayer samplers before she could read. Why do we teach women to read anyway? All they do is correspond with each other the livelong day and tattle on their menfolk."

By which means, family and social ties were preserved despite great distances and years of separation. "Are you drunk already?"

"Believe I am. Drunk with joy at the prospect of putting aside the lonely tedium of bachelorhood and accepting the responsibilities I was born to shoulder. Certain funds will come under my control when I marry—certain needed funds—and my lady wife will add to those funds nicely. Should have married long ago, but never met the right sort of female."

"What sort would that be?" Besides desperate.

"One wants a wife whom one can control," Dunstable said, downing half his wine. "I need look no farther than my dear parents to see what havoc a female can wreak when she don't know her place. I won't have that problem."

"You'd marry a simpering featherbrain?" Luddington shuddered to contemplate the offspring of such a union.

"I'd marry a mature woman who knows how to respect her duke. Fortune is smiling on my choice. I've had an omen." He nodded sagely and finished his wine.

"You've taken to reading bird entrails."

"Mock me all you please, Luddy." Dunstable helped himself to another bumper of merlot. "That dreadful property Papa tried to foist upon me when I came of age has caught the interest of a buyer. Have you another bottle of this vintage? It's quite good."

Luddington set aside his empty soup bowl. "I generally buy by the lot when I find a wine I enjoy. I didn't know your Brighton property was for sale."

"It's not. The damned solicitor said I'd have to load it up with furniture and art and servants to get a decent price for it. I'm letting it go for a mere bagatelle, but between us, the construction ain't sound. Papa said. Damned place will be somebody else's problem. Caveat empty, and all that."

"*Caveat emptor,*" Luddington murmured. *Let the buyer beware.* "I congratulate you on your good fortune, both as regards the real property and the marital prospects. Might I know the name of your intended?" He asked out of simple expedience, for he himself was in the market for a spouse. No need to court another man's prospective duchess.

"You may ask, though you are sworn to secrecy. Have to inform Papa of my choice, and he'll have to talk Mama 'round. I intend to offer for none other than Eugenia, Dowager Duchess of Tindale."

Luddington nearly got a snoutful of merlot. "You think *she* will make you a biddable and docile duchess?" The lady had brooked no nonsense from her haughty husband and was held in very high esteem by the matchmakers. The fortune hunters had learned not to approach that citadel, and King George was said to owe her favors.

"I'm certain of my ability to maintain the upper hand in the marriage. For me, the duchess will be the epitome of domestic subservience."

"Have some more wine," Luddington said, though clearly poor Dunstable was already either half-seas over or showing signs of early dementia. "Did I mention that I'm removing to London at the end of the week? You're welcome to bide here as long as you please, but I must look in on my sister."

For under no circumstances did Luddington want the task of consoling Dunstable when the duchess sent the marquess packing with a flea in his ear.

* * *

With Genie tucked against his side, Adam could think more efficiently. She was snoring gently, spent from unburdening herself, while he mentally constructed a project schedule complete with elevations, landscape plans, and a budget.

He would need the services of one duke and one duchess—possibly two of both—and the timing would be delicate. Funds would be required and some luck.

The most critical asset, however, was determination. "My love, wake up." He kissed Genie's temple, because he could.

"Chocolate."

"I can think of many ways to wake a lady that are more enticing than chocolate."

She straightened to peer at him. "You are a resourceful man. I must look a fright."

"You look splotchy and tired, also lighter in spirit and very dear. If you can gather your wits enough to plot a strategy with me, I have need of your keen intelligence and remarkable powers of observation."

She kissed his cheek, lingering near enough that the scent of her addled Adam's wits. "Nobody has ever valued my keen mind before."

"When you are the wealthiest sheep farmer in Derbyshire, they'll learn of their error." For she would be. She'd see which flocks prospered in which fields, which ewes produced the most twins, which shepherds truly loved their occupation, and soon, fat, fluffy sheep would dot every hillside she owned. Adam would build snug byres for the sheep and model cottages for the tenants...

"We will own property in Derbyshire?"

Why hadn't anybody, not her damned ducal cousin, not her brothers, not her man of business, bought her an estate in Derbyshire?

"You will own property in Derbyshire. We'll tie it up in a trust for our daughters, and when you are wroth with me, you will remove there to torment me. I won't dare trespass, or you'll have me ejected and bound over for the assizes, and your neighbor, His Grace of Devonshire, will see me transported."

Genie curled down to rest her head in his lap, as she had on their picnic blanket. "Your vivid imagination is surely why you are such a success as an architect, but before I become a sheep nabob, might we decide what to do with Lord Dunstable?"

Might we decide. Adam had never taken a partner for his building projects. He suspected that was about to change.

"What is needed," he said, "is truth, and somebody with enough consequence to make that truth compelling, for the same source authored my father's downfall as can author Dunstable's."

"His Grace of Seymouth."

"*Their* Graces of Seymouth. I know not what role Her Grace played in Papa's troubles, but if she'd taken so much as a single tour of the Brighton property, she might have intervened. The house was built to her specifications."

Adam closed his eyes, the better to learn the curve of Genie's cheek against his palm, the better to savor the texture of her skin. Her face was warm, her hair silky. For the first time in years, he felt the urge to take up a mallet and chisel to craft cold stone into a living form.

Instead, he must sculpt a solution to Genie's troubles, and to his own.

"Her Grace is formidable," Genie said. "Quite the force of nature. I've arranged to buy that house. I'd thought to sell it to you for your gentlemen's club."

An odd effervescence cascaded through Adam's heart. "You bought my father's house for me?"

"You needn't get all masculine and affronted. The business called for some subtlety, and nobody suspects a duchess of anything other than self-indulgence. I will charge you exactly what I paid for the place, and you may do with it as you please."

She'd bought the property, protected Adam's pride, and done so with Dunstable prancing about her parlor. She was a terror in a tiara, and if Adam hadn't been in love with her before…

He was in love and he was in awe, a stirring combination of sentiments. "What are you paying for the house?"

She named a figure, perhaps one-tenth what the dwelling was worth, and Adam just had to hug the stuffing out of her.

"The Duchess of Seymouth might be intimidating," he said when he had stopped laughing, "but you are the more formidable, for you bring the element of surprise to every battle. You are so gracious and charming that others miss your determination and strength. I must learn to be formidable as well."

Genie patted his thigh. "You can be grouchy and direct. That's a fine start on formidable, and an aptitude for numbers helps."

"Anybody can work an abacus and eschew idle talk."

"I've done what I could, Adam, but Dunstable will now have the funds from the sale of the house, and he'll be pleased with himself for having liquidated an asset his father could not. He means to offer for me and to create serious trouble for Augustus and for the man I love if I refuse."

The man I love.

"I cannot have a mincing dukeling vexing the woman I love with threats of marital servitude."

Genie sat up and situated herself in Adam's lap, her arms around him. For a long, lovely moment, Adam reveled in their mutual declarations. His breeding organs clamored to celebrate the occasion intimately, but first he must conclude the strategy session.

"You have kindly given me the means to make the truth of my father's situation known to all and sundry," Adam said. "I need only execute the task I dread most in the entire world—other than losing you—to see the plan put in motion."

Genie left off teasing his earlobe with her tongue. "What task is that?"

"I must give aid to a duke and ask him to aid me in return."

* * *

"A bear in morning attire is pacing about in the formal parlor," Anne, Duchess of Tindale, said. "I like the looks of him."

Augustus more than liked the looks of his duchess, a circumstance which weeks of marriage hadn't changed. Anne passed over a silver salver with a single card on it.

"I intercepted Jenkins," she said. "He would not have offered this visiting bear tea. What manner of ducal household fails to offer hospitality to all who call?"

"One recovering from years of priggish posturing. Shall you join me in receiving"—Augustus glanced at the card—"Mr. Morecambe?"

"He's an architect. I'm not in need of any buildings or renovations, while you own property in six counties and the City. I'll leave you to it."

She sashayed from the room, grinning over her shoulder as she passed through the doorway, because of course, Augustus had watched her departure with a worshipful devotion that only grew the longer they were married.

He tucked Mr. Morecambe's card into his pocket, buttoned his morning coat, and prepared to set down a presuming fellow who should have made an appointment rather than stormed the ducal residence. Augustus appreciated initiative wherever he found it, though, so he'd at least hear the bear—the fellow—out.

Anne hadn't exaggerated regarding Morecambe's appearance. He was large, dark, and possessed of shoulders worthy of a blacksmith. His countenance was far from refined, and his blue eyes held not a hint of deference.

"Mr. Morecambe." Augustus bowed. "I don't believe we have been introduced."

Morecambe bent from the waist. "I'm madly in love with your cousin by marriage. We can discuss that later."

Being a duke was tedious. One wasn't to brawl, not physically, not verbally, not financially, not ever, and as Mr. Morecambe turned an imperious glower on his host, Augustus realized how much he'd missed brawling.

"We'll discuss it now, sir. Who the hell are you to fall in love with the Dowager Duchess of Tindale?"

"I'm the man who will get her free of Lord Dunstable's clutches, and you are the man who will listen to what I have to say before you summon footmen to do what you yourself don't dare attempt."

"Toss you out on your presuming ear?"

"*Attempt* to lay hands on me. I'm not very toss-able, Your Grace. I suggest you take my word on that, for your duchess doubtless values the present arrangement of your features."

Augustus nearly burst into whoops, but he was learning to be a duke—to be Anne's duke. "Before I return the favor and rearrange your features, would you care for some tea, Mr. Morecambe?"

"No, thank you. I'd care to enlist your aid in ensuring that Lord Dunstable is shamed for his presumption."

"You have a pretty way of asking for help."

Morecambe smiled, and his resemblance to a large, hungry, wild beast was complete. "The Dowager Duchess of Tindale finds my ways pretty enough."

Genie hadn't thought to warn Augustus of Mr. Morecambe's call. She must finally be recovering from her marriage to Charles.

"The dowager duchess was gracious to me when the rest of my family barely acknowledged me. Trifle with her, Morecambe, and I will kill you."

"As well you should. Lord Dunstable is attempting to trifle with her, but she won't let me call him out. A fate worse than death is to live with dishonor, and I'd like to sentence Lord Dung-stable to at least that."

Augustus held out his hand. "Welcome to the family. What have you in mind?"

Morecambe's grip was crushing, though Augustus knew that Genie's pet bear would be the soul of tender delicacy with her. Anne would be so pleased, and Augustus was damned happy for Genie too.

CHAPTER NINE

Genie's nerves were in a state, balanced between hope and despair. She received her guests with the Duke and Duchess of Tindale at her side, for she'd appropriated the ducal town house in Brighton for her ball.

Her guest list had skimmed the cream of summer Society from the seaside towns, and no less personages than the Duke and Duchess of Seymouth had bestirred themselves to accept her invitation. Dunstable had called upon her nigh daily, while Adam had taken himself back to London with every appearance of having ended their association.

"You have the document?" Augustus asked during a lull in the receiving line.

"Adam sent it by express earlier today," Genie replied.

"And where is your Mr. Morecambe?"

"On his way." Though Genie had no idea if that was the case. Construction at the club had been plagued by the usual sorts of delays and setbacks, and cold weather would arrive without regard to an architect's schedules. Horses went lame, coaches overturned, and plans went awry.

"I saw the house you purchased for your architect," Augustus said. "Lovely property."

"The ceilings," Anne murmured. "I want those ceilings. Tindale, you are warned."

"Our ceiling renovations will start in the bedroom." Augustus and his duchess exchanged a look that confirmed where the couple spent most of their time when at home.

"The eighth biblical plague approaches," Genie said, pasting her own darling-duchess smile in place and curtseying to Her Grace of Seymouth. "Your Grace, welcome. So glad you could join us."

Genie endured the same sniffy perusal she'd been treated to a thousand times before, a copper heiress's lot when she aspired to become a duchess. Now, though, she was a duchess, and she was soon to become Mrs. Adam Morecambe.

She returned the older woman's rudeness.

"Dunstable told us to expect an announcement," the older woman said. "I'd best not have spent three hours in a coach only to learn one of your protégés has snagged a mere honorable, madam."

"We assure you," Augustus said, "this evening will figure in your memories for years to come."

The greetings proceeded at the pace of a turtle navigating a sandy beach, with Dunstable all but licking Genie's glove, and still, no Adam. The time came to open the dancing, and fortunately for Genie, the Tindale dukedom had nearly a century's precedence over the Seymouth dukedom, or she would have been forced to dance with Dunstable's papa.

"This feels right," Augustus said as he escorted Genie to the center of the dance floor. "I danced with you at your presentation ball, and now you dance with me at my first formal appearance in Society as a ducal host. Where the hell is Morecambe?"

"Adam will not fail me," Genie said, sinking into the requisite curtsey, "and Dunstable has already appropriated my supper waltz, exactly as planned."

The next two hours were spent in the usual fashion for Genie—matching wallflowers with bachelors, diffusing spats among the ladies in the retiring room, monitoring the punch and those who partook too often from the men's bowl.

Dunstable's gaze followed her everywhere, and when Genie spent a few minutes visiting with the Duchess of Anselm, a friend from the days of Genie's court presentation, Dunstable went so far as to stand in Genie's line of sight and pat his pocket.

Wherein a ring doubtless nestled.

The supper waltz arrived, and nothing would do but Genie must dance with Dunstable.

"Do I mistake the matter, my dear, or are we to make an announcement when our guests have sampled the buffet?"

His gaze dropped to Genie's décolletage; she tramped on his foot.

"I have not the gift of seeing into the future, my lord, but I do hope Augustus will make an announcement by the end of the evening."

"I suppose His Grace of Tindale is the host, though Papa does a fine job of commanding the attention of a large company. I thought we'd make our wedding journey to Paris, but then, everybody goes to Paris."

"You have creditors waiting for you in Paris, and they will seize your coach and horses, if not my jewels, to settle the debts you've run up." Adam had passed that tidbit along. Dunstable's situation in London wasn't much better, which explained his weeks by the sea sponging off of Lord Luddington.

Also his desperation to plunder Genie's fortune.

"If Tindale has been looking into my finances, then I must assume he has raised no objection to our match. I thought a special license would suit, so that we can be married at Seymouth House."

He tried to twirl Genie under his arm and ended up clipping her on the jaw with his elbow. The blow stung, not her first in the course of a polite waltz, and he had the grace to look horrified.

"Too much punch," he said. "I do apologize."

"If it happens again, Augustus will doubtless provide you instructions on how to properly stand up with a lady, though by the conclusion of his lesson, you will be hard put to stand without assistance yourself."

The waltz came to an end, and Dunstable clamped his hand around Genie's. "Tindale doesn't plan to be an interfering sort of relation, I hope."

"You know how fond I am of Cousin Augustus," Genie said. "I expect if I remarry, he'll be very much in evidence until he's satisfied the union is happy. I did the same when he and his duchess were courting. Family looks after family, you know."

"Any more looking after you with close embraces on secluded stairways after we're married, and His Grace will become an outcast, his duchess with him."

You will become the outcast, God willing.

They took their places in the buffet line, though Genie had no interest in the food. The Duke and Duchess of Seymouth were looking bored and impatient—also tired—and Augustus was nowhere to be seen.

Anne, however, caught Genie's eye over the offerings of *soufflés à la vanille* and smiled like the cat who'd devised how to open the canary's cage.

"He's here," she whispered.

Genie wanted to dump her plate over Dunstable's head, but instead comported herself like a duchess, nibbling this and that, tasting none of it. All the while, Dunstable chattered about Continental destinations he'd never seen and sat so close his knee constantly bumped against Genie's.

She felt sorry for him, despite his bullying and arrogance, for he'd very likely be living in one of those far-off cities unless his papa agreed to again pay off his debts.

At the top of the steps, the herald was consulting with a late arrival, a tall man with broad shoulders, his evening attire accented with a red rose *boutonniere.*

"I have a late-arriving guest," Genie said, setting her plate aside. "Perhaps you'd like to greet him with me?"

Dunstable stuffed another strawberry into his mouth and rose. "Of course. My duchess is the soul of graciousness, and then we can find some library or parlor and get the bended-knee bit over with. Paid a damned fortune for the ring. Had to sell my Brighton property because the jeweler would only take cash."

Good for the jeweler.

Adam smiled faintly as she approached.

"I don't recognize him," Dunstable said. "Looks familiar, though. Probably got some of his blunt at the gaming tables. Are you sure he was invited?"

"He is the guest of honor," Genie said, gaining the top of the steps. "Mr. Morecambe, a sincere pleasure to see you here tonight. Have you met Lord Dunstable?"

Adam sketched a bow. "I have had that honor. My lord, good evening." Adam was breathtaking in his formal clothing, and the mere sight of him settled Genie's nerves.

"Morecambe. Suppose you've come for the free food and drink. Don't bother the women, or this will be the last ball you attend."

"Do you promise?" Adam asked, taking Genie's hand and tucking it over his arm. "To be spared the tedium of Society balls would be a great blessing."

Dunstable looked like his cravat had abruptly grown too tight.

"Shall we repair to the formal parlor?" Genie suggested. "Mr. Morecambe has some news to pass along to you, my lord."

"Mr. Morecambe's news had best not take long," Dunstable said, starting down the corridor. "I have plans for that formal parlor that do not include him and his clumsy attempts at flirtation."

Adam bent close to Genie. "You are well?"

"I will be. The letter is in the parlor, and I hope Augustus awaits us there with Their Graces."

"Two dukes, a duchess, and a presuming disgrace of a lordling. Promise you'll not abandon me in such company, Genie."

"Never."

"Then all shall be well."

* * *

Disaster had struck, in the form of bad eel pie served at the pub nearest to the club's construction site. For most of a week, Adam had had barely half a crew at barely half strength. He'd carried hod, he'd laid brick, he'd wielded saws, mallets, and hammers, while Tindale had passed along each debt and bet Dunstable owed money on.

The sum was astounding and showed a capacity for industry, albeit mischievous industry. Adam ached in every particular as a result of the past week's exertion, but sore muscles and scraped knuckles faded from his awareness at the sight of his Genie.

He'd never seen her in a ball gown, and the shimmering russet velvet showed her off exquisitely. She'd chosen rubies for her jewels—fittingly precious—and gold settings. By candlelight, she glowed, while Dunstable looked pallid and effete.

When Adam arrived to the formal parlor, Augustus had served the Duke and Duchess of Seymouth glasses of wine. A missive sat on the escritoire's leather blotter, the red seal unbroken. Augustus was looking severe, while Her Grace of Seymouth was looking dyspeptic.

"There you are," she said when she caught sight of Dunstable. "Have you an announcement to make? I came all this way, braved the dust of the road and the heaving of that dreadful coach, because I was promised by your father that the evening would result in cheering news. The sea air does not agree with me, I can tell you that straightaway, young man, so you'd best be about your business."

"Lord Dunstable will appreciate his parents' support, I'm sure," Adam said, withdrawing a folded paper from his pocket. "He's considering paying his addresses to the dowager duchess, but sought to compel her agreement to his proposal by force."

The Duke of Seymouth was on his feet in the next instant. "Who the hell are you, and what gives you the right to make any accusations against a ducal heir?"

"I am the lady's intended," Adam said. "I make no accusations, I state facts. This is a list of your son's debts, Your Grace. If you ask him, he'll tell you he sold his Brighton property to satisfy a few of his creditors. In fact, he spent a pittance with the jewelers on Ludgate Hill, then gambled away the rest."

Dunstable sank into a chair. "Every gentleman has debts. His Grace knows that, and the Brighton property was falling in on itself."

Dunstable's mother glowered at Adam. "The Brighton property was an eyesore, which you'd know if you'd ever set foot inside it. Nothing was done as it should have been, because the architect was a cheating scoundrel who thought to ill-use his betters. Be off with you, whoever you are, and don't think to show your face among polite society again."

Adam bowed. He did not withdraw. "I am Adam Morecambe, son of the man who designed, financed, and oversaw the building of your Brighton property, madam. My father died in penury and disgrace because he was cheated, lied to, and taken advantage of by a pair of high-born scoundrels whose perfidy will soon become common knowledge. If Your Grace of Seymouth will please read the letter awaiting you on the escritoire?"

Seymouth stalked over to the desk and slit the seal. "To whom it might interest," he began…

I have had the pleasure of recently examining the dwelling located at the corner of Monmouth and Exmoor Streets, Brighton, which dwelling first became known to me when a late associate in the architectural profession, one Peter T. Morecambe, consulted with me on plans for the building more than fifteen years ago. My inspection was undertaken in anticipation of the sale of the property by Lord Dunstable to a dear acquaintance of longstanding, the Dowager Duchess of Tindale. Though the house was in want of a thorough cleaning, I found all appointments carried out exactly according to the plans signed for by the late Mr. Morecambe, which plans I did examine in detail prior to visiting the premises.

A better example of domestic elegance on a tasteful scale does not come to my mind, and several of the innovations—plumbing on the upper floors, speaking tubes to accompany the bell system, a solar on the uppermost floor—have been incorporated into my own subsequent designs.

I cannot fathom why such a lovely and commodious home suffered so many years of disuse and neglect, but I hope that in future, the prospective owner will do justice to this jewel of architectural art.

John Nash, Architect to King George IV

Seymouth tossed the letter onto the desk. Tindale took it up.

"What do you want of me, Morecambe?" Seymouth asked. "The house has been sold. Your father is long dead. Take the matter to court, for all I care, but don't expect me—"

"Seymouth." The duchess spoke softly. "I told you not to believe a man of business who knew nothing of building. I told you to have a look, to get another opinion."

"Your Grace," Seymouth retorted, "now is not the time to air old and much-wrinkled linen."

Dunstable looked from one parent to the other. "You mean to tell me that I sold a house John Nash has deemed *a jewel of architectural whatever*? Sold it for a *pittance*?"

The duke and duchess spoke at the same time. "Hush."

"You did," Adam said, "and I now own the property. I'll convert it into seaside quarters for the members of my gentlemen's club, once it has been cleaned and refurbished. My wife will oversee the decorative scheme once we return from a protracted wedding trip to Derbyshire."

"Derbyshire is lovely this time of year," Augustus observed.

"Derbyshire is lovely any time of year," Genie added.

"What's the rest of it?" Dunstable's mama snapped. "There has to be more, or you wouldn't have gone to all this trouble. Your father has been exonerated of cheating us. What else can you want?"

"Your son has attempted to extort not only an enormous sum of money from my intended, but also to force her to join him at the altar. In an effort to placate his ambitions, she has surrendered at least two personal heirlooms. Dunstable saw, years ago, an embrace between cousins by marriage during a private moment of grief and chose to misconstrue that memory when it became to his advantage to do so. He is no gentleman."

"Now see here," Dunstable began, "I cannot be responsible for the foolish fancies of a widow whose recollections are as inaccurate as they are unflattering to me. I never threatened, implied, or intimated in any way

gone to his reward. I will recommend your services to all and sundry, Mr. Morecambe, and admit my part in the misunderstanding that sent your father into retirement. Honesty from me now won't give you back your father, but it will allow me a very small measure of self-respect."

He bowed and withdrew, his duchess at his side.

"That went well," Augustus said. "I do believe Seymouth and his duchess consider themselves in your debt, Morecambe."

"Honor is not the exclusive province of the titled," Adam said.

Genie kissed his cheek. "Nor of those who wear breeches. Away with you, Augustus. Adam has something he wants to ask me."

Tindale stayed right where he was. "If it has to do with capitals and astragals, then an estimate would be the first—"

"Out," Adam said. "Now."

Augustus scampered from the room—in as much as a largish duke could scamper—and Adam took Genie by the hand and led her over to the sofa.

"Your Grace," he said, lacing his fingers with hers. "Would you do me the very great honor of reserving all of your future picnics for me and me alone?"

"Yes," Genie said, wrapping her arms about his neck, "or yes, unless children come along, in which case, we will have to let them accompany us at least some of the time."

Oh, that was the best, best answer. Adam kissed her and kissed her and kissed her, and only Augustus rapping on the door prevented Genie from holding their first picnic as a betrothed couple on the rug before the formal parlor's hearth.

EPILOGUE

Genie mapped out a wedding journey that wandered from Yorkshire to Lancashire, then down to her beloved Derbyshire, the better to inspect properties for purchase. She also frequently inspected her husband's unclad person.

She settled on a lovely estate in Derbyshire and promptly named it Farmdale. The lintel over the drawing room was Gibbons's work, and the portrait gallery included plasterwork by Bradbury and Pettifer.

"I do so love my sheep," she said, lounging back on the blanket. "They seem happy."

Adam, upon whose chest she reclined, propped his chin on her crown. "They seem woolly and happy."

She turned in his arms, feeling like the luckiest woman in the realm. "Are you happy?"

Adam nuzzled her ear, which gave her the shivers in the best possible way. "Not quite."

Oh dear. She'd worried. She had never quite felt like a genuine duchess—and thank heavens she no longer had to try—but would Adam ever feel comfortable as the husband of a dowager duchess?

"What's amiss?"

"Another viscount has petitioned for membership in the club." The gentlemen's club in London was simply named Morecambe's, nicknames notwithstanding.

Adam had the loveliest steady heartbeat. "How many is that?" Genie asked.

"This will be our fourth if we approve of his application. He's an earl's heir."

Three months ago, Genie might have scampered off to the nearest copy of Debrett's, where she'd research the courtesy lord in question and all of his family connections. The Farmdale library held no such volume.

"Is he a decent fellow?" she asked.

"Seems to be. Two current members vouch for him. He pays the trades on time."

Genie struggled into a sitting position as an inquisitive lamb sniffed at the blanket. "But you don't want his business?"

"I want the business of any decent man who appreciates a place to spend time with others of like temperament, but this man will be an earl someday. Viscounts can be relatively unassuming, but an earl…"

Genie waited, because Adam considered his words and what he had to say mattered.

"Life was simpler when I could resent the entire peerage and dukes in particular," he said. "We've been invited over to Chatsworth for dinner."

"His Grace of Devonshire is a lovely man," Genie said. "He's a bit hard of hearing, but a great patron of the arts and sciences." He was also their neighbor, by country reckoning, and a genial host.

The lamb grew bolder, sniffing at the wicker basket on one corner of the blanket.

"He's a duke," Adam said. "This part of the country is positively infested with them. I'm an architect."

"My favorite architect, who is wrestling with some conundrum which you've yet to share with me."

Adam distracted the lamb by scratching its woolly forehead. "Devonshire's invitation included a note. He'd like my opinion on some renovations."

"Ah."

He scooped up the lamb and cradled the lucky little creature against his chest. "Am I a tradesman, a respected professional, a neighbor?"

"What would you like to be?"

"Mostly, I'd like to be your husband." The lamb leaped off of Adam's lap and gamboled away. He watched it go, and Genie took the lamb's place.

"You are concerned," she said, pushing his hair back from his brow, "that a gentleman does not engage in trade, much less in commercial undertakings. As an architect, you were a gentleman with a profession. Now you are in the middle of Derbyshire, with me."

"My favorite place to be."

He meant that, and he'd given up much to make it so. "Adam, you don't have to choose. You don't have to remain penned here at Farmdale like one of my rams. You can be Devonshire's neighbor and consult on his renovations. Chatsworth is a perpetual work in progress and enormous. If the duke isn't modifying his house, he's tinkering with the stables, the gardens, the conservatory, the landscaping, the fountains... I'm sure you will assist him if you can, and if he offers a professional arrangement, and you'd enjoy the work, then do it."

Adam passed her a clover plucked from the grass. "For pay? You would not object to my taking commissions?"

He'd found a lucky clover, hadn't even had to hunt for it.

"You trained long and hard to develop your expertise, and Devonshire has pots of money. Why should you work for free? I don't intend to give my wool away." That Adam would trouble over this decision and discuss it with her was all the morning gift Genie would ever need.

"I never want you to regret marrying me, Genie. You learned to move in circles I never aspired to reach, and I..."

"You love to build things." He'd built her the most marvelous barn, for example, with winches and trapdoors and chutes and clever lifts.

"Mostly, I want to build a life with you. I'll have a look at the renovations at Chatsworth." He fanned his hand over the grass again, as if he could feel the four-leaf clovers. "Worksop apparently needs some interior redesign as well."

"That's the family seat of the Dukes of Norfolk."

Adam was smiling. "His Grace of Newcastle has invited us to Clumber House at a time of your convenience. I think your peers are rallying to your cause, madam."

Genie tackled him, because what were blankets—and husbands—for? "They are rallying to *your* cause, you daft man. Not all dukes are like Seymouth or Dunstable. They are the exceptions, in fact. Most dukes are simply gentlemen with complicated estates."

"I am a gentleman," Adam said, frothing Genie's skirts up. "I am *your* gentleman."

He was so much more than that. He was Genie's partner in every regard, her lover, her companion, her favorite architect.

"You will be very busy," she said, kissing his nose. "I might have to hire you to ensure our home is kept in good repair."

"You will come with me on reconnaissance," he said. "I don't intend to take on these dukes without you."

"We'll take them on together, just as you assist me to manage my flocks, and—oh, Mr. Morecambe." Adam had situated himself behind her, so they lay spooned on the blanket. His hand had found its way between her legs, and Genie's thoughts went scampering off like spring lambs.

"We should reply to Devonshire's invitation, Mrs. Morecambe." He called her that when they were private, and it was Genie's favorite endearment. "Also to Newcastle and Norfolk. You'll help me compose my replies?"

"No dukes right now, please, Adam. Not on my picnic blanket, please." What he could do with his big, talented hands…

He leaned closer and kissed her temple. "No dukes for now, then, only the architect of your fondest wishes and most intimate dreams."

To my dear readers,

I hope you enjoyed Adam and Genie's happily ever after, meaning no disrespect to all those dashing dukes. For my next full-length novel, *My Own True Duchess* (June 2018), I recruited a ducal heir, Jonathan Tresham, to woo the fair maid. Suffice it to say, Jonathan's dashing needs some work—a lot of work—and Theodosia Haviland has a few pointers for him. Order your copy by visiting my website.. Enjoy an excerpt below.

If you simply must have another duke, you'll be pleased to know that the first story in my **Rogues to Riches Series**, *My One and Only Duke* (Nov. 2018), features Quinn Wentworth, who doesn't find out he's come into a ducal title until he's kicking his heels in Newgate prison. Jane Winston come along, and then things really get interesting. Enjoy an excerpt below.

I hope to have another **True Gentlemen** on the shelves in September 2018, but that will require the cooperation of a certain stubborn earl—I'm looking at you, Grey Birch Dorning—and a widow with a mind of her own. Wheeee!

If you'd like to keep up to date regarding my upcoming deals, pre-orders, or new releases, following me on **Bookbub** is a handy way to do that. Find me at https://www.bookbub.com/profile/grace-burrowes. If you're more the type who enjoys cover reveals and author-chat in addition the new release announcements, you can **sign up for my newsletter** at http://graceburrowes.com/contact/

Happy reading!
Grace Burrowes

MY OWN TRUE DUCHESS

Mr. Jonathan Tresham, heir to a dukedom, has sought the privacy of an unused parlor to negotiate with Mrs. Theo Haviland for certain personal services. The negotiations are off to a bumpy start…

"I don't want a perishing duchess!"

Mr. Tresham had raised his voice, though he was insisting rather than shouting. Theo was pleased with his reaction nonetheless. He'd managed the situation with Bea, managed Diana's obstinance in the park, and managed any number of presuming debutantes. Theo was cheered to think Mr. Tresham had found a situation he could not confidently handle on his own.

"What *do* you want, Mr. Tresham? You are to become a duke, God willing. Dukes are married to duchesses."

"Might we sit? I'll spend the rest of the evening enduring bosoms pressed to my person while I prance around the ballroom with a simpering, sighing, young woman in my arms. My feet ache at the very prospect."

Theo began to enjoy herself. "Poor dear. You must have nightmares about all those bosoms."

He smiled, a rueful quirk of the lips that transformed his features from severe to… charming? *Surely not.*

Theo took a seat and patted the cushion beside her. "Speak plainly, Mr. Tresham. The bosoms await."

He took the place beside her. "Plain speaking has ever been my preference. I left England after finishing at Cambridge, and went abroad to make my fortune. In that endeavor, I was successful, but the whole time I ought to have been finding my way among polite society, making the right associations, being a dutiful heir, I was instead making money on the Continent."

Without any partners, he'd said. "Why Cambridge? You would have met more young men from the right families at Oxford."

Theo really ought to scoot a good foot to the side. She'd taken the middle of the sofa, and Mr. Tresham was thus wedged between her and the armrest. There was room, if they sat improperly close.

He was warm, however, and he wasn't shy about discussing money. Theo stayed right where she was.

"Cambridge offers a better education in the practical sciences and mathematics. I am something of an amateur mathematician, which skill is helpful when managing one's finances." He gazed at the fire, his expression once again the remote, handsome scion of a noble house.

Theo had the daft urge to tickle him, to make that charming smile reappear. He'd doubtless offer her a stiff bow and never acknowledge her again if she took liberties with his person.

"You offered me plain speaking, Mr. Tresham, yet you dissemble. No ducal heir needs more than a passing grasp of mathematics."

He opened a snuff box on the low table before them. Taking snuff was a dirty habit, one Theo had forbid Archie to indulge in at home.

"Would you care for a mint?" Mr. Tresham held the snuff box out to her.

Theo took two. "Tell me about Cambridge."

He popped a mint into his mouth and set down the snuffbox. "My father went to Oxford. He earned top marks in wenching, inebriation, stupid wagers, and scandal. I chose not to put myself in a situation where his reputation would precede me."

Most young men viewed those pursuits as the primary reasons to go up to university. "I gather he was something of a prodigy in the subjects listed?"

"Top wrangler. So I became a top wrangler at Cambridge."

Ah, well then. "And you've taken no partners in your business endeavors. Can't your aunt assist you in this bride hunt, Mr. Tresham?"

"Quimbey's wife doesn't know me, and she's too busy being a bride herself. She and Quimbey are..." He fiddled with the snuffbox again, opening and closing the lid. "Besotted, I suppose. At their ages."

Clearly, Mr. Tresham did not approve of besottedness at any age, and Theo had to agree with him. Nothing but trouble came from entrusting one's heart into another's keeping.

"They are off on a wedding journey of indefinite duration," Mr. Tresham went on. "They are reminding me that soon, Quimbey will not be on hand. He's an old man by any standards, and I have put off marriage long enough."

"You want me to help you find a bride?"

"Precisely. I haven't womenfolk I can turn to for first-hand information, haven't friends from school who will warn me off the bad investments. In this search, I need a knowledgeable consultant, and I am willing to pay for the needed expertise."

A consultant, but not a partner, of course. "Why should I do this? Why exert myself on behalf of a man I don't know well. I could end up with another woman's eternal misery on my conscience."

Another smile, this one downright devilish. "Would you rather have *my* eternal misery on your conscience?"

Well, no. Mr. Tresham was little more than a stranger, but he'd been kind to Diana, he was dutiful toward his elderly relations, and he'd make a woman of delicate sensibilities wretched.

"How would my matchmaking to be compensated?"

"Your role has two aspects: Matchmaker and chaperone. I will accept only those invitations where I know you have also been invited. You will simply do as you did with Dora Louise's ambush in the library—guard my back. You will also keep me informed regarding the army of aspiring duchesses unleashed on my person every time I enter a ballroom."

Theo got up to pace rather than remain next to him. "And my compensation?" Five years ago, she would have aided Mr. Tresham out of simple decency. Archie's death meant she instead had to ask about money—vulgar, necessary money—and pretend the question was casual.

Mr. Tresham rose. Manners required that of him, because Theo was on her feet, but must he be so tall and self-possessed standing in the shadows? Must he be so blasted, *everlasting* attractive?

"Name your price, Mrs. Haviland."

Order your copy of ***My Own True Duchess***!

MY ONE AND ONLY DUKE

Quinn Wentworth has escaped the hangman's noose only to find a ducal title slung around his neck. He married Jane thinking they had no future, but fate has other plans. Now, when he ought to be bringing his enemies to justice, he's instead besotted with his duchess...

Having no alternative, Quinn went about removing his clothes, handing them to Jane who hung up his shirt and folded his cravat as if they'd spent the last twenty years chatting while the bath water cooled.

Quinn was down to his underlinen, hoping for a miracle, when Jane went to the door to get the dinner tray. He used her absence to shed the last of his clothing and slip into the steaming tub. She returned bearing the food, which she set on the counterpane.

"Can you manage? I'm happy to wash your hair."

"I'll scrub off first. Tell me how you occupied yourself in my absence."

She held a sandwich out for him to take a bite. "This and that. The staff has a schedule, the carpets have all been taken up and beaten, Constance's cats are separated by two floors until Persephone is no longer feeling amorous."

Quinn was feeling amorous. He'd traveled to York and back, endured Mrs. Daugherty's gushing, and Ned's endless questions, and pondered possibilities and plots, but neither time nor distance had dampened his interest in Jane one iota.

Her fingers massaging his scalp and neck didn't help his cause, and when she leaned down to scrub his chest, and her breasts pressed against Quinn's shoulders, his interest became an ache.

The water cooled, Jane fed him sandwiches, and Quinn accepted that the time had come to make love with his wife. He rose from the tub, water sluicing away, as Jane held out a bath sheet. Her gaze wandered over him in frank, marital assessment, then caught, held, and ignited a smile he hadn't seen from her before.

"Why Mr. Atherton, you did miss me after all." She passed him the bath sheet, and locked the parlor door and the bedroom door, while Quinn stood before the fire and dried off.

"I missed you too," Jane said, taking the towel from him and tossing it over a chair. "Rather a lot."

Quinn made one last attempt to dodge the intimacy Jane was owed, one last try for honesty. "Jane, we have matters to discuss. Matters that relate to my travels." And to his past, for that past was putting a claim in his future, and Jane deserved to know the truth.

"We'll talk later all you like, Quinn. For now, please just take me to bed."

She kissed him, and he was lost.

Order your copy of *My One and Only Duke*

Pursuit of Honor

Kelly Bowen

CHAPTER ONE

Brighton, England, 1823

"He's here."

Diana felt an arm wrap around her waist, and she was almost yanked off her feet as she was pulled behind a potted fern that was starting to wilt. "Good Lord, Hannah, where have you been? You can't just up and disappear for an hour—"

"Hide," her friend urged frantically, crouching behind the massive pot at the far edge of the ballroom and dragging Diana down with her.

Diana's right knee hit the ground, though she covered her wince with a light laugh. "Very funny, Hannah."

"I'm not trying to be funny. I'm trying to keep him from seeing you. Or me."

Diana sobered at Hannah's urgent tone and cast a wary eye about them, but no one seemed to have noticed that she'd been all but wrestled to the ground. With the champagne flowing, conversation competing in volume with the music, and small, selfish dramas playing out all over the crowded room, no one even looked their way. Which had been Diana's general objective in the first place. Stay in the background. Avoid notice.

And the idea that the Duke of Riddington had managed to follow her yet again made her both uncomfortable and furious at the same time.

Furious because the abhorrent man had the power to make her uncomfortable. Furious because she was reduced to crouching behind the imported shrubbery, on her hands and knees in a manner she hadn't done since she was nine. Furious because her well-intentioned friend believed this was a better option than another conversation with him, or another round of not-so-subtle suggestions that Riddington would do Diana the honor of allowing her to warm his ducal bed, if only she would come to her senses.

"This is crushing my skirts," she muttered.

"Who cares about your skirts?" Hannah slowly stuck her head over the top of the pot, pushing aside a spray of fronds. The theme for tonight's ball was the wilds of the Far East. Swaths of embroidered crimson and tangerine silk were tacked to the walls, and potted ferns lined the perimeter of the entire room. Ropes of ivy had been hung from the chandeliers in an attempt to create a canopy of vines. A handful of peacocks strutted through the chairs and refreshment tables, occasionally voicing their displeasure over the sound of the music. Someone had even come up with a tiger hide, and that was draped over the dais upon which the orchestra sat. Its glass eyes stared unseeingly at the crush, its teeth bared in an eternal snarl. Diana rather felt that the entire display belonged on a stage and not in a ballroom, but Hannah adored such spectacles.

"I am not hiding behind a pot all night," Diana said, making an effort to rise. Her pride was worth far more than the Duke of Riddington.

Hannah yanked her back down with more strength than should have been possible for a small, red-haired, green-eyed pixie. "Well, I can't go out there."

Diana finally extricated herself from Hannah's grasp and staggered to her feet. The Duke of Riddington was her problem, not Hannah's. Diana would deal with him again if she had to, but her more immediate concern was dealing with the woman who was still cowering behind the décor, looking pale and panicked and disheveled. In truth, Hannah hadn't been herself in awhile—withdrawn and secretive and seemingly avoiding everyone, Diana included. She'd tried many times to gently extract the source of her friend's discontent, but her efforts had been met only with mumbled apologies and no real explanations. Yet since the redhead had arrived in Brighton last week, the vivacious, cheerful Hannah Burton seemed to have returned.

"He shall see you." Hannah's eyes darted between Diana and the far side of the room.

Diana followed her gaze and saw nothing but a wall of people in a dizzying array of colors, none of whom seemed to be looking in their direction.

"And then he shall see me." Hannah crouched lower behind the greenery. "He can't see me. I'm not ready to see him. Promise me you won't let him see me."

Diana was aware she was scowling now, and she forced her expression to relax. "I don't see the duke," she told Hannah. A horrible thought struck her. Had Riddington threatened or propositioned Hannah in his vile manner? Had—

"The duke?" Hannah's gaze snapped to Diana's face. "What duke?"

"Riddington." He was, in part, why Diana had left London in the first place, though that had been pointless, given the man had appeared in Brighton not three days later. The relentless gossip that linked Diana and the duke had followed hard on his heels.

"Riddington? He's here too? Oh, good God, this is a disaster."

"Wait, who were you talking about?" Diana asked.

Hannah pushed the fern fronds a little farther to the side and scrambled back. "No, no, no. I can't do this now."

Diana looked across the room again, half expecting to see a bloody troll with a great lurching gait and a mouthful of sharp, pointy fangs headed their way. But all she could see were knots of people standing and talking and drinking and laughing. One group of dandies, dressed obnoxiously and speaking in tones to match, were clearly well on their way to being utterly foxed. A dark-haired gentleman with his back to her stood just past them, a tall, masculine figure in well-tailored, elegant evening clothes. Those dandies would do well to take a lesson from him, she thought idly. There was nothing more attractive in a man than one who was confident enough that he felt no need to posture.

"Don't tell him you saw me," Hannah said, and Diana twisted to find her friend crawling from behind the pot toward the wall. "Promise me. I was never here." Hannah reached the wall on her hands and knees and stood, sidling under a hanging swath of crimson silk.

Diana followed her, wondering if she should fetch Hannah's aunt, who was somewhere in this crowd, and have her take her niece home. Because her niece had clearly taken leave of her senses.

"I need your word that you won't mention me at all." Hannah's disembodied demand was frantic.

"You have my word. But, Hannah, this is ridiculous," Diana started, though she was speaking now toward nothing but a curtain of crimson silk hanging on the wall. "I can handle the duke or anyone else who—"

"It's not the duke or anyone else," Hannah hissed. She poked her head out, making frantic gestures in the direction of the dance floor. "It's Oliver."

CHAPTER TWO

"Say, who is that woman talking to a potted fern?"

Oliver Graham, third and youngest son of Viscount Hambleton, drained what was left in his glass of a middling-quality brandy. He'd been trying to ignore the three young dandies who were having a very loud, somewhat drunken conversation behind him, but that comment had piqued his interest.

He turned casually, his eyes sweeping past them and over the crowd, finding the object of the dandies' discussion near the far wall. She had her back to him, gleaming wheat-gold curls artfully arranged at the back of her head, a few spilling down over the champagne hue of her gown. Even from this distance, he could see the gracefulness of her movements and the slide of satin over curves that would make any man with a pulse look twice.

Even if the fact that she did, indeed, appear to be talking to a potted fern did not.

This was absurd. Oliver had been in Brighton barely twenty-four hours, and this was not how he had envisioned spending his time. Wasting his time, in truth. There were things that legitimately required his attention, the least of which was finding Madelene. A dull fury rose, one that had been festering since he had stopped in London and discovered that his sister was not in Boston as he had believed. As he had been told. The story had been something that his parents used to explain away the fact that his sister had abruptly left London six years ago for whereabouts unknown.

Unknown, save for a single, unopened, unread letter she had sent the unforgiving viscount and viscountess a year after her departure, postmarked Brighton. A letter that confirmed Oliver's worst suspicions and made his heart break and his anger ignite.

"That woman is the Duke of Riddington's mistress," one of the dandies behind him stage-whispered loud enough for half the room to hear.

This wasn't absurd, it was intolerable. Nothing had changed in the dozen years he had been gone. It was still a never-ending agenda of balls and assemblies and musicales where the same small people gossiped about the same small things. He wasn't sure how he'd managed to be persuaded to partake in it all tonight, but he blamed his bad judgment solely on his friend.

You should accept your invitation to the Montmartin ball, Maxwell Thorpe had suggested. *You'll see some old friends,* he'd promised with a wink and a knowing look. That assurance had finally convinced Oliver to go, yet he had not seen anyone he even remotely recognized, much less knew. Something that didn't come as any sort of shock, since he'd been away from England for well over a bloody decade.

"Not his mistress," the second dandy was arguing behind him. "I heard she won't have him."

"But the scandal sheets said he's already had her. In all sorts of—"

"You can't believe everything you read," the second dandy scoffed.

Dandy One snorted into his glass and promptly choked. "I'd have the duke," he snickered when he'd recovered. "Wherever and whenever he wanted. If only for the wardrobe he'd buy me."

"She's only the daughter of a damn baron." His friend giggled drunkenly. "Almost a nobody. You at least have the advantage of rank. Perhaps you should ask His Grace when he plans to give up on her and if he'd consider you."

Oliver's eyes swiveled back to the woman talking to the fern. Only now, she had moved and seemed to be conversing with the swath of silk hanging against the wall, her back still to them. The color of her hair was faintly familiar. Or maybe it was her height. Or— He stopped, discarding his conjectures and far-fetched ideas. He knew a blond-haired girl who was the daughter of a baron, but she didn't possess curves like that. And she wouldn't be talking to ferns. Or walls.

"If a woman like that turns down a damn duke, what chance do we have?" It was said morosely by the buck who had asked the original question. "Is she holding out for a bloody prince?"

"A woman who looks like that could. She's already turned down two earls and a marquess since she was widowed. I hear the pot at White's is up to two thousand pounds on who will bed her first."

The seed of suspicion was starting to sprout despite the part of his brain that was telling him it was impossible. Well, unlikely at least, that his childhood friend would be here. A childhood friend who had written him hundreds and hundreds of letters and entertained him with stories from home during his absence. But she had said nothing about Brighton in her last one, after he had written to tell her he was coming back to England.

You'll see some old friends, Thorpe had told him.

Oliver stared harder. It couldn't be. And yet—

"But she was just talking to a plant," one of the dandies tittered.

"No one said she was sane. One doesn't have to be sane to be taken to bed and fu—"

"Excuse me." Oliver shoved through the knot of dandies with more force than was necessary. There were numerous mutterings and exclamations, but Oliver ignored them, making his way across the room, heading for the blond vixen who had turned down a duke, two earls, and a marquess. A vixen who was still talking to a swath of crimson silk.

The fact that he knew nobody worked in his favor as he cut across the expanse, because no one stopped him to speak to him, and in fact, a few people stepped hastily out of his way. He made it past the looming pots with their wilting vegetation just as the fern whisperer turned away from the wall to face him.

And the ground shifted beneath him.

Or at least he thought it did, but the edges of his vision were a little bit fuzzy and the sound of the crowd behind him faded away to the point that he could hear only the pounding of his pulse in his ears.

She was gazing up at him, her unmistakeable cerulean-blue eyes wide and not a little startled. Yet her eyes were all that was unmistakable, because the woman who stood before him in a Brighton ballroom looked nothing at all like the girl who had waved goodbye to him on the London docks. That Diana, who had hugged him and wished him well over a dozen years ago, had had bony elbows that stuck out in all directions, just like the wheat-colored curls she'd tried to tame into braids. That Diana had had eyes a little too big for her face, a dress a little too big for her body, and a wide, ready grin that told him she didn't really care.

The woman staring up at him was a stranger. A beautiful, breathtaking, incandescent stranger. Her body had matured from awkward angles into tantalizing curves, and each and every one was displayed in an elegant embroidered gown that fit her to perfection. Her arresting eyes were set into a fair complexion, her cheeks a pretty pink, her unruly curls now glossy waves that fell softly around her face before being caught at the nape of her neck. This stranger who stood before him was the very definition of the classic, demure beauty that this society admired and went to preposterous lengths to achieve.

And then she grinned at him and became simply Diana once more.

"Oliver," she half shrieked, half gasped before she launched herself into his arms.

"Dee." He caught her easily, thinking that this was the first time he'd really felt like he was home since he'd stepped foot on England's shores again. He tightened his arms around her and breathed in, the scent of orange blossoms and woman filling his nose. Joy bubbled up, pure and effervescent and instant, catching him off guard.

"I can't believe it's really you. I can't believe you're here," she said against his neck.

Here being the grand country ballroom of the Marquess and Marchioness of Montmartin. Where he was embracing her in a scandalous fashion in public. Not that he should be embracing her in a scandalous fashion anywhere else, for that matter. He pulled back, hating the loss of her touch. It was all he could do not to reach out and clasp her hand in his. "I'm sorry. I might have just put you in an awkward—"

"Don't worry," she said. "No one pays much attention to the wallflowers and the widows."

Oliver didn't bother to correct her.

"Besides," she added, smoothing his rumpled cravat back into place, "I don't know many people here anyway."

"Is that why you were talking to a fern?" he teased, feeling happier and lighter than he could remember feeling in a long time.

If he hadn't been watching so carefully, he might have missed the way she stiffened slightly. And then she laughed, the corners of her eyes crinkling, and he wondered if perhaps he'd imagined it. "There is something to be said for a conversation partner that doesn't ever argue."

He smiled back, trying to reconcile the fact that he hadn't seen her in a dozen years, and yet the awkwardness that he might have expected was completely absent. Perhaps because he had heard her voice every week in the letters she had unfailingly sent him. Perhaps this was merely a continuation of a conversation that had last ended across an ocean.

"Well, then," he said, "maybe I should go. I can't guarantee myself to be so agreeable as a fern."

She shook her head. "Two minutes. Meet me out front by the fountain in two minutes."

"Sounds mysterious."

"Not mysterious," she assured him. "Just selfish. I haven't found you after this long just to lose you again. I'm not letting you out of my sight, and I don't want to share you."

Oliver knew that those words were spoken out of friendship, yet a peculiar warmth and longing curled through his chest. A feeling akin to the way he would feel if a lover had spoken them.

She hesitated. "Unless, of course, you wish to stay?"

"God, no. When I saw you, I was contemplating striking up a conversation with the fellow over by the dais."

Diana shot him a questioning look.

"You know, the one with the orange and black striped outfit?" Oliver prompted. "He looks like he's enjoying himself as much as I."

Diana laughed again, and Oliver grinned in response. And wondered how he had lasted as long as he had without hearing that infectious laugh.

"I need to speak to the aunt of a friend before I go." She ducked past him, heading toward the tall doors looming on the far end of the room. "Two minutes," she called happily over her shoulder once more.

He watched her go, his grin fading as he fought the urge to bolt after her. Because that was what a lovesick puppy would do, not a man who had just reconnected with a dear friend after a dozen years and had been asked to wait one hundred and twenty seconds longer. But now that he had found her again, he didn't want to let her go, even for a minute. He wanted to keep her close. Pull her back into his arms and—

Oliver stopped himself. He had clearly been on his own for too long. That urge, no doubt, was simply a side effect of the plaguing loneliness that he had never truly shed in all his travels, but that had evaporated instantly in her presence. He had so many questions for her. So much he wanted to talk about. Things that had been kept from him, things he hadn't discovered until he'd arrived home. Like, what had happened to his sister? What was going on with Diana that had landed her in the betting books at White's?

And of course, where was his intended bride, who had seemingly dropped off the face of the earth?

He shifted, a feeling of restlessness crawling through him. He'd come back to England knowing that it was well past the time he finally honored a promise he'd made long ago. Well past the time he finally made good on the agreed-upon arrangement between families that would neatly unite position and wealth.

Except, his dutiful messages to his intended's home that he'd sent as soon as he'd arrived in London had gone unanswered. He'd shown up at her door, only to be advised by a stoic butler that the family was summering in Bath. He'd sent messages there, but thus far, they'd gone unanswered too.

Oliver shifted again, trying not to remember how Diana had felt in his arms, or the joy and sense of home that had overtaken him. Such thoughts were not those of an honorable man.

He was getting married.

And not to Diana Thompson.

CHAPTER THREE

He was getting married.

Married, married, married. Diana repeated this to herself as she slipped from the Montmartin House and out into the dark coolness of the night. Married, married, married.

Not to her, but to Miss Hannah Burton.

Diana had known this since she was eight, when the Burton and Graham families had cordially agreed upon the union. She'd known it every minute of every hour she and Oliver had spent together, exploring the dales up north every summer where their parents had both kept modest country estates. She'd known it as they had played in the ponds and the barns and the forests. She'd known it as they had become older and their time spent together had lessened, but their friendship had strengthened. She'd known it with every letter she'd ever sent to him as he had worked his way through Eton and Oxford, and then after he'd departed for India to seek his fortunes with the East India Company.

She'd known it the entire time she'd fallen hopelessly, irrevocably in love with him.

And now Oliver was back in England, no longer a young buck with something to prove, but a confident man who had made his fortune and had come home to claim the bride he had promised to marry and the new life that was waiting for them both.

Somehow, this made Diana want to weep.

Which was indeed selfish, because if she were a better person, this union between Hannah and Oliver, her two closest friends, would be cause for boundless joy. Diana had thought she had accepted this reality. But the second she had turned around to find Oliver Graham standing behind her, she'd no longer wanted to accept it. The moment she had thrown herself into his arms, the moment she had felt them tighten around her as he held her close, she'd known she had made a monumental mistake. In his arms, she'd finally felt whole.

He wasn't the slim young man she had hugged goodbye on the docks. He was bigger and stronger and harder. His shoulders were broader, his muscles honed to a steely strength that was obvious even through the layers of his evening clothes. His features had sharpened too as they had matured, his cheeks more distinguished, his jaw more defined. His hair was as dark as she remembered, his skin the same rich olive, and his chocolate-colored eyes held the same warmth and humor.

He had transcended handsome to become compelling.

Yet, he still had a quick smile, and the time apart had not dimmed the ease with which conversation had always flowed. Until, of course, he had asked why she had been talking to a fern. And she had dodged his question because Hannah had made her promise not to give her away.

No doubt because the reality of the man Hannah would spend the rest of her life with, the man who would be at her side during her days and dominate her nights, needed adjusting to. She didn't blame Hannah for wanting time to prepare herself in the face of his sudden, unexpected appearance. Had she been the woman who would marry this man, perhaps she too would have asked for distance—

Diana made a face. Who was she trying to fool? If she were going to marry Oliver Graham, she'd be kissing him right now. Not reminding herself why that could and would never, ever happen.

"Dee."

She whirled to find him behind her in the shadows, the soft, flickering light of the torches along the sweeping walking paths highlighting his silhouette. "There you are," she said brightly, clasping her hands behind her back.

"This was a good idea, Dee. You can hear yourself think out here."

"Yes," she agreed, thinking that she was thinking entirely too much.

He smiled, his teeth bright in the darkness, and offered her his arm. She eyed it uncertainly.

"I promise not to kidnap you and ravish you in the bushes."

Diana's mouth went dry as she tried not to consider just how much she might enjoy being ravished by Oliver Graham. She pasted on what she hoped was a benign smile, counting on the shadows to hide any deficiencies, and slipped her hand around his arm.

She would not dwell on the heat of his body beneath her bare hand. She would not pretend that he was taking her on a romantic moonlight stroll. She would not imagine that he had come back from India to be hers.

"I still can't believe you're here," she said as they began to walk. "You didn't mention visiting the coast at all in your letters."

"I hadn't planned on it," Oliver replied after a brief hesitation. "But what are you doing here? There were no Brighton plans in your last letter either."

"My last letter was months and months ago. I didn't know I was coming here until last week, when Belinda and Eugenia invited me." She was careful not to mention Hannah. "You've met them, I think."

He nodded slowly. "A very long time ago. But you've spoken of them often enough in your letters."

"They thought a break from London would be… therapeutic."

"I can imagine."

No, she thought, he couldn't. Because Oliver hadn't been reduced to a bloody bet in the ledgers at Boodle's and Brooks's and White's, like a high-priced whore whose services were up for auction. Though she certainly wasn't going to discuss that with Oliver. Not here. Not now. Probably not ever.

"How was your voyage back?" she blurted.

Oliver shrugged, his arm moving beneath her hand. "No storms, no pirates, no outbreaks of anything deadly. By all measures, a positively decadent trip."

"When do you start at the college?" she asked, continuing with reasonable, rational questions a friend would ask.

"In a fortnight."

"I'm so pleased for you. You deserve it." She meant it. Teaching positions at the East India College were rare opportunities, and they were wildly sought after, awarded to individuals who were truly masters in their field.

"Thank you," he said, putting his hand over hers where it rested on his arm. "But I want to talk about you."

"I think I've talked about me enough in my letters, don't you? There's not much more to tell," she answered. She didn't really want to talk about herself. Because then there was the risk that she might say the wrong thing and ruin everything.

"I was so sorry to hear about your husband."

Diana looked at his hand covering hers, a familiar feeling of guilt bubbling from somewhere deep. "Laurence was a good man," she said. A good man she had married at her family's urging. A man she had admired and respected and cared for deeply. But she'd never been in love with him, and the guilt that came with that knowledge lingered, as it had right after Laurence Thompson's death eight years ago. He'd been killed in Belgium fighting the French barely three months after they had wed.

"Did he make you happy?" Oliver asked.

"Yes," Diana answered. Any shortcomings in her happiness were hers and hers alone.

"Good," Oliver replied with more vehemence than she'd expected. "Not everyone is so lucky to find happiness in a marriage arrangement."

Diana resisted the urge to look at him. The arrangement between her family and that of Laurence Thompson's hadn't been much different than the arrangement between Oliver's and Hannah's, though Diana didn't point that out. She waited instead for Oliver to bring up his own impending nuptials.

He didn't.

Though, perhaps he was as reluctant as Hannah was to discuss their planned marriage until he had had a chance to properly prepare and speak to his bride and her family. Diana had, after all, left Hannah hiding behind the wall décor in a ballroom. Not talking about it was fine with her. She'd rather run naked through a forest of nettles than discuss Oliver's wedding.

They continued down the path, the quiet broken only by the faint crunch of gravel beneath their feet. The torchlight flickered, sending fingers of light dancing wildly across the manicured lawns, and the breeze was laced with the salty tang of the sea.

"How's your family?" she asked, unable to stand the awkward silence that the topic of marriage had left behind.

"I came to Brighton directly from London," Oliver said, and without warning, he stopped in the middle of the path. "Madelene never went to Boston."

Diana stumbled into him before righting herself. She cursed herself, knowing she should never have asked that last question without being better prepared. She knew that this was the part when she was supposed to feign shock. Instead, she felt only faint surprise that it had taken Oliver this long to discover that his sister had never sailed for Boston.

"No," she said. "She didn't."

"You knew that? And yet, you let me believe the same story my parents fed everyone else?"

"Yes."

"Why?" he asked, his voice rough. "Why wouldn't you tell me?"

"Madelene asked me not to."

His muscles went stiff beneath her hand. "Madelene asked you not to," he repeated slowly.

"Yes."

"I know why she left."

Diana hesitated, wondering just how much he knew. "I'm not sure you—"

"I recovered a letter she tried to send to our parents. A letter they didn't open and tossed into the hearth to be burned. Our housekeeper saved it and kept it all these years. Gave it to me when I went back to the house."

"Ah." Diana sighed. "Then you might know why she felt ashamed. Afraid."

"She's hardly the first woman who's been seduced, believing herself to be in love. What would she be afraid of?"

"When you talked to your parents, your brothers, what did they say?"

Oliver flinched. "They told me that they no longer have a daughter. Or a sister."

"That. She was afraid of that same reaction from you."

"My parents and my brothers are punishing her. And they're wrong to do so."

"They are. And I'm glad to hear you say it. Madelene would be too."

"Who did this to her?" Oliver asked, and his voice was like cut glass. "Who took advantage of her?"

Diana cursed herself again for not having a better response prepared. "That is Madelene's secret." She'd made a promise to Madelene a long time ago to keep her secret, and Diana was not about to break that promise now. God only knew what Oliver would do. "Does it really matter after all this time?"

"Yes, it matters," he growled. "It's all that matters. It matters that the bastard who ruined her life didn't have to answer for it." He pulled away from her and stalked a few paces ahead before turning back. "I wasn't there to protect her then, but such a transgression will not go unaddressed now. Whoever he is, I will make sure he answers for it."

"And do what?"

"Whatever it takes." He sounded unnaturally calm.

This was what she had been afraid of. "Oliver—"

"You helped Madelene, didn't you?" Almost an accusation.

Diana lifted her chin. "She's your sister, Oliver. And a friend. Of course I helped her."

"How?"

"I gave her the means and money to leave the rot of London without looking back. To start over." She frowned. "And I'll not apologize for it."

Oliver exhaled heavily. "I'm sorry. Thank you. For being there for her when I wasn't."

"Of course."

"Where is she?"

"I don't know, exactly. I did not require or expect her to take anything from her old life with her. Including me. In fact, I encouraged her not to."

"I think she's here somewhere. Somewhere near Brighton."

Diana glanced up in surprise. "Why do you think that?"

"She mentioned Brighton in her letter." He paused, a look of anguish chasing itself across his features. "That letter also had a lock of baby hair in it. Madelene has a son."

"Yes."

"You knew that too?" It sounded raw.

"Yes," Diana murmured. "She's sent me similar letters over the years."

"And you've never looked for her?"

"If she wanted me to know where she is, she would have told me. I've respected that."

"You should have told me."

"It wasn't my secret to tell."

"I need to find her."

"Perhaps it would be better if Madelene was the one who—"

"I need you to help me."

"Oliver—"

"Do you remember when we were twelve and Madelene was ten, and she followed us when we trekked up to the old ruins near Reeth without us knowing? And got lost somewhere on the way?"

Diana bit her lip. "Yes."

"I remember feeling sick when we got back and realized what had happened. That my little sister was somewhere in those forests on her own. This is like that, only a hundred times worse." He came back to her, catching her hand in his. "You helped me then, Dee. You helped me keep my head, and you helped me search, and in the end, we found her. And I'm asking for your help again." Oliver took a ragged breath. "She's my sister and I love her, and I haven't seen her in a dozen years, and whatever she did or didn't do changes none of that. And I have a nephew I haven't met." The words came out in an anguished jumble. "Please."

Diana tightened her hand in his. Because she couldn't wrap her arms around him and lean her head against his chest and listen to the beautiful heart that beat inside this beautiful man. "Yes," she said.

"Yes?"

"Yes, I'll help you find her."

"Thank you." Oliver slid his free arm around her shoulders and drew her close.

Diana let him and pretended that everything might have been different. Pretended that in another time, in another place, she might slide her hand up the front of his lapel to his face so that her fingers might explore the angles of his jaw and the softness of his lips. Pretended that she might tangle those fingers in his thick, dark hair and pull his head down to hers—

"Mrs. Thompson." The voice cut through the shadows. "If you're not careful, you'll catch your death out here."

* * *

Oliver felt every muscle in Diana's body go rigid.

She spun away from him, and Oliver was left gazing at a man standing in the center of the gravel path before them, the wavering torchlight casting uneven shadows across his features. Not that Oliver needed much light to recognize him. Even after all these years, Ludlow Thrup still had the same smug expression, the same arrogant set to his mouth, the same haughty cast of his eyes. He still possessed the good looks he had always taken an inordinate pride in, and combining that with the wealth and power of the dukedom he now held, Oliver could understand why such a man would believe that he was entitled to everything he desired. And everyone.

I heard she won't have him.

Diana, it seemed, had not been swayed. A petty satisfaction gripped him.

Oliver spoke first. "Your Grace, it's been a long time."

Riddington's dark eyes narrowed as he stared at Oliver, before they widened in recognition. "Graham," he said and seemed to falter slightly.

"Nothing gets past you, does it, Your Grace?"

Riddington's lips thinned. "I almost didn't recognize you. You barely look like an Englishman anymore. It's clear you've been living too long in whatever backward place you hared off to all those years ago."

"You've been, then?" Oliver inquired flatly.

"Been?"

"To India? China? Mongolia?"

"Of course I haven't." The duke straightened his shoulders. "Those places are nothing but barbaric cesspools of disease and violence. Places Englishmen go to die. I've heard all the stories."

"It's a pity you remain so sheltered, Your Grace, for it's clear you've not, in fact, heard all the stories. You fail to mention the wealth of culture and beauty in each of those places. The rich history and knowledge that those lands and their people possess. It is both humbling and exhilarating to have had the privilege of being there. To have learned and experienced new and incredible things."

The duke was staring at him, an unpleasant expression on his face.

"Any worthwhile endeavor has risks," Oliver continued with a shrug. "A man must simply have the courage to face those risks."

"How dare you imply that—"

"I'm not implying anything, Your Grace. I'm telling you that the world is shrinking. That the future and the men who will control it lie beyond this island."

"The future of this empire lies with men like me," Riddington bit out. "I am a very influential man, with more power and wealth at my fingertips than you will ever have. If you doubt that, you only need to read any newspaper in London and every other city and town I travel to. I am mentioned almost daily. Something you wouldn't be aware of, scraping out an existence in the jungles for as long as you have, Graham."

"Mmm."

"Though Mrs. Thompson can certainly enlighten you, can't you, darling?" The duke bowed to Diana, his eyes lingering on her bodice before he straightened.

Diana stared back at him, expressionless.

Oliver resisted the urge to wipe that smug, satisfied smirk off the duke's face with a well-placed right hook.

Riddington brought his fingers up to brush a stray curl from Diana's shoulder. "You shouldn't be out here in the cold and in the dark, Mrs. Thompson. It would be my pleasure to see you back inside and attend to your every comfort."

"Thank you, but no," Diana replied, edging away. "I was retiring early."

"Then allow me to escort you. You're staying at Ainsworth House, correct?"

"That is not necessary, Your Grace."

"Come, Mrs. Thompson, I—"

"She said it was not necessary," Oliver cut him off.

A dark look passed over Riddington's face before it cleared. "Of course. I will call upon you tomorrow, then, Mrs. Thompson."

"I'm sorry, Your Grace, but I won't be available."

"Mrs. Thompson, I do think that you should reconsider very carefully." The duke leaned toward Diana. "And remember who I am."

"Otherwise?" Oliver prompted.

"I beg your pardon?" Riddington's jaw was set.

"If Mrs. Thompson doesn't reconsider?" Oliver asked, deliberately and gently brushing at an ivory-colored moth fluttering near the sleeve of his coat. "You sounded like you were making a threat," he continued. "Though I'm sure I was mistaken."

"I'm sure you were." The duke's words were tight. He turned his back on Oliver and picked up Diana's unproffered hand, pressing a kiss to her knuckles. "Another time, then, Mrs. Thompson. When we are not so... encumbered."

Diana said nothing, only pulled her hand from his and buried it in her skirts.

"Good evening, Your Grace." Oliver shifted, once again offering his arm to Diana.

She moved to take it without hesitation.

The duke glanced at Diana's hand on Oliver's arm. He looked as though he might say something further, but instead, he merely sniffed, turned his back on both of them, and stalked away in the direction of the house. Oliver forced himself to relax. Riddington would not ruin this night.

Beside him, Diana remained silent.

"Dee? Are you all right?"

She sighed. "I'm fine. And I don't need you to fight my battles for me."

"I know. I've been gone too long to have earned that honor. My lance and armor are rusty, and my noble steed is most surely out of condition."

Diana laughed, the greatest reward she could have given him. "He's not worth it," she said.

"Agreed. But knocking him on his pompous backside would have been exceedingly gratifying."

"Maybe next time." Her fingers slid more securely around his arm.

He covered her hand with his free one, as if that gesture could keep her with him beyond this night. "I didn't think Riddington could get any more detestable than he was in school, but it appears as though I was mistaken."

"He despises you."

"He despises everyone. The things that most people admire in a man— or a woman, for that matter—have only ever threatened Riddington. All the way through Oxford, he loathed anyone with courage and athleticism, and hated those who possessed creativity and industriousness. Simply because their abilities were greater than his. He is a small man with a small mind who can't understand that title and fortune cannot ever compensate for talent and character."

Diana made a funny sound. "He must have abhorred your academic success."

"He abhorred the fact that I was a nobody and that no matter what he bribed or threatened me with, I wouldn't cheat for him. I refused to sacrifice my honor and integrity for him. Worse, I never apologized for it when he failed. I think Riddington hated me most of all."

"Mmm." It was a pensive sound.

"If a man like that still hates me, I suppose I've done something right in my life," Oliver said, trying to lighten the saturnine turn that the conversation had taken. "But enough about detestable dukes. This night is about you and me."

He glanced down at her just as she looked up, her eyes luminous and her lips slightly parted. And he found himself ambushed by a desperate impulse to kiss her. To catch her mouth with his and run his tongue over those lush, seductive lips. To draw her into his arms and slide his hands over those lush, seductive curves.

He looked away instantly, horrified at the desire and arousal flooding through him. These feelings were unacceptable. They were not part of any plan for any part of his life and, in fact, threatened to obliterate his neatly ordered responsibilities and duties, the way artillery fire annihilated neatly ordered infantry squares.

"Thank you. For what you said. For what you did. For your… friendship. No matter how rusty your armor might be."

"Always," Oliver replied, trying to regain his bearings.

Friendship. Something he'd always taken for granted with Diana. Yet, friendship did not adequately explain the possessiveness that seemed to be getting stronger with every minute. Friendship did not address the way his blood raced when he touched her. Nor did it explain his overwhelming urge to kiss her.

But friendship was all he could have with Diana Thompson. Because he was a man of honor who had made promises. Without honor, a man had nothing.

"Come, Dee," he said, his cheer sounding forced even to his own ears. "Let me see you safely home before we come across a dragon that requires you to ride to my rescue. I might not recover from the indignity."

Diana laughed again.

And Oliver reminded himself that he was an honorable man.

CHAPTER FOUR

Diana spread the letters out across the surface of the desk.

In the late afternoon, the house was quiet, both Belinda and Eugenia gone for the day, and only the sound of a whitethroat singing outside the open window broke the silence. Which suited her just fine. At the moment, she did not want to explain why she had left the ball early. Why she had slept late after tossing and turning all night.

She would not have been able to look either woman in the eye and remark in a blasé manner about what a lovely coincidence it had been to run into Oliver Graham, and what a pleasant conversation they had had, and how splendidly he seemed to be doing. Not without both women seeing right through such inanity.

Diana rearranged the third and fourth letters so that they reflected the dates chronologically. She needed to do better. With Oliver back in England, she would need to set aside her emotions. He did not belong to her, but he was still her friend. And she would have to learn to settle for that.

A soft breeze drifted in, bringing with it the scent of roses and lifting the edge of the letter closest to Diana. She picked up the folded paper, turning it over. It was the second-to-last letter she had received from Madelene, and the only letter that did not have a Brighton postmark, but instead, a mileage mark. Which, in theory, should tell Diana exactly how many miles that that letter had traveled to London. Which, in theory, should allow Diana to take an educated guess at the town or village close to Brighton that it had been posted from. Except, mileage marks could be notoriously inaccurate, and even if it was somewhat precise, that left a wide swath of possibilities that surrounded Brighton.

She frowned and sat back, gazing at the collection of little glass goats arranged on a table by the window. A dozen pairs of beady, glossy eyes stared back at her, offering her no answers. But at least this was a start. She'd give these letters to Oliver. At the very least, he would want to read them and see for himself that Madelene had—

"What did he say?"

Diana jumped and nearly upset the inkpot near her elbow. "Saints, Hannah, you need to knock."

"I came in the back through the kitchens." Hannah strode into the room, her eyes darting into the corners as though she thought someone might be lurking behind the curtains. She was wearing a plain gray cloak over her yellow dress, even though the day was warm. "What did Oliver say last night before you encountered Riddington?" she repeated as she paced back and forth. "Did he talk about me last night? Did he say anything about me or a wedding or—"

"No." Diana moved the inkpot to a place of safety in the center of the desk. "And how did you know we encountered Riddington?"

Hannah blinked at her, looking a little abashed. She paused long enough to thrust what looked like a crumpled newspaper in Diana's direction. It landed on the corner of the desk, and Diana made no move to pick it up.

"The social pages," Hannah mumbled.

"The fictitious gossip pages, you mean." Diana refused to read them, but for as long as Diana had known her, Hannah had always had a weakness for the frivolity. There was rarely a column she missed.

"Whatever you want to call them, they say that you and the duke were seen together, out in front of Montmartin House last night."

"With Oliver." She snatched up the paper, crumpling it in her hand, and tossed it in the direction of the dustbin. She missed. "Oliver was there too."

"Oliver didn't get a mention. But they've speculated that you are now… intimately acquainted with His Grace."

A familiar revulsion gripped her. "Again? Based on what?"

"Ambiguous comments by the duke, of course."

"Perhaps I should have let Oliver knock him on his pompous backside."

Hannah picked up one of the glass goats. "What's he doing in Brighton? Oliver, I mean."

Diana forced the contemptible Duke of Riddington from her mind and slid the letters in front of her into a neat pile. She turned them over, reluctant to speak of Madelene or Oliver's search for her. Which was foolish, because Hannah would eventually be Oliver's wife and would know everything then. But it seemed as though perhaps this, being a close family matter, was something that Oliver should impart, how and when he wished.

"A visit, I suppose, until he heads to Hertfordshire to assume his post at the college," Diana told her instead, consoling herself that it wasn't actually a lie, just not the complete truth.

"Right. Hertfordshire."

"Where you will live with him once you are married," Diana said slowly and in the most matter-of-fact voice she could manage. She wasn't sure whose benefit that was for.

Hannah nearly dropped the goat before she recovered and set it back on the table with exaggerated care.

"What's going on, Hannah?" Diana asked, impatience and concern rising in equal measure.

"Nothing."

"Nothing," Diana repeated. "That's what you said when I asked last time. And the time before that. And the time before that. You've been avoiding me for months—"

"I'm sorry. That's not what I intended—"

Diana held her hand up. "I'm not angry. Just worried. Whatever is going on with you, you can tell me."

Hannah pinched the bridge of her nose with her fingers, looking wretched.

A terrible thought struck Diana. "Are you ill?"

"What?" Hannah's head came up, her eyes wide. "No. Of course not."

Relief washed through her. "Then whatever it is, just tell me. Perhaps I can help."

"You can't."

"It's clear that this has something to do with Oliver."

"Yes. And no." Her words were barely audible, but at least they resembled an answer.

"Oliver hasn't changed," Diana tried. "He's still decent and honorable." And handsome and strong and loyal and kind… She stopped before she made a fool of herself.

The pretty redhead's fingers twisted and untwisted around the edge of her cloak. "That is what I am afraid of."

"He'll make a wonderful husband." It was hard to force the words past the mass of awful, unwanted jealousy that lodged in the back of her throat. She would be happy for them if it killed her.

"Yes," Hannah said slowly. "He will make a wonderful husband. But to the right woman."

Diana swallowed a horrified gasp, wondering if her jealousy was that transparent. Dear Lord, she was a terrible friend. "Don't be ridiculous. You are that woman. You always have been."

"Have I?"

This conversation was starting to slide into places Diana had no intention of going. She was always so careful, especially around Hannah. She had never, ever spoken to anyone about how she truly felt about Oliver Graham. Nor did she intend to. Doing so would be pointless. The die was cast long ago.

"You have," Diana said loudly. Too loudly.

"Will he still want to marry me, do you think? After all this time?"

Diana stared at her. "Of course he will—" She stopped abruptly as understanding dawned. "You don't want to marry Oliver." It wasn't really a question.

"It's complicated." That wasn't really an answer.

"Complicated?"

"I thought I'd have more time," Hannah whispered.

At least, that was what Diana thought she heard her say. Because another voice from somewhere in the house intruded.

"Dee? Where are you?"

Hannah's eyes went as wide as saucers, and her face went even chalkier. "Mother of God. Oliver's here? Why is he here?"

Diana stood behind the desk. "Because I asked him here." A completely inappropriate thrill of anticipation shot through her, making her pulse kick and her breath quicken. "Whatever it is that is going on with you concerns him too. Even if you don't want to tell me, you need to talk to him," she said firmly, as if that would rectify her response.

"This is as good a time as any."

"I can't. Not yet." Hannah looked around wildly.

"Well, you're not hiding behind the plants or the curtains this time to avoid him." Diana put her hands on her hips. "We're in here," she called.

Hannah blanched.

"Perhaps he can—Hannah?" Diana felt her jaw slacken. "What are you doing?"

"Promise me you won't tell him I was here." Hannah had shoved the window all the way up and was levering herself out the opening. "I just need one more day."

"What?"

"Promise me," Hannah hissed as her legs swung over the sill. She stuffed her yellow skirts in front of her with frantic movements.

"You can't do this." Diana hurried to the window, but Hannah had already dropped out of sight into the rose garden below.

She landed in a thorny maze of bushes with a loud curse and clambered awkwardly to her feet. The redhead crouched and pulled the hood of her cloak up over her head, but not before she was forced to untangle hair that had become snagged on an errant branch. She scrambled through the greenery before disappearing over a manicured hedge in a flurry of petticoats and more curses.

"I think the butler forgot about me in the hall. I got tired of waiting. Hope you don't mind."

Diana spun just as Oliver appeared in the door. He was dressed simply, in dusty boots and a well-worn coat and snug breeches that only emphasized the impressive lines of his body. Her heart skipped a beat. He had never looked so touchable. So real.

And so concerned.

He glanced around the empty room. "Who were you talking to?"

"There was a... bird. There was a bird."

"Well." He raised a dark brow. "I suppose that's a step up from ferns."

Diana shoved the window closed, knowing there wasn't anything she could say that would make her sound less daft.

"There is an entire conservatory of flowers in the hall," he continued, his forehead creasing. "The butler tells me you've exhausted their supply of vases. It seems you have a lot of suitors." He didn't sound pleased.

"Competitors," she muttered.

"I beg your pardon?"

"Competitors, not suitors." All vying for her bed or her fortune or both.

"What does that mean?"

"It doesn't matter. It's not important." She should not have mentioned it. "Here," she said, returning to the desk and picking up the pile of letters to distract him. "These are from Madelene. I've spent the morning rereading them. I want you to have them now."

Oliver lunged forward before catching himself and took them carefully from her hand. "You kept them."

Her face heated. "Of course I did. They were important." She gestured at her battered mahogany writing box that sat open on the desk. Which was the wrong thing to do, because now he was staring at the box and the bundle of correspondence resting inside, tied with a sky-blue ribbon.

"You kept my letters."

Diana moved to close the box as casually as she could manage. "Of course," she said again. But she wouldn't tell him just how valuable each and every one of his letters was. She wouldn't tell him how often she read them, imagining him in the far-away world he described. Just imagining… him. "You were gone a long time."

"Yet, you were with me every step of the way. Your letters, Dee—it was like you were there with me. I should have written you more."

"Don't be ridiculous. You were busy. And you wrote plenty. It wasn't as good as having you here, in person, but it was better—"

"I missed you terribly."

The air in the room seemed to thicken, and breathing became a chore. She should say something light. Something flippant and funny that would diffuse whatever this was that was happening between them.

"I missed you too," was what she said.

"Diana—"

She cleared her throat. She couldn't do this, whatever *this* was. "Madelene sent me one letter a year. Usually around Christmastide. They're not terribly long, but they let me know that she is doing all right."

He looked down at the letters in his hand. "She should have told me," he said eventually, and when he looked up again, frustration and unhappiness etched lines across his features.

"She told me," Diana said. "Came to me for help. Knowing, I think, that I would make sure that when you returned, these would be passed on to you if…"

"If I forgave her."

"Yes."

"There is nothing to forgive. Save, of course, for her lack of faith in me."

Diana stepped closer to him, unable to help herself. "They're postmarked in Brighton," she said, resisting the longing to smooth the lines of worry from his face. "All of them except this one." She reached for one of the letters in his hand. "This one only has a mileage mark. Which means she sent it from a smaller village somewhere around Brighton, because in it, she still speaks of the sea and the construction of the Pavilion."

"She sent it from where she lives." He sounded hopeful.

"That's what I was thinking."

"Does she mention anything else in any of her letters that would give us a clue where that might be?"

"She mentioned a church once. An old one, with a crenellated tower. She said her son pretended he was riding to besiege the castle when they went to church."

He smiled, and his eyes went soft. "What else?"

"A river. She talks of fishing in a river."

"We need a map of Brighton and the surrounding parishes." He glanced around as though one might suddenly appear in this elegant morning room.

"The Dowager Countess of Ainsworth keeps a lovely home here, but I'm afraid that local maps are not one of the things that she collects. Glass goats, on the other hand…" Diana eyed their caprine audience.

"I thought those were donkeys," Oliver said. "Or maybe llamas."

"Llamas? Really?"

"Doesn't matter. There is a bookseller on Church Street who has maps. He'll have one of Brighton."

"How do you know that?"

"Because I sold him a map yesterday that I brought back from India. Besides books, he has hundreds of maps. From all over." The hope in his expression was unmistakable. "Let's go." He tucked the small bundle of letters inside his coat.

"Now?"

"You have other plans for the day?"

"Um." Her only other plans for the day had included avoiding anywhere the Duke of Riddington might be so that she wouldn't be tempted to kick him. Now, she was wondering if her other plans should include avoiding anywhere Oliver Graham might be so that she wouldn't be tempted to kiss him.

"Dee, I need you," he said, catching her hand in his like it was the most natural thing in the world.

The echoes of those words lodged deep in her belly, sending waves of want through every nerve ending.

"Um." She needed to gather her wits and drag her mind from the indecent depths to which it had sunk. He needed her help. This was simply another adventure that they were undertaking. Though they were older now, and the stakes were much more real than hunting an imaginary dragon to its imaginary lair deep in the dales. "Of course." She couldn't refuse him this, help with finding his sister.

"Thank you." He squeezed her hand, pulling her closer. "Thank you for doing this for me. For doing what you did for Madelene."

Diana might have nodded, but time seemed to have slowed, the sounds of the house around them strangely muffled. He had gone utterly still, her hand caught tightly in his and pressed against his chest. He was looking down at her, his brows drawn together, his eyes intense as they held hers. And then they dropped to her mouth, and on his face, she saw a reflection of the desire that was coiling through her with exquisitely excruciating force.

Oliver brought his free hand up and touched a loose curl that had escaped its pins. He tucked it back over her ear, the backs of his fingers brushing the side of her neck. He let them drift lower, coming to rest at the edge of her bodice.

Surely he would feel the way her heart was thundering in her chest. Surely he would feel the shudder that coursed through her, evidence of the want and longing that rendered her immobile and unable to breathe. She wanted his lips on hers, his hands on her skin, his body where she needed it the most. She wanted all of him. In this moment, right now.

Oliver remained right where he was, within kissing distance. His hand drifted from the edge of her bodice, along the side of her breast, to her waist. His mouth was only inches from hers. All she had to do was push herself to her toes and take everything that she had wanted since forever.

But she would not. For the same reasons that had existed since forever.

"We should go," she managed, a little surprised that her voice still worked, though it was hoarse and uneven. She pulled her hand from his, because if she kept touching him, she was not going to have enough willpower left to do the right thing.

Oliver steadied himself against the side of the desk, and it didn't escape Diana's notice that his breathing was fast and shallow, his forehead creased, his color high. She wasn't sure if she should be happy or horrified.

She needed to stop this. She was walking a very dangerous line, one that could have no happy endings and could cost her friendships.

"The dowager has allowed me the use of her carriage if I need it," she continued, doing her best to pretend that the last minute never happened. Because it couldn't happen. "I think we should take it in the event we need to travel further afield."

She was babbling now, but she needed to put some normalcy back between them. Right the ship, as it were.

Oliver nodded. "Yes."

"Good." Diana clasped her hands together. "I'll see to the arrangements."

"Yes."

Diana fled.

CHAPTER FIVE

I almost kissed Diana Thompson.

Oliver leaned against the bookseller's counter and jabbed his fingers through his hair before resting his forehead in his palms. For the hundredth time, he wondered what the hell he had been thinking. Nothing, he realized. He hadn't been thinking at all. He had just been... feeling. Feeling the way Diana fit in his arms and feeling how right that was. Feeling the softness of her hair and her skin. Feeling the arousal that ignited as she looked up at him, sending sparks and electricity arcing over his skin and down his spine.

He slid his hands to his eyes, making spots dance behind his lids. But the pressure didn't erase the vision of Diana's lush mouth as she smiled. Or the graceful curve of her neck, or the way her bodice strained over the swell of her breasts. He had never experienced desire of that intensity before. It sent his thoughts to dark, libidinous places, as he imagined all the things that he would like to do for her. All the ways he would have her gasping with pleasure, arching mindlessly under his touch.

Oliver cursed softly. He needed to stop feeling and start thinking again. And he would. Start thinking, that was. Just as soon as his blood returned to his brain from areas south.

He would stop this. Now. Because no good could ever come of the lust-fueled imaginings that had followed him from that morning room all the way here. He was a man of honor. Or he had been, at least.

"I've found it." The bespectacled man emerged from a room behind the counter, and Oliver straightened abruptly, glad the man's attention was on the scroll he held in his hand and not on Oliver. "Not so many people looking for local maps," he said as he placed the long paper on the counter. "Since they built that Pavilion, everyone wants something more exotic. Unusual. Like what you brought me yesterday. Sold it already, you know. Just this morning."

"Glad to hear," Oliver said, not really caring. The map had been one of his old ones, and the fantastical illustrations around the edges had not made up for the lack of detail of the Indian terrain. He was interested in the Sussex terrain now. Oliver fixed his attention on the lines and illustrations unfurling before him, delineating the southern coast and countryside. He glanced back to see Diana approaching from where she had been browsing the bookseller's shelves. And keeping her distance.

Just like she had kept a polite, careful distance in the carriage on the way here, not in space, of course, but in words, and he hated himself for that. He had, no doubt, made her horribly uncomfortable.

The bookseller set paperweights at the four corners of the map as Diana came to the counter next to Oliver. She didn't look at him, and he didn't really blame her.

"How accurate are these distances?" she asked the proprietor as she leaned over to view the map in more detail.

The gray-haired bookseller shrugged. "Can't say for certain." He gazed up at Oliver for a moment. "Are you looking for something in particular?"

"Somewhere," Oliver corrected him. "We'll buy the map."

The bookseller shrugged again. "I don't mind you just looking," he said with a crooked smile. "You made me quite a bit of profit this morning with your map. Makes me feel a bit like I'm taking advantage."

"Don't apologize for good business," Oliver said.

"Hmph. Well, maybe I can help?" the elderly man asked. "I've lived in this area all my life."

Oliver pulled out Madelene's letter with the mileage marker. "We're looking for a place near Brighton. A place that has a church that looks like a castle and a river nearby."

"Ah. That's easy. You're looking for Beddingham," he said.

Diana's head came up, and Oliver straightened.

"I expected to see knights on top of that old church when I was a boy," the bookseller continued with a chuckle. "I was always a little disappointed to arrive and find that there were no great destriers tied up in front." His gnarled finger traced a winding river from the sea inland. "That's the River Ouse. Beddingham is just here." His finger stopped to the northeast of Brighton, on a village that couldn't be more than eight miles from where they stood.

Oliver met Diana's eyes, the well of excitement overcoming whatever awkwardness lay between them. It seemed too easy, this. Or perhaps he had just been afraid to hope.

"Thank you," Oliver said, trying to caution himself that this offered no guarantees. Madelene might not be there. They might have the location wrong, or she might have moved.

Behind them, the door opened, a gusting draft sending a handful of papers fluttering off the surface and behind the counter. The bookseller bent to collect them.

"I need to go to Beddingham," Oliver said to Diana in a low voice. "Right now."

Diana put a hand on his arm. He kept his own hands where they were, remembering what had happened last time he touched her.

"It'll be nearly dark by the time you get there."

"So? I'll wake everyone up if I have to. Knock on every door. Someone will know where she is."

"That will go over well, I'm sure," Diana said wryly. "People are usually very forthcoming when they bolt from their beds, certain their homes are being broken into by strange men. Besides, you don't even know if Madelene lives in town. She might live in the surrounding area."

If she even lived there at all, Oliver added in silent frustration. He chafed at the delay, but Diana was right.

"We can leave first thing on the morrow," she said. "We'll start at the church. Because she's described it in such detail, it's likely that she's attended. Someone in the clergy might know her."

"You'll come with me?"

"I'm far less threatening than a strange man stomping about town demanding answers to the whereabouts of a young woman," she teased. "Of course I'll go with you."

"Going somewhere, Mrs. Thompson?" a familiar voice inquired from behind them.

Oliver froze. Not again.

Diana's face instantly shuttered, and he turned to find the Duke of Riddington standing between the counter and the door, smoothing the front of his embroidered waistcoat with a gloved hand. A slighter man, dressed in dark, nondescript clothes, was standing behind him with what looked like a journal tucked under his arm.

"Riddington," Oliver said.

"Mr. Graham," the duke replied with a curl to his lip. "And darling Mrs. Thompson. I thought it was you I saw through the window. I couldn't pass by without offering my salutations and complimenting you on your appearance. You look positively fetching today."

Diana mumbled something that Oliver couldn't hear.

"Your Grace." The bookseller tossed his own greeting into the fray. "I was going to have your map delivered when it was ready." He sounded worried. "The frame is not quite finished."

"Yes, yes." The duke gave a dismissive wave. "You'll be envious to see what I picked up for a song this morning, Graham," he said to Oliver. "An Indian map of the future, illustrated in fine detail. Mark me, only the best will do."

"The future?" Oliver asked, wondering at the duke's sudden interest in a place he had referred to as barbaric and backward only last night.

"The world is shrinking, Mr. Graham. Beyond our borders lies a world of culture and knowledge. The future and the control of it lies there, for men with the courage to face the risks that come with such great rewards." Riddington sniffed and turned slightly to the man behind him. "Did you get that, Mr. Rhodes?" he asked. "I wish to be quoted directly. So many of the peerage remain sheltered from the beauty to be found in such places."

Diana made a funny sound in her throat, and Oliver willed his face to remain impassive.

The man seemed to sigh and pulled out his journal. From somewhere in his coat, he produced a pencil stub and dutifully jotted something down.

"And you will be one of these men?" Oliver asked.

The duke preened. "Of course I will."

The journalist finished writing and closed his book.

"Mr. Rhodes writes for the *Herald*," the duke said. "He covers all the important people and their contributions to this empire. People like me."

"Really?" Diana's silky-smooth tone had a decidedly brittle edge. "Did he write about you last night?" She shot the journalist a hostile stare.

"Ah. You saw the social pages this morning. The mention of our... affair." The duke smirked.

Actually, truly smirked before he rearranged his expression into what Oliver suspected was supposed to be grave concern. Oliver's fingers curled into fists, and for the second time in as many days, he resisted his baser urges to simply knock the man's teeth out.

"That bit was not from the *Herald*. That was the *Gazette*," Riddington continued with a shrug. "Though I understand it came from a credible... source."

"A credible source?" Diana said, her color high. "You?"

The duke waved his hand. "You know just as well as I that these papers must pander to their audience. An audience that delights in the details of the lives of their betters." He patted his artfully styled hair. "And my name sells papers."

"What they suggested was not only false, but utterly implausible." Diana's words were tight.

"Implausible? You wound me, Mrs. Thompson." Riddington put a hand to his chest, annoyance flickering over his features. "You know, perhaps it is only you who does not see how well suited we are. You are too beautiful to be wasted on anyone else."

Diana looked away.

"Come now, Mrs. Thompson. Don't be like that. It's not my fault that every paper from London to Brighton wishes to write about me and my ambitions, personal or otherwise." He paused, his expression becoming patronizing. "I will, of course, speak to the editor on your behalf if such idle gossip unduly distressed you."

"It's too late. The damage can't be undone."

"Damage?" the duke repeated archly. "I am a duke, if you've forgotten. Having your name linked with mine in any sort of fashion can only improve your own popularity and prestige. It is futile to resist me. I have the power to open doors for those who please me. Or close doors for those who do not. You would do well to remember that."

Oliver stared at Riddington, considering the damage he would do in this bookshop if he hurled the duke through the window.

"Mr. Graham?" the journalist asked. "Oliver Graham? You aren't, by any chance, recently returned from India yourself?"

"Indeed, he is," Diana replied before he could answer. "Further, Mr. Graham will be assuming a position at the East India Company's college, teaching science and natural philosophy."

The journalist perked up at this. He opened his notebook again. "You don't say? My editor would love a piece about someone with firsthand knowledge, and I would very much like to—"

"Mr. Rhodes will be far too busy covering important matters this week to waste his time on such drivel," Riddington interrupted. "Though, perhaps, Mr. Rhodes, if you're looking for a deliciously scandalous tidbit that will put you and your paper ahead of the *Gazette*, you might want to ask Mrs. Thompson here about the Double Duchess. They are very close. Staying together here in Brighton, in fact."

Diana stiffened. Oliver frowned, having no idea what that meant. Who, or what, was the Double Duchess?

Rhodes said nothing, only glanced at the duke from the corner of his eye, looking faintly annoyed.

"Mr. Rhodes, I'm giving you an inside track," Riddington said sharply. "I would expect you to be grateful for the advantage."

The journalist seemed to sigh. His pencil was still poised above the pages. "Of course, Your Grace," he said, not sounding very enthusiastic. Or remotely grateful. "Can you get me an interview with the Double Duchess, Mrs. Thompson?"

"No." Beside him, Diana's fists were clenched in her skirts, her mouth set in a hard line.

The reporter sighed again. "Do you have a comment on your own—"

"Mrs. Thompson has no comments," Oliver said. "About anything." He wasn't familiar with all the nuances of this conversation, but he knew Diana did not deserve to be subjected to another moment of this. "I see that your driver waits outside, Mrs. Thompson. Do enjoy your evening. I will send a message to Ainsworth House regarding the matter that we spoke of?"

Diana shot him a grateful look. "Yes, thank you, Mr. Graham. That will be suitable." She picked up her skirts and nodded curtly. "Your Grace, gentlemen. Good day."

The reporter merely closed his notebook and stepped to the side as she swept past him. Oliver watched her disappear through the door before turning back to Riddington. "Petty gossip is a little beneath you, don't you think, Your Grace? It wasn't amusing at Oxford, and it is certainly not amusing now."

"Watch yourself, Graham," the duke said.

"Or what? You'll spread rumors that you and I are involved in a scandalous affair?"

"You do not want me for an enemy. You are a nobody, while I am a very powerful man."

"Yes, you keep saying that."

"It would be a shame if your appointment to the East India College were revoked," Riddington sniffed. "A well-placed word from me could become quite troublesome for you."

"Is that a threat, Your Grace?" His voice was deceptively soft.

"You're not a foolish man, Graham."

"No," Oliver agreed. "Nor am I afraid of you." He'd faced far more intimidating men in his life than this poor excuse for a duke. Emperors. Sea captains. Chieftains. Soldiers. Faced them and learned that real power was born not from a title but from cleverness and confidence and courage.

"Mrs. Thompson doesn't belong to you," Riddington spat, his face flushing a mottled red.

Oliver smiled, a slow, pitying smile. "No, she most certainly does not." He met the duke's eyes without flinching. "And it would serve you well to remember that she doesn't belong to you either."

CHAPTER SIX

Diana didn't get back in the carriage.

Instead, she told the driver to wait for Oliver and struck out down the narrow street, heading for the vista of ocean that she could see spread out across the horizon in front of her. She was angry and shaking and wished with all her heart that she was one of those supremely clever, cool women who could cut a man down to size with her wit. Yet everything she wished she had said usually came to her about two hours too late.

She despised the duke and all his spiteful conceit. She despised the vindictive gossip that she couldn't get away from. And she despised that she didn't really know what to do about any of it.

Those thoughts dashed around in her mind until she found herself past the last shops and inns and houses, and the beach opened up before her. She turned west, her feet sinking into the rough sand as she walked blindly into the setting sun. The blue in the sky above her had yielded to amber and rose, the wispy clouds gilded with streaks of orange. The surface of the sea glittered with gold, the surf leaving a coral sheen on the sand where it crashed and receded. Here, the salty tang of the sea was rich on the breeze, the cry of seabirds the only other sound that could be heard over the waves.

The fashionable set, out taking the air, had long ago left the shore, as had the seamen and fishermen, and Diana had the wide expanse nearly to herself. She walked until the buildings fell away and the beach narrowed to be hemmed in by the sea to her left and rolling, grassy dunes to her right. She changed direction, climbing up into the dunes, and lowered herself to the ground among the lengthening shadows. The sand was still warm from the day, and Diana lay back, closed her eyes, and let the cooling air wash over her. Perhaps she would stay here forever, she thought. Here, gossip couldn't touch her. Here, she didn't have to pretend to be a good person who wasn't horribly jealous that the man she loved belonged to another.

She opened her eyes and stared up at the sky, the orange hues starting to surrender to the pale wash of twilight. With enough food and water, she could happily spend her days in this wild isolation—

The sound of feminine laughter nearby startled her. Not as isolated as she'd thought, Diana realized, pushing herself to her elbows. Just off to her right, slightly below where she was, a couple had emerged, the man's arm around the woman's shoulders. He spun her around, the woman's cloak swirling around her yellow skirts, caught her face in his hands, and kissed her deeply. Diana could feel herself blushing. They wouldn't be able to see her where she lay, and she felt like a voyeur. Perhaps she should slip away. Or make herself known. Or—

She froze. The last rays of the setting sun touched the woman's hair, setting the red tresses on fire. The woman pulled away slightly, her hands slipping around her lover, her face buried in the crook of his neck. The blond man had his back to Diana, and she couldn't hear what he said, but the woman nodded and lifted her head. With infinite care, she touched his face, and he caught her hand, holding it against his heart.

And then he let it go and disappeared back up into the dunes, leaving Hannah Burton gazing wistfully after him. After a moment, she pulled the hood of her cloak up over her head and picked up her skirts before she too vanished into the dunes, taking a different direction.

Diana stared sightlessly at the spot from which Hannah had departed, unable to move. She dragged in a breath, trying to sort out the tumult of emotions crashing through her. After a few minutes, her mind started working again, and she wondered how she could have missed it. How, given everything that had happened in the last days, had it taken her this long to see it? See that Hannah was in love.

And not with Oliver.

She got to her feet, feeling strangely numb, not bothering to brush at the sand and bits of dried vegetation that clung to her skirts. She made her way to the very edge of the surf, the water nearly touching her feet.

It's complicated, Hannah had said, and Diana should have guessed what *complicated* meant. In fairness, she hadn't seen Hannah in the months leading up to their time in Brighton, and the distance her friend had put between them now made sense. It also explained Hannah's decision to come here with her aunt instead of traveling to Bath with her family. And her reluctance to face Oliver. It explained everything.

And yet, in the end, it changed nothing. The engagement between Hannah Burton and Oliver Graham still existed. Oliver had too much honor to ever break such a contract. And if Hannah hadn't already done so, or wasn't going to do so—

"Who is the Double Duchess?"

Diana nearly jumped out of her skin. She put a hand on her chest, as if that would slow the pounding of her heart and turned.

Oliver stood before her, the last vestiges of light making the paleness of his shirt unnaturally bright in contrast to the shadows.

"Who is the Double Duchess?" he asked again. "And why are you a leading wager in the betting books in every gentlemen's club in London?"

"Did you follow me?" she demanded. Of course he had followed her, but she was stalling, unsure how she felt about that. She didn't yet have her thoughts in order. She didn't have answers to anything in order.

"Yes, I followed you," Oliver replied unapologetically. "The driver said you walked down to the beach. I was worried about you. I'm still worried about you."

"I'm fine. If you had concerns about tomorrow, you could have left a message at Ainsworth House, like you said." Her heart was still racing out of control beneath her palm.

"I'm tired of writing letters to you. Especially when I can see you whenever I want."

Diana glanced down the empty beach beyond him and moved away, following the edge of the surf. She was afraid that if she continued to stand in the twilight, next to this man, she might do something stupid. Something more foolish than she already had.

"Tell me what's going on, Dee. Please."

The woman you're supposed to marry is in love with another man. She couldn't bring herself to say it. That was something that needed to come from Hannah. Not her. That was something that was between the two of them.

And I'm in love with you. She couldn't bring herself to say that either, and she cursed herself for the coward she was.

"Belinda Collins, Duchess of Winchester, pursued by the Duke of Pomperly now that she's a widow," Diana replied instead, because bringing up Belinda made her incensed and indignant on her behalf all at once. Which were better things to feel on a deserted beach than reckless and overwhelmed. "Labeled in every damn gossip sheet in London as the Double Duchess. She thought she might escape the scandalmongers here in Brighton." She continued down the beach.

Oliver fell in beside her. "But she hasn't."

"No."

"And neither have you. Tell me about the wagers."

Diana flinched. "How do you know about them?"

"Does it matter?"

"I suppose not."

He was walking close enough to touch her. Close enough that if she chose, she could slip her hand in his. She curled her fingers around her skirts.

"I've been a widow for eight years," she said. "Too long, according to popular opinion, to be without a new husband. Or, at the very least, a lover."

Beside her, Oliver was silent.

"When Laurence died, his estate went to a cousin, but he left me more money than I could ever spend in a lifetime. There has been no shortage of men who believe that they are best suited to control it. Who tell me that I am helpless on my own without a man to guide me."

"You don't have to do anything you don't want to," Oliver growled. "And you are far from helpless."

"I know that. But in their eyes, I am but a prize to be won. By marriage or other means." Anger simmered. And she embraced it because it was safe and real. "The fact that I have refused them all has generated the expected speculation and rumor. The idea that I simply want to be left alone is insupportable."

"Dee—"

"Did you know that the victor of the wager at Boodle's and White's is only required to bed me, not marry me? And that he is entitled to twenty-five percent of the purse if he can prove he did so?"

From somewhere beyond the dunes, an owl hooted, its call eerie.

"I'm sorry," Oliver said.

"For what?"

"For… everything." He sounded unhappy.

"It's not your fault."

"Would you ever," Oliver asked, his voice rough, "get married again?"

Diana was silent, her eyes on the horizon, where the last vestiges of twilight were finally and inevitably succumbing to darkness.

"Yes," she finally whispered. "But only to a man I am in love with." That was the truth. A horrible, unavoidable truth.

That man was walking next to her. Close enough to touch. Hers to want but not hers to have. While the woman to whom he supposedly belonged was somewhere else in these dunes. Avoiding Oliver so that she might be with her own love. Because she didn't want him.

This entire situation was unfair. And absurd. And it sent a furious frustration punching through her.

"Were you in love with Laurence when you married him?" Oliver asked.

Diana stopped and whirled. "What difference does that make?"

Oliver took a step back. "I'm sorry, I didn't mean—"

"Are you in love with the woman you're going to marry?" It was harsh.

He gazed at her, his features hidden by shadow, his eyes glittering in the darkness. "No. I'm not."

Her anger and frustration suddenly drained, leaving her hollow and wobbly.

"Perhaps I could come to love her," he said, and his words were bleak. "With enough time, perhaps—"

"All the time in the world cannot make you fall in love with someone when your heart already belongs to another," Diana said. "No matter how much you wish it otherwise." She couldn't bring herself to be gracious anymore. Her heart was aching, and a gaping, empty hole was opening up within her. "I can't be with another man who I don't love. I just can't."

"Dee." Oliver stepped toward her.

Diana shook her head, afraid that if she looked at him, she would burst into tears. And tears fixed nothing. So she stared up at the rising moon in the darkening sky instead.

She felt his warmth before she realized that his fingers were on her cheek and that, despite her best intentions, a tear had escaped. Oliver brushed the drop of moisture away, but then his hand slipped down to cup her cheek, and God help her, she couldn't step away. Her eyes closed, and she pressed the side of her face into his palm, allowing the heat of his skin to seep into hers against the cool air of the night.

Nor did she step away when his other hand came up, slipping over her shoulder and caressing the back of her neck. Instead, her fingers curled into the lapels of his coat, as if she were afraid that she might be lost if she let go. Very gently, he tipped her head back, and she could feel his breath against her skin as his lips grazed her forehead.

And then his lips found hers, and she was utterly lost.

He kissed her in a way she had never been kissed, in a way that set her entire being aflame. He held nothing back. This kiss wasn't soft, and it wasn't gentle. It was hard and a little desperate, and Diana felt the power of it, the power of him, flood through as the world dropped away. Distantly, she understood that this wasn't a kiss at all. It was a claim.

But then, she had always belonged to him.

His hands moved over her back, pulling her to him, crushing her against the hard planes of his body. Which was good, because Diana was no longer sure her legs would hold her up. He deepened the kiss with a tortured groan, a sound that did dangerous things to her insides and made dampness gather at the juncture of her legs. She whimpered and kissed him back, her hands sliding up the front of his coat and around the nape of his neck, her fingers tangling in the inky thickness of his hair in the way she had dreamed of doing.

His tongue teased hers, clever and hot, and his hands fell to the curve of her buttocks. Held against him, she could feel his arousal, which sent sparks showering through her belly. She wondered if, when he took her, it would be like this too. No tentative fumbling, no uncertain touches, only the raw surety of a desire suppressed for too long.

His lips slid from hers and caught her earlobe before dropping to scorch a trail of flames down the side of her neck. Her head tipped back, sensation sizzling through her, making her feel drunk.

His mouth was at the hollow of her throat, chasing fire over the skin beneath her collarbone and then down the slope of her breast. His hands moved up over her hips, exploring the curve of her waist and her ribs, to cup the weight of her breasts. His thumbs played over the sides, brushing her nipples through the confining fabric, and Diana gasped in pleasure, arching farther into his touch.

He was everywhere, touching, tasting, filling her senses, and she couldn't tell where she ended and he began. He was everything that she had ever wanted. Everything that was perfect and complete and right.

And still wrong.

She felt the moment he came back to himself. The moment when he surfaced from the vortex of impulse and need. He rested his forehead on hers, his breath coming in harsh gasps, his hands shaking where they caged her ribs.

"What are we doing?" His voice was rough.

She couldn't answer.

His hands dropped, and he stepped away from her. His heat was replaced by the cool night air, leaving her chilled. "I'm sorry."

Diana started walking back toward the lights of the town that had appeared in windows and on streets. Walking away from him so that he couldn't see her face and the grief that she knew was carved upon it.

"Dee?" he called, but she kept walking.

She too was sorry. Sorry that he could never be hers. Sorry that there would be no happy ending to what had started on this beach.

But she couldn't bring herself to be sorry that he had kissed her.

CHAPTER SEVEN

Oliver stared out the carriage window, watching the rolling countryside fall away, resisting the urge to glance at the woman who sat across from him.

The night before, he'd followed Diana back to town, but at a distance, until he'd seen her slip safely back into Ainsworth House. And then he had walked the darkened beaches for hours, dazed and aroused and cursing himself alternatively for not stopping that kiss before it had ever started and ending it when he had. He wanted her. Wanted her with such single-minded desperation that it made him think he might simply be reduced to ash from the inferno of need that had razed his control and his inhibitions. That kiss had left him shaken. Left him completely adrift, every predictable and familiar anchor to which he'd thought he had his life moored obliterated in a single minute.

Returning to his rented rooms, he'd discovered that Diana had sent him a concise message, stating that the dowager's carriage would collect him at eight o'clock sharp. No mention of anything that might be construed as remotely personal. No clue as to what she might be thinking. Oliver had tossed and turned until dawn crept through the windows. He told himself over and over that that kiss had been a mistake. A mistake that tarnished whatever honor he still had left. No matter how much he wanted Diana, no matter how much his heart hurt with the thought of losing her, he couldn't simply abandon Miss Burton. He couldn't renege on a promise he made to their families a lifetime ago.

Abandoning his promise to Miss Burton and her family would make him no better than the blackguard who had undoubtedly made promises to his sister and then left her because she was inconvenient. He was not that man. He could not be that man and live with himself.

Yet, kissing Diana Thompson hadn't felt like a mistake. Kissing Diana had felt like heaven. Kissing Diana had felt perfect and real and right.

Except now he sat opposite her in a comfortable carriage feeling anything but right. Her greeting this morning had been polite, her demeanor distant, her subsequent conversation almost non-existent. Oliver had had no idea what to do from there. So he sat, looking out the window, until he couldn't stand the silence any longer.

"Why did you come today?" He pulled his eyes from the countryside and faced her.

"Because I promised you I would."

"Are we going to talk about what happened last night?" he asked recklessly.

"Should we?"

Her voice was quiet, and he tried not to remember the way it had caressed him on that beach. Tried not recall the soft sounds she had made as he had explored her skin first with his hands and then with his mouth. Tried not to dwell on the way her body had felt against his—

He ran his hands over his thighs, his palms damp, hating that his composure was slipping away from him despite his best efforts. "I kissed you."

"You did."

"I shouldn't have done that." *Even though I want to do it again. Right now. Badly.*

"Perhaps." Diana looked out the window. A muscle flexed near the underside of her jaw. "She's in Brighton, you know."

"Who?"

"Hannah. She's staying with her aunt at their country home."

"What?" Oliver sat up straighter, the mention of Hannah Burton's name slicing through his desire like an icy knife.

"I thought you should know."

"I was told that the Burtons were in Bath."

"The rest of her family is. Hannah came to Brighton with her aunt."

Well, that would explain why none of his messages had been answered.

"Why is she not with her family? Why did she come to Brighton?"

Diana shrugged, the movement looking forced and stiff. "Maybe you should ask her."

Guilt chased away whatever lust lingered. Diana was right. This was a conversation he needed to be having with Miss Burton.

Oliver frowned as another thought struck him. "Does she know that I am also staying in Brighton?"

Diana kept her eyes averted. "Yes."

But avoiding him, it would seem. Oliver had no idea what to make of that, other than it was a reminder that since he'd been back, he'd allowed himself to become distracted. He needed to focus on the future and his duty to it. A future that did not and could not include kissing Diana Thompson.

The carriage turned sharply and lurched to a halt.

"We're here," Diana said, gathering her skirts.

The door to the carriage swung open, and she allowed herself to be helped down by an ever-efficient servant in Ainsworth livery. Oliver followed, glancing up at a sky that was starting to darken ominously, bruised clouds heavy with rain approaching from the west. His eyes fell on the stone building in front of them, its crenellated tower jutting up from the end of the steeply pitched roof as if to challenge the elements.

"A castle," he mumbled, hope flickering.

"But no destriers."

Whatever this was between them, it would have to keep for now. For now, he would concentrate on finding the family that had been lost to him. Concentrate on feeling nothing but gratitude toward the woman who had helped Madelene and was now helping him.

Diana picked up her skirts. "Let's go find your sister."

Oliver nodded, unable to answer. He led them up the crooked, uneven path toward the arched entrance that was tacked onto the base of the tower like an afterthought. They passed under the covered entrance and pushed open the iron-bound door.

The hinges squealed as the door closed behind them, and they took a moment to let their eyes adjust to the dimness. Above their heads, the ceiling soared, unlit chandeliers hanging in neat intervals. To their right, at the far end, a long window reached toward the heavens, divided and framed, and putting Oliver in mind of a great cathedral. The air was thick with the scent of candle wax and wood polish.

"Good morning, friends." An elderly clergyman was approaching them. He wore the collar of a priest, and a heavy crucifix hung from his neck. "May I offer you assistance?"

"I hope so," Diana answered. She was dressed in a blue so pale it was nearly white, and with her beautiful eyes and golden curls, she looked rather like an angel. By the slightly transfixed expression on the priest's face, it seemed he thought so too.

"We're looking for a woman," she said in a soft, musical voice. "We think she lives here."

"In Beddingham?" the priest asked, his eyes drifting over Diana's shoulder to where Oliver stood.

"Yes."

"Does she have a name?"

"Madelene." Oliver spoke up for the first time. "Madelene Graham." Belatedly, Oliver realized that if Madelene had started a new life, she might not be using her real name any longer.

"Indeed." The old priest folded his hands in front of him, his bushy gray brows furrowing. "And who is this woman to you?"

Oliver nearly came out of his skin. The priest hadn't said, *I don't know her*, or, *I can't help you*. As in the bookseller's shop, Oliver was struck again by the feeling that this was all dreamlike. That finding Madelene after all these years couldn't be this simple. "She's my sister," he croaked.

"Yes, I can see the resemblance." The priest nodded slowly.

It was all Oliver could do not to grab the priest and shake Madelene's whereabouts out of him.

"Where is she?" Diana asked in a much more civilized fashion, as if sensing his unrest. "May we see her?"

The priest tipped his head. "I think that those are questions best put to Madelene." He paused. "I will send her a message and leave those answers to her."

He should be grateful to the priest, Oliver knew. He should be thanking him for taking such care with Madelene's well-being. If he wasn't wound tighter than a clock, he would be.

"That's fair," Diana said. As if all this subterfuge was expected.

"What message would you like to pass along?"

"Tell Madelene that Oliver is here," he said hoarsely. "And that I'm not leaving without seeing my little sister."

The priest glanced back at Diana, who only nodded.

"Very good," the old man said. "I'll see it done. Wait here."
The man shuffled away through a door off to their left.

"Wait here?" Oliver ran his hands through his hair in agitation. "What does that mean? Wait here for how long? A minute? A day? A week?"

"I don't know." Diana looked at him helplessly, her blue eyes wide and almost violet in the hazy light.

Outside, thunder rumbled menacingly.

"I'll direct the driver to the nearest inn," she said, glancing out the thick-walled window nearest them. "There's no point in subjecting him or the team to the elements when we don't know how long we'll be."

"I can do that."

"No," she assured him. "You wait here in case the priest comes back. I'll be but a minute." She slipped from the church before he could answer.

Oliver heard the door close, and he paced through the nave, stopping in front of a thick, wide arch that loomed above his head. On the surface, in an ancient, dark paint almost the color of dried blood, a robed figure was drawn, his hands clasped in silent prayer. A savior, no doubt, meant to—

"Who are you?"

Oliver started and turned to find a girl of no more than four years standing in the center of the aisle, gazing up at him. In a blinding flash, he was whisked back in time, a four-year-old Madelene gazing up at him, begging to be allowed to come along with him as he and Diana had set out on one of their adventures in the dales. He blinked, and the present reasserted itself.

"Oliver," he said, unable to tear his eyes away from the brown eyes and dark hair so like his own. So like Madelene's.

"My mama knows a man named Oliver. But she says he lives in a country far away."

Oliver put a hand out to steady himself against the side of the arch. "Do you and your mama live here?"

"No one lives in a church." She giggled, making a face. "Except mice. And Father Hubert."

"Father Hubert is the priest?"

"No, silly." She laughed again. "Father Hubert is the cat. He eats mice."

"Ah." Oliver was having a hard time thinking. This girl wasn't old enough to be the child Madelene had been carrying when she fled London. But the coincidences were stacking up in neat, orderly rows, and all Oliver could think was—

"My mama says I can have a cat when I'm older. Do you have a cat?" she asked, her face solemn now.

"No," he managed to answer. "I don't."

"I'm going to call my cat Queen Eleanor. My mama says she was a good queen."

"Your mama is right. What if your cat's a boy?"

"Then I'll call him King Eleanor."

"Sounds reasonable. What's your name?"

"Diana," she said proudly. "Diana Seymour."

"Diana," he repeated faintly.

"My mama says she named me after a beautiful, kind lady," the little girl continued. "She says she hopes I grow up to be just as kind. That's why I came to talk to you, even though I'm supposed to be helping my mama clean the church," she confided. "You looked sad."

Oliver crouched, afraid his legs were going to betray him if he didn't. "I think you're already very kind. And I think your mama is very wise."

She smiled at him, and Oliver's heart melted into a messy puddle. "Do you know my mama?"

"He does."

Oliver staggered to his feet and whirled. A woman, clad in a plain brown dress, a dusty apron tied over the front, her dark hair pulled back into a simple braid, and tears in her warm brown eyes, stood before him.

"Welcome home, big brother."

CHAPTER EIGHT

They didn't bother to collect the carriage or the driver from the inn. Instead, they walked the half mile to Madelene's farm, Oliver's sister tucked against his side, the little girl skipping ahead of them. Diana followed at a discreet distance, her cheeks aching from smiling and her heart full to bursting. When she'd returned to the church, she hadn't expected to find another woman in Oliver's arms. She hadn't expected to be drawn into the embrace amidst laughter and happy tears. She hadn't expected to look into the beautiful eyes of a beautiful little girl and be introduced to her namesake. Which had brought her to tears all over again.

They beat the storm, closing the door of the small cottage just as the rain came down in sheets. Within minutes, the door crashed open again, and a man and a young boy tumbled in, both laughing and drenched to the skin. And Diana and Oliver were introduced to Madelene's husband, Jack, and her son, Miles.

Diana hadn't been sure how their sudden appearance would be met. Years had passed since Diana had embraced a tearful but determined Madelene in the yards of a coaching inn, a single trunk at Madelene's feet and a small fortune sewn into her skirts.

It had been even longer since Oliver had seen her, and the girl he would remember was nothing like the woman he had found. She and Oliver had barged into her life uninvited and with no warning. But now, watching Madelene and Oliver tease each other, hearing the buoyant flow of conversation and the laughter that echoed throughout the cottage, Diana wondered why she had ever been worried.

The day seemed to pass in a heartbeat. The time wasn't enough to make up for the years that they had been away from each other, but it was a start. The promise of more days like this one made it easier to face the lengthening shadows and the knowledge that Diana's time with Madelene's family was almost at an end tonight.

"How did you find us?" Madelene asked as she and Diana cleaned up after dinner.

Diana stacked a plate on the sideboard and came back to the table. "The castle church you mentioned. As it turns out, more than a few young imaginations have been captured by those ramparts."

Madelene smiled.

"You didn't, however, mention in any of your letters that you had married," Diana said, wiping the crumbs from the table.

Madelene ducked her head. "I meant to. It seemed an awkward thing to blurt out in a letter."

"Like the birth of your daughter?" Diana teased.

"That too." Madelene's cheeks were pink. "Perhaps I knew deep down that you would find me." She folded and refolded the cloth in her hands. "I'm sorry I didn't tell you where I was. Seems rather foolish now."

"You don't have to apologize. I understand that you were protecting yourself. Your family." Diana picked up a bowl from the table. "I was worried that you might be angry."

"Angry?"

"That we inserted ourselves into your peaceful existence. I told myself that I would always respect your privacy and your choices," Diana said. "But then Oliver came home, and all he wanted was to find you. He would have done it with me or without me."

"I could never be angry," Madelene said vehemently. "In fact, it is you who should be angry with me. You were my guardian angel. You deserved my faith. You deserved better." She shook her head, her gaze settling on her brother on the far side of the cottage. "Oliver too."

Oliver was crouched on a stool, his hands waving in the air, the children utterly transfixed by whatever tale he was telling them. A vision of what it might be like to belong to this man as his wife crowded into her mind. An impossible, unattainable vision.

Madelene was looking at her expectantly, and Diana fumbled for a response. "You only did what you thought was best." She congratulated herself on how normal her voice had sounded.

"Not just for me." Madelene's gaze went from Diana to Oliver and back. "But for Oliver too." She set the cloth on the table and then picked it up again, her fingers playing with the edges. "He had just started his position in India. I did not want gossip of a scandal to reach him there."

"Because he would have come back."

"Yes. He would have abandoned everything he ever worked for without a second thought." Madelene looked beseechingly at Diana. "I don't want him to do something reckless on my behalf. I didn't want that then, and I don't want that now. Do you understand? He can't know everything."

Diana bit her lip. "I understand. His belief that honor is the measure of a man hasn't changed."

"And I'm afraid that it will blind him to reason." Her forehead creased. "Miles's father was not a good man. But I was young and gullible, and he possessed the ability to be charming and dashing when he needed to. He made me feel, for a while, like I was the only woman in the world. Until, of course, he got what he wanted from me. I carried around a fair bit of humiliation at my naïveté for a long time. But no longer. Because everything that happened was supposed to happen. I regret nothing, because it all brought me to where I am now."

"You need to tell Oliver that," Diana warned. "Before he starts polishing his armor and lance."

"Tell me what?" Oliver asked, wandering into the kitchen and leaning against the edge of a heavy sideboard.

"Tell you that you'll keep my children up all night with stories about creatures like that," Madelene replied smoothly. "And when my daughter starts asking for a tiger instead of a kitten, I'm going to send her to you."

"I hope you do." Oliver grinned, and Diana's knees went a little weak. He looked so devastatingly handsome. So perfectly... happy.

"Thank you for a wonderful meal," she said to Madelene. "For a wonderful day. I'd like to come again."

"You're always welcome," she replied, giving her a hug. "Eternity lacks enough meals or days that would adequately repay you for everything that you've done for me."

"You're not leaving, are you, Dee?" Oliver pushed himself away from the sideboard. "You're staying tonight." It was more of an order than a question.

"I'm going back to Brighton. You have a lot of time to make up as a family."

"You're family," Oliver said with a frown.

"No. I'm not." She was a friend. A good friend to both of them. But she wasn't family, and she didn't belong here right now.

"You have to stay."

Diana shook her head. "Jack has already gone to the inn to ask our driver to come and fetch me. I imagine they will be back shortly." As if on cue, she heard the steady thump of hooves and the rattle of carriage wheels outside. "Stay, Oliver," she said gently. "Enjoy every minute. And help your sister clean up the dishes." She tried to make that last part light, because inside, she felt that by leaving here, she was leaving her entire heart behind. But she did not belong to Oliver, and she did not belong to his family.

She squeezed Madelene's hand and went to say good-bye to the children. From there, she went directly outside, unwilling and unable to look at Oliver anymore.

Jack had finished putting his own gelding away and met her outside the door. The carriage and its driver were waiting at the end of the short, narrow lane that led up to the house. She glanced at the sky, the sun peeking over the edges of the clearing clouds as it started its descent to the horizon. If she left now, she would be back in Brighton before night fell.

"Thank you," she said to Jack. "For fetching the driver. And for today. And for being... a good man."

"I am a lucky man," he said, "who owes you his thanks. Without your kindness, I would never have found Madelene." He kissed her on the cheek. "You are always welcome here."

Diana started down the lane. She hadn't made more than a dozen steps when a hand caught her arm and spun her around.

"Dee." Oliver was standing in front of her, slightly out of breath, his brow furrowed. "Don't go."

"I'm not going to argue with you, Oliver," she said, starting toward the carriage again. She couldn't do this. She couldn't stay. She couldn't listen to him ask her for impossible things.

He moved and was standing in front of her again. "Stay. Just one night."

Diana closed her eyes briefly, those words making it difficult to draw a full breath. "I can't."

"Why not?"

"Because I don't belong here. I don't belong to you." There. She had said it out loud.

She heard him catch his breath. His eyes searched hers, and he reached for her hand, tightening his fingers when she made to pull away. He stared down at their joined hands, his hair falling over his forehead, his brows knit.

"But what if I belong to you?" The question was barely audible.

Diana's heart broke. Piece by piece, it fell, until nothing was left but a horrible, aching void. "Don't do this, Oliver. This can't happen, and we both know why."

"Jesus." He let go of her hand, walking away three steps. He ran his fingers through his hair in agitation before spinning. "You're right. I didn't mean to—I don't—I just—" He stopped. "I'm so sorry, Dee."

"So you've said."

His eyes clashed with hers across the distance, his miserable. "I'm trying to be an honorable man. I am trying to do the right thing."

"And marrying Hannah is the right thing," Diana said dully. She already knew what his answer would be.

"Yes."

"And what if the honorable thing isn't the right thing?" The familiar furious frustration was rising again, and Diana welcomed it, because it was keeping every other emotion at bay. It was keeping her from falling apart.

"That makes no sense."

She supposed that, to Oliver, it wouldn't. "What if Hannah doesn't wish to marry you? What if her heart lies elsewhere?"

"She's never given me any indication that she doesn't want to marry me. And she would have done so by now if that was the case. Because I know Miss Burton to be an honorable woman. She'll marry me because we are both bound by promises. By our word. If you don't have that, you have nothing."

Diana gazed back at him, suddenly feeling tired beyond words. It was likely that Oliver was not wrong.

I thought I'd have more time, Hannah had whispered miserably in a pretty morning room. More time with the man she loved before circumstance and honor would ensure that she did exactly as Oliver had said. Keep her promise to her family and to his. Just as Oliver would.

"So you'd sacrifice love for honor. Hers and yours."

"You're twisting this."

"I'm not twisting anything, Oliver." She took a shaky breath. "Tell me you don't love me."

He took a step toward her, but she backed away. "Dee."

"Tell me that you don't love me, Oliver. And then I'll tell you that I don't love you, and you can go on your way knowing that you've sacrificed nothing for your precious honor."

He held her gaze, his face a portrait of anguish. "I can't."

Diana closed her eyes briefly, not sure if she was going to survive this. "But you'll marry Hannah anyway."

He flinched. "Yes."

She stepped farther away from him, and he let her. "Then you can't ask me to stay. You have to let me go, Oliver," Diana said, knowing that she wasn't talking about tonight.

She was talking about forever.

* * *

Oliver stepped out into the night, breathing deeply and thinking how the fates amused themselves at mortals' expense.

Tonight, with his sister and her beautiful family, he had found joy and peace. He had been given an invaluable gift that he would always hold dear to his heart. Yet, at that same moment, when he believed he truly had everything, he had let the person who owned his heart slip away. He had lost Diana, not just for tonight, but forever. Because he couldn't make her stay. That knowledge pressed down on him mercilessly, an acute ache settling into his chest.

"Had enough of storytelling?"

Madelene sat on the other side of the small kitchen garden, perched on the edge of the low stone fence that enclosed the pasture. The full moon cast a pale ghostly light over the yard and was reflected in the puddles on the ground. The wind blew cool and fresh, bringing with it the scent of everything washed clean after a hard rain. Somewhere in the darkness, a cow lowed over a chorus of crickets.

"I have a lot of years to make up," he said, picking his way across the wet yard. "I think they'll have enough of me long before I have enough of them." He lowered himself next to Madelene.

His sister smiled. "Be careful what you wish for."

"What I wish is that you had told me all those years ago."

Madelene was quiet for a moment. "I'm sorry, for what it's worth. But you were a world away."

"I would have come back. In a heartbeat."

"I know that. And I did not want my foolishness to cost you everything."

"Nothing you did would have cost me anything."

"Perhaps."

Oliver swept leaves scattered by the storm from the top of the fence. Droplets of water clung to his fingertips, and he wiped them on his breeches. "You're not a fool. You made a mistake."

"You sound like Diana," Madelene said. "That's exactly what she said. Right after that awful day that I showed up at her door with nothing but the clothes on my back and the certainty that my world was coming to an end."

"You should never have been put in that position."

"I put myself in that position, Oliver," she scoffed. "I wasn't forced to do anything. I made choices that had consequences."

"Who was he?" Oliver asked, trying to keep his voice even.

"It doesn't matter."

Oliver made a rude noise. He had tried not to think about that, tried not to let it color the happiness of the day, but it was always there in the back of his mind. Someone had hurt his sister. Someone had used her and then turned his back on her when she'd needed him the most.

Regardless of what she told him or didn't tell him, someone would answer for that. He would find the man who'd behaved in such an ignoble manner, of that he was certain.

"Promise me that you'll let this go, Oliver."

"He deserves to pay for what he did," he said through gritted teeth.

"It's done, Oliver. The past is the past. Nothing you do now will change anything. I don't want to change anything. I've found my happiness. I have a husband I adore who loves me for me. Two beautiful children and a warm, safe home. A generous and compassionate friend who had the wisdom to know that I had to find those things for myself." She rested her head against his shoulder. "And, of course, a bloodthirsty brother whom I love anyway."

"I will find out, Madelene," he warned. "You should just tell me."

"No," she snapped. "You will honor my wishes and leave this be. For your sake and mine. For my son and my entire family. Promise me."

Oliver pressed his lips together. Madelene might have made peace with the past, but he certainly hadn't. He wasn't going to make promises he had no intention of keeping.

His sister sighed. "Life is too short to dwell on things that cannot be changed. I want you to find the same happiness I have, Oliver. To be loved completely and unconditionally is the greatest gift anyone can ever have."

"I'm glad you're happy, Madelene, I am. But—"

"When I met Jack, he believed that I was a widow living with my son," Madelene interrupted. "That was what I told everyone. When he asked me to marry him, I confessed the truth. And I was afraid he would be angry."

"Was he?"

"Only that I would ever think that that would matter to him." Madelene straightened. "Love isn't pretty or perfect. But when it finds you, you hold on with all your might. You defy everything to keep it."

Oliver dropped his head, loss hollowing out his insides. He hadn't done that. He had watched that sort of love disappear down a country road back to Brighton.

"You haven't told her, have you?" Madelene asked.

"Told who what?"

"Told Diana that you love her."

"You can't possibly know that."

Madelene snorted. "Now who's the fool? The two of you were inseparable when we were young. The best of friends as you got older. And tonight, you looked at her the way that every woman wants to be looked at at least once in her life."

"I kissed her," Oliver mumbled.

"It's about time. But you didn't tell her how you feel, did you?"

"I can't."

"Why not?"

"Why not?" Oliver dug his fingers into the stone hard enough to send sparks of pain shooting through his hands. "Have you forgotten that I've promised to marry Hannah Burton?"

"You never promised anything. When you were eight, our parents instructed you to marry Hannah Burton."

"It's the same thing."

"No, it's really not."

"No matter how the arrangement came about, it's binding, and I still have my honor. A man is nothing without it."

"And marrying a woman you cannot possibly love because you're in love with another is honorable?"

Oliver cursed under his breath. "I will not do to Miss Burton what was done to you. I will not abandon her."

"And what does Miss Burton think?"

"I don't know."

"You don't know?"

"I haven't talked to her since I've been back."

"Perhaps you should."

"She's in Brighton. Miss Burton, I mean. But I haven't seen her yet."

"Has it crossed your mind that she doesn't want to see you?"

Oliver dug the toe of his boot into the soft earth.

"If I have learned anything in these last years, Oliver, it's that life is a little like love. Messy and random and scary, and most of the time you must make it up as you go along. But to live a life without happiness, without love, is no life at all."

"How poetic. And trite."

"It might sound poetic and trite, but it's also the truth, Oliver. If I had to go back and do it all over again, I would do nothing differently. Nothing." She stopped. "I won't pretend it wasn't hard. Those first months were awful. To be shunned by your family is not something I think anyone can prepare themselves for. I struggled with the thought that I disappointed them by not following the directives and ideals that were neatly laid out for me by others. That I failed them, somehow."

"Madelene, that's not—"

"Let me finish."

Oliver fell silent.

"As time went on, I realized that in fact, it was they who disappointed me. My life is my own, to live as imperfectly as I wish."

"This is all wrong."

"What is?"

"I'm your big brother. I'm supposed to be giving you advice."

She laughed softly. "If you truly believe yourself to be an honorable man, then you will be honest with Miss Burton. You will be honest with

Diana." She stood and put a hand on his shoulder. "You will find the courage to be honest with yourself. And choose the right thing."

What if the honorable thing isn't the right thing? Diana had asked.

He had never believed one to be independent of the other. He had never believed that he would ever choose between them. But now there was something gathering within him, something that crackled like an impending storm. A feeling of hope that made his heart pound and his skin prickle, and it made him believe that perhaps the fates weren't as cruel as he had thought.

They had brought him here, after all. And presented him with a choice.

Madelene withdrew her hand and started toward the cottage. She stopped by the edge of the garden. "Are you coming in?"

Oliver remained frozen where he was. "No," he said slowly. "I'm not."

Madelene smiled. "I didn't think so." She came back and bent to kiss Oliver's cheek. "Bring our gelding back before Saturday."

CHAPTER NINE

Hannah Burton was as pretty as he remembered, though if he were to be honest, his recollections of her were somewhat vague.

Once a year for the past dozen years, Oliver had sent her a single, polite letter inquiring about her health and the weather. And once a year, he received a single, polite reply inquiring about his health and the weather. He had a vision of what their life might look like. A never-ending parade of days in which they politely discussed their health and the weather.

Tonight's ball was mercifully free from trailing ivy or dead tigers or wilting foliage, and Oliver sipped his punch as Miss Burton danced with a blond man he didn't recognize. Her eyes were sparkling, and her cheeks were flushed. Possibly from the heat, but perhaps her present company had her glowing. She was wearing a pretty green dress that complemented her pretty red hair and pretty green eyes, and Oliver felt… nothing. Only a heightened sense of determination that he needed to do the right thing. For all of them.

He put his empty glass on the tray of a passing footman as the music wound down. Miss Burton and her partner bowed to each other, and the man made to lead her off the floor. Oliver stepped smoothly into their path.

"Miss Burton," he said. "Perhaps you would do me the honor of the next dance?"

He watched as Miss Burton's face went the color of bleached linen. Her eyes darted around the room, and her entire demeanor put him in mind of a rabbit cornered by a fox. The man beside her shifted so that he stood almost between them.

Oliver bowed, mostly to give the lady time to recover her wits. Or possibly bolt.

Her dance partner cleared his throat. "Miss Burton? Are you all right?"

Her eyes flew from Oliver to the man at her side, and she seemed to collect herself somewhat. "Thank you, Mr. Fitzroy. For the dance."

The blond man hesitated. "I can stay."

"I need a brief moment with Mr. Graham." Her gaiety sounded forced.

The man bowed and nodded and moved away, glancing over his shoulder numerous times.

"Mr. Graham," Miss Burton squeaked. "I wasn't expecting you. I thought you were out of town."

"I was. I'm back."

"I see. How did you find me?"

Oliver's frown deepened. "I spoke to a stable lad at your aunt's house who told me this is where I would find your carriage. And you."

"I see." She was rotating the gold bangle on her wrist, around and around.

A phalanx of couples moved into position for a quadrille. To his left, a gaggle of dowagers were staring in Oliver's direction, their painted fans covering whatever gossip was coming out of their mouths. Given Miss Burton's reaction, he was beginning to think that it was best that they did not have an audience.

"Perhaps, Miss Burton, instead of a dance, there might be someplace we can go where we can have a conversation?"

Miss Burton swallowed hard before she nodded. He offered her his arm, and she took it after a brief hesitation. He could barely feel her hand, but she followed him willingly enough out through the polished halls. Her face was even paler if that was possible, and now her eyes were swimming. She looked like he was leading her to her execution.

Outside of the ballroom, Oliver ducked into the nearest doorway, Miss Burton still at his side. He found himself in a drawing room of some sort, a collection of ornate couches interspersed with several carved tables scattered around the room. On the nearest wall, a wide hearth loomed, the coals that had been lit against the evening chill still glowing.

Oliver pulled the door closed behind them.

"It's lovely to see you again, Miss Burton," he started, trying to put her at ease, but Miss Burton had already pulled away from him and was pacing the room like a caged animal looking for a way out. Which, he supposed, was better than a frightened rabbit, but it certainly didn't encourage small talk.

Perhaps this had been a mistake. Perhaps he should have sent a message ahead to her aunt's house. But sending a message would have meant that he'd be required to speak to her aunt, and any other family members who might be in Brighton. It would have meant he wouldn't be able to have the brutal, forthright conversation that he needed to have with Hannah, and Hannah alone. And this was the only way he'd thought he could do that.

"Miss Burton," he said again, with more force. She was clearly distressed, and there was no point in drawing this out. "I'm sorry to catch you unaware like this," he began, reaching for the words he had so very carefully rehearsed in his mind. "I know it's been a long time."

Miss Burton didn't even turn to look at him, just kept pacing at the far end of the room.

"I think you know why I'm here. And I will get straight to the point. Our families made an agreement on our behalves many years ago." He took a deep breath. There was no easy way to say it. "But we can no longer get married."

She looked like she was about to cast up her accounts. "No," she croaked.

Oliver tried to soften his voice. "Miss Burton, I—"

"Stop," she cried, putting her hands over her face. "Just stop."

Oliver winced. He knew in his heart that this was the right thing to do, but that didn't make it any less awful. He didn't want to hurt this woman.

Miss Burton sank onto one of the couches, her hands still over her face. "Diana was right. You are a good man, Mr. Graham." The last was said on a sob that came out more like a hiccup.

That made him feel even worse.

"You don't deserve this. You don't deserve any of this."

He blinked. That made no sense. "I beg your pardon?"

"I'm so sorry."

"Miss Burton, you've done nothing wrong." He wasn't sure if she heard him over her sniffling. He raised his voice. "It is I who owes you an apol—"

"You owe me nothing." Miss Burton's hands dropped to her lap, and she stared down at them, her eyes puffy and her face splotchy red. "Nothing at all."

Oliver approached the miserable woman with the care he usually reserved for wild, unpredictable creatures. "I've come back to England a wealthy man," he said carefully. "If you need—"

"You think I wouldn't marry you unless you were rich?" she cried. "You think that's what I care about?"

"That isn't at all what I was about to suggest." Somehow, this conversation had got away from him. "But in all honesty, Miss Burton, I don't know what you care about. I barely know you."

She slumped. "Which is just as well. Hating me will be easier."

Oliver sat gingerly on the couch opposite her. "I don't hate you."

"You will."

"Why would I ever hate you?"

She swiped at her tears and stared at him. "Because I can't marry you."

"Yes, I believe we've covered that." He passed her the kerchief from his pocket.

She took it and glanced down at the small *G* embroidered on the corner of the fine linen. "I assume it was Diana."

"It was," he said quietly. "It is." That was a truth that she deserved.

Hannah kept her red-rimmed eyes fixed on the kerchief, her lips quivering. "I've betrayed you in the most grievous of ways. And I've been a horrible, selfish friend to Diana. How did she find out?"

"What?"

"You just said Diana told you that we can't wed." She looked askance at him.

"I didn't say that."

"Then how did you know I can't marry you?"

"You've got this all wrong, Miss Burton. It is I who cannot honorably marry you, no matter what past arrangements our families made. I am in love with another. With Diana."

She was blinking at him furiously, utter confusion stamped on her petite features. "You're in love with—" She stopped abruptly. "You're in love with Diana."

"Yes."

A strangled sound escaped from her lips. "Oh God. She didn't tell you anything. Because she still doesn't know."

"Know what?"

Hannah put a hand to her forehead and closed her eyes.

Oliver cursed silently. This was ridiculous. "Miss Burton," he said firmly, seizing control of the muddled, bizarre shreds of this conversation. "I take full responsibility for this decision, even if it means sacrificing my honor for love and happiness. I hope with all my heart that you are able to find the same one day. But for as long as you need, you will have my protection and support and whatever resources you require. I don't know what it is that you think you did or said that would make me hate you or ever prevent you from marrying me—"

"I'm already married."

Oliver blanched. "You're what?"

Miss Burton's chin rose a notch. "I'm already married."

Somewhere deep inside of him, something turbulent and exultant rose in his chest. And it kept rising, making further speech impossible, until it burst like the froth released from a corked champagne bottle, fizzing and flooding everywhere. And he laughed. Not just chuckled, but great, heaving gasps of laughter that had tears running down his cheeks. He bent double, his head in his hands, and by the time he got himself under control, Miss Burton was staring at him, her eyes dry.

Wordlessly, she passed his kerchief back to him, and he wiped his own face.

"Congratulations," he said when he was able. "What should I call you now?" She wasn't Miss Burton any longer.

"Hannah," she said. "Hannah Fitzroy." She twisted her fingers in her lap.

He watched her, the fragmented pieces of their conversation falling together to make sense. "I must assume that there were no banns or flowers or wedding breakfast."

"There was a breakfast." She blushed but did not look away. "A breakfast for two. In Scotland."

"I see."

"We've only been married a month. No one knows."

"Except me."

"Except you," she agreed. "I'm sorry. I should have written to you long ago. Ended our betrothal properly, when I knew that I couldn't possibly marry you."

"When you fell in love."

"Yes."

"I'm happy for you," Oliver said. "I admire your courage."

"My courage?" She gaped at him. "I'm not courageous. I got married in secret because I knew I would never be allowed to marry the man I love. I knew what sort of scandal it would bring down on my family. And yours. I've booked our passages to New York, leaving in a fortnight, and I've begged my husband not to tell anyone. I thought that once we were gone from here, my entire existence could merely be forgotten." She looked like she was going to cry again. "When I saw you here, in Brighton, I panicked. Hid behind ballroom décor so that I didn't have to face you. Fled through morning room windows. Those are not the actions of a courageous person."

"Hannah—"

"I've treated you horribly. Didn't even consider what it would be like when you were left here, fielding all the gossip and speculation about why the woman you were supposed to marry ran away."

Oliver put a reassuring hand on her arm. "Hannah, I'm fine. Given everything I've survived these last years, I think I can weather a little gossip without too much trouble. Whatever you decide, know that I'll support you."

She sniffled. "Thank you."

"Of course."

"My family is going to be furious. I'm going to disappoint a lot of people."

"But not me. And more importantly, not yourself."

Hannah sniffed again and smiled. "Not myself."

"You chose love, not because it was easy, but because it was right. A very smart person recently told me that that takes courage."

Hannah laughed weakly. "Perhaps." She looked at him. "Do you forgive me?"

"There is nothing to forgive."

"I hope Diana will too."

"I'm sure she'll understand."

Hannah gazed at him, her eyes clear. "She loves you too, doesn't she?"

"I'd like to think so."

"She's never said anything to me."

"The two of you make a fine pair, then," Oliver said lightly.

"Will you tell her that I'll come see her tomorrow?"

"I beg your pardon?"

She tipped her head. "I'm not sure what you're still doing here with me, Mr. Graham," she said. "I think that there is somewhere else you need to be right now."

Oliver swallowed and nodded. "Yes."

Hannah got to her feet, and Oliver rose with her. "Good luck, Mr. Graham."

Oliver caught her hand and pressed a gentle kiss to the back of it. "Good luck, Mrs. Fitzroy."

She smiled at him and moved toward the door, pausing as she lifted the latch. "Perhaps I might send you a letter from New York sometime," she said, almost shyly.

"I'd like that," he replied. "I'd like that very much."

CHAPTER TEN

The candle sputtered in the breeze coming through the window but didn't extinguish.

She should get up and blow the flame out, Diana thought idly, but she couldn't seem to move. Instead, she stared up at the ceiling, her eyes tracing the same crack in the plaster in the way she'd been doing for the last three hours. The crack started at the very edge of the west wall, fine and delicate, but by the time it got to the center, the edges were rough and wide.

Not so different than how her heart had cracked. Cracked and then shattered beyond repair. Perhaps she would leave Brighton tomorrow. Maybe travel north, back to her family's country house. At least until she knew that Oliver had left for Hertfordshire. Leaving was cowardly, she knew, but the idea of staying here where she might run into him over and over was unbearable. It was different between them now. They couldn't pretend anymore. She couldn't pretend anymore. She loved him too much.

A soft tap at the door had her sitting up. Worried, she slipped from the bed and went to the door, her hand on the latch.

"Genie? Belinda?"

"Dee." Her name was muffled and barely audible.

Diana froze for a heartbeat before her fingers fumbled with the latch, and she yanked the door open. "What—"

It was all she managed to say before his mouth was on hers, his hands tangled in her hair.

"Oliver," she gasped, and he released her just long enough to close the door behind him with exquisite care, sliding the latch back into place.

"What are you doing here?" Every part of her instantly, inescapably ached for him.

His eyes were hungry, devouring her where she stood, and she realized that she wore only her chemise. Though, that seemed unimportant in the face of the precipice that they were standing on.

"I'm here to tell you that I'm not letting you go. That I refuse. No matter what."

She was fevered and chilled all at once.

"I belong to you, Dee. I've belonged to you since we hunted dragons in the dales. Since I couldn't wait to come home from school at Christmastide, knowing that I would get to see you. Since the night I drank myself into oblivion when you'd written to tell me that you'd married Laurence. Since I saw you in that ballroom, talking to a fern."

"It wasn't a fern I was talking to." Her thoughts and emotions churned wildly.

"I know. You were speaking to Hannah Fitzroy, who was trying to avoid having to tell me—and you, for that matter—that she up and married the man of her dreams."

Diana put a hand out against the wall to steady herself. "What?"

"I went to see Hannah tonight. To tell her that I couldn't marry her because I am already in love with someone else. As it turns out, she's already beaten me to it."

"Hannah's married?"

"Happily. Secretly also, in the event that wasn't obvious."

A sound Diana didn't recognize emerged from her throat, something between a sob and a laugh.

"I should have waited until morning to see you, I know," he said. "But I couldn't. I'm so tired of waiting, Dee."

"So you broke in?" She was terrified that this was a dream. That any second now, she would wake up and find herself alone.

"I didn't break in," he said, moving toward her. "The kitchen door was open. Hannah told me which room was yours."

She stared up at him in the soft light, his beautiful brown eyes holding hers captive.

"Marry me," he said, and his voice was ragged.

"Yes," she whispered.

She wasn't sure who moved first, but in the next second, she was in his arms, his mouth on hers, this kiss just as desperate as the one on the beach. She lost track of time, lost track of how long they kissed, aware only that she couldn't seem to get enough. She was pressed against him, his heat bleeding through the layers of his clothes as his hands stroked her back, her hips, her shoulders. She groaned, needing, wanting more. Wanting everything.

"Tell me to stop," he gasped. "Tell me you want to wait until after we're married. No matter what I said, I can wait."

Diana nipped at his lower lip, her hand sliding beneath the lapels of his coat. "I can't."

Beneath her hands, Oliver shuddered, and she shoved his coat from his shoulders, letting it fall to the ground. He bent his head and kissed her again, this time slowly and deliberately, as she unknotted his cravat and then worked the buttons of his waistcoat. Those too fell to the floor, and she made a noise of frustration because he was still wearing too many damn clothes.

She yanked the bottom of his shirt from his trousers, and he ducked his head long enough for her to pull it off. And then he stood in front of her wearing nothing but his trousers, his chest rising and falling, every ridge of hard muscle beneath all that glorious skin displayed to perfection. A scattering of dark hair across his chest narrowed and trailed off into the waistband of his trousers. She would get there soon enough.

But right now, she would savor what was in front of her. Explore his magnificent body the way she had fantasized about doing too many times. Her hands went to his shoulders, her fingertips running along the edges of his collarbones and then down over the slopes of muscle. She circled his dark nipples, feeling him shudder again, and bent her head to let her lips trace where her fingers had already gone.

Her hands roamed lower, her fingers splayed over the sides of his rib cage and around to his lower back. His own hands were still at his sides, allowing her this freedom, but she could feel him nearly vibrating under her touch. She lifted her head, pressing kisses along the underside of his jaw as her fingers moved to the fall of his trousers. He made a tortured sound, his hips arching into her touch, his erection straining at the fabric.

She fumbled with the buttons, the overwhelming desire that was spiraling through her robbing her of dexterity. Her legs were shaking, and a throbbing ache was building at her core, demanding release. Without warning, he bent and lifted her, holding her hard against him and tumbling her back onto the bed.

He covered her mouth again, this kiss deep and slow as he swept into her mouth. He braced himself above her, teasing and torturing with his lips and tongue. Without pausing, he reached for the bodice of her chemise, yanking at the ribbon that secured it. The thin fabric released with a faint tearing sound, and he reared back, using both hands to strip it down her body and away. He knelt above her, his eyes hot and his face a mask of desire.

He slid back to the end of the bed, his eyes never leaving hers as he discarded his trousers, leaving him gloriously, magnificently naked. Diana watched him from where she lay on her back, every fiber in her body screaming with anticipation, the heat between her legs becoming slick with need.

He climbed back onto the bed and crawled forward. His warm fingers slid up the inside of her thighs. Her eyes closed, and her legs fell apart. His hand caressed the mound of curls between, his thumb trailing behind to stroke through the folds of her sex. She whimpered, pleasure coursing through her. He shifted, and now his mouth was on her abdomen, his tongue flicking over her navel before sliding upward. He grazed the edges of her breasts before taking one of her nipples into his mouth and swirling his tongue around the peak. She gasped and arched, and as she did, he slipped a finger deep inside her.

"Oliver," she managed. "That's too... I can't..."

"Stay still." His fingers were doing unholy things, and she writhed beneath him.

"I can't."

"You can." He bent his head, kissing her neck. "Wait for me."

Her eyes were still tightly shut, and little white lights danced behind her lids. He explored and worshipped every inch of her body with his mouth, tasting, teasing, leaving her breathless and bowed tight. Need built, twisting and coiling.

"Oliver. Please." She was begging, and she didn't care.

His fingers slipped from her, and he caught her hands in his and brought them up over her head. "Wait for me."

The head of his erection pressed against her, and her hips strained up off the bed. She opened her eyes, drowning in the heat of his.

"You belong to me," he whispered and thrust into her.

The throbbing, pulsing need he'd built within her detonated into waves of pleasure. She might have cried out, but he caught the sound with his mouth, his tongue stroking hers as he moved deeply inside of her. She arched into him mindlessly, artlessly, desperately. He groaned, thrusting hard, his hands tightening around hers, and she wrapped her legs around his waist.

She felt the moment he lost control, felt his body contract and shudder, and he came with a hoarse cry, his face buried in the side of her neck. Felt him pulse deep inside her, the eddies of her own orgasm still swirling and sending showers of sparks through her boneless limbs.

He collapsed against her, breathing as hard as she. The world slowly reasserted itself, and her surroundings came back into focus. After what might have been a minute or an hour, he rolled to the side, pulling her with him, cradling her against his chest. The night air pushed in past the curtains and over their damp bodies, and Oliver pulled the coverlet over both of them.

Diana reached up, running a hand over the stubble of his jaw, her fingers tracing the outline of his mouth. Tracing the planes of his jaw, the bridge of his nose, the ridge of his brow, committing the feel of them to memory. She had known this man forever, this man she had loved for so long, but never like this.

"Oliver?"

He caught her hand in his, pressing a soft kiss to her palm. "Dee?"

"You were worth the wait."

CHAPTER ELEVEN

Oliver woke, though he kept his eyes closed.

Morning had arrived—he knew that without needing to see the light intruding past the edge of the curtains. Outside, birds squabbled, while inside, the occasional clang of a pail told him the household was likewise awake. He'd had full intentions of being gone by now, but the door was latched, Diana still slumbered beside him, and he had waited a lifetime for this.

He rolled to his side, pressing himself against the silky smoothness of her back. He kissed her shoulder, caressing her arm. The feeling of possessiveness, of rightness, of love that gripped him was overwhelming. He belonged to this woman, heart and soul. No matter how far he traveled, no matter what place he returned to, in her arms he was home.

Diana stirred, and he was instantly hard. They'd made love twice more in the darkness of the night, neither of them seemingly able to get enough of the other. He knew he should let her rest. Knew that he should get up and get dressed and slip from the house before a well-meaning servant fetched the housekeeper and all her keys, certain that something dreadful had happened to Diana.

He stayed right where he was, content to hold her as she slept.

She stirred again, and he swallowed a groan as her beautiful backside rubbed against his straining erection. He might never have the willpower to get out of this bed—

A warm hand closed over the length of his cock. This time, he couldn't muffle his soft groan.

"You're insatiable," she said, her fingers stroking down the length of him.

"You do this to me." He leaned forward, kissing the intimate spot behind her ear as her hand continued its ministrations between them. "You should go back to sleep."

"Mmm." She withdrew her hand, and Oliver nearly wept at the loss, but then she turned into him, the sheets drifting from her body, her hair cascading over her shoulders in glorious disarray. She slid one leg over his hip and pushed him to his back, coming to rest over him on her hands and knees. Very slowly and very deliberately, she lowered herself so that his erection slid between her legs.

Oliver nearly came right there.

"That would be a terrible waste, don't you think?" she asked.

He tried to answer, but she reached between them, positioning the head of his cock at her entrance. Her hair had fallen forward, the silken ends brushing against his chest and sending electricity skating across his skin. And then she lowered herself completely, and any ability to speak coherently was lost.

He let her set the pace, giving himself up to the feel of her above him, around him. He fought for control as her movements became quicker, the tiny sounds she made as her hips ground against his the most erotic thing he had ever heard. He felt the first ripples as she started to come, heard her gasp, saw her eyes close and her head tip back. He caged her hips in his hands, surging up into the spasms pulsating around him. His own release was bearing down on him, and he held her hard against him, plunging deep.

She leaned forward, kissing him as he came, smothering the shout that would have brought the household running. The intense pleasure rolled on and on, spinning him away into an abyss with no bottom.

"Dee." It was all that he could manage.

"You're going to have to learn to do this more quietly."

Oliver could barely catch his breath. "I don't care who hears when my wife is pleasuring me witless," he panted.

"I'm not your wife yet," she said wryly. She went to slide off him, but he caught her in his arms.

"Don't move. I like you right here."

"We'll scandalize the servants."

"I don't care about that either. Let them know that you own my heart and my soul. All of my nights, all of my days."

"And all of your mornings?" she asked with a wicked grin.

He kissed the underside of her jaw. "And all of my mornings," he confirmed. "Especially if they're like this."

* * *

In the end, he did get up, dressing quickly and taking inordinate pleasure in the simple and intimate task of helping Diana dress as well. The dowager countess did not keep a large staff, and it was surprisingly easy to slip unnoticed through the house. As he soundlessly closed the door that led out into the rear gardens and mews, he congratulated himself on his stealth. Until he turned and nearly ran into another body.

He cursed and stumbled, almost pitching into the rosebushes growing beside the entrance.

"Mr. Graham?"

Hannah stood in front of him.

"Good morning," he said automatically.

"Yes, I can imagine it was," she said, a knowing grin on her lips. Her eyes dropped to his clothes, the same ones he had on when he'd left her last night. "Is she awake?"

Oliver plucked a white rose from the nearest bush, careful of the thorny stem. "She is."

"Dressed?"

"Yes."

"Well, that's something." Hannah was clearly enjoying this.

"What are you doing here?" he asked. "In the back, I mean? Is something wrong with the front door?"

"The front door is guarded by a butler who has lost all patience recently with callers for Diana. He no longer discriminates between male and female, just leaves them in the hall for a good quarter hour before he remembers to fetch her." She shrugged. "So I use the back."

That certainly explained his earlier reception.

"Marry her soon."

A thorn jabbed into his thumb. "I beg your pardon?"

Hannah's smile slipped. "She puts on a good face, but it wears on her. The asinine bets at those gentleman's clubs, the constant competition for her money, for her bed. They're all abhorrent, and no one is worse than the Duke of Riddington. He won't leave her alone. He won't stop until he gets what he wants."

Every muscle in Oliver's body tensed. "If he touches her, I'll kill him."

"I'm surprised you haven't done so already," she said. "Especially after the rumors about your sister and him."

The temperature in the garden dropped. The birds stopped singing. "I beg your pardon?"

Hannah took a step back. "Um."

"I'm not sure what you're talking about," he said, using every ounce of his control to keep his voice steady. "Please explain."

"Diana always says I shouldn't read the gossip columns," she said. "Nothing but lies and conjecture. And she's right. And it was a long time ago. Forget I said anything."

"No," Oliver said, and even he could hear the warning in his voice. "You owe me this. You owe me a truth."

"There were a few rumors," she started unsteadily. "In the social pages of some of the smaller dailies. Nothing that anyone took seriously, because by then your sister had left for America, and there was nothing else to say."

Oliver's vision went a little hazy, hues of red and black crowding the edges.

There were a few rumors in the social pages—

He squeezed his eyes shut, trying to put his thoughts in order, a difficult task with the fury and the sense of betrayal hammering at his skull. Was he the last to know? The last person to be let in on a secret that wasn't a secret at all? Had he been taken for a fool?

Oliver opened his eyes. "Did Diana know? That it was Riddington who seduced and discarded my sister when he was done with her?"

"Yes," Diana said from the doorway behind him. "I knew."

* * *

Oliver spun to face her.

"You forgot your watch," she said. She tightened her fingers around the pocket watch, the metal cool against her skin.

He was trying to form words, but no sound was coming out. The white rose he held in his hand was slowly being crushed between his fingers.

"Perhaps, Hannah, you might come back this afternoon?" Diana said.

Hannah's eyes darted between Diana and Oliver, and she nodded, beating a hasty retreat through the low garden gate and disappearing through the mews.

"You knew," he said, a harsh accusation. "You knew all along that it was Riddington."

"Yes. Madelene told me at the very beginning."

"You knew who ruined my sister, and you didn't tell me." He looked like he wanted to hit something.

Diana squared her shoulders. He was furious and upset, and he had every right to be, but she needed to make him listen to reason. "First, it wasn't my place to tell. Second, he ruined nothing. He is a loathsome and deplorable excuse for a man, and what he did was wrong, but your sister emerged on the other side of it stronger. Strong enough to live her own life and find her own happiness."

Oliver was shaking his head. "My sister—"

"Is living her life. Making her own decisions. Decisions you need to respect. Including the one she made not to tell you who Miles's father was."

"I don't have to—"

"She's trying to protect her family," Diana told him. "Riddington knows nothing. She never told him she was pregnant. By the time she realized she was with child, he had already disposed of her and moved on to his next conquest."

"She should have—"

"She should have what? What were her options? Stay and let your family sink into scandal? Or leave and start over?"

The stem of the rose Oliver was holding snapped, and a drop of blood from his palm splattered onto the snowy petals. He didn't seem to notice. "He should have married her."

"He would never have married her, and you know it," Diana bit out. "If every titled man wed every woman he took to his bed, every woman he had a child with, half the aristocracy would have a dozen wives. The world doesn't work like that, and you know it, and in this case, Madelene is better off for it."

Oliver cursed loudly. "This is my fault. Riddington did what he did to Madelene because of me."

"I beg your pardon?"

"He hated me. I told you that. And he is a resentful, bitter, spiteful man who would seek his own brand of retribution. He couldn't ruin me, so he ruined my sister."

"You know nothing of the sort. Don't you dare make this about you."

"I will not let what he did go unpunished." His voice was cold.

"Then tell me, what will you do? Call him out?"

"Yes!"

"So you'll shoot him? Run him through?"

"Maybe both," he snarled. "I'd like nothing better."

"And then what?"

"What do you mean, 'and then what'?"

"What happens when a duke is dead by your hand? What will that change?"

"It's not about change, it's about honor."

"This honor you speak of will cost you everything. You are not immune to the law."

"I'll take that chance."

Diana closed her eyes and tried not to scream in frustration. "'Before you embark on a journey of revenge, dig two graves.'"

He made a disgusted sound. "You're quoting Confucius to me? Now? Really?"

"Yes, really. Because you didn't survive everything you did to come home and die in a damn ditch in some useless duel. Or swing from the gallows."

"I will not look the other way, Diana."

"I thought you understood that the right thing is not always the same as the honorable thing. I thought you chose love over honor."

"This is not the same, Dee. This is not the same at all."

"But it is. I will not stand by and watch you sacrifice everything for something—someone—so worthless."

"I thought you, of all people, would understand," Oliver said through clenched teeth. "It is my duty to protect my family. I would do the same for you. Because I love you."

"Oliver." She exhaled. "I understand that you're angry, and I understand that you want your pound of flesh. But this isn't about you. This is about a sister who loves you very much. This is about two small children who deserve to have an uncle who will be there for them as they grow up. This is about me. This is about our future. What we started last night. Because I love you too, Oliver."

He tossed the rose aside, and it landed on the packed ground, broken and bloodstained. "If you loved me, you wouldn't make me choose. You'd understand."

"Last night you told me that you wouldn't let me go. No matter what. Don't let me go, Oliver. Don't do this."

He stared at her, breathing hard, before he spun wordlessly and stalked to the end of the garden.

"Oliver." A bubble of terror and helplessness that danced along the edge of hysteria was expanding into her throat and making it hard to breathe. "I can't lose you again."

He paused, his back to her, his hand on the gatepost.

"Where are you going?" She was fighting back tears, because she already knew the answer.

"I'm going to do what I should have done a long time ago," he said.

And then he was gone.

CHAPTER TWELVE

Oliver sat on the edge of his bed in his rented rooms, the battered trunk that had seen him across two continents open in the corner, its contents strewn across the room. Late afternoon sun slanted through the window, carving long shadows around the space. He stared down at the long, flat box in his hands.

The box was made of rosewood, elaborately carved and inlaid with ebony and ivory. It had been a gift from a chieftain, a token of thanks after Oliver had defended the man's young son from a pack of feral dogs. At the time, he'd had only a club and his bare hands, and the chieftain had sought to rectify that.

Oliver released the ornate latch and opened the box, the hinges silent. Nestled in a bed of midnight velvet, two officer's pistols lay. They were Turkish, decoratively engraved, and as beautiful as they were deadly. The wooden stocks gleamed, and Oliver withdrew one of the pistols, its familiar weight settling into the palm of his hand like an old friend.

The debilitating fury that had gripped him in the garden had become a dull, agitating throb. The look on Diana's face when he left her had shaken him more than he cared to admit. The principles of honor that he had once believed to lie in straight, razor-edged lines of black and white had become a haze of gray.

He set the pistol on the bed between the two piles of letters. The small pile on the right, the letters Diana had given him from Madelene, slid to rest against the muzzle of the pistol. His fingers hovered over the second pile, this one thick and tied with a simple leather string. These letters were worn and travel-stained, the bold, feminine handwriting unapologetic and steadfast. These letters were the piece of home that he had looked for every day, every week, every month that he had been gone. These letters made him feel like he was never alone.

Oliver cursed and picked up the pistol again. From his coat pocket, he withdrew a torn scrap of paper, an address scrawled across the crumpled surface. He'd asked Thorpe for this address, and his friend had given him a long, measuring look but, in the end, had provided it. Oliver stood, shoving the pistol under his coat into the holster strapped across his chest, feeling very much like the corsair from whom the chieftain had taken the firearms in the first place. He looked down at the scrap of paper, stuffed it back into his coat pocket, and strode from the room.

The sunshine faltered as he walked through the town, thick, dark clouds drifting across the sky and plunging the streets into an ever-shifting gloom. The gathering storm perfectly suited his mood. It perfectly suited what he was about to do.

The address was easy to find. The building loomed in front of him, its whitewashed façade stark against the darkening sky. He checked the address once more, the weight of the pistol heavy beneath his coat. He ascended the stairs, the stone beneath his boots cracked and the blue paint on the wooden door starting to peel. He banged on the warped wood with his fist, and the sound echoed in his ears. From the bowels of the building, he heard a voice, and he pounded again.

He had raised his fist a third time when the door was yanked open by a man, his expression going from irritation to surprise and then confusion. "Mr. Graham. May I help you?"

"I believe we can help each other," Oliver replied.

The man looked at him for a moment before pulling the door wide. "Then, by all means, come in."

Oliver stepped over the threshold.

"Thank you, Mr. Rhodes."

CHAPTER THIRTEEN

Diana wondered if she was destined to spend the entirety of her remaining sojourn in Brighton hiding behind shrubbery. The ferns on this night had been replaced by staked hibiscuses, meant again to capture the romantic ideals of the Far East, in case the architecture of the Pavilion itself did not. Diana wondered what Oliver would make of it. And then she cursed herself for wondering.

Five days.

Five days had passed since Oliver had left her standing in the back of the dowager's house, and in those days, Diana's emotions had ricocheted from terror to fury to heartbreak to hope. Terror that, any minute, she was going to be brought news of Riddington's death and an announcement that Oliver Graham had been arrested by the authorities. Fury that he had left her in that garden the way he had. Heartbroken that, in the end, the future hadn't been enough to overcome the past. She hadn't been enough. He had chosen an antediluvian, skewed sense of honor that would accomplish nothing except tragedy. The ensuing silence was exhausting and nerve-racking, and she could barely concentrate on anything any longer.

And yet, with each passing day, hope glimmered because Riddington still breathed. Diana tried not to let that hope in, because she knew very well that this might simply be the calm before the storm. This might be the time that Oliver Graham required to plan the demise of the Duke of

Riddington.

She raised her glass to her lips, her fingers shaking. She cursed again and set the glass on the edge of the hibiscus planter, a crimson flower falling from the vine to settle at her feet like a pool of blood. She never should have come here tonight. She never should have let Hannah dress her and all but drag her from her rooms. Hannah might have wanted to see the king, but Diana couldn't have cared less that he was in attendance tonight. The king solved none of her problems. The king offered no solutions to a man bent on honor at the expense of everything else.

The king only made this room horrifically overcrowded and hot.

She bent down to pick up the fallen flower.

"Dance with me."

Diana straightened, her heart lodging in her throat. "Oliver."

"Dance with me," he said again. He had never looked more devastating, his inky hair and rich complexion foils for the perfect whiteness of his elaborately knotted cravat. He was wearing his evening clothes again, though they had been brushed and pressed back into pristine condition.

Her heart returned to its rightful place, banging so hard against her ribs, she was afraid that they would crack. Heat flared and receded, only to smolder deep within her. Through sheer willpower, she kept from touching him.

Very slowly, he took the crimson flower from her unfeeling fingers and tucked it behind her ear. "Beautiful," he murmured. "You're so damn beautiful."

"What are you doing here?" The terror of the unknown crowded into her mind. He had come here to finally end things. With the king here, the Duke of Riddington would be here too, somewhere in this crush. Oliver would know that. Everyone would know that.

"I'm asking you to dance. Because I've never danced with you. Not once, in all the time we've known each other."

Diana hesitated. "Oliver—"

"There are a lot of things I haven't yet done with you." Oliver's eyes held hers as he extended his hand. "I want to remedy that."

She stared at him, hope pushing through the terror and the anger and the heartbreak and making it difficult for her to think.

"So I'm asking you to dance." He held out his hand. "And I'm asking you to trust me."

She nodded because her voice no longer seemed to be working.

Oliver caught her fingers in his and led her through the crowd, the music swelling over the buzz of voices. He slid his other hand around her waist, pulling her closer than was proper.

"I choose you," he whispered against her ear as he led them into their first steps. "I choose you, and I want everyone to know it."

Hope burst through her, and the room around them dissolved into a blur of color. And on the heels of that hope, love. She hung on to him with all her might, the way she had on a Brighton beach what seemed like a lifetime ago.

"I love you, Oliver," she said, her throat thick. "I will always love you. No matter what."

She meant it. It didn't matter what had happened or what might yet come—

"Mrs. Thompson. I believe that I am owed a dance. And I believe that I'll have that dance now."

Oliver stiffened beneath her hands as he stopped at the edge of the dance floor.

Diana closed her eyes and rested her forehead on his shoulder, as if that could block everything out. As if that would keep Oliver with her, the Duke of Riddington reduced to nothing more than an inconsequential nuisance that could be ignored.

He chose you, a small voice in the back of her head intoned frantically. *He chose you, he chose you, he chose you.* Yet, Oliver was only a man.

She raised her head and faced the duke, aware that Oliver's hand had not moved from her waist. "I owe you nothing," she said, not looking at Oliver. Afraid to look at Oliver.

Riddington's eyes narrowed. "I think you've led me on more than enough, Mrs. Thompson. While I won't deny I've enjoyed the chase, publicly choosing to spend your time with an unexceptional man such as Graham over me is not doing either one of us any favors. We both have reputations to uphold. We both must make smart choices, don't you agree?"

The fury and terror were back. Fury directed solely at this man who lacked integrity and character. Terror that the man beside her had too much.

"I've heard that," Oliver said beside her.

Diana's eyes flew to his. He sounded almost... amused.

"I beg your pardon?" the duke said scornfully.

"Reputations." Oliver waved a hand airily. "I heard that they are often thorny to manage and maintain. Especially when there are, indeed, so many choices."

Diana was staring at him. Oliver's muscles were still rigid beneath her touch, but he looked like he hadn't a care in the world. He did not look like a man who had very clearly stated that he would happily kill the duke. He did not look like a man who was still planning to do so.

"Have I missed something here, Graham?" the duke sneered. "I've only just arrived and thought to honor Mrs. Thompson with my undivided attention, yet she seems not to understand the privilege of that—"

"Your Grace!" The address hailed from just behind Riddington.

The duke turned, annoyance creasing his face. "Lord Lowell," he replied, not bothering to keep that annoyance from his voice.

The portly marquess who was puffing as he approached them seemed not to notice. "Let me be the first to congratulate you on such an intrepid undertaking!" he boomed, raising his glass of liquor in a salute to the duke. "I can only say that more of our countrymen should be so ambitious and courageous."

The duke stared at him, annoyance replaced with blankness. "I'm sorry?"

"And humble too!" The marquess thumped Riddington on the shoulder, the liquor in his glass sloshing a little over the side. He looked at Oliver. "His Grace won't tell you this, but even the king was impressed. He said he couldn't think of a finer emissary."

Diana was looking between the three men, wondering what was going on.

"The king? Indeed?" Oliver said, doing an admirable job of looking impressed. "Do tell."

"I don't have to tell you," the marquess said. "You can read it all for yourself in the *Herald*. A splendid article, if I do say so myself. Very flattering to His Grace, but then, you already knew that. I heard that the *Times* has even picked it up back in London. A bloody good show, Your Grace!"

The duke nodded, confusion gouging lines around his mouth even as his chest swelled. "Of course," he murmured.

"I understand that you will be leaving us for India shortly," Lowell continued. "We'll miss you here, of course, but it is so inspiring to see a man such as yourself go on to greatness."

The duke stumbled back, knocking into a passing footman carrying an empty platter. The silver clanged loudly against the floor, drawing two dozen sets of eyes as the hapless servant scrambled to retrieve the tray.

"I beg your pardon, Your Grace, my lord," the footman sputtered.

Lord Lowell waved him away with impatience, though Riddington seemed oblivious.

The marquess turned back to Diana and Oliver. "His Grace spoke so eloquently and so passionately, it moved me beyond words." He tapped his fingers against his jowls, looking up as he recited, "'Beyond our borders lies a world of culture and knowledge. The future and the control of it lie there, for men with the courage to face the risks that come with such great rewards.'" He clapped his hands. "Truly inspiring, Your Grace. Truly." He gave Riddington one final thump and moved off, back into the crowd.

"Good heavens, Your Grace, but you've certainly left an impression. And with the king, no less." Oliver's face was inscrutable.

Riddington had paled. "That wasn't at all—I never said…" He trailed off and ran a finger around the edge of his cravat.

"Your Grace! Excellent news, excellent indeed," another expensively dressed gentleman said as he strolled past, an equally extravagantly dressed woman on his arm. "You'll do us all proud, I'm sure! Splendid coverage in the papers. Felicitations and best wishes!"

The duke nodded, an angry flush starting to creep up his neck. "You did this," he hissed at Oliver.

"Did what, Your Grace?" Oliver asked. "Those were your words, recorded for your audience, who delight in the details of the lives of their betters. Also your words." He paused. "Given that you so boldly declared your ambitions, you should be grateful if, somewhere along the way, an individual uttered a well-placed word to make those ambitions a reality."

"You bastard," the duke wheezed. A line of perspiration beaded on his forehead.

Oliver simply stared back, his face like granite.

"I can't go to India," Riddington rasped. "People die there. Of heat and disease and all manners of foulness."

Oliver shrugged. "I didn't."

"I won't go."

"I'm sure the king will understand if you change your mind. I'm sure everyone in this ballroom right now will understand if your courage fails you."

The duke opened his mouth, but there was a commotion just beyond them, a buzz of voices as people parted to the sides.

Oliver glanced over the duke's head. "Ah. It appears that the king approaches, no doubt to impart his support and salutations." He tipped his head. "I believe I'll take my leave so as not to intrude. Bon voyage, Your Grace, and best of luck."

"What did you do, Oliver?" Diana asked as he led her through the crush, every man and woman craning their necks to get a view of the king. No one took any notice of them.

"I did what I should have done a long time ago," he said. "I came home and asked a beautiful woman to dance with me and—"

"Oliver."

He tightened his hand around hers and pulled her through the soaring halls of the Pavilion, leading them out into the darkness of the night. He stopped only when they reached the pool of water in the center of the lawns, torchlight reflected on the glassy surface.

"The Duke of Riddington is not the only man who has the power to open doors for those who please him. Or close doors for those who do not," he said quietly. "I merely expedited his ambition. I'm made to understand that the company has created a special position for him in Bombay."

Diana touched his face, her fingers slipping along the edge of his jaw. "I love you. And I'm proud of you. I know that this wasn't easy for you."

"There is more than one way to vanquish a dragon without getting my lance all bloody," he said.

"You hope he dies?"

Oliver shook his head. "No. I'm hoping he might learn a little something about living." His arms slid up her back, and he pulled her to him. "I meant what I said, Dee. I will always choose you. I will always choose the woman who holds my heart and my soul and my future."

Diana wrapped her arms around his neck, joy and love burning the backs of her eyes. "I love you, Oliver."

"And I love you." He bent his head and kissed her tenderly before he stepped away from her, catching her hand and bowing low. "Now, if you wouldn't mind, I'd like to finish our dance, since we were so rudely interrupted."

Diana laughed. "Of course."

He took her in his arms once again and led them in a waltz across the lawn, with only the stars as an audience.

"I've made a list, you know," he said against her ear, "of things I've yet to do with you." His lips grazed her cheek. "Of things I've yet to do to you."

She shivered even as heat blazed through her.

"Would you like to hear them?"

Diana caught his lips with hers, knowing that this kiss was the beginning of her forever. She smiled and let her fingers drift to the front of his chest, where his heart pounded beneath her palm.

"Yes," she whispered. "Do tell."

Dear reader,

Thank you for taking the time to read Diana and Oliver's story – I hope you enjoyed it! The best laid plans go spectacularly awry when nothing is as it seems on the surface, and that is a premise which I adore writing. If you're new to my books and are in the mood for a full-length tale of said subterfuge, I'd recommend the first novel in my Season for Scandal series, *Duke of My Heart*. (For the record, the subterfuge continues in the rest of the series!) The **ordering links are here**: http://www.kellybowen.net/a-season-for-scandal-series.html.

I've also finished putting the final touches on *Last Night With the Earl*, the second book in my brand new Devils of Dover series, which comes out this September. This story introduces Eli Dawes, fourteenth Earl of Rivers, assumed dead at Waterloo, but finally back on English soil. Wishing his arrival to go unmarked and his presence unheeded, he heads directly to the isolated wilds of Dover — and straight into the path of Rose Hayward. A sneak peek at their reunion is in the excerpt below and the **ordering links are here**: http://www.kellybowen.net/the-devils-of-dover-series.html.

If you'd like to keep up with my releases, you can sign up for my **newsletter** at http://www.kellybowen.net/about---contact.html, or follow me on **Bookbub** by visiting https://www.bookbub.com/authors/kelly-bowen. All of my books are listed on my **website**: http://www.kellybowen.net/home.html.

Happy reading!

Excerpt from

LAST NIGHT WITH THE EARL

"Don't move."

Eli froze at the voice that had come out of the inky darkness. He turned his head slightly, only to feel the tip of a knife prick the skin at his neck.

"I asked you not to move."

Eli clenched his teeth. It was a feminine voice, he thought. Or perhaps that of a very young boy, though the authority it carried suggested the former. A maid, then. Perhaps she had been up, or perhaps he had woken her. He supposed that this was what he deserved for sneaking into a house unannounced and unexpected. It was, in truth, his house now, but nevertheless, the last thing he needed was for her to start shrieking for help and summon the entire household. He wasn't ready to face that just yet.

"I'm not going to hurt you," he said clearly.

"Not on your knees with my knife at your neck, I agree." The knife tip twisted, though it didn't break the skin.

"There is a reasonable explanation." He fought back frustration. Dammit, but he just wanted to be left alone.

"I'm sure. But the silverware is downstairs," the voice almost sneered. "In case you missed it."

"I'm not a thief." He felt his brow crease slightly. Something about that voice was oddly familiar.

"Ah." The response was measured, though there was as slight waver to it. "I'll scream this bloody house down before I allow you to touch me or any of the girls."

"I'm not touching anyone," he snapped, before he abruptly stopped. Any of the girls? What the hell did that mean?

The knife tip pressed down a little harder, and Eli winced. He could hear rapid breathing, and a new scent reached him, one unmistakably feminine. Soap, he realized, the fragrance exotic and faintly floral. Something that one wouldn't expect from a maid.

"Who are you?" she demanded.

"I might ask the same."

"Criminals don't have that privilege."

Eli bit back another curse. This was ridiculous. His knees were getting sore, he was chilled to the bone and exhausted from travel, and he was in his own damn house. If he had to endure England, it would not be like this.

In a fluid motion, he dropped flat against the floor and rolled immediately to the side, sweeping his arm up to knock that of his attacker. He heard her utter a strangled gasp as the knife fell to the floor and she stumbled forward, caught off balance. Eli was on his knees instantly, his hands catching hers as they flailed at him. He pinned her wrists, twisting her body so it was she who was on the floor, on her back, with Eli hovering over her. She sucked in a breath, and he yanked a hand away to cover her mouth, stopping her scream before it ever escaped.

"Again," he said between clenched teeth, "I am not going to hurt you." Beneath his hand her head jerked from side to side. She had fine features, he realized. In fact, all of her felt tiny, from the bones in her wrists to the small frame that was struggling beneath him. It made him feel suddenly protective. As if he held something infinitely fragile that was his to care for.

Though a woman who brandished a knife in such a manner couldn't be that fragile. He tightened his hold. "If you recall, it was you who had me at a disadvantage with a knife at my neck. I will not make any apologies for removing myself from that position. Nor will I make any apologies for my presence at Avondale. I have every right to be here."

Her struggles stilled.

Eli tried to make out her features in the darkness, but it was impossible. "If I take my hand away, will you scream?"

He felt her shake her head.

"Promise?"

She made a furious noise in the back of her throat in response.

Very slowly Eli removed his hand. She blew out a breath but kept her word and didn't scream. He released her wrists and pushed himself back on his heels. He heard the rustle of fabric, and the air stirred as she pushed herself away. Her scent swirled around him before fading.

"You're not a maid," he said.

"What?" Her confusion was clear. "No."

"Then who are you?" he demanded. "And why are you in my rooms?"

"Your rooms?" Now there was disbelief. "I don't know who you think you are or where you think you are, but I can assure you that these are not your rooms."

Eli swallowed, a sudden thought making his stomach sink unpleasantly. Had Avondale been sold? Had he had broken into a house that, in truth, he no longer owned? It wasn't impossible. It might even be probable. He had been away a long time.

"Is it my brother you are looking for? Is someone hurt?"

The question caught him off guard. "I beg your pardon?"

"Do you need a doctor?"

Eli found himself scowling fiercely, completely at a loss. Nothing since he had pushed open that door had made any sort of sense. "Who owns Avondale?"

"What?" Now it was her turn to sound stymied.

"This house—was it sold? Do you own it?"

"No. We've leased Avondale from the Earl of Rivers for years. From his estate now, I suppose, until they decide what to do with it." Suspicion seeped from every syllable. "Did you know him before he died? The old earl?"

Eli opened his mouth before closing it. He finally settled on, "Yes."

"Then you're what? A friend of the family? Relative?"

"Something like that."

"Which one?"

Eli drew in a breath that wasn't wholly steady. He tried to work his tongue around the words that would forever commit him to this place. That would effectively sever any retreat.

He cleared his throat. "I am the Earl of Rivers."

* * *

Preorder a copy of Last Night With the Earl

The Double Duchess

Anna Harrington

Dedicated to my darling Mel

A very special thank you to
Sara Kortenray, Head of Charity
Greenwich Hospital, London
for her help in researching this story

PROLOGUE

Fort St George, India
October, 1813

Lieutenant Maxwell Thorpe stared at the letter in his hand, for once oblivious to the hot rains that poured endlessly over the white stone fort. The candle lighting the small writing desk in the quarters he shared with five other junior officers sputtered as a drop of water dripped through the ceiling and onto the flame.

... to notify you that I will be asking for her hand in marriage.

A burning clawed at his gut, helped along in no small part by the now-empty bottle of whiskey sitting on the desk, one last swallow of the stuff in the glass beside it.

She will become a respected woman of rank and fortune within the Collins family, protected by my brother, Duke of Winchester. I will offer a generous settlement that will erase her father's debts. She will never want for anything.

Hell... that's what this was. He had seen torment and suffering on the battlefields. Had endured weather that killed lesser men. Had once even been in such physical pain that he'd wished for death. None of that compared to the agony that pulsed through him now.

So I ask you, as one gentleman to another, to let her have the life she deserves.

Slowly, he set it down and picked up a second letter. This one had arrived the same day as the first, dated nearly two months ago. Two months that he'd lived thinking that his fate was still his own, his future his to claim. In reality, his heart had been killed then, but the damnable thing only now knew to break.

… a terrible position. Papa wants me to marry Lord George Collins. He sees that as the salvation for our family's future. But I want only you for a husband, my love. Please come home—come home and help me.

With grim determination, he tossed back the last swallow of whiskey, then reached for the inkpot and paper. She would think him a bastard for this. But let her place the blame on him, let her hate him to the end of her days. Small price to pay for the life that he could never give her otherwise. Scribbling quickly before he changed his mind—

My dearest Belinda, I cannot return to England. My life is in the army here. I want you to forget me…

CHAPTER ONE

Brighton, England
July, 1823

Belinda stared across the meeting table toward Maxwell Thorpe and bit out, "You are a heartless monster."

The monster himself said nothing. He silently continued to gaze at her with brown eyes that had always reminded her of melted chocolate, with a face that most women would have said was handsome enough to give sweet dreams but which had brought her nightmares.

Around them, the other members of the board of the Royal Hospital who had arrived in time for this meeting shifted awkwardly in their chairs. The tips of Mr. Peterson's ears turned red, and Lord Daubney was downright shocked. But when had she ever cared what Society gentlemen thought of her?

And she certainly couldn't care less what the monster at the head of the table thought. Maxwell Thorpe had lost that right a very long time ago.

Colonel Woodhouse leaned forward. "Your Grace, if you would consider—"

She slid a narrowed gaze at him, silencing him with a look. Nor did she care what opinions the colonel—or any actively commissioned officer, *especially* the one leading the meeting—held about this matter. Those same officers were now conspiring to shut down the Royal Hospital, home to more than sixty military pensioners, and she refused to let that happen.

"Of course *you* support him, Colonel." Her calm words belied her anger. "I'm certain the orders came down from the highest level in the War Office, and a good soldier never questions his orders. Not even when it destroys the home of elderly men who have lost the best years of their lives—and several dozen eyes and limbs between them—protecting England."

That silenced the colonel. He leaned back in his chair and busied himself by shuffling through the papers in front of him.

It silenced all protests from the other board members as well. *Good.* They needed to know that she was resolute in carrying out the remaining few months of her late husband's three-year tenure on the board. Once a new board was seated, she'd lose the influence she held as a voting member. But until then, she planned to fight to keep those men in the only home they had left, and the one they deserved.

"As I explained," Maxwell interjected, "the army needs another training facility in the south of England, and because the garrison barracks are already located here, Brighton is the most logical choice."

"Very well." She kept her hands folded demurely in her lap, not once reaching for the tea tray that the flustered aide-de-camp had hurried to ready and bring into the room, once his surprise had worn off at a woman arriving unannounced for the meeting. The widow of a duke, no less. One who spoke her mind on military matters and held her own against peers and His Majesty's officers. "Then, by all means, you should build one."

And leave the Royal Hospital and its pensioners alone. The unspoken challenge hung in the air between them.

She'd received word only yesterday about this called meeting of the board and the War Office's plans, which had taken her completely by surprise. And she certainly hadn't expected that the man who was leading the meeting, as special War Office liaison to the board, was the same one who had once shattered her heart.

Now, apparently, he was also set on turning pensioners out of their home, just so soldiers could learn to more effectively wage war.

But he had another think coming if he thought he could come sweeping in and so easily close the hospital.

She flashed a saccharine smile. "Other properties are available where the academy can be constructed."

"Unfortunately, that's not feasible." Maxwell's answer was calm, although she was certain he wanted to throttle her for raising objections to his plans. "We need the academy to be operational within six months, which means we need these existing buildings."

"Without regard to the men whom the army no longer has any use for?" She held up the list of pensioners' names. "What's to become of them?"

"They're not being kicked out into the cold, Your Grace." His forced smile proved that she was wearing on his patience. *Good.* "They'll be relocated to other hospitals, including Chelsea."

"But their home isn't Chelsea. It's Brighton."

"They will adapt to their new home, wherever it is." His hard expression told her that he was through attempting to win her over by persuasion. So did the way he leaned back in his chair, reminding her of a tiger studying his prey. Right before it pounced. "His Majesty's soldiers are all loyal men who are used to doing what's needed of them."

"Are they? My experience tells me differently."

His eyes glinted at that private cut, the only outward reaction that her arrow had hit home. But she'd noticed. After all, there was a time when she'd noticed everything about this man.

"With respect, Your Grace," Mr. Peterson interjected, perhaps fearing the two of them would come to blows if someone didn't intercede, "your experience with the military is limited. I'm certain Brigadier Thorpe is doing what's best for both the pensioners and the cadets."

"While my experience with the military might be limited"—she leveled her gaze on Maxwell to make certain he understood that she'd neither forgotten nor forgiven how he'd used her for his own advancement all those years ago—"my experience with *military officers* is not. In addition to serving on this board in my late husband's stead and being the hospital's leading patroness, I am also a patroness for the Royal Hospital Chelsea and the Greenwich Hospital."

As the Duchess of Winchester, she wielded a great deal of influence, and her role here couldn't be dismissed out of hand. That was the greatest gift that her late husband, George, had ever given her—the power of a duchess, along with a dower that ensured she'd be able to give financially to whatever charities she favored. Winchester had known since the day he married her that her heart lay with her charity work. He'd probably laugh to know that she was using his old position on the board to put a thorn in Maxwell Thorpe's side.

She straightened her shoulders to become as imposing as her twenty-eight years could be. "Gentlemen, need I remind you that those pensioners are here because they have no money and no families to look after them? It is up to us to defend them."

"And it is up to His Majesty's active army and navy to defend *all* of England," Maxwell countered. "Sandhurst has proven a grand success, and the War Office believes—and I concur—that more academies are needed. Of course, we want to work with the board, not against it, to ensure a smooth transition."

In other words, the War Office was going ahead with the academy whether the board liked it or not.

"And if the board refuses?" she pressed.

The men all looked at her as if she'd sprouted a second head. After all, they'd have to be mad to go against the War Office's wishes.

Except for Maxwell, in whom she saw a flash of admiration for her tenacity.

Perhaps, though, it wasn't admiration at all but simply acknowledgment of an adversary. If so, he had no idea how stalwart an opponent she could be.

Colonel Woodhouse gently cleared his throat. "I believe, Your Grace, that the board agrees with Brigadier Thorpe."

"Does it? By my count, only a third of the board is present." Eleven men—and one lone widow—sat on the board, but because of the rushed nature of this meeting, only four of them were present. "Do we really want to expose ourselves and the War Office to the hostilities that might ensue if sixty pensioners are expelled from their home based upon the agreement of only one-third of the board?"

The men exchanged troubled looks. Only Max's inscrutable expression remained unchanged, as if he'd expected a fight from her all along.

"What are your terms, Your Grace?" he asked. The same words, she noted, that generals used when negotiating surrender. The question was... which one of them did he think was surrendering?

"That we hold a formal vote by the entire board in a fortnight. Delaying the decision will give the others the opportunity to weigh in or send their proxies."

And give her time to sway them all to vote against the academy.

Woodhouse's patience snapped. "This is absurd!" He dismissingly waved a hand at her. "To let this woman—"

"*Colonel.*" The force of that word reverberated through the room as Maxwell rose from his chair. "You forget yourself."

Woodhouse snapped his mouth shut, but his nostrils flared. "Yes, Brigadier."

"Apologize to Her Grace."

Woodhouse hesitated. "Sir?"

"Apologize."

Clenching his jaw, Woodhouse was anything but apologetic as he ground out, "My apologies, Your Grace."

Well, that was a surprise—Maxwell coming to her defense. Yet Belinda regally inclined her head to coolly accept the apology.

"Her Grace has a valid point."

That surprised her even more. Did Maxwell truly mean it, or was he simply flattering her in an attempt to appease? Especially since he remained standing at the head of the table in a posture of pure command.

"Of course, the War Office can petition Parliament to claim the property if it likes," he explained. "But the secretary would prefer the cooperation of both the board and the town, and avoiding rancor will be more pleasant for everyone."

For everyone… For King George, he meant.

While the War Office might very well have the influence to take over the property, the soldiers—and King George himself—would find Brighton a very inhospitable place if the board voted against them. She'd use that to her advantage and personally appeal to His Majesty on behalf of the pensioners, if she had to.

"So we'll adjourn for today and take up the discussion again when the other board members arrive." He closed his portfolio. "But if they are not all here within the fortnight, we proceed without them. Lord Palmerston wants a new academy established by Christmastide."

Belinda forced her shoulders not to sink. A fortnight would barely be enough time for the others to travel to Brighton, let alone for her to sway them to her side.

But she would have to. Somehow.

"Gentlemen and Your Grace." Maxwell nodded at the room at large, then at Belinda. "Thank you for your time."

He moved toward the door, where he spoke to each man in turn as they left. But when Belinda rose from her seat, the devil closed the door instead of following the men from the room, shutting them inside together.

With his curly black hair highlighted against the red of his uniform and his broad shoulders accentuated by the cut of his jacket, he leaned a hip against the closed door in a posture so rakishly alluring that her belly knotted. That was one undeniable facet of Maxwell Thorpe—the sight of him had always taken her breath away.

Apparently, some things never changed.

"It's been a long time, Belinda."

She trembled at his audacity to use her given name. When she'd stepped into this room, she'd thought she was seeing a ghost. But she wasn't fortunate enough to simply be haunted. Oh, no. He was blood and flesh… and oh, what flesh. Even now her fingertips ached with the sudden memory of how it had felt to touch him, the soft warmth of his skin, the hardness of his muscles. Only the faint lines at the corners of his eyes and mouth gave proof that he'd aged beyond the image of him she still carried in her mind from the last time she saw him.

"How have you been?"

Ha! As if he cared. "I was perfectly fine until you came along."

His eyes gleamed at the sharpness behind her comment. As if he'd also expected *that*.

Not daring to challenge her, he said sincerely, "It's good to know that you're still dedicated to helping the pensioners. Your kind heart has always been your very best trait."

At that unexpected compliment, she fought to keep her well-studied composure in place. The *very* last thing she'd allow was for him to see how much he still affected her. And most likely always would. "It's easy to be kind… to those who deserve it."

Instead of rising to the bait, he returned to the table and reached to pour a cup of tea from the tray, putting in milk and sugar. Then he held it out to her. A peace offering.

Her irritation spiked that he would remember how she took her tea. But then, didn't she remember every detail about him, right down to the small scar at his right brow?

He murmured, "You're also just as beautiful as I remember."

Damn her heart for stuttering! And double-damn the dark emotion that squeezed her chest around it like an iron fist, because she knew better than to fall for his charms. She'd learned the hard way how little his word was worth.

Ignoring the offered tea, she stepped past him to the buffet cabinet to withdraw a bottle of port that was kept there for after the board meetings when the men finished their business. She filled a tea cup and offered it to him.

For a moment, they held each other's gaze. Two adversaries now on even ground, both filled with such determination that tension pulsed between them.

"If you're attempting to flatter me into conceding," she warned, "it won't work."

He accepted the cup, then lifted it to his nose to draw in the port's sweet scent. "I would never dare to presume such a thing."

And *she* was certain that he'd dared to presume a great deal more about her in the past. A presumption that had made her beg her father to ask favors from his friends in order to give Maxwell a high-profile post in India where he could more easily distinguish himself.

Oh, she'd been so naïve!

He offered the tea again. This time, she accepted it… only to set it down, unwanted.

"Why are you doing this?" She folded her arms over her chest. There was no need for pleasantries between them.

The small tea cup in his hand served to remind her of how large and solid he was. Ten years ago, he'd been a young man just beginning to fill out his frame. Now he was a man in his prime. Every inch of him displayed the powerful officer he'd become. "As I told you, your cooperation makes establishing the academy easier."

"I mean the orders from the War Office that brought you here." *And back into my life.* "Why are you closing the hospital and putting those men out of their home?"

"Because we need a training academy."

"You already have Sandhurst."

"It isn't enough."

He set down the cup and stepped up to the large map of the world that decorated the wall. Red pushpin flags were scattered across it, one flag for each place the pensioners had served.

A frown creased his brow as he studied the map. "Do you have any idea how limited training was during the wars with France? The army needed men on the battlefield immediately, with no time for instruction except for a cursory overview of how to use their guns and bayonets. We had good generals with solid battle plans, but the lower-ranking officers and foot soldiers didn't know enough to carry them out. Our men were little more than cannon fodder. We won only because of sheer numbers and our cavalry. Two years." His voice grew distant as he touched one of the flags in the mass of those pressed into the Iberian Peninsula. "Two years of the worst bloodshed in British military history…" He flicked the flag with the tip of his finger. "How much of that carnage could have been avoided if they'd had better training? How many wives and children could we have kept from mourning their dead?"

His hand dropped to his side.

In the silence between them, Belinda shivered. He'd been wounded himself in the fighting in Spain, before her father arranged for him to be posted in India. The summer she'd met him.

"If I have the chance to save men's lives—even if just a handful—I'm going to take it." Then he turned away from the map, and the vulnerability she saw in him vanished. He was once more a brigadier, straight-spined and impassive. Once more the man sent to close the hospital. "No respectable officer would refuse that."

Her chest tightened with empathy, but the pensioners needed to be defended. "At the cost of men in their golden years who have sacrificed all for their country, including the loss of limbs?"

He picked up his port and swirled it gently. "Wouldn't it be better to have an academy to instruct soldiers so they don't lose limbs in the first place?"

Damn him! He was twisting everything around, refusing to see the situation from the perspective of the pensioners. But then, hadn't he always gotten his way? Hadn't what he wanted always come first, no matter whom he hurt in the process?

She arched an imperious brow. "What do you gain from this?"

A haunted expression came over him, onne as dark as the port in the white bone cup.

"The knowledge that there will be fewer widows and orphans."

She was no fool and refused to let that arrow pierce her. His answer was meant solely to pull at her heartstrings… and dodge her question. "What do *you* gain from this, Maxwell?"

He took a slow sip of port before answering, "The War Office thought I would be the best officer to present the plans to the board. They knew I'd been a patient at the hospital once myself."

She inhaled sharply. The *very* last thing she needed was that reminder of how they'd met. He'd been wounded and was recuperating at the hospital, while she'd been doing charity work there as a way to fill the long, dull days that summer. Her father had insisted that the family spend their season here in Brighton, where there was nothing for a young lady her age to do except volunteer. Only later did she discover that her father was on the verge of being thrust into debtors' prison and needed to ask favors of several men who had followed the Prince Regent down from London to keep the creditors at bay. She hadn't discovered until season's end that Papa was already ill. Or until the following year how much the medical expenses had added to the debt, sending her family into financial ruin.

She pushed away the flood of memories. *All* in the past. She had to focus on the present. "And a promotion for you, perhaps? I imagine it would be advantageous for your career to found a school that rivals Sandhurst."

"Perhaps." He set down the port. "But that's not my prime motivation."

"Forgive me if I don't believe you." She reached a hand to the table to steady herself as ten years of hurt and anger rose inside her. The old bitterness returned in force. "I have firsthand knowledge of how you advance your career."

She felt him stiffen, as surely as she felt the tension filling the air around them.

With the ghosts of the past rising between them, she expected him to deny it. To defend himself and claim that he'd not used her all those years ago, only to abandon her once he'd no longer needed her. To strike out and attack—

Instead, his eyes softened as he took a slow step toward her.

Her heart skipped, the foolish thing momentarily forgetting what he'd done to her. But then, hadn't it always loved him, even when he didn't deserve it? Didn't it even now remember the kind and caring man he'd been before he left for India, and how they'd healed each other that summer—her with his physical wounds, him with her heartbreak over her father?

Oh, he'd changed, certainly, both in appearance and in demeanor.

But she could still see in him the only man she'd ever loved. Which was why she didn't slap his hand away when he raised it to caress his knuckles across her cheek.

She gasped at the touch, pained by it.

"And what do you gain from this, Belinda?" His deep voice seeped into her, warming her as thoroughly as his hand against her cheek. "Why fight so hard when you know that the pensioners will be taken care of?"

"Split up and shipped off to other hospitals, you mean?" She'd wanted to sound determined and strong. Instead, her voice emerged as a whisper. "This place is their home, and those men have no other family but the men living with them. To force them apart…"

The knot of emotion in her throat choked her.

He reached for her hand and gave her fingers a soothing squeeze. "Why?"

She trembled, then cursed herself that he might be able to feel it. That he might dare to believe he still possessed even an ounce of influence over her. It certainly wasn't a yearning for the old days. It was anger and pain… memories of how she'd placed her trust in him, only to have it destroyed. She'd *never* make that mistake again.

"An act of decency." Her answer was a blatant challenge. "In your world of war, surely you can appreciate that."

Then she stepped out of his reach. He didn't deserve to know the real reason or to lessen his guilt about the past by attempting to console her now. They had a long fight ahead of them over the hospital, and she had no intention of making one second of that any easier on him.

"I won't give up this fight." She snatched up his tea cup of port and finished it in one swallow.

Something unreadable sparked in his eyes, and he quietly confessed, "I'd be disappointed if you did."

CHAPTER TWO

Twenty minutes later, Max strode into the Honors Club with determination. Good Lord, how he needed a drink!

When he'd first approached the War Office about creating the new academy, he'd known that winning the board's support wouldn't be easy. Neither was seeing Belinda again, even after all these years. But he hadn't realized until he saw the fire in her green eyes exactly how difficult his task would be.

Or how much he still loved her.

"Cognac," he ordered the attendant behind the bar, who nodded and promptly set to pouring a glass.

He squelched a tired sigh. He was getting too old to fight battles like this.

At thirty-two, he certainly wasn't young anymore, and the years spent distinguishing himself in the army had left more scars than he wanted to admit. But he'd made a good life for himself, rising from lieutenant to brigadier, one hard-won promotion at a time. From the youngest son of a minor baron to a man who commanded legions.

But those days were done. He was tired of foreign posts and wanted to return to England. He'd grown sick of sending men to their deaths and wanted instead to train them to survive the carnage and destruction that battle brought. When he couldn't bear to write one more letter home to yet another widow, informing her of her husband's death, he knew he needed a new purpose. This academy would give him exactly that.

He hadn't been exaggerating when he said that the governing board's support would make the transition easier for everyone. Peace had lasted long enough that the British people were no longer willing to accept without question such a decision by the military.

And Belinda, Duchess of Winchester, held the balance of that decision in her delicate little hands. The same woman who had healed him all those years ago and made him believe in the possibility of a future that was more than simple survival. A future that had purpose, wonder, goals… a home.

The same woman he'd so brutally hurt. Fate was surely laughing at him.

No difference that he'd rejected her for her own good—he would go to his grave letting her think the worst of him in that. What mattered now was that her trust in his character would be an enormous part of the board's decision, and in that, she believed he'd failed her.

Worse. Based on her comments today, she believed he'd used her.

He could have asked to be replaced in this mission. *Should* have asked for that, in fact, when he'd discovered that Belinda was serving out her late husband's term on the board. But the academy was his idea, one he needed to follow through to the end.

He'd also needed to see Belinda again, the way that thirsty men needed water to live.

"Brigadier!" a fellow officer called out and stepped up to the bar, with a half-dozen others following.

They announced their greetings as they pressed in around him. A few slapped him on the back.

"Thorpe! Good seeing you here."

"We were wondering when you'd stop by."

"Can't keep a soldier away from his brothers-in-arms, eh?"

Max's lips curled wistfully. Perhaps not, but he wasn't here for military brotherhood. He was here in search of drink and solace.

"Heard you were back in England." Another officer slapped him on the back. "When I heard that, I knew you were putting yourself up for a new position."

He grimaced. Rumors were more reliable than military intelligence these days. "I am."

"Ha!" The officer nodded toward two young captains in their group.

"Told you that Thorpe was here to pursue that new post in Africa."

"No," another soldier interjected from behind Max's shoulder. "The brigadier's returning to India, aren't you?"

He hesitated to answer. But what could it hurt to share his plans? They'd all find out as soon as the board members started spreading news of the meeting. "I *am* interested in a new position. But not in India or Africa. I'm pursuing a much more dangerous location, gentlemen."

Curious murmurs surrounded him, along with bewildered frowns.

He accepted the glass of brandy from the attendant and raised it high. "Brighton!"

Laughter exploded from the soldiers. They all thought he was bamming them.

"The army needs a new academy, and the Royal Hospital is being converted into one." He took a long swallow. "I'm here to carry it out."

That sobered the group. They stared at him as if he'd just admitted to attempting to kill the king.

After several awkward moments while it became clear that Maxwell was serious, the senior officer commented, "I'd heard rumors that they were seeking battle-tried officers to train cadets."

"Not rumors. They are."

"Is that truly to be your next move, Thorpe? Retiring to the seaside like some old woman past her prime?" One of the captains didn't bother with holding out his glass to the attendant for a refill but took the bottle from the bar and began topping off glasses himself. He pointed the bottle at Max and jokingly asked, "Earning your commission by putting young lords through their paces on their bellies?"

Before he could answer that he was here only to establish the academy, not run it, the senior officer interjected, "Bollocks! He won't retire to the seaside if he's offered the African post. It's the perfect place for a career army man on the verge of becoming a major-general, which is assured."

"Far from assured." The *only* thing he was certain of at that moment was his need for Belinda's understanding. Professionally and personally. He'd had no choice before but to let her hate him. He'd not do it again.

"An *academy?*" a lieutenant who had served briefly with Max on a short stint in Egypt repeated with disdain, as if he hadn't heard properly. "Don't need no fancy academy to train officers. Those cadets are just a bunch o' coxcombs who'll piss their britches the first time a ball whizzes by 'em!"

More laughter rose from the group, but Max only sipped his cognac, saying nothing.

"A good soldier cuts his teeth on th' battlefield," one of the weathered officers explained. "Not on books in some academy lecture hall. Thorpe knows that, don't ye, Brigadier? That's how ye did it, an' a fine officer ye became, too."

Another soldier shook his head, tapping his glass against the older officer's chest to impress his point. "Can't study battle strategy while the artillery's targeting your arse."

Max hid his smile behind the rim of his glass.

"What's your game, Thorpe? Truly—you'd give up a good post to teach a bunch of dandies how to march in line and point their muskets at the enemy?"

It was so much more than that. None of the soldiers here would understand, even if he tried to explain it. But someday they would, when they'd had enough of the slaughter of battle themselves, when they were ready to return home.

"Actually, I've always liked the idea of academies, even though I chose a different path. I'm all for anything that can make for better soldiers on the battlefield, especially if the training they receive comes from officers who have been through the fire." He leveled his gaze on the older officer. "And it's damned hard to cut your teeth on battle when the wars are over and there's none to be fought."

Laughter went up from the group of men, until Max raised his glass in a toast.

"But we should all pray to God that our memories of war are long, even in times of peace," he added somberly, quashing the men's amusement. "Lest we forget the hell of it and rush too easily back into the fray."

The men soberly raised their glasses with his to drink to fallen comrades and a continuation of peace. One of them murmured, "Hear, hear."

The men moved away, now that the novelty of having Max among them had worn off, to return to their card games and cigars.

He set down his empty glass and gestured for a refill, grateful to finally have the peaceful drink he'd sought when he entered the club. And a moment to himself to contemplate what to do next about Belinda. If he didn't complete his orders, his military career would be over. There would be no more promotions, no more command posts. He'd be lucky not to be sent to some godforsaken post in northern Canada.

But if he succeeded, he'd never win Belinda's forgiveness.

Either way he was damned.

The attendant placed the glass in front of him. Just as Max raised the drink, a large hand slapped him on the back, causing him to nearly spill the brandy.

Oliver Graham grinned at him. "Heard you and Colonel Woodhouse just had a set-to."

"I was a dashing hero, I'll have you know." He took a gasping swallow and welcomed the burn down his throat. Thank God Graham was in Brighton this summer. The way things were going, he could certainly use an ally. "I was defending a woman's honor."

"So that's what they're calling it these days." Graham signaled for a drink. "And here I thought you'd simply struck out at a man for daring to criticize the woman you once loved, then shut the two of you together into a small room." He paused. "Alone."

Max grimaced. Apparently, rumors were faster than military intelligence, as well.

"Were you hoping to hold her captive until she declared her undying devotion to your cause?" Graham joked.

"Holding her captive is on tomorrow's agenda." He was only half teasing. If tying up Belinda until she agreed to champion him to the board would have worked, he'd have done it right there in the hospital.

Graham's amusement sobered. "I take it that your meeting didn't go well."

"As well as can be expected."

"That badly, huh?"

In answer, Max tossed back the brandy and signaled for another.

Graham was one of his oldest and most trusted friends, and fate had tossed them together in Brighton this summer. But even after years apart, they'd fallen back into their fast friendship. Graham was one of a handful of men in the world whom he trusted unquestioningly with his life, and the only one who knew the real reason why he'd broken off with Belinda. He knew he could count on his advice. And when his advice failed, he could count on Graham's silence to let him wallow in misery in peace.

Graham arched a brow. "Well?"

Usually.

"Circumstances weren't the best." Max rubbed at the knot in his nape. "I surprised her by being the officer in charge."

Surprised? Hardly. He'd downright stunned her. The look of wounding that had gripped her beautiful face when she'd walked into the room and seen him had torn his breath away. So had the hatred that immediately replaced it.

He hadn't reacted much better, staring at her throughout the meeting like a smitten pup. He simply wasn't prepared for his visceral reaction to seeing her again. One that had come like a punch to his gut when he saw her face, those sparkling green eyes, and that auburn hair that was even softer than it looked. And the way he'd chastised Woodhouse—*Christ*. He'd have to seek out the colonel to offer his apologies.

But seeing her again changed nothing. "I have no intention of giving up trying to win her support." The academy was too important.

"What about winning her over in other ways?"

His gaze snapped to his friend. Surely he didn't mean… "Pardon?"

"You haven't heard?" Graham eyed him warily. "Pomperly's arrived in Brighton."

A rush of jealousy burned through him at the mention of the duke, followed by an unreasonable flash of hatred that Pomperly would dare try to claim her—

Then he felt like a damned fool.

Good God. Less than an hour in Belinda's presence, and he was already losing his mind.

What did it matter to him if rumors were flowing through London like the Thames that the Duke of Pomperly had determined to marry Belinda? So many rumors, in fact, that all of Society believed just that would happen, so confident in it that the gossips had begun to call her the Double Duchess. What difference did it make to him whom she chose to let into her life… or into her heart?

Still, he couldn't stop his hand from shaking as he raised the glass to take a bracing swallow.

"So if you want to pursue her yourself, then—"

"No." He said that with more force than he'd intended. But good God, he wasn't here because of *her*. He was here exactly for the reason he'd given her—to turn his experience into saving men's lives rather than leading them to their deaths. To think he'd come here wanting anything else was preposterous. "It's no concern of mine who courts her."

And yet, he was shaken by seeing her again, hearing her voice, and breathing in the sweet lavender scent of her… by seeing firsthand that she still possessed the same fiery spirit and kindness of heart that had made him fall in love with her. Just as he couldn't help experiencing again the old jealousies and desires he'd once felt over her. He wouldn't be a warm-blooded man if he didn't, even if he had no intention of acting upon them.

"Seems to me you've been given a second chance," Graham said thoughtfully. "You might consider taking it."

He laughed, although in truth he didn't find the suggestion at all amusing. "All I want is her vote."

"Are you certain?"

"Absolutely." A damned lie. He wasn't certain at all.

He'd loved her once, he couldn't deny that. And ten years ago, he'd convinced himself that he loved her enough to let her go, just as he'd convinced himself that a life in the army was all he needed. He'd had to, in order to keep getting out of bed in the mornings once she was gone. In order to simply keep breathing. He'd hoped that eventually, with the passage of enough time and distance, he could purge her from his heart the way he'd purged her from his life.

He'd been a damned fool to ever think that.

* * *

Belinda slumped down onto the bench in the town house's garden and hung her head.

Maxwell Thorpe... *good God.*

Of all the places to encounter him again, of all the ways she'd always imagined in her mind for how they'd meet after all these years, if ever— *this* certainly wasn't it. She'd planned to pretend not to recognize him at all at first, then give a well-practiced look of bored disdain, followed by a haughty sniff and a toss of her head, then casually pass him by as if he meant nothing to her... actions she'd replayed countless times in her mind. Not one of which had involved a fight over elderly pensioners.

She bit back a groan. Only Maxwell would reappear in her life at this very moment and completely invert it, now that she'd finally found her footing after Winchester's death nearly three years ago.

But then, hadn't he always taken her off guard?

She sucked in a pained breath as the memories rushed over her like a tidal wave. The day she'd met him, when her eighteen-year-old eyes had never seen a more handsome man, even wounded and covered with bandages... Their first dance at the assembly rooms, first picnic in the park, first stroll… Their first kiss, when she could never have imagined a more magical moment. Until he'd said he loved her and wanted to marry her. And *that* had been simply perfect. Because she'd never expected to find love.

To say that her prospects for marriage had been limited would have been a grand overstatement of how bleak they'd actually been.

Bleak? *Black*, more like.

Despite empty flattery from gentlemen about how beautiful and brilliant she was, those compliments never turned into courtship. Not once those same gentlemen discovered that she had no dowry because her father had made bad business decisions and stumbled far into debt. She'd been destined for spinsterhood.

Until she met Maxwell.

The biting irony was that she'd met him right here in Brighton, recuperating in the very hospital he now wanted to destroy. He'd been wounded during his first engagement on the Peninsula, by the slice of a French bayonet across his chest that nearly killed him. He'd needed doctors' care and a place to heal before he could return to his post.

Love had been immediate for both of them, she'd been so certain of that then. Both had helped heal the other, with Maxwell accepting her help in mending his physical wounds and Belinda relying upon his strength and resolve when she learned that her father was dying. When she was with Maxwell, she'd felt healed, whole… loved. They'd given each other hope for a brighter future, one with a happy home and loving family. Together. But fate had had other plans, and less than one year later, their future was over.

Maxwell Pennington Thorpe… Heavens, what *was* she going to do?

Because the problem wasn't speaking her mind and telling him what she thought of him and his plans. Oh, she'd done a fine job of that!

No. The problem was that even now, despite the hell he'd put her through, a part of her still loved him. And always would.

"There you are!" Eugenia swept through the open French doors of the town house into the garden. Diana followed closely behind.

When the three of them had decided to share the town house this season, escaping London for the seaside with her two oldest and dearest friends had seemed like a godsend. The perfect way to put distance between her and the Duke of Pomperly until he found another woman to cast his attentions upon.

Now it felt as if she'd been tossed from the pan into the fire.

A distraught expression marred Diana's pretty face. "I just heard—*Maxwell Thorpe?* How are you holding up?"

She forced a smile. "I'm fine. There's nothing to worry about."

But the two joined her at the bench, with Diana reassuringly clasping her hand. Her throat tightened with emotion at their concern.

"Truly. He's here only for military business." When the two women exchanged dubious looks, Belinda reminded them, "I deal with military officers all the time. I know how to hold my own against them."

Neither woman replied to that. They'd been friends since their school days, and they knew each other well enough to spot when one was dissembling. Or, in this case, outright lying.

Then Eugenia arched a brow in silent recrimination.

Belinda sighed and, biting her lip, admitted quietly, "There *is* more to the story."

"I knew it!" Diana clapped her hands, then turned toward Genie. "I told you that something was amiss. That Maxwell Thorpe just *happened* to be in Brighton at the same time as she is. That he just *happened* to be there when she needed to be rescued from Colonel Woodhouse—"

"I did *not* need to be rescued," she ground out in aggravation, then felt immediately guilty over poor Colonel Woodhouse and the spurious stories being spread about him already. Apparently, the Brighton rumor mill was operating at breakneck speed. And as inaccurately as ever.

"Oh, I think we *all* need to be rescued by tall, dark, and handsome men in uniform," Genie drawled.

"Especially when we don't," Diana finished with a smile.

Belinda rolled her eyes. "And do we need to surrender as well?"

Genie's smile faltered. "He said that? That he wanted you to…"

"Surrender?" Diana whispered breathlessly.

"Of a sort."

She stood and stepped a few feet away, presumably to study a bloom on the rosebush, but more because she simply couldn't sit still. Her heart pounded too hard, her breath came too ragged. Maxwell's unexpected arrival had flustered her, and it wasn't just the confusion and anger that set her trembling. Because he'd looked good. *Very* good. The years had matured him into a man who was very much confident in himself, one used to getting what he wanted.

She straightened her spine with as much courage as she could muster.

"Maxwell is here in Brighton to close the hospital."

Shock flashed across their faces, yet they listened silently as she told them about the meeting. Both were remorseful when she explained what really happened with Colonel Woodhouse, and neither reacted at all to Maxwell's caress of her cheek… because she conveniently forgot to tell them.

"He's truly going to do that?" Diana paled, her hand going to her throat. "Turn the hospital into an academy?"

She grimaced. "If I cannot find a way to stop him."

"Then he's just as terrible as before, isn't he?" Genie's question was a statement.

More like sisters than friends, they both knew what had happened between her and Maxwell. They'd been at her side during those wonderful months when he'd said that he wanted to marry her—only an understanding, not a formal agreement. But at the time, she'd thought that had been for the best. After all, he'd been at the start of his career and off on a bad foot at that. Or rather, on a bayoneted chest. It might have been years before he rose in the ranks high enough to provide a home for her and the children she'd dreamed of having, but she had been willing to wait… sort of. Because she'd gone to her father, to ask Papa to use his influence to help Maxwell with his career. It had worked, and he was assigned to Fort St George in India, where he would be able to quickly distinguish himself while staying out of the fray of the wars.

Maxwell had been away less than a year when her father's debts became so out of hand that creditors began beating at the door, when Papa's illness grew worse and death became a certainty. In desperation, she'd written to him, begging him to come home and help her… only for him to reply that his future lay with the army. In India.

But out of the ashes of that love came salvation for her family, if not for her heart. Lord George Collins offered for her, and she married him. He saved her family from ruin, taking them in after Papa's death and paying off their debts, and eventually, he made her a duchess when his brother died. Overall, it was as good a Society marriage as could be hoped. Winchester was kind and generous, dedicated to his position in Parliament and to his family… but she never loved him, not the way she once loved Maxwell.

Inhaling a jerking breath, Belinda answered, "It appears so."

"I don't mean to defend him," Diana said delicately, "but he does have a good point about the soldiers needing better training."

He did, drat him. "But at the expense of the pensioners' home?"

"Perhaps you could talk with him," Genie interjected. "Convince him that the hospital isn't at all the kind of facility that cadets in training need."

"Yes!" Diana's face lit up at the possibility. "Surely he's receptive to reason."

"He's a brigadier who will most likely be promoted to major-general in recompense for starting this new academy." She shook her head. "I don't think logic matters."

"But he wasn't always a brigadier," Genie reminded her.

Belinda knew that well. Despite the agony he'd caused her, she still hadn't been able to bring herself to let go of him completely in the intervening years. She'd followed him as best she could through newspaper reports and shared acquaintances, knowing every place he'd been stationed since leaving England… first at Fort St George, then stints in Egypt and Nassau, before heading back to the Continent to help restore Europe after the wars and ensure the peace. Just as she knew every heroic act he'd committed to save his men in battle, every promotion he'd received that raised him from lieutenant to brigadier. She couldn't help herself. He was an addiction she couldn't quit.

Yet he'd picked now to reappear, when she was least prepared for him. How had she managed to keep from screaming from the searing pain at the sight of him? No idea. But she would *never* let him know how much he'd wounded her. Or that the reason she clung so fiercely to the pensioners and worked tirelessly on their behalf, both here and in London, was because they reminded her of that summer when she was in love and happy… before everything turned black.

"He loved you once, I'm certain of it," Genie assured her.

Belinda was far less certain.

"Perhaps he still holds a soft spot in his heart for you and will listen."

Her shoulders sagged wearily. "He chose the army over me—"

"Ten years ago," Diana reminded her.

"And is even more firmly entrenched in the ranks now."

Nothing that she'd seen in him today proved otherwise. Yet her foolish heart held out hope… and her past experience quashed it.

She shook her head. "What guarantee do I have that he'll listen?"

Her two friends pondered that for a moment. Then Diana conceded,

"None, I suppose."

That was the crux of it. He'd shattered her heart ten years ago, brutally breaking her trust. If he wounded her a second time, how would she survive it?

"I'm not certain you have a choice but to try," Diana said somberly. "And quickly."

A dark smile tugged at her lips. "Knowing Maxwell, I'm certain he's already prepared for siege warfare."

"Unfortunately, you don't have time for a siege."

No. She had less than a fortnight. "I'll just have to—"

"His Grace has arrived in Brighton."

Cold dread shivered through her at that quiet announcement.

"Pomperly?" she breathed, barely louder than a whisper. The earth tilted beneath her as aggravation added to the confusion and frustration already swirling inside her.

Genie confirmed that with a nod. "The Duke of Pomposity."

Belinda rolled her eyes. She disliked that nickname. Yet she also had to admit that, in his case, it certainly fit.

Oh, Pomperly meant well, she supposed. But a more arrogant man she'd yet to meet, which was saying a lot, considering she knew King George. And one she had no intention of letting court her.

With a snap of its stem, she plucked one of the roses from its bush. "I'll rebuff him in Brighton as I did in London."

Her friends didn't seem at all confident about that. But *she* was certain of it. Pomperly might have missed the hint in London that she held no interest in becoming his new duchess, loathing the nickname, the Double Duchess, that the gossips had given her. As if marrying the man was an absolute certainty. But while he might believe that she'd make an excellent wife for him, *she* had other intentions. She'd refused to receive him at her town home whenever he called, just as she'd refused every request he made to dance with her at balls, to sit beside her at soirees, to join him in his box at Vauxhall... She'd returned every gift he'd sent her, including two doves. The most inappropriate—and ironic—gift of courtship she'd ever seen. Did he think that symbolized what their marriage would be like... her imprisonment in a gilded cage?

The fact that he'd chased after her to Brighton changed nothing. "I'll refuse his overtures here just as I did in Mayfair."

"He already stopped by the town house while you were with Maxwell,"

Diana informed her.

She grumbled, "I wasn't *with* Maxwell." At least not the way Diana had implied.

Genie pulled a note from her pelisse pocket. "He left this for you. An invitation to dinner at the Pavilion."

"Then I'll refuse him." Her rejection was surely routine for him by now. Soon, he might just give up completely and—

"You cannot."

Just watch me. She smiled confidently. "A lady always has the opportunity to forgo a soiree." Especially a duchess.

"Not when the king is in attendance."

Her stomach sank. "No," she whispered, "not with the king."

Their slender shoulders sagging, the three of them seemed to deflate in unison, all falling into contemplative silence. They were all part of the *ton*, all knew what an invitation to the palace meant. A command appearance. She nearly laughed at the irony. Thrust inside a gilded cage after all—one that resembled an Asian pleasure palace.

Then her stomach plummeted right through the floor as the full realization of what this meant fell over her. "Not when Pomperly sits on the board."

And not when she desperately needed every vote she could get.

Her friends were right. There was no way out of the dinner, no way to keep from having to attend on Pomperly's arm.

"Unless…" The two looked at her hopefully as a desperate thought struck her—"Maxwell."

That made their brows shoot up.

With a smile like the cat who'd gotten into the cream, she plucked the petals from the rose. "I cannot very well accompany Pomperly if I've already agreed to attend on the arm of another, now can I?" The petals fell to the ground, one by one. " As one of the highest-ranking officers in Brighton, the brigadier has surely been invited."

Oh, it was turning into a perfect idea!

Almost.

It would mean having to be in close proximity to Maxwell all evening, to tolerate the ghosts of past heartbreaks and pretend that nothing was wrong between them.

But she would suffer through it. After all, what was one evening in his presence compared to the torment of the past decade?

"I'll simply make certain that I arrive as Maxwell's guest." *Somehow.*

Her friends exchanged unconvinced looks, before Diana asked, "But why would the brigadier agree?"

Because he has no choice. "He wants my support with the academy, so he'll do whatever he can to win my favor."

"Are you certain about this plan?" Genie asked.

She tossed away the bare stem. "Absolutely."

Maxwell Thorpe might be the devil himself, but if he thought he could once more take her soul and cast her into hell without a fight, oh, he had another think coming!

CHAPTER THREE

Maxwell waited on the far end of the promenade the next afternoon, where he'd sent word for Belinda to meet him, and tugged at his jacket sleeves. Good Lord, he was nervous! He hadn't been this much on edge since the last time he'd charged into battle. But then, this *was* Belinda. Little difference between her and the French.

Both had good reason to shoot him.

She'd surprised the devil out of him by asking to speak with him, but it wouldn't be to simply reiterate that she thought him a monster and that she had no intention of supporting the academy. That could have been put into the message itself, with no need to see him face-to-face. Most likely, she planned to attempt to cajole him to her side and, when that failed, toss him onto the first ship bound for Australia.

Still, the best defense was a good offense, and an experienced soldier never gave his opponent time to regroup. Which was why he'd told her to meet him at the edge of the town, right where the cliffs began to rise from the sea. And why he'd called in every favor he had with the men in the barracks to arrange the surprise waiting for her.

As if out of a dream, her lithe figure appeared on the promenade.

She walked toward him, with the skirts of her ivory dress stirring around her legs in the sea breeze and her bonnet shielding her face from the sun, and his pulse spiked. Old desires—and dreams—died hard.

Dear God, she was beautiful, and not because of how she looked. Oh, she was pretty, certainly, but not classically. Not with that pert little nose that turned up slightly at the tip, those green eyes that were too big for her face, and that auburn hair that couldn't decide if it wanted to be red or brown and never stayed in its pins.

No, it was her soul that radiated beauty and commanded a man's attention. While other women were content to follow, Belinda led with her heart. Always had. Indeed, he'd fallen in love with her because of it.

And it was her kind heart that once again had them at odds.

She stopped in front of him. When her eyes met his, an electric jolt sped through him so intensely that he lost his breath.

"My apologies for being late." The ribbons from her bonnet fluttered in the sea breeze, and she tucked them inside her jacket. "I dropped off a basket of sweet rolls at the hospital. It took longer than expected."

"No apologies necessary." His gaze languidly drifted over her. He felt like a blind man given back his sight, and he couldn't stop staring. "You look lovely."

"Maxwell, please don't." A faint blush pinked her cheeks, but he couldn't have said whether from pleasure at the compliment or aggravation. At that moment, he didn't particularly care which.

"You'd rather I'd lie and say the exact opposite?" When he reached for her hand, she didn't pull away. Perhaps she didn't think him a complete monster after all. "Very well. You're the most hideous woman I've ever met, and every time I'm near you, I want to flee."

She laughed at the absurdity of his words. But the urge to kiss her was simply too great to resist, and he turned over her hand to place a tender kiss against her palm.

Her laughter died. She stiffened, as if waiting for him to wound her again.

Her reaction eviscerated him. But he hid the pain by forcing a grin and adding, "I want nothing more than to put as much distance between us as possible."

"You do, do you?" Suspicion thickened her voice.

"Absolutely." He pressed his advantage by looping her arm around his and leading her down the steps to the rocky beach below. Her sweet scent of lavender filled his senses. "I cannot think of anything I'd rather do less than spend hours in your company."

"Then it's a good thing that we'll only have to suffer a brief conversation this afternoon."

He stopped short. When she slipped her arm free and walked on ahead a few paces, he stared after her. Did the little vixen mean that as part of their teasing in opposites, or was she serious?

Once again, Belinda had him on his toes. No wonder dukes fought for the privilege of courting her. There was never a dull moment in her company.

He caught up with her and took her arm, guiding her along the beach. "This way."

"Where are we going?" She blinked against the late afternoon sun as it sank toward the horizon. "I was hoping we could talk."

"We will. But first, just a short walk along the beach." When she hesitated, he purposely misread her reaction and assured her, "Don't worry. The tide won't be in for several more hours."

"It isn't the tide that I'm worried about," she muttered.

His lips crooked into a half grin. "Worried that I'll tie you down and hold you captive until you see reason and support the academy?"

"I think you'd enjoy it."

A sharp pang of yearning reverberated shamelessly inside him at her unwitting innuendo. When they'd courted before, he'd never been anything more than a gentleman with her, no matter how much he'd longed to lay her down and strip her dress away. With his teeth.

He cleared his throat, but it didn't keep a husky rasp from his voice. "A man has to do what a man has to do."

She slid him a dubious sideways glance. "Including ropes and sailors' knots?"

"I'd never use sailors' knots against you."

"Well, thank good—"

"I'm a soldier," he continued, deadpan. "We use irons."

Halting in her steps, she jerked her arm away. The hard look that she narrowed on him could have cut glass.

He chuckled at how easily she'd risen to the bait, how much he'd always liked stirring the fire inside her. Ignoring her irritated but surprisingly adorable sniff at his teasing, he once more took her arm.

He led her farther down the cliff face, until they were out of sight of the town and on an isolated stretch of beach fronted by tiny coves and other indentations carved into the soft limestone rock. Until they were alone.

"Perhaps we should stop and talk now," she suggested, the nervousness visible in her.

"Perhaps we should explore what's just beyond that next cliff." Whatever it was that she wanted to say to him would keep until she saw the surprise. It was mercenary, he'd admit that, and done more than just to gain her favor with the board—he also did it simply because he wanted time alone with her. "There's a stretch of sandy beach there that I think you'll appreciate."

She arched an unconvinced brow. "And *I* think you're simply hoping to get me alone so you can charm me into supporting the academy."

"You've given me no choice. When diplomacy fails, a good soldier attacks."

He sensed immediately that he'd said the wrong thing, despite his joking tone. The *very* worst thing because she stiffened, turning instantly cold.

"I don't need reminders of your military career, Maxwell," she said into the wind, turning her face away as if she couldn't bear to look at him. "I'm well aware of exactly how dedicated a soldier you are."

Damnation. He should have known better. "Then how about a reminder that I'm more than just a soldier? I'm out of uniform. Hadn't you noticed?"

"Oh, I noticed." Yet she slightly turned her head back toward him in a surreptitious glance.

He stopped her and tugged her around to face him. "Take a good look, Belinda." She startled slightly at his order. "A good, *long* look."

For a moment, her bright eyes never left his as she stubbornly refused to do as he asked.

Then, as if unable to resist, she slowly lowered her gaze, trailing it over him, from the neckcloth his man had taken great pains to knot to perfection, to the tan cashmere jacket and brown and white diamond-pattern waistcoat beneath. He was certain she'd stop her perusal there, but the audacious woman continued on, her eyes drinking in the cut of his brown trousers all the way down to his boots.

When she began a languid return up the length of him, he nearly groaned at the torture that her heated look spiraled through him.

A stray curl had escaped the confines of her bonnet, and using it as an excuse to touch her, he reached to tuck it back into place.

"See?" He opportunistically caressed her cheek as he pulled his hand away, then thrilled at the soft shiver that sped through her. "This afternoon, I'm simply a civilian. Don't think of me as a soldier."

"I don't think I can," she admitted. Ignoring the affectionate touch he'd just taken, she busied herself with securing the ends of the ribbons that once more danced in the breeze. But she couldn't hide the shaking of her hands. "I've only ever known you as a soldier."

Feeling as if he were plunging right over the cliffs above them, he corrected, "You knew me as a man, Belinda."

"I thought I did." Her breathless voice was so soft that it was almost lost beneath the noise of the wind and waves. "I was wrong."

"You knew me better than anyone."

"No." She gave up on securing the ribbons and tossed them away in irritation. "The man I knew would *never* have abandoned me."

He didn't attempt to lessen the wounding those words sliced into him, knowing he deserved it. Instead, he deepened the punishing pain by confirming her worst thoughts of him. "The man you knew would have done exactly that."

And did.

When she opened her mouth to reply, he cut her off. "The past is over." And nothing that he wanted to discuss with her. "We're different people now, with different responsibilities and concerns, and there's no point in arguing about the past when nothing can be done to change it."

She arched a piqued brow. "When we're so able to argue about the future, you mean?"

"When I'd rather not argue with you at all." Solemnly, all teasing gone, he held out his hand in invitation to continue their walk. "You once trusted me. Give me the chance to earn back that trust."

She hesitated.

"Please."

For a long moment, she didn't move. Then she gave a jerking nod.

Not letting himself think about the racing of his heartbeat when her hand slipped into his, he guided her carefully over the rocks as they gave way to sand just beyond the rounded front of the cliff face towering above them. Overhead, in the last light of sunset, gulls cried out against the din of the rolling waves striking far across the wide stretch of beach exposed by the outgoing tide.

"What was it that you called me in yesterday's meeting?" Although he knew very well. Despite not allowing it to show, he'd been pierced by the accusation. "A monster?"

Remorse flashed over her face, yet the stubborn woman didn't apologize. But he hadn't expected her to.

"I'm not a monster, Belinda. I'm simply trying to save as many lives as possible." He stopped, turning so that he blocked her view into the narrow cove behind him. "Give me the opportunity to convince you that I have only the best interests of everyone at heart. That's all I'm asking for. Just the chance to be heard."

He stepped aside to reveal the surprise waiting for her.

* * *

Belinda gasped. "A picnic?"

She blinked at the sight, unable for a moment to believe her eyes. No, she was wrong—this was so much more than a picnic. This was... oh, this was simply magical!

A sailcloth lay spread across the patch of powdery white sand, anchored in place against the wind on all four corners by large brass lanterns whose flames danced in the sea breeze, their oil giving off a spicy scent. Scattered across the cloth were several dishes covered with lids so that she couldn't see what they contained, along with several pillows in jewel-tone satins and a long and narrow Turkish rug edging the side of the sailcloth. A small fire of driftwood flickered on the rocks a few feet away.

All like something out of *The Arabian Nights*... exotic and romantic, complete with red rose petals scattered across the white cloth.

"How..." She was too stunned to finish. Thank goodness that amazement covered her face, because it hid the confused thrill pulsating through her that Maxwell had gone to all this trouble for her.

"With the aid of the men at the barracks." He led her to the rug and helped her to gracefully lower herself. "Do you like it?"

She loved it. And yet... "I won't support the academy, if that's what this is about."

He repeated pointedly, matching her own stubbornness, "Do you like it?"

"It's tolerable," she grudgingly admitted.

Quirking a knowing smile, he placed one of the pillows behind her so she could recline. Then he sat beside her.

She gestured at the spread. "Why go to all this trouble?"

"Because you're right. I want your support." He reached to pour her a glass of wine. "I'm not above being the type of man who charms his way into a woman's affections."

At that, she couldn't prevent a little laugh. *Charming.* He was definitely that, all right. But she knew the truth. That he didn't have to charm his way back into her affections because he'd never completely left them, despite everything. Which was what had always bothered her most... How could a man whom she'd known well enough to love with all her heart fool her so well?

He held out the glass to her. "Surely you don't begrudge a man the opportunity to use every weapon at his disposal?"

"I suppose that would depend upon how the weapon was wielded," she clarified, accepting the wine.

His eyes shone knowingly. "And who was doing the wielding?"

She pressed her lips tightly together. *Drat him.* She couldn't properly answer that without digging herself deeper. The devil knew it, too. He was nothing if not razor-sharp, always had been. His mind had been one of the things she'd loved best about him. That and his understanding of how much her charity work meant to her, how much purpose she found in helping others.

Yet she wasn't a dolt herself. "Since when does a picnic count as a weapon?"

"Wait until you've had my cooking." He winked at her.

Her breath hitched. She stared at him, speechless. She couldn't have replied right then even if she'd known what to say.

He stretched out casually across the length of the rug behind her, propping himself up on one elbow. He reached to pluck a grape from the cluster lying on a platter in front of them. "You always liked picnics, and I thought this might be a good way for us to catch up on what our lives have been like since we last spoke."

Not wanting to reopen old wounds, she waved a hand toward the spread. "You spent your life lounging with Scheherazade by lantern light?"

"Actually, when I wasn't being shot at, I spent my summers mostly laboring in the hot sun, the rainy seasons fighting off mosquitoes, and my nights sleeping in cramped barracks with thirty other men." He blew out a long-suffering sigh and popped the grape into his mouth. "Every last one of whom snored loudly enough to shake the rafters."

When she laughed, he plucked a second grape and held it up to her lips.

Her belly pinched. Fearing that he was offering far more than a mere grape, she raised her wineglass to her lips like a shield. "If you think a picnic can sway me, you're mistaken."

"Not a picnic. I told you. A chance to get to know each other again."

In one last desperate attempt to cling to her pride, she sat up and busied herself with uncovering the dishes, each more exotic than the one before. Focusing all of her attention on a bowl of yellow rice, she mumbled, "I think we know each other well enough already."

"Not nearly well enough."

His low voice sent a warm tingle spiraling through her, which did nothing to put her at ease and everything to cause her hand to tremor as she lifted the lid on a plate of red chicken.

"I want you to know the man I've become, so you can understand why I'm set on opening the academy. Perhaps we can find common ground."

She wasn't certain she wanted to know him any better. "That depends." She sat back, her fingers tightening around her wineglass. "What do you want to know about me?"

"Nothing."

"*Nothing?*" she squeaked out. *That* pricked at her pride.

Mischief sparkled in his eyes, as if he could see right through her and knew exactly how much his comment baited her. Then he took the glass out of her hand, set it aside, and raised the grape once more to her lips.

She hesitated, then opened her mouth to let him place it on her tongue. She simply couldn't resist. Being with him like this felt too familiar to deny. Too *right*.

"I don't need to know about you," he explained, suddenly solemn, "because I made a point of always knowing what your life was like, what you were doing, all the charities you were involved with. No matter how far I traveled, I was never able to put you behind me."

Instead of lowering his hand, he audaciously stroked his thumb over her bottom lip. She shivered, but she couldn't tell which was making her head spin more—the deep, husky purr of his voice or the way he caressed her mouth, as if pondering whether he wanted to kiss her. Or devour her.

Then he dropped his hand so suddenly that she nearly whimpered at the loss of his touch. He reached for a plate and began to spoon out small bites of the various dishes. "But there is one thing I still need to know."

She inhaled a deep breath to steady herself. "Which is?"

"Why are you so concerned about the pensioners?" He held out the plate to her, as casually as if they were friends lunching on the green in Hyde Park instead of adversaries on a secluded stretch of beach. "They'll be taken care of, I promise you. They'll have good homes, perhaps even in Chelsea or Greenwich."

She took the plate and held it awkwardly. For one desperate moment, she wanted to tell him, in case it made a difference in keeping the men here in their home. But how could she share the awful truth? That it was the pensioners who comforted her and gave her strength and understanding when he'd abandoned her, choosing the army over her. That she was right here in Brighton when she received word that her father had died, helping in the hospital. Over the years, being a hospital patroness gave her a feeling of closeness to both of the men she'd lost, a connection she hadn't yet been able to relinquish. The pensioners had helped her survive when the darkness had closed in upon her. Now it was her turn to protect them and help them survive, just as they'd helped her.

How could she ever make him understand all that? *If* he even deserved to know in the first place.

She set the plate down, untouched, and threw his question back at him. "Why are you so concerned about training cadets? Surely they can learn battle tactics and leadership better on the field than in classrooms and on parade grounds."

His face hardened with a small deepening in the lines at the corners of his eyes. "Because I'm fed up with a system in which promising young men never have the chance to reach their full potential or demonstrate what they're capable of becoming. If we can enroll more cadets, then we can train better officers, and everyone has the opportunity to rise in the ranks as high as their competence and skills allow." He turned away from her, squinting into the sun that was sinking in a blood-red ball toward the horizon. "And perhaps more men can return alive from the battlefield."

She bit her lip. All good points. But... "Once they return, don't they deserve to be taken care of? To be given a permanent home and not be shuffled about from place to place whenever the army decides it no longer wants them around? What does that say to the men who risk their lives for England?"

"That once a soldier, always a soldier."

She leaned toward him, unwilling to let him dismiss her concerns so easily. "They have every right—"

"The real question," he interrupted, countering her offensive with one of his own, "is why you asked to meet me this afternoon." He rested his forearm across his bent knee, his hand clenching lightly into a fist as if to

238 | ANNA HARRINGTON

keep himself from reaching for her. "Obviously, it wasn't to tell me that you haven't changed your mind."

Guilt sparked inside her. When she'd schemed to avoid Pomperly, she'd still believed Maxwell to be the horrible, selfish blackguard who'd used her and cast her away, who deserved to be used in kind. But now, knowing how much it meant to him to have proper training for the soldiers, he seemed far less of a monster.

"Because I need you," she answered grudgingly.

He chuckled, a low sound that rumbled into her. "Why do I think it's not the way a man wants to be needed by a woman?"

Oh, that devil! Her face flushed hot. "That is *not* what I meant, and you know it!"

Without a repentant bone in his body, he stroked his knuckles across her cheek. "Pity."

Stunned, she clutched at the rug beneath her, desperate to hold on to anything as the world rocked around her. He couldn't *possibly* mean... could he?

Then the reality of their past crashed over her. What a fool she was! To let herself think it, even for a fleeting heartbeat—no. She doubted he held a single affection toward her. Even the trouble of this picnic wasn't for her but to try to persuade her to his side.

She pushed his hand away to hide her mortification that the devil could affect her even now. And to quash an unexpected pang of sadness that she didn't have the same effect on him. "There's a dinner at the Pavilion with His Majesty." She busied her empty hands by pulling at the yarns in the rug beneath her. "The Duke of Pomperly has invited me to be his guest. But I prefer not to attend with him."

"Then refuse." His blunt response startled her. So did the suddenly sharp edge to his voice. With any other man, she would have claimed he was jealous.

"I cannot refuse an invitation to dine with the king, even if it comes from a man whom I'd rather avoid." Nor could she afford to offend a board member. "But I *can* refuse if I'm already attending the dinner with someone else."

"Who?"

Guilt at using him to avoid Pomperly added to the knot sitting in her belly like a lead ball, and she bit her bottom lip. "You."

"I see," he drawled, his face inscrutable.

"You're a brigadier, one of the highest-ranking officers in Brighton," she rushed out. "Surely you'll receive an invitation or can wrangle one. Or *I* can contact the Pavilion and request that you be put on the guest list. So I thought—I thought that you'd—" Now that the scheme was hatched, the words poured from her as she attempted to find purchase in her persuasion. And failing. Because he returned her gaze with an unreadable expression, with no indication if he were sympathetic to her situation. Or simply thought her mad.

She fell silent, realizing with embarrassment that her explanation was paltry justification for using him.

He covered her hand with his, stilling her nervous fingers against the rug. "I'll accompany you."

She blinked. "You will?"

"But not to spite Pomperly." Masculine pride underpinned his voice. "I'll do it on two conditions."

She felt as if she were negotiating terms of surrender with the enemy. "Which are?"

"I'll escort you to the dinner if you agree to accompany me to the barracks to meet the soldiers."

Suspicion prickled at the backs of her knees. "Why?"

"Just to talk to them." His deep voice curled softly around her, nearly lost beneath the sound of the rolling waves breaking against the shore. "To find out what their lives in the army have been like."

Without agreeing, she asked a bit breathlessly, very aware of the warmth of his hand still covering hers, "And your second condition?"

"That you want to spend the evening with me because you want to be with me."

Clinging to what little pride she had left, she lifted her chin with an imperious sniff, but succeeded only in drawing a grin from him. Oh, that infuriating devil!

"Why would I want to spend the evening with you?" she asked, determined to pretend that he wasn't affecting her when he was actually shaking her to her core.

He smiled with arrogant charm. "Because you like me."

"Ha!" Her indignation flared at that. But blast it, she couldn't bring herself to pull her hand from his. "I don't like you."

His eyes gleamed. "A great deal."

"A very little," she shot back. Then she grumbled, "And less with each passing moment."

With a quirk of his brow, he lifted her hand to his lips to place a kiss to her palm. She managed to fight down the tremble that threatened to sweep through her. But when he slid his mouth down to her wrist, her pulse spiked tellingly against his lips, and he smiled.

"A great deal," he repeated in a rakish murmur.

He slipped a hand behind her nape and tugged her gently toward him before her confused mind had the chance to realize what was happening so she could stop him. Then his lips found hers, and stopping him was the *very* last thing she wanted to do.

Closing her eyes against the agonizing flood of bittersweet memories that his tender kiss unlocked, she placed her hand against his chest for something solid to cling to as the world around her fell away completely. His heart pounded beneath her fingertips, an echo to her own racing pulse, and she knew she was lost. The achingly sweet kiss tasted of the past, of love and promise... of *home*.

When he shifted back, breaking the kiss, the loss of contact was so powerful that a whimper rose on her lips.

He stared at her wide-eyed, as if he couldn't believe that he'd kissed her, with a bewildered expression that she was certain mirrored her own. But for all the confusion that kiss created, the pull of it had been irresistible.

"Maxwell," she whispered, her right hand rising to touch her lips. She could still feel the heat and strength of his kiss, like a shadow of the love they'd once shared. A ghost pain of the life together that fate denied them.

"Forgive me." He reached to once again gently take her hand, this time covering it with both of his. And this time, she couldn't hold back the trembling.

"Of course." But her voice sounded strained, as if every lie she was telling herself was audible in it. "It was only a kiss." Oh, it was so much more than that! "It was nothing." It was simply breathtaking. "We both got caught up in old memories and feelings and..." And something inside her had desperately wanted that kiss. "It won't happen again." Even now she yearned to be taken back into his arms, kissed breathless, and told that everything was going to be all right, as if the past had never happened—

But the past couldn't be changed. She was a fool to wish that it could.

"It was only a kiss... nothing," she repeated. This time, she meant every word.

"No." He gave her fingers a tender squeeze. "I meant about what happened ten years ago."

That small touch of affection raced up her arm and landed warmly in her breast. Heavens, she desperately needed an anchor! But the soothing caress of his fingers over the backs of hers only increased the spinning inside her head. So did that stunning declaration.

"Forgive me, Belinda." The hard set of his jaw told her how difficult this was for him. "I made what I thought was the best decision at the time."

One that ended up nearly destroying her. She pulled her hand away and pressed her fist to her chest to physically hold back the pain of old wounds that were once more bleeding as if still fresh.

"Why should I forgive?" Somehow, she kept her voice even. She wanted to scream!

"Because I'm not the man I was before."

Oh, *that* was certainly true. She could see the changes in him with her own eyes. Age had mellowed his brashness, and maturity had dulled the impulsive edge she so clearly remembered in the young man he'd once been.

But was he truly repentant for what he'd done, or was he simply playing her for a fool... again?

As if reading her doubts, he slowly pulled at her bonnet ribbons, untying them with a gentle tug. She inhaled sharply at the far-too familiar gesture but couldn't find the resolve to push his hands away.

"Say that you'll forgive me," he cajoled, removing the bonnet and setting it aside.

Then he reached up to her hair and scandalously pulled loose the pins holding her chignon. Spurred on by the sea breeze, her hair spilled free, stirring in the wind around her shoulders.

He stilled as his eyes drank her in. Not moving, not touching, only looking... yet the heated intensity in him coiled a powerful longing deep inside her.

Somehow finding the strength to keep her wits about her, she rasped out in a breathless whisper, "I don't want your apology."

"Good. Because I'm not giving one."

Surprise darted through her, and her lips parted. Taking her reaction as an invitation, he brushed his thumb over her bottom lip. His eyes softened as he focused on the caress, as if touching her like this was the most important thing in the world.

"I've made a lifetime of mistakes," he admitted, remorse roughening his voice, "and I've learned that apologies are meaningless. I would never demean you by offering one." She stiffened beneath his touch, so stunned that for a moment she forgot to breathe. "An apology, no matter how sincere, can never make up for the pain I caused you. And for *that*, I am truly sorry."

Fresh anguish sliced into her heart, and she flinched at the pain, so fierce it was visceral. There was a time when she would have given anything to hear those words from him. But that was ten years ago—a different lifetime. Hearing them now brought only torment at the reminder of all they'd lost.

He stared at her so intensely that the little hairs on her arms stood on end. As if he had so much more he wanted to confess. But he said nothing and instead dared to comb his fingers through her hair.

Her heart skipped. In that missed beat, she saw everything her life could have been with him, the family and home they could have made, the dreams and hopes they could have shared—

Then it was gone in a flash of brutal reality.

The pain was vicious. Because her heart knew the truth... that Maxwell didn't regret what he'd done. What he regretted was that fate had brought them together again while she still blamed him, when he needed her on his side in the fight over the academy. When he once more needed her help to advance his career.

"I can't forgive you." She slowly pushed his hand down and moved away, unable to bear his touch a moment longer.

Wisely, he remained where he was, as if sensing that reaching for her again would be the worst mistake he could make. "Not now," he asked solemnly, "or not ever?"

Unable to find the courage to put full voice to how much he'd wounded her, how the darkness of that time nearly destroyed her, she whispered instead, "I think... I think our picnic's over."

* * *

Richard Marbury, Duke of Pomperly, watched the two figures walking together up from the beach in twilight's darkening shadows. He noted the way Belinda rested her hand on Thorpe's arm, how his hand reached up to cover hers—only for a moment before dropping back to his side. A gesture of tenderness and affection. One she marked by stiffening ever so slightly, but in her connection to him not shifting away.

Then Pomperly turned away from his carriage window and signaled with a sharp rap of his cane to the roof for his driver to move on.

So the rumors he'd heard about the duchess's youthful liaison with Maxwell Thorpe were true after all. And from the looks of things, the two were picking up right where they'd left off.

"Not if I have anything to say about it," he grumbled.

Belinda was the perfect choice to become Duchess of Pomperly, and nothing was going to get in his way of making her his. Certainly not some upstart baron's son turned army officer who didn't have the good sense to realize when he was overstepping. *Very much* overstepping, in fact, to think that he could win himself a duchess.

Oh, she might find him pleasant enough as an old friend. Or attractive enough for an assignation or two, to take care of whatever physical needs hadn't been satisfied since Winchester died. But certainly nothing beyond that.

A *brigadier's* wife? He snorted. Even Belinda wasn't reformer enough for that.

No, she was meant to be a duchess. *His* duchess. Well-cultured, already familiar with the demands of the rank and how to navigate the highest levels of Society, possessing a nice fortune of her own and so would never need to touch his—she was perfect. Doubly so, considering that she was barren and that he already had heirs from his previous duchess. There would be no children to interfere in their marriage.

No mere army officer was going to steal her away.

He'd just have to make certain that Thorpe was put in his proper place... all the way to Africa.

CHAPTER FOUR

When Max reached inside the carriage stopped in front of the barracks to help Belinda to the ground, she hesitated to slip her hand into his. Only a heartbeat's uncertainty, but in that moment, he knew she remembered their kiss from two days ago, and her regret ripped through him.

Then she put her gloved hand into his and descended gracefully to the cobblestones.

She'd arrived for her visit to the barracks, and not a moment too soon. He'd spent all of yesterday with her at the hospital, meeting the pensioners and watching as she read books to them, helped mend their clothing—even helped one dress himself, a man whose leg and foot had been badly damaged in an explosion. If anyone from the *ton* had seen a duchess do such a thing, they surely would have suffered apoplexy on the spot. But Belinda behaved as if she were privileged to help.

She'd made her point. The pensioners needed her, and they needed one another.

He only hoped that today she'd realize how much the army needed well-trained cadets.

"You look lovely," he told her as he bowed over her hand, then placed it on his arm to lead her through the gate. He was acutely aware of every curious stare cast their way from the soldiers gathered in the yard.

"Please stop saying that," she admonished with an exasperated sigh. "Your charms won't work on me."

He clenched his jaw. "I'm not saying it to—"

"And you cannot seduce me to your side either."

That brought him up short. He halted, stopping her next to him. "Pardon?"

She fussed with her gloves, not daring to spare him a glance. "Your kiss."

"*My* kiss?" As if she'd had nothing to do with it. As if he routinely staged elaborate picnics on beaches only to have his wicked way with unsuspecting ladies. "That kiss was *not* a seduction." Not by a goodly ways, although for the life of him, he couldn't have said why he'd done it. Except that he couldn't resist. "And you were a willing participant."

"That doesn't mean that you should have done it."

Oh, he was pretty certain that was *exactly* what it meant, and she knew it, too, which was proven by her careful dodge. But he didn't want to risk a slap in front of the men and silently led her forward, toward the enlisted men's mess hall.

"I spent a great deal of time yesterday thinking about it," she continued. He was confident she had. He'd thought of little else himself, especially when they'd been together at the hospital. Close, but never alone so they couldn't repeat the encounter. "It cannot happen again."

"Absolutely not."

She began to nod, as if satisfied with his answer—only to freeze as his comment sank through her.

Her bewildered gaze darted to him. She'd obviously been expecting a different answer, and her mind surely whirled at a million miles a minute to figure out his reply. If he had agreed with her or was refusing.

Finally, unable to bear the uncertainty any longer, she scowled and demanded, "And what, exactly, do you mean by that?"

He had no intention of answering. Especially when he didn't know himself. Instead, he dodged, "I don't have to charm you to win your support, and I certainly wouldn't attempt to seduce you." Although he'd lost count of the number of times over the years he'd imagined doing just that. He added bluntly, "You're an intelligent woman who trusts in logic and reason, and I'd be a fool to try to use your heart against you. We both know how ineffective that would be."

She hesitated with what he was certain was a cutting reply poised on the tip of her tongue. Then she softened as that unusual compliment sank in. "Then why did you kiss me?"

He purposefully avoided her question. "If that kiss was wrong, it wasn't for the reason you think."

"I *think* we already have enough problems between us," she answered, getting in the last word as they reached the dining hall door. "We don't need to add more, not ones like that."

"Absolutely not."

Her shoulders slumped in exasperation. "Maxwell—"

"Brigadier!"

The shout went up as soon as they entered. As more men took up the call, it echoed through the building and out across the barracks grounds that stretched along Church Street, just a stone's throw across the park from the Pavilion. Infantrymen scrambled up from the benches lining the long tables to snap to attention, then were relieved when Max signaled for them to fall at ease. A comforting sense of familiarity rose inside him as he led her through the hall, a place he knew well, surrounded by men whom he'd trust with his life.

"Brigadier in the barracks!"

She tensed at his side, and her eyes widened as she glanced around the room. He fought back a twitch of his lips at her discomfiture, this woman who was usually so confident that she charged through the world without hesitation.

Briefly placing his hand over hers as it rested on his sleeve, he leaned down to quietly explain, "If it helps, you should know that they're all more concerned about my presence here than yours."

"Oh?"

"I can order them to serve guard duty. You can only order them to serve tea."

The tension drained out of her, and a faint smile of irritation tugged at her lips. "Enjoying yourself, are you?"

"Of course." He patted her hand with mock condescension. "For once, I outrank a duchess."

When she opened her mouth to give him the set-down he deserved, he interrupted, "You've entered a different world, Belinda." He gestured behind them at the dozen or so men who had returned to their seats at the table but were still craning their necks to stare curiously at them. "The army is a world unto itself, with its own laws and traditions, its own expectations and loyalties." They reached the end of the mess hall, and he took her hand to help her sit on the wooden bench at the head of the long table. Standing behind her, he took her slender shoulders in his hands and leaned over to murmur into her ear, "Today, consider me your guide to that world."

He removed his hat and tossed it to one of the nearby men, with unspoken orders to hang it from one of the pegs on the wall. The soldier stared at him in surprise. Officers rarely entered this mess hall and certainly few of high rank.

Then the soldier grinned as he hung the hat, apparently deciding that all the stories he'd heard about Max were true. That he'd rather spend his time with infantrymen than officers.

"Why do I need a guide?" she challenged. "I've spent a good amount of time around soldiers, you forget."

"Around officers." Instead of joining her at the table, he crossed to the little cast-iron stove in the corner, where a pot of coffee sat heating. He lifted the lid and peered inside. "You've probably never had a conversation with an enlisted soldier."

"Many of the pensioners were enlisted men."

"Retired, not actively serving." He returned the lid and turned away, cursing himself for not thinking ahead to have a tray of tea ready for her. But then, hadn't he wanted to show her the way the average soldier lived? Expensive china and tea had never graced the doorway of this dining hall.

"No difference."

"A *world* of difference." He signaled for the men to gather near. Good soldiers all, they joined them at the front of the room without a single grumble.

"Your Grace," Max introduced with as much formality as if they were meeting in a Society drawing room, "these are the men of the Royal Fusiliers."

"The 7th Regiment of Foot, sir," one of the older soldiers interjected.

"Of course." With a deferential nod, he smiled at the man's pride over his regiment. The grizzled sergeant had reason for being proud. Every man in His Majesty's army knew the heroism of the 7th Regiment of Foot and how much they'd sacrificed over the years. "Men, this is Her Grace, Duchess of Winchester."

He held her gaze as the men stared at her in surprise. Most of them had never seen a duchess in person before, let alone been introduced to one, and were uncertain of the proper way to greet her. They shifted nervously, until the sergeant pulled at his forelock and nodded. "Your

Grace."

The others followed suit, and Belinda gave them a bright smile, as if she were being introduced to peers of the realm instead of coarse soldiers.

"I'm very pleased to meet you, gentlemen." Her soft voice lilted through the dining hall and drew relaxed smiles from the men. Already she was winning them over, exactly as Max knew she would. "The 7th Regiment of Foot... My! That sounds like a very fine regiment."

The men didn't know if they were supposed to make replies to that, and an awkward silence followed until Max cleared his throat and said, "One of His Majesty's bravest. They fought in America and the West Indies before taking on Napoleon on the Peninsula at Talavera and Bussaco."

"Also at Albuera," one of the older soldiers added proudly. "'Twas me first fight."

"A bloody one, from what I've heard." Max's eyes never moved from Belinda.

"Aye," the sergeant agreed somberly. "Gave it to 'em right good, we did!"

"And the sieges, don't forget," another soldier piped up. Although he was too young to have fought on the Peninsula, he openly showed his pride at being part of the storied regiment. "All three of 'em."

Then the men all jumped into the conversation. "Salamanca, too—"

"And Vitoria—"

"Then we stuck it to Boney by chasing him right o'er the Pyrenees and back to France!"

"Stuck it to 'em good."

"Right there on their own soil!"

"Toulouse."

At that, the men all turned their gazes to the sergeant who had quietly spoken that last. Including Max.

The sergeant lowered his eyes to the floor, but not before a haunted expression darkened his face. He added solemnly, "Never forget Toulouse, boys."

A grim silence fell over the room, broken only by the faint popping of coals in the stove and the muted noise of horses and wagons moving in the barracks yard outside.

Belinda glanced from man to man, attempting to understand what she'd missed, before her puzzled gaze landed on Max. "What happened at Toulouse?"

"Hell," he answered quietly.

"*All* hell," the sergeant corrected.

Her lips parted slightly as she pulled in a stunned breath. She gracefully rose to her feet and stepped toward the sergeant.

"You were there, weren't you?" Not a question.

With a curt nod, he looked away. "Yes, ma'am."

Silently, Belinda held out her hand. The sergeant hesitated, then took it in his. She leaned close, bringing her mouth to his ear.

Max had no idea what she whispered to the man, but the sergeant's eyes glistened, and he nodded again. When she released his hand and stepped back, the old soldier blinked rapidly and turned completely away to hide the raw emotions on his face.

Instead of returning to her seat, Belinda went through the group of men, holding out her hand in greeting to each of them, asking their names, where each called home, and how long they had been part of the Royal Fusiliers. Each man beamed when she spoke to him, captivated by her interest in them and by her kindness.

"You've been with the Fusiliers for a long time," Max interjected when she laughed at a joke that one of the oldest of the soldiers told her.

"Aye, sir." The man straightened. Even though Max was here unofficially and doing his best to put the men at ease, none of them forgot his rank. "Over twenty years since I enlisted."

Which would have been right at the start of the wars with the French. Seizing on this opportunity, Max asked, "What was your first engagement?"

His eyes took on a faraway look. "Copenhagen. Been in the army less than three months 'fore they shipped us off to Denmark."

"How old were you?" Belinda asked.

"Just turned one and twenty, ma'am."

Max fixed his eyes on Belinda to gauge her reaction. "Were you prepared for it?"

He snorted in disgust. "The trainin' they gave us was little more than instructions on which end o' the rifle to point at the enemy an' t' keep our heads down when the artillery goes to boomin' off. And marchin'." He scowled in distaste. "Hours o' marchin'."

Belinda asked innocently, "What's wrong with marching? Order and discipline among the ranks are surely important in a battle."

"Aye, ma'am." His nod turned into a frustrated shake of his head.

"Until th' first shots are fired. Then it's a scramble on the field, wi' no one knowin' what to do, where to charge, or when to fall back."

"But isn't that what the officers are there for? To give direction to the men?"

He spat on the floorboards. "Officers who themselves ain't had more than a few weeks of trainin' at best? An' trainin' not at all like what they'll encounter i' th' fray, when bullets come a-whizzin' at 'em."

She folded her hands demurely in front of her. "I see."

Max was certain she did. After all, this was why he'd brought her here, so she could understand how little training most soldiers were given before being rushed into battle, along with field officers who were just as inexperienced.

She confirmed her understanding of his scheme when she answered dryly, "I suppose not all officers can be as clever as Brigadier Thorpe." Then she slid a sideways glance at him. "Occasionally, he makes quite good decisions under the pressure of battle."

He fought to hide the amused twitch of his lips at her sly innuendo. She always had been one of the sharpest women he'd ever met.

"So soldiers need more training," she announced. "Do you all agree?"

A round of ayes and emphatic nods went up from the men, and Max gave a silent sigh of relief. If Belinda was ever going to be swayed to support the academy, it would be the soldiers themselves who convinced her.

"What are your career plans, then?" she asked with a sincere smile.

The abrupt change in conversation didn't surprise the men, but a warning prickled at the back of his neck. What was she up to?

One by one, the men all shared their plans with her, and to a man, they all wanted to serve out their army careers as part of the Fusiliers. Not one wanted to be pensioned before he'd given his all to crown and country. The pride Max felt in them warmed his chest and reminded him that he'd not been wrong to pick the military as his life's path. Not when he could serve with men like these.

"And when you're no longer able, what then?" Another question that seemed innocent to the men but which sliced into Max, because he knew where that quick mind of hers was headed. "Once you're too old to charge into battle, or God forbid, should you be wounded? What would you do then, if you couldn't be a soldier any longer?"

One of the younger men shrugged. He was so young, in fact, that freckles still dotted his nose. "Go home to our families, ma'am. Start over there with them."

She pressed, "So you all have families to depend upon?"

Most nodded, except for three men who remained still. One of them was the old sergeant who had fought at Toulouse.

"And your family, Sergeant?"

"Got none, ma'am," he answered quietly, as if a bit embarrassed to admit it. "The regiment is my family, till the day I'm pensioned."

"What a great loss that day will bring to the Fusiliers," she said sincerely. Then she turned toward Max. "Did you know, Brigadier, that in order to be a pensioner at one of the royal hospitals, a man cannot have any family?"

"Yes, Your Grace," he answered with chagrin. "I did know that."

"Hospitals that might otherwise keep a dedicated soldier who has given the best years of his life to crown and country from a life of starvation and suffering on the streets?"

He clenched his jaw. "Yes, ma'am."

Satisfied that she'd made her point, she smiled warmly at the men. "Do not worry. You'll all be given the respect and rewards you deserve, both now and when you retire." Then she added with such conviction that it pulsed through him like an electric tingle, "I give you my word."

Max quietly dismissed the men and took her arm to escort her out. Instead of cutting directly across the yard to the barracks gate and her waiting carriage, he guided her the long way around, along the brick wall that separated the barracks from the inn and houses fronting Marlborough Place.

When they were well out of earshot of the soldiers, she commented dryly, "I think I made my point about the hospital."

She had. And yet... "And I mine about the academy."

"Then it seems that we're right back where we started."

Not back where they'd started, but more firmly entrenched than before. Due in no small part because of their past. Even now, the tension flowed around them as palpably as the salty sea air and only increased with each step they took leading them away from the main part of the yard and past the service buildings framing the perimeter.

"The War Office wants the academy," he reminded her as gently as possible. "I think it's time you accepted that and turned your kindnesses toward helping the pensioners relocate."

"Why can't you see any other perspective but your own?" Aggravation colored her voice.

"I am trying to see your point. But you're an outsider. You have no idea what the army needs to protect its men and—"

"Do not dare to try to put me in my place by telling me that I don't know what army life is like. The War Office will be breaking their promise to those men." He could feel her breath grow short as her frustration mounted, and not with the War Office but with *him*. "I know what it means to place your trust in someone, only to have it destroyed."

He halted as the words slammed into him, grabbing her elbow and pulling her to a stop. "You are letting the past cloud your judgment."

"Cloud my judgment?" With a bitter laugh of disbelief, she tried to yank her arm away, but he held tight, refusing to let her go. All of her pulsed with anger as she accused, "You used me!" She drew her hands into fists. "I loved you, and you used me just to advance your career."

Fury flared inside him. *Enough.*

He pulled her into an open storage room and kicked the door closed behind them. In the dim light cast by a small window high up in the wall, his gaze bore down into hers as he stepped her back against the stone wall. No surrender, no quarter—

This fight was ten years in coming, and he'd be damned if he'd retreat now.

"I didn't use you," he bit out. Every ounce of his will fought for restraint against the anger and pain he'd kept locked inside him all these years. "And I sure as hell didn't break my promise to you."

"You told me you loved me, that you wanted to marry me—"

"I did want that." *Christ!* He'd wanted that more than he'd wanted anything in his life, save for wanting the best possible life for *her*.

She pushed at his shoulders to make him step back, but he refused to budge. "You let me believe it just so my father would arrange for a better post for you. One that gave you a better chance at promotion. When you didn't need me anymore, you abandoned me."

"I *never* abandoned you." Her accusations ripped fresh wounds into him.

"You refused to return to England when I needed you, and it nearly destroyed me." Even in the dim light, pain shone in her eyes. "Why, Maxwell?" Ten years of confusion choked her as she forced out, "For God's sake—*why?*"

That single word was the one question he'd *never* wanted to answer, preferring to take the truth to his grave. But he should have known that Belinda would make him walk through the fires of hell.

"I made a choice." The *right* choice. He was as certain of that now as he'd been ten years ago. "I did what was best for you."

"For *me?*" Disdain darkened her face. "The best thing for me would have been for you to return to England and marry me."

The very *worst* thing. He bit back a curse that she refused to let this go. "You would have resented me."

"*Never.* I loved you. I wanted to marry you and—"

"For God's sake, Belinda! Don't you understand?" Furious that she refused to let this go, he grabbed her shoulders and humiliatingly confessed, "I wasn't good enough for you!"

She stared at him, shocked speechless.

"I wasn't good enough for you," he repeated, the guilt over hurting her so brutal that he shuddered with it. "I couldn't give you the help you needed, but I *could* give you a better life. A life without me."

He released her shoulders with a jerk and stepped away so that he couldn't see any more of her pain. It would absolutely undo him.

"I loved you enough to let you hate me for it. *That's* why I asked you to forget me." The powerlessness he'd felt then rushed back over him now with full force. A cruel reminder of the man he'd once been, of how far he'd come since then. Without her. He forced out around the tightening knot in his throat, "And it *killed* me, Belinda. I had no money, no rank of consequence, mounting debts—" Now that he'd made his confession, the words poured out of him in a wave, carrying with them all the guilt and anguish he'd kept inside him since the night he wrote that letter beneath the monsoon's rains. "You deserved better than being married to some junior officer stationed halfway around the world, with no prospects back in England and no other way to provide a living."

"You're a brigadier." She touched a shaking hand to his arm. "We would have married and—"

He yanked his shoulder away, out of her reach, and wheeled on her. "I was *nothing* then!"

When a tear slipped down her cheek at his outburst, he raked his fingers through his hair to resist the urge to reach for her, to brush it away and stop the trembling of her lips with his own.

He sucked in a ragged breath to gain back his control. "It took years to be promoted—years in which you would have been forced to live in near poverty on whatever few pounds I was able to send home from my pay. You deserved so much more, and Winchester gave it to you." Even now the thought of her in that man's arms sparked fury and anger inside him. "I knew you'd hate me for what I did, and I was willing to pay that price. For you."

"You had no right—*no* right—to make that decision for me!"

"I had every right," he replied quietly, closing the distance between them. "Because I loved you."

"Because you thought I wouldn't be—"

"Because I loved you." Another step.

She fiercely shook her head. "No! How could you have done—"

"Because I loved you," he repeated firmly. That was the answer to all her protests. The *only* answer.

One more step, and she was in his arms, shaking violently and sobbing openly in both anger and anguish. Raw pain seeped from her, and he held her close, taking on her pain for himself.

"I loved you, Belinda," he murmured into her hair, "with every ounce of my being."

She shoved at him to push herself free of his embrace, but he tightened his arms around her. He was *not* letting her go. Not this time.

"I couldn't help you." He squeezed his eyes closed against the cost to his pride that this admission forced him to pay. He'd never felt less like a man than the moment ten years ago when he realized the truth of that. "In order to help you, I *had* to let you go."

"But we loved each other!" A sob gripped her. "We could have… We could have…"

When words failed her, a great shudder pierced her. She finally understood the same truth that he'd realized all those years ago. That they could have done nothing.

She buried her face in his chest and cried, harder than he'd ever seen a woman cry in his life. Every sob was an agonizing slice into his heart.

Not letting her go, he lowered them both slowly onto a large grain sack resting on the floor and held her in his arms as she cried out all the torment fate had thrust upon them. She clung to him, and he'd never seen her more fragile than at that moment, when she cried as if she might break. He hadn't been there to see the pain he'd caused her when she received his letter, but he was living it now. A brutal torment.

"Don't cry, love," he whispered, his lips at her temple. "No more tears, please." God, he couldn't bear it!

But he might as well have been begging the tide not to rise or the sun not to set. And truly, the only way forward was through the hellfire of the past. So he let her cry and provided whatever comfort he could. The only words were soft whispers to soothe her, the only movement the consoling caress of his hand against her back.

When her cries lessened into soft sobs, then finally subsided into nothing more than little gasps for air, he shifted her in his arms to rest her cheek against his shoulder and stroke her back. Eventually, her breath came gentle and even, but he didn't release her. Neither did she shift away, remaining vulnerable in his arms.

Yet the difference in her now was palpable. Pain still lingered inside her; he could feel it with every delicate beat of her heart against his chest, pulsing inside him until he couldn't tell where her heartbeat ended and his began. But it was no longer the harsh anguish she'd held inside her all these years or the confusion over why he'd abandoned her. Now there was at least understanding, if not yet acceptance.

He placed a soft kiss to her hair.

Then he whispered what had tormented him since that night in India. "I regret every day that I couldn't be the man you needed, but I have never once regretted giving you the life you deserved." He sucked in a deep breath to steel himself. "Was he a good husband to you?"

"Yes," she breathed out, so softly that it was barely audible. But his heart heard, and the emotions that crashed over him were a mix of love and fierce protectiveness. Two emotions that he suspected she would always stir inside him. "He was kind and generous. He never spoke a word in anger, never threatened… denied me nothing. We were as happy as could be expected."

The swift stab of jealousy tore through him, and he couldn't find the power to speak. To tell her how glad he was for her. How thrilled he was that she'd lived the wonderful life he'd always wanted for her.

"But I never loved him," she finished. As if compelled, she added, "Not the way I loved you."

That soft confession revealed fully to him all he'd lost by letting her go, and instant mourning for that life nearly brought him to his knees. But he needed to ask the question whose answer he feared most—"Do you hate me?"

Her heartbeat's hesitation nearly broke him.

Then she gave a soft shake of her head against his shoulder. "How can I hate you when you loved me so much?"

His eyes stung, and he squeezed them shut. Her voice lacked conviction, but she'd said the words, and he'd desperately needed to hear them. Hope stirred inside his hollow chest that he'd be able to eventually persuade her to forgive him. No matter how long it took.

"Maxwell." His name was a plea for compassion, an entreaty to give her guidance as to what to believe about him.

He cupped her face in his palm and rasped out, "I never stopped loving you, Belinda, even after you forgot about me. You need to know that."

Her hands twisted his uniform in her fists, and her heart pounded against his chest as she pressed into him. "I never forgot you, you damnable fool," she chastised in a gentle whisper. "Not one day."

Both seeking absolution and giving solace, he touched his lips to hers.

She inhaled sharply at the tender contact but didn't pull back. Instead, she softly returned the kiss, her trembling lips moving tentatively beneath his.

In that kiss he tasted the forgiveness he sought. More, that kiss held a second chance at the future they'd been denied, with Belinda back in his arms. Where she'd always belonged.

* * *

"Give me a second chance," he whispered entreatingly against her lips.

A second chance? Belinda pulled away and stared at him. His quiet declaration simply stunned her.

Taking her surprised reaction as an invitation, he reached up to trace his thumb over her chin and back along her jaw. That small touch of affection sped through her, blazing a trail of warmth and need in its wake.

"Seeing you again and holding you in my arms makes me realize how much I still want a life with you. The one we'd planned." His deep murmur seeped into her, filling her with the happiness she remembered. "Say that you'll forgive me and give me that chance."

She pressed her fist to her chest to physically calm her racing heart. A second chance with Maxwell… All of her yearned to have just that— the life with him that they'd been denied. She was still drawn to him as strongly as ever. Perhaps even more now that she knew the truth about why he'd broken off with her, now that she knew how much he'd loved her. At that moment, with Maxwell holding her in his arms, she could almost believe the past ten years and all the grief had never happened. As if anything could be possible again.

And yet…

"If you're saying all this only to gain my support for the academy, it won't work," she warned, putting voice to her worst fears that all this was only a lie. That the second chance he wanted was simply another opportunity to break her heart.

"Then how about to gain your love?"

Did he really mean… *love?* She was too stunned to answer as he brought his lips to hers again and kissed away her surprise.

Despite her reservations, she sighed as his mouth moved gently against hers. At first, the kiss was tender and hesitant, then growing more bold with each passing heartbeat in which she didn't stop him from claiming more. How could she, when this was exactly what she'd always wanted, what she'd longed for years to experience just once more? His lips on hers, the masculine taste of his kiss, his strong arms slipping around her to draw her against him…

She surrendered with a whisper. "Maxwell."

All those kisses he'd given her in the past had been nothing like this. For heaven's sake, she could *taste* the difference in him. The maturity that the years had brought to him, the tempering of experience, even an underlying patience that certainly hadn't been there before—it all worked together to sweep her away, until there was only the strength of him beneath her fingertips as she splayed her hands over his shoulders, only his presence filling her senses until she shivered.

When she melted against him, boneless in his arms, a groan sounded from the back of his throat, and his tongue plunged between her lips to capture all of her kiss. She reveled in his need for her and enjoyed her own answering passion. A passion that now had her stroking her tongue over the length of his and encouraging him to claim even more.

"Belinda," he rasped out. Awe laced through his voice, as if he couldn't quite believe that she was real.

"Yes," she whispered. *I'm real. I'm here with you. The way I always wanted to be.*

He kissed down her neck to her collarbone. He tongued the pulse pounding wildly in the little hollow at the base of her throat before trailing his mouth lower to the scooped neckline of her dress.

Belinda wrapped her arms around his shoulders and clung to him, rolling back her head with sheer delight.

"Dear God, how good you feel." He nuzzled his face against her shoulder. "I'd forgotten how soft you are, how tempting... how much I missed you."

As if to prove his words, his hands caressed up her body to her breasts to strum his thumbs against her hardening nipples through the dress. He'd touched her like this before when they'd been courting, but his hands hadn't been as expert then. His attentions had never been on her as intently as they were now to gauge every reaction he drew from her, no matter how small.

Belinda shamelessly arched herself against him, wishing her clothes weren't between them. Wishing her body was bare to his eyes, his hands, his mouth... wishing he was working to quench the burning ache throbbing between her thighs now instead of so devilishly stoking it with each touch and kiss. She was a widow and knew what intimate pleasures a man could bring to a woman. But only Maxwell could make her heart ache just as fiercely with love as he made her body burn with desire.

"I—I missed you, too," she forced out the admission between increasingly harder breaths that were quickly becoming pants.

Lifting her onto his lap, he buried his face against her cleavage with chuckle. "Only *missed*, hmm?"

He licked into the valley between her breasts in a brazen allusion to what he would do if he could strip her dress off her right there in the supply room. If he could lie her back on the flour bags and feast on her as if she were one of the exotic dishes he'd presented to her at the picnic. She couldn't fight off a soft moan as that deliciously wicked image filled her mind. For one desperate moment, she wanted him to do exactly that.

Then he audaciously tugged down her neckline, and she gasped. The tight stays and chemise beneath made it impossible for him to set free her entire breast, but her nipple was visible to his hungry eyes, then to his greedy lips as he captured it in his mouth and suckled her.

"Perhaps—" She forced out the admission chokingly between alternating gasps of surprise and whimpers of need as he tortured her with sucks, licks, and soft bites. "Perhaps it was... a bit more... than simply missing."

He smiled against her flesh, and the devilish expression curled liquid flame through her, so hot that her thighs clenched. She watched without a trace of shame as his mouth worshipped at her breast, as he rolled her nipple between his teeth and then placed a delicate kiss to the sensitive point.

"Good," he purred as his mouth captured hers in a languid yet sultry kiss that held the promise of all the wanton things he wanted to do to her. "Because I sure as hell longed for you." His words were an enticing torment. "So many sleepless nights when you were all I could think about, when I wanted nothing more in the world than to spend just one night making love to you."

She closed her eyes against the pleasure he gave her and against the soft confession poised on the tip of her tongue that she'd wanted the same.

"Give me a second chance." He nipped at her neck in an erotic cajoling that pulled straight through her, down to the ache building between her thighs. "Let me prove to you the man I've become."

"Yes," she whispered breathlessly.

A deep sigh swept through him as his shoulders sagged and his forehead rested against hers. He placed another tender kiss to her lips. Then he pulled away, climbing quickly to his feet.

She fluttered her eyes open, confused. A surge of cold loss passed through her with a shudder. He was... *leaving?* After giving her the most thrilling kisses of her life?

As if reading her mind, he leaned over to touch his lips to hers. Then he murmured in a husky voice that was more promise than explanation, "If we don't leave now, I'll have no choice but to make love to you right here."

His audacity sparked a low heat inside her, and she nearly begged him to do just that.

"You'll not have to worry about dinner with Pomperly then if anyone should happen along and find us." His lips quirked into a lazy grin. "The scandal of it would drum me right out of the army and keep you from ever being invited to a royal affair again."

A bubble of laughter spilled from her, and she didn't fight his help in rising to her feet, straightening her dress, and leading her from the supply room. Or how he wrapped her arm around his to escort her back toward the gate, walking so closely to her that he could whisper in her ear simply by lowering his head... whispers of love and desire that stirred such happiness and longing through her that her insides melted.

Everything had changed between them.

Again.

CHAPTER FIVE

Max watched Belinda over the rim of his wineglass. His attention tonight focused solely on her, despite being in the company of sixty other guests at His Majesty's small dinner in the Pavilion's grand banqueting hall.

He couldn't tear his eyes away from her. Dressed in a gown of dark blue silk that shimmered beneath the lamplight of the three-tiered crystal chandeliers, she was simply radiant. Her skin was luminescent against the sapphires she wore around her neck and at her ears, made to appear even more satin-soft by the curls of her auburn hair piled high onto her head. Every inch of her was perfection, and he couldn't help but wonder if she'd taken such care with her appearance tonight because of him. Because this was the first time he'd seen her in all her formal splendor.

But knowing Belinda, it wasn't to show herself off or titillate with how breathtaking she was. No. It was an imperious warning of exactly what he was getting himself into with such a powerful duchess.

Yet she had no idea how proud he was of the woman she'd become. Or how captivated he was by her.

She belonged at his side. Tonight proved that. A connection stretched between them like a ribbon tying them together. One that had always been there, even during the years when half the world—and her marriage—had been between them.

She felt it, too, based upon the way she'd leaned close to him during the reception in the saloon before dinner, when she'd not removed her hand from his arm even as they'd chatted with the other guests. The little gesture was just possessive enough to spin heated arrogance through him to think that every other man in the room wanted to be in his boots tonight when he escorted her home. Alone. Even now, seated by precedence at opposite ends of the massive table, she took surreptitious glances in his direction.

Another glance... He rakishly raised a brow as his lips curled in private innuendo.

Caught, she quickly turned away, but not before a flustered blush pinked her cheeks.

Seated beside her, Pomperly narrowed his eyes in irritation. But Max only gave the man a slow, confident smile, and the duke haughtily lifted his nose into the air.

Her rank as a duchess had put Belinda right beside Pomperly, despite her scheme to be free of him. Against Belinda's best attempts to keep conversation balanced between guests on her left and right sides, Pomperly was always turned toward her in his effort to monopolize her attention. But he never managed to keep it long before her gaze strayed once more down the table.

Surprisingly, Max felt not one jot of jealousy toward Pomperly. Belinda was on his arm tonight, and his world pulsed electric because of it.

The last course finished. Everyone stood, the women to go through to the saloon and the gentlemen to rise in courtesy to the women.

Seizing the moment, Max circled the table to come up behind her and stopped her with a touch to her elbow. Then he leaned down to bring his mouth close to her ear so that he wouldn't be overheard.

With an amused roll of her eyes, she interrupted before he could speak, "If you're going to say that I'm lovely, then—"

"Not lovely."

That surprised her. She glanced at him, wide-eyed, over her shoulder.

"Tonight, you're simply breathtaking," he murmured. She'd always appreciated bluntness, so... "I'm out of my mind with desire for you."

She caught her breath. That soft inhalation pulsed through her and into him, warming him through with a longing he hadn't felt in ten years.

"I want nothing more tonight than to get you alone to prove it," he admitted quietly.

For a moment, she didn't move, letting that possibility whirl inside her mind. Then she admonished gently in a breathless whisper, "Maxwell, the pensioners…"

"Let them find their own women," he teased, purposefully diverting her from the objection she was about to raise, the problem that now stood between them like a wall. "I want you all to myself, Belinda." Hospitals and academies be damned. After spending the evening in her presence, seeing the sparkle in her eyes and hearing the soft lilt of her laughter, his patience hung by a thread. It was all he could do not to toss her over his shoulder at this very moment, to march her straight down to the beach and make love to her. "And I intend to have you."

He released her elbow and stepped back before he lingered too long and gained unwanted attention from the other guests.

Not daring to look at her again, now that he'd made a frontal charge and significantly raised the stakes of the attraction between them, he snatched up a cigar and bottle of port from trays carried into the room by half a dozen footmen. But he knew she was staring, because he could feel the heat of her bewildered gaze on him the entire time she slowly left the room to join the ladies.

"So it's Brigadier Thorpe, is it?"

He didn't recognize the voice at his side as he turned back toward the table. But he should have known—

The Duke of Pomperly, who had clearly sought him out on purpose during these few moments when the men were all changing seats and settling in for conversation over port and cigars.

"Yes, Your Grace." Max smiled coolly as he set the bottle of port on the table, claiming a new chair halfway down the table but still toward the bottom of the hierarchy. "I don't think we've yet had the pleasure of being introduced."

"Surprising, since we have such a dear friend in common." He ignored the opening for proper introductions and plucked at an invisible piece of lint on his kerseymere coat sleeve. "Her Grace seems quite enamored of you."

Dear God, he hoped so! "We've known each other for years."

If Pomperly caught the territorial presumption in that casual reply, he didn't show it. "General Mortimer assures me that you're very well respected within the ranks. That he knows no one else currently serving His Majesty who is as fine a soldier as you."

Max reached for the brazier the footman placed in front of him to light his cigar. "General Mortimer is too generous."

"He also feels that you would be the perfect man for the new post in Africa." Pomperly tugged at his jacket sleeves, his old-fashioned ruffled cuffs getting in the way. "Whoever gets that position will be a very fortunate man. His career opportunities will be endless."

A warning pricked at his gut. "A very fortunate man, indeed."

And a man who wasn't him. His future was right here, in Brighton.

Pomperly's attention returned to the invisible lint on his sleeve. "You should know that I have connections within the War Office and, of course, as you've seen tonight, a close relationship with His Majesty."

Max's gaze flicked across the room to King George, who most likely wasn't even aware that Pomperly was in attendance.

"I'm also an old friend of the duchess." Pomperly's nose tilted into the air with an arrogant pride. "A very *dear* friend, you understand."

Max tensed at the innuendo that Belinda's acquaintance with the duke was an intimate one, unprepared for the hot jealousy that flashed through him. And for his pity for the duke that immediately followed, because Pomperly was a fool to think that Belinda would ever give herself to a man like him.

"I could help you acquire the Africa post."

Ah, there it was! The reason Pomperly had sought him out.

"I would be happy to put in a good word for you."

Yes, Max was quite certain of it. After all, it would be damned hard for him to interfere in the duke's pursuit of Belinda if he was in Africa.

"I appreciate your generosity, but I'm committed to the Brighton academy." He puffed at the cigar, sending a cloud of smoke into the air. Then he pointed it at Pomperly and smiled. "But I'll be certain to let Her Grace know of your offer… when I escort her home tonight."

Snatching up the bottle of port, Max walked away, ending the conversation before Pomperly said something that made him pummel the man senseless and get himself court-martialed.

Blowing out a hard sigh, he sank into an empty chair near General Mortimer and poured himself a glass. He nearly laughed to see his shaking hand, which was trembling with equal desire to both punch Pomperly and to caress Belinda.

Then he leaned back in the chair, letting his pounding heart slowly return to its normal beat. At *that* he did chuckle to himself. Because nothing about his heart would ever be normal again.

If he successfully established the academy, he would be promoted, and everything he'd ever wanted would be his. A successful career in the army, a post in England...

But not Belinda. The one thing he wanted most of all.

He thought he'd put the past behind him and found a way to move on without her. But that was before he'd seen her again. Before he'd kissed her and remembered all the reasons why he'd once fallen in love with her. And why a part of him had never stopped.

Yet old scars often gave way to new wounds, and if he couldn't find a compromise for the hospital and academy—and soon—he feared he would lose her all over again.

Led by the king, the gentlemen launched into animated stories about horses and hounds, as was to be expected in after-dinner conversation, along with the more bawdy stories that were certain to follow once the port was half gone. In Africa or India or England, whether of rank or not—none of that made any difference whenever a group of men gathered after dinner. The stories were all the same, the boasts just as unbelievable, the jokes just as coarse. Only the fineness of their clothes and the quality of their drink signified any difference.

Including King George, who was proving himself to be the loudest and bawdiest of all. Max had never been in such close proximity to His Majesty before tonight. Despite being a baron's son, he'd certainly never moved in the kinds of circles that gave access to royalty, and he wasn't prepared for the way the king insisted that the men behave as if this were no different from any other after-dinner gathering in any other gentleman's house.

The forced sense of casualness should have unnerved him, along with the way Pomperly continued to send him narrowed glares when the duke wasn't doing his best to ingratiate himself with the king. But all he could think about was Belinda and how beautiful she looked tonight. How flustered she'd become when he said he wanted her. How much he longed to hold her in his arms and caress her, to taste her sweetness and hear the soft mewlings of pleasure that would fall from her lips—

He rose to his feet. "Would you excuse me for a moment, Your Majesty?"

No one cared that he'd breached protocol by addressing the sovereign before the king had spoken to him. Least of all King George, who waved a drunken hand in his direction to signal that he didn't care what Max did.

"Unable to tolerate all the fine food and drink, eh, Thorpe?" General Mortimer called out. "Thought His Majesty's officers were made of stronger stuff than that!"

He laughed good-naturedly, not falling for the bait. "I'd like to catch a bit of air to clear my head before we return to the ladies." He paused just long enough for effect before adding, "As Her Grace's escort, it's best to have all my wits about me."

The men laughed at that, having been on the receiving end of Belinda's razor-sharp wit themselves. Except for Pomperly, whose mouth tightened into a hard line.

Even as Max sauntered from the room, his mind whirled to figure out a way to clear Belinda from his head long enough to get through the evening without embarrassing—

He stopped. And slowly smiled.

Belinda waited in the hallway, as if they'd planned a rendezvous.

"Tired already of all those pleasures you men insist on keeping secret from us ladies?" Despite her teasing, an unspoken challenge laced through her words.

He stalked toward her, shamelessly raking his gaze over her. His gut twisted, the urge to possess her so strong that he throbbed with it. "Those aren't the pleasures I'm craving tonight."

As he stepped in front of her, so close that he could feel her body warming his, she replied in a throaty murmur, "What pleasures would those be... exactly?"

"The kind that will leave you breathless and begging." Not caring if a passing footman might see, he lifted his hand to shamelessly caress the side of her breast.

The heated tone to his voice was undeniable, even to his own ears. But then, all of him was on fire as he dared to strum his thumb over her nipple through the silk of her dress and draw it into a hard point.

She forced out between pants, "I don't beg... for anything."

Grinning at her obstinate pride, he slid his hand down her body to clasp hers and promised wickedly, "You will."

Then he strode away, pulling her quickly behind him as he led her deeper into the palace. His willing captive.

When they reached the end of the long gallery, he shot a quick glance behind them to make certain no one would see where they'd gone.

Snatching up the candle from the wall sconce, he led her inside the dark waiting room near the king's apartments, then closed and locked the door.

He backed her against the door and kissed her. A whimper fell from her lips, and a glorious sensation of triumph poured through him. She wanted him as much as he did her, both physically and emotionally, her heart eagerly waiting for him to reclaim it.

He let the fierce possessiveness he felt for her invade his kiss, certain from the way she trembled that she could taste it in him. *Good.* Because nothing and no one—not a post in Africa, not a hospital or academy, not even another damned duke—was going to take her away from him again.

* * *

"I plan on giving you all kinds of pleasures tonight, my love," Max purred. "But we'll start with this." Then he licked his tongue around the outer curl of her ear and sent a shiver of raw need coiling through her to land in a heated ache between her legs.

A soft moan fell from her lips. She could barely believe this was happening, that he was here with her, kissing her. That he wasn't simply a dream from which she would awaken into tears, exactly as she'd done countless times before. But he *was* real, and so were the liquid flames of need heating through her.

He'd changed. He wasn't the same man she'd fallen in love with all those years ago—he was *better.* The connection between them was stronger than ever, so was the desire to physically reveal the emotional bond that had never vanished. She loved him, always had. If possible, she loved him even more than before, now that she'd seen firsthand his dedication to his men, now that she'd experienced first-hand his strength and resilience.

He'd asked for a second chance, and as the old feelings engulfed her anew, she offered up a silent prayer that he'd take this opportunity to love her… tonight and always. Which was why she didn't stop him when his hands shoved up behind her to unfasten the tiny pearl buttons holding her bodice snugly in place.

The silk sagged over her breasts, then fell away completely as he swept his hands over her shoulders and pushed the soft material down her arms, baring her to the flickering shadows of candlelight.

A low growl sounded from the back of his throat as his hot gaze raked over her. "You're not wearing stays."

She wasn't wearing *anything* beneath the silk except for stockings. This dress fit too tightly, its specially made bodice reinforced to lift her bosom and hold it in place. She'd chosen this dress tonight precisely because of that, hoping in the secret recesses of her heart that something exactly like this would happen.

But now that it was—

She inhaled a nervous breath and asked softly, "Am I... am I what you'd imagined?"

"No," he admitted. That single word seared through her, nearly undoing her before he added, "You're more beautiful than I'd ever dreamed."

Happiness burst through her. The way she'd always imagined this moment was nothing compared to the heated reality of it, with his smoldering gaze lingering over her flesh as if he'd never seen a woman before. Her nipples drew up taut as he drank in the sight of her, and arching her back as a wave of female power surged through her, she shamelessly let him look his fill.

Then she granted him the permission he sought. "Give me the pleasure of your touch, Maxwell."

"Like this?" He lightly traced his thumb over her nipple. Barely a touch at all, but electricity jolted through her. As he continued to circle her in a reverent, featherlight caress, a damp heat grew between her thighs.

She bit back a pleading whimper, wanting more. He obliged and claimed her breasts in both hands, her fullness nearly spilling over as he massaged them against his palms.

She gasped as he lowered his head to take one between his lips and suck. Oh, simply exquisite! She brought her hands to the back of his head and dug her fingers into his soft curls to press his mouth harder against her.

He laughed at her eagerness, and the deep sound rumbled into her. Her breath came so labored now that her breasts rose and fell fiercely against his mouth, and he suckled at her again, this time drawing her deep with each hard suck that left his cheeks hollow from the ferocity of it. She felt each great pull shoot through her to the merciless throbbing at her core, and a low moan tore from her.

"You like that," he murmured against her breast. The tip of his tongue teased at her nipple before he nipped playfully at her.

Oh, she did! But now that he was hers, now that her love for him could be set free, she wanted so much more and panted out in a wicked challenge, "What... other pleasures... do you crave?"

In answer, he grabbed her hands and pinned her arms over her head as his mouth captured hers, surprising her with his swiftness and catching her openmouthed. His tongue plunged between her lips to ravish the kiss in great, deep sweeps of possession.

"This," he rasped hotly against her mouth as he pressed his hips forward into hers. The hard bulge jutting into her lower belly was unmistakable, and she shivered at the tantalizing contact and all the pleasures it implied. "I crave this, with you."

He bent his knees slightly, low enough that when he pressed into her as he rose up, the hard ridge of his erection slid enticingly into the valley between her thighs. The skilled motion caught the top of her crevice and the little nub buried within, grazing across it just hard enough to send an electric tingle spinning through her.

She wasn't an innocent. She knew what his hard body was capable of doing to hers, and she yearned for it. She tightened her arms around his neck, holding her breath in anticipation of another, harder stroke. Her sex clenched tightly even as it longed to be invaded.

But the next stroke didn't come, and her eyes fluttered open in confusion.

As she stared up at him, she realized why he'd hesitated. This moment had to be a meeting of souls and hearts, a meeting of true lovers... a meeting halfway. And it was her turn to express how much she wanted this. How much she wanted *him*, now and for the rest of her life.

She reached a shaking hand down to tug up her skirt, feeling no shame in what she was asking. She grasped his hand and placed it on her inner thigh, mere inches from the hot ache he'd flamed inside her.

"I want your touch." She slowly slid his hand up her leg until it reached her intimate folds, then she guided him in long, slow strokes as she rubbed his palm against her.

Oh, sheer heaven! She couldn't keep from quivering against his fingers in wanton invitation. Only a fleeting embarrassment swept through her that her wetness slicked his hand, so great was her need for him.

"I've longed for this since the first time I laid eyes on you. I wanted your hands on me, exploring, pleasing... My love." She leaned up to place a kiss of permission against his throat. "Touch me."

With a groan, he stroked his hand against her, stealing her breath away and leaving her sagging against the door. All of her yearned for an even greater pleasure, for the release her body begged from his, and she stepped her legs farther apart to claim it.

His finger slipped inside her, and she shivered at the delicious sensation. But his intimate strokes only grew the ache, not quenched it. With a cry of frustration, she thrust her hips forward to meet each stroke of his hand.

But even that wasn't enough. Desperate for release, she wrapped her leg around his, spreading herself even wider. When a second finger filled her, she rolled back her head as the pleasure gripped her. All the tiny muscles inside her clenched down hard around him, greedily drawing him deeper to satiate the unbearable hunger—

With a single flick of his thumb, she broke with a gasping shudder and buried her face in his shoulder to stifle her cry. But he held her close with his arm around her waist as he continued to stroke into her to prolong her climax and give her as much pleasure as possible.

Bliss overtook her, and she fell bonelessly into his arms.

"I craved the pleasure of *you*, Belinda," he murmured against her temple as he slowly peeled off her dress and left her in only her stockings. "Every ounce of your love. Every moment with you."

Then he lifted her into his arms and carried her to a chaise longue. She luxuriated in the feel of the velvet beneath her as she leaned against the sloping back, but not nearly as much as she relished his stare as he stood at her feet and gazed hungrily down at her, removing his cravat and loosening the buttons on his waistcoat. Then he dropped to his knees and rapaciously crawled up the length of velvet cushion toward her, every tigerlike move boldly proclaiming what he intended.

With a sigh of surrender, she closed her eyes and spread her legs. A heartbeat later, his mouth claimed her.

The kiss stole her breath away. Her intimate flesh was already sensitized from his fingers, and this new pleasure nearly undid her. She could scarcely bear the way his lips and tongue plundered her—no, he was *worshipping* her, and it was the most erotic, most exquisite sensation she'd ever experienced.

"I craved you." His hot breath tickled against her. "The pure deliciousness of your heart. The sweetness of the sparkling girl I fell in love with."

Then he placed a single kiss so reverently against her that she couldn't stop a soft sob from escaping her lips.

Yet regret swelled inside her. She wasn't that innocent girl any longer.

Fate had given that innocence to another man, and she would never be able to share that special intimacy with Maxwell now.

Except...

Her heart pounded furiously as the idea struck. She couldn't give him her innocence, but she could give herself to him in a way she'd never given herself to any man before.

She pushed at his shoulder to shift him away as she slipped out from beneath him.

A confused expression clouded his face, but he let her go, only for that look to change to one of predacious hunger when she lowered herself to her knees at the edge of the low-rising chaise and draped herself across the velvet cushion on her belly.

"And I craved *this* with you," she breathed out as she turned her head to look at him. With her hips perched at the edge of the cushion, her bottom rose into the air in decadent enticement, and she spread her knees, offering herself to be taken.

"Please, Maxwell," she begged. "I've waited so long for you, for this moment... please. Let me give myself to you, just like this."

All of him shook fiercely with desire and emotion as he slid himself over behind her. "Are you certain?"

The sweetness of his hesitation nearly broke her. She nodded and rested her head on her folded arms. "But I've never before..."

Her breathless words were so soft that she wasn't sure he'd heard, until he leaned up to place a tender kiss between her shoulder blades. As his large hand caressed a slow and possessive circle over her bare back, she knew that he understood what she was offering. That he was experiencing this special moment as magically as she.

She closed her eyes in anticipation as she felt him rise up on his knees behind her and reach between them to unfasten the fall of his breeches. A tremor shivered through her when he slowly slid his erection between her thighs and against her folds. He grew slippery from her wetness. Each smooth glide across the length of her cleft made her quiver with need, each push forward brought his tip to tease at the aching nub buried within.

A whimper of need strangled in her throat. She writhed against the edge of the chaise, less to ease the fire inside her than to tempt him into giving her the release she craved... his body inside hers, making love to her. "Maxwell, please!"

This time when he slid forward, he changed the angle of his hips and pushed inside her. Her body expanded around his, and she moaned with pleasure as he moved deeper, sinking into her until his pelvis pressed against her buttocks, until he was sheathed completely in her tight warmth. She inhaled a ragged breath, wanting to engrave upon her mind the exquisite sensation of having him inside her, filling her completely. When he clasped her hips and began to stroke—oh, it was simply heaven!

She'd dreamed for years about Max making love to her, but nothing in all those fantasies compared to this. Because this was so much more than physical pleasure. This was a meeting of hearts and souls, an exchange of the strength and resilience that underpinned the affection they shared.

This was pure love. And it undid her.

Her hands gripped tightly onto the cushion as she welcomed his hard thrusts that brought him as deep inside her as possible, filling her body with his and inundating her senses with the raw masculinity of him—the scent of port and tobacco, the rough friction of his breeches rubbing against the backs of her thighs, the hardness of his muscles as he strained into her.

With a plaintive moan, she pushed back to meet each oncoming thrust with one of her own, until he shoved his hand between her belly and the edge of the chaise to search for the aching, swollen nub buried there. His finger delved down, stroking against it hard and fast, relentlessly—

"Maxwell!" The choking cry tore from her as her hips bucked up against him and her thighs spasmed.

She shattered, a shivering and shaking climax that sent ripples of bliss pouring through her.

"I love you!" She arched into him as she tossed back her head and let her release claim her. "I love you so much!"

He grabbed her hips, holding her tightly to him as he gave a final thrust deep inside her. She gasped at the desperate sensation of vulnerability that pierced her, only to shatter a second time when she heard the low groan of his own release, when she felt him jerk inside her and spill himself. Her greedy body drank him in, quivering around him as he strained to empty every drop of himself inside her—giving her every bit of his heart and soul.

Whispering her name, he collapsed on top of her. His body folded over hers, enveloping her beneath him as his strong arms went around her and gathered her close, his cheek resting against her bare back. As if he never wanted to let go.

Sheer happiness blossomed inside her. There would be more battles between them, more conflict over the hospital and the academy in the days to come. But at that moment, held safe in his arms, she knew he loved her.

CHAPTER SIX

Max sat sprawled across the chaise longue and watched Belinda dress, certain he'd never been happier in his life.

She loved him. He could barely fathom it. But she was also giving him the opportunity to prove that he deserved her. In that, he'd never let her down again.

He pushed himself to his feet and leisurely approached her to button up her dress. But he couldn't help slipping his arms around her waist and bringing her back against him. He placed a lingering kiss to her nape and smiled against her flesh when he felt her tremble.

"If you keep that up," she warned as she straightened her bodice and smoothed down her skirt, "we might very well end up right back on the chaise."

He groaned at the temptation. "While I would love nothing more"— he took another kiss before stepping back—"we need to return to the party before we're missed."

She laughed, her eyes gleaming at him in the mirror over the fireplace as she fixed her hair. "Not at one of King George's dinners." She reached up to pin her hair into place. "Before this evening is over, half the guests will be finding their own unused rooms."

"Is that what Pomperly hoped with you?" Oddly enough, he felt not one prick of jealousy.

"Most likely." She twisted a stubborn curl into place and pinned it securely. "But it would have been a very cold day in Brighton before I fell for his entreaties."

"You fell for mine."

She smiled like the cat that got into the cream. "Because yours are irresistible."

In reply, he lifted her hand to his lips and placed a kiss to her palm. Goose bumps sprang up along her arms. Like magic.

"If you keep that up," she repeated, her voice suddenly husky, "we won't need the chaise."

When she cast a meaningful glance at the rug in front of the fireplace, all kinds of deliciously wicked thoughts spun through his mind.

If she kept saying things like that, he might very well have her naked again before she could speak his name. Reluctantly, he released her hand and stepped away.

"The next time I make love to you," he promised, "will be in a soft bed with all the silks, velvets, and down you deserve."

Turning back toward the mirror as her cheeks pinked, she tried to hide the effect that his comment had on her by focusing on the last hairpin. But she couldn't hide her breathlessness as she asked as casually as she could muster in mid-blush, "So there's going to be a next time?"

"That depends." His heart stuttered. He was afraid of her answer. "Do you want there to be?"

Her gaze slid across the room to the chaise. She hesitated before answering, just long enough to lick her lips. "Very much."

His restraint broke. He closed the distance between them with a single step and had her back in his arms, his mouth ravishing hers, before she could finish her soft gasp of surprise. The sound changed into a throaty moan, and he drank it in, reveling in the happiness she sparked inside him. *Never* had he met another woman like her, and he never would again.

When she arched her breasts against his chest, he groaned with frustration. "We can't, love."

She twirled her fingers in his hair. "Oh, I think we can."

He laughed and wrapped his arms around her to pull her into a large hug. He nuzzled her hair. "We didn't take precautions," he reminded her gently, although not regretting making love to her. "We can't take that risk again."

She stiffened in his arms, then slowly pulled back. "You don't know? I thought everyone knew…" She turned away as she explained softly, "I'm barren."

He cupped her face in his hands, gently forcing her to look back at him. "Why do you say that?"

A brave smile tugged at her lips in what she must have thought was the proper expression for grim acceptance. The same way experienced soldiers sometimes smiled before the inevitability of battle. "I must be, to have been married for so long and not gotten with child."

"It takes two to create a child. Perhaps Winchester couldn't father children."

She gave a sad shake of her head. "I didn't get with child tonight." Then, slipping out of his arms to turn back to the mirror and finish the last adjustments to her hair, she forced out teasingly, "So you'll have to find another way to get me to marry you."

When she reached for her discarded gloves, the shaking in her hand was unmistakable. So was the grief over not having children.

"Then how about because we love each other?" he quietly proposed.

She froze, the first glove halfway on her hand. Sudden tension filled the room, and a long, awkward silence passed between them before she busied herself again with tugging her glove the rest of the way on.

"You don't have to say that. Just because we…" She gestured with the gloved hand in the general direction of the chaise longue. "I don't expect marriage."

"Too bad. Because I do."

She startled. The other silk glove slipped through her fingers and piled softly on the floor at her feet.

He picked it up, then took her hand and slowly helped her into it. A satisfied warmth twined through him. Who knew that dressing a woman could be as erotic as *un*dressing her?

"You—" She forced out the words, moon-eyed, "You truly want to marry me?"

"Always have." He lifted her hand and kissed her gloved fingertips. "I was hoping you wanted the same."

"I do, but…" The soft whisper died on her lips.

"The pensioners." He knew her nearly as well as he knew himself.

She nodded, her worry about the men darkening her eyes. He loved her all the more that she would so selflessly think of a group of old men in the middle of his marriage proposal.

"I cannot marry you, Max," she said achingly, as if the words pained her. "If we cannot find a way to save the hospital, then this will always be between us. I'll never be able to look at you without thinking of them, how you were sent to remove them and how I couldn't stop that."

Her words twisted inside him like a knife. The academy was still wedged between them, the tension surrounding it as thick as ever. "I'm not giving you up, Belinda. So we're just going to have to find a way."

With a faint nod, she echoed quietly, "We'll find a way." But doubt furrowed her beautiful brow, and she said the words as if she didn't fully believe them.

Yet, for the first time, she spoke as if they were working together to find compromise rather than as adversaries. She was acknowledging the possibility of a future together. And he liked it. A great deal.

"I've been thinking." She tentatively bit her bottom lip. "The academy needs to be opened too quickly for the War Office to construct new buildings, correct? Which is why you need the hospital."

"Correct."

"So the cadets cannot be moved to another building. But what if the pensioners could?" Her face shone with hope. "What if we found another building that could be turned into a home for them? That way, they could all stay together, right here in Brighton."

He took her hands in his and gave them a sympathetic squeeze as she eagerly waited for his reaction to what she was certain was a grand compromise but which in reality wouldn't work. "The War Office would never agree to the expense of purchasing and maintaining a second property, not when there are other hospitals where the men could be sent."

Her slender shoulders sagged as her hopes were dashed. "Then what do we do?"

"We find a solution." He touched his lips to hers. "Together."

She nodded and stepped into his embrace.

He rested his cheek against her hair and sighed out a silent breath. Thank God she didn't ask how, because he didn't have a bloody clue. But even as he held her encircled in his arms, he knew he would lose her if they didn't.

* * *

As Belinda had predicted, no one paid any attention when they slipped into the saloon to rejoin the party, least of all His Majesty. He was too busy staring at Lady Roquefort's bosom to care about anything at that point, except how to be rid of Lord Roquefort.

They entered separately, of course, and fifteen minutes apart, for which Belinda was glad. It gave her time to calm her soaring heart and catch her breath before Maxwell could stride into the room and steal it away again.

"Coffee, please." She smiled at the footman as she stepped up to the buffet where tall, silver urns sat surrounded by delicate bone china cups and silver spoons edged with gold. All of it was monogrammed with the king's initials.

"I thought it best to tell you this in private," a deep voice said quietly over her shoulder.

Her smile froze, although her heart stuttered with dread. "Yes, Duke?"

Pomperly gestured with a scowl at the other footman to pour him a cup. "You have my full support with the hospital."

Relief poured through her, and her smile turned genuine. "Thank you, Pomperly."

"Of course, my dear. I know how much that place means to you."

"To the pensioners, you mean." She accepted her coffee from the footman. She would still have to fight an uphill battle to persuade the War Office to keep the men here in Brighton, but at least now she had an ally. "Your support will help convince the rest of the board."

"And I'm hoping that the new post in Africa will help convince Thorpe," he muttered as he sniffed at his own coffee. "I plan to send a letter to Lord Palmerston."

She frowned, not understanding. "The secretary?"

Taking a sip of coffee, he smirked. "He's a close acquaintance. If I tell him how much Thorpe is hoping to be reassigned to the new African command, I'm certain he'll send the brigadier off packing immediately for Egypt and spare your hospital. That's why he's here, after all, pressing so hard for his academy."

"You've misunderstood." She gave a faint laugh, despite the prickle of unease that rose inside her. "Brigadier Thorpe wants to start an academy here because he believes soldiers need better training. He's hoping that this academy might save men's lives."

"Is that what you think?" He clucked his tongue as if she were a naïve child who needed to be placated.

"I know so. The brigadier told me himself."

"Then he's lied to you."

The brusqueness of that slammed into her.

Maxwell picked that moment to walk into the room, looking every inch like the commanding officer he'd become during the years they'd been apart. Tall. Strong. Proud. Instead of glancing her way, he approached the group of fellow officers who had gathered by the French doors.

As doubt began to creep into her bones, all pretense of a smile faded. "No, he was quite earnest with me." *Look my way, Maxwell... Make me believe... Dear God, look at me!* "His motivation is to create better officers."

"His motivation is to gain a promotion to major-general." Pomperly set his cup back into his saucer with a jarring clank, as if finding the coffee—and Maxwell—distasteful. "Thorpe couldn't care less about those old men or the cadets. The only man he cares about is himself. Surely you've noticed that. General Mortimer claims he's just as ambitious as when he was younger." He gestured impatiently for the footman to add liqueur to his coffee. "You knew him then. Surely you can see the same in him now."

She lowered the cup from her lips. The coffee tasted like acid on her tongue.

"If he's offered that commanding post in Africa—one that's a jewel in His Majesty's imperial crown—I'm certain he'll accept immediately." He took the freshened cup from the footman. "And forget all about those of us he's left behind in Brighton."

Her stomach tightened into a sickening knot. "You are mistaken." Maxwell had told her that he loved her, that he wanted a second chance with her, that he wanted to marry her...

"Don't be fooled, Belinda. That man will do everything in his power to establish that academy and help himself to a promotion." He lifted the cup to his mouth and mumbled from behind the rim, "Even charm you into believing he's sincere."

Numbness gripped her, except for her heart, which had already started to ache. She clung desperately to what Maxwell had told her, to the tenderness she'd felt when he made love to her, when he asked her to marry him. They *would* be married...

But not until after they found a solution for the pensioners, after he no longer needed her help to establish the academy and secure his promotion.

Her chest burned as she realized what the timing of that meant. And she'd been foolish enough to suggest it.

Yet she forced out, "He would never do as you're suggesting." She *had* to believe that, had to believe that he was a different man now than the one who'd so selfishly used her before. "You're only saying this because you don't like him, because you want to court me yourself."

"I *do* want to court you. But I'm telling you this as a friend who doesn't want to see you be hurt." He gestured around the room with his coffee cup. "But you don't have to believe me. Others will tell you the same. General!" Pomperly called out as General Mortimer circled through the room. "A word, if you please."

The portly general stopped in front of them with a nod to Pomperly and a shallow bow to Belinda. "Your Graces."

"General." Pomperly made the man wait while he took a long sip of coffee, then fussed with his cup as he returned it to its saucer. "I was just commenting about the new African command post, how Brigadier Thorpe would be the perfect man for it."

"Indeed!" Mortimer folded his hands behind his back, which only made his belly jut out farther. "I'd recommend him for it myself, if Thorpe were open to the idea."

Her heart stuttered hopefully. "Then he doesn't want to go to Africa?"

"Heavens, no!" He looked at her as if she'd gone daft. "Deserts and camels, sandstorms and wild beasts... Who in their right mind would want that?"

"Someone who's hoping to be promoted to major-general, I suppose," she prompted gently, fishing for any denial on the general's part that would prove Maxwell's innocence.

Mortimer laughed. "Thorpe has better plans for himself than Africa, I daresay."

She stiffened, her fingers tightening on her cup. "Oh?"

His eyes sparkled with admiration at Maxwell's audacity. "If the creation of the academy goes well, he gets the post he's wanted since the day he purchased his commission." He leaned toward her, as if sharing a grand secret. "London!"

Her gaze darted to Maxwell, whose attention finally wandered away from his group as he glanced around the room, but not yet finding her.

She somehow summoned the strength to ask, "And a promotion to major-general?"

"That goes without saying. He knew he'd be promoted when he made the suggestion to the War Office to open an academy here."

"*He* suggested the academy?" She prayed she'd misunderstood, prayed that this whole conversation was a mistake—

"Directly to the secretary himself."

Dear God… No, that couldn't be. She stared at Maxwell, oblivious to the rest of the room around them, even as his face blurred beneath the hot tears welling in her eyes. Still, she held her head high and somehow managed to replace her well-practiced smile, even as her heart cried out that she was a fool to ever let him back into her trust. But she couldn't react, *had* to keep calm no matter how much she wanted to scream… because she was a duchess, after all. And a duchess would never let the world know that the only man she'd ever loved had once again used that love against her.

"Had an entire proposal worked out, including a six-month timeline for implementation. Said we needed another academy to train officers. Said Brighton was the best place for it and that he knew people on the hospital board he could sway to support his cause." General Mortimer smiled at her, not realizing that he'd just cut out her heart. "He must have meant you, Your Grace."

Somehow, she forced her smile to grow brighter. "He must have." She set aside the coffee before her trembling hands spilled it. Or worse, let it smash against the floor.

"If you'll excuse me." Mortimer sketched a bow that included both of them. "I promised Lady Agnes Sinclair that I'd share with her what's been happening in the Americas." He chuckled with amusement. "The old bird's ready to send the cavalry against the Americans again, just for spite!"

"As good a reason as any, I suppose," Pomperly drawled, lifting his coffee to his lips. Once the general strode away, he added in that same condescending tone as before, "Perhaps now you'll believe me when I say that *I* have your best interests at heart."

Her heart… Nothing was left of it.

"Go away," she whispered, her smile still firmly in place. "I no longer wish for your company."

Pomperly's mouth fell open. "Belinda, how can you—"

"Leave me alone! Tonight and for the rest of my life."

His face turned red, and he gestured at Maxwell with his cup. "You don't mean that you still believe that arrogant bastard's story that he—"

"What I believe is none of your concern." Now that the floodgates had opened, revealing what she truly thought of Pomperly, she found it impossible to hold back the venom, even knowing that he would turn the board against her, that she would lose all support in saving the pensioners' home... but hadn't she been destined to lose this battle from the beginning? "It never has been, and it *never* will be."

"I could have made you a duchess!" he seethed. In his anger, he grasped the coffee so tightly that his fingertips turned as white as the bone china cup.

"I *am* a duchess."

"A barren widow." He laughed scornfully. "Not even a true dowager."

The vitriol behind that snapped her polite patience. "I would rather be a light-skirt than become your duchess." She arched an imperious brow and added, "Although I strongly suspect that there would not be much difference."

Enraged, he slammed down his cup and splashed coffee onto the tablecloth. He glared murderously at her and stalked way, without deigning to spare her a word in reply.

She looked up and saw Maxwell staring at her from across the room. The anguish returned in a brutal blow so fierce that she flinched. She glanced away before tears could fall and give her away to the other guests. None of them would care that she'd given herself physically to him tonight. No, they'd cut her for daring to love him.

Love? She nearly laughed at the bitter irony. Oh, so much more! Because tonight, when happiness had flowed in her veins, she'd dared to imagine a future with him.

His brow furrowed as he stared at her. She couldn't look away. Even with all the pain pulsing through her with each heartbeat, knowing once again that he'd plotted and schemed to use her, she couldn't break the spell that this devil held over her. And most likely always would.

But it didn't mean she had to sell her soul.

Summoning her strength, she walked toward the door, to walk out without a word to anyone, without permission from King George—to just *leave*. To walk into the cool night and disappear into the darkness. To drown herself in misery until no more tears would come. Then, when the pain subsided and she could breathe again, she planned on waging war on Maxwell, the likes of which he'd never seen before in his entire military career. If he thought he could so easily use her again for his own advancement, to harm old soldiers—

A hand at her elbow stopped her. "Belinda."

She sucked in a harsh breath through clenched teeth at the sound of Maxwell's voice, even now having the audacity to twine its way so heatedly down her spine and remind her of all the love she'd thought they'd shared, the coming together of hearts and souls... *Ashes.* It was nothing but ashes!

"Are you well?" Concerned thickened his voice, but was that worry for her or for his precious academy? Did he think that she'd been wounded and needed solace, or had he come over to find out if she'd persuaded Pomperly to protest the closing of the hospital? "Did Pomperly upset you?"

"Yes," she answered, not turning to face him. She somehow found the strength to remain calm. "As a matter of fact, he did."

He stiffened imperceptibly, but she could feel it. God help her, she noticed everything about this man, and always had. It devastated her that she was still so connected to him that she couldn't stop it, even now.

"What did he say?"

"He told me the real reason why you're in Brighton." Her numb lips surprised her by being able to form words. "Why you want this academy."

"To save men's lives." The same excuse he'd given her from the beginning.

The same excuse she could no longer bear! "To earn a promotion and new post in London, you mean. After all, that was why you proposed the academy to the War Office in the first place, wasn't it?"

She glanced over her shoulder, needing to see his reaction. Needing to sear closed the fresh wounds he'd given her tonight.

He tightened his jaw, not denying it. With each damning heartbeat's silence that passed, the burning anguish inside her grew more intolerable. All the while, she was keenly aware of the room around her, of the guests who might be watching and waiting for her to show any sign of vulnerability that they could use against her.

"Such an easy plan for your success... convince the board to support the academy, and you get to return to London as England's glorious hero. All you have to do is cast out a few dozen old men from their home." Then she forced out, each word a knife to her heart—"And pretend you love me."

His fingers tightened on her arm. "*That* is not true."

"Stop lying!" She'd been such a fool to believe his words of affection. But no longer. "I know why you're here—why you're with me tonight—why you... why you..." Oh God, she couldn't even say it! *Why you seduced me.* "Because once again you wanted to advance your career at the cost of my heart."

"What I wanted, Belinda—what I have always wanted—is *you.*"

"No. You want an academy so you can be promoted and assigned to London, and you want it so badly that *you* approached the War Office with the idea for it." Only summoning all her strength kept her from clenching her hands into fists. "General Mortimer explained everything."

"*Not* everything." He stiffly glanced at the other guests to gauge whether he and Belinda were drawing attention. But anyone who happened to glance their way would see nothing out of place. Just two old friends and dinner companions looking as if they were discussing how long they wanted to remain at the party tonight after the king retired. "This is neither the time nor place for this discussion." He gestured toward the open French doors. "Walk with me in the garden, and we'll talk."

"Never." She would *never* let herself be alone with him again.

"Give me the chance to explain. Because I do love you, Belinda. I always have."

"No." She blinked rapidly, needing all of her will to keep back her tears. "*Not* always."

His head snapped back, that harsh reminder striking him like a slap.

"When did you realize that you were losing the fight over the academy, Maxwell, and that you had to increase your attack in order to win against me? That you needed to do more than throw a picnic?"

"Is that what you think tonight was?" Subtly, so that no one else would see, he pulled lightly at her glove to remind her of how he'd stripped her bare. "That I seduced you in order to win you over?"

She pulled her arm away so he couldn't touch her. "I learn well from my experiences, and you used me once before. Why should I think you're no longer that selfish cad, when you're simply repeating all the motions?" Despite the heat of her anger, her blood turned to ice. "Congratulations, Maxwell, you've proven yourself to be a bastard." Her voice cracked as she added, "Again."

Unable to stand the torture of this evening a moment more, she walked on through the door and out of the palace.

CHAPTER SEVEN

"Oh no, you don't!" With the fear of losing her already pounding away inside him, Max caught up with Belinda just as she reached the line of carriages waiting in front of the palace. "You are *not* leaving."

She hurried to her carriage. "I'll claim illness. His Majesty will understand."

"I don't give a damn about His Majesty." That drew a wide-eyed reaction from the tiger who opened the door for her that bore the Winchester insignia. The same door that Max wanted to drive his fist through. With an angry grimace, he waved the man away and took her arm to help her into the carriage himself. "I care about *you*, Belinda."

"You can stop with the empty flattery." She yanked her arm away and stepped up into the compartment unassisted. "There's no point in it now."

"More than you realize." Without invitation, he swung inside and shut the door, calling out to the driver, "Go!"

The carriage jerked to a start as it moved away from the palace, fast enough to keep her from jumping out to flee. Although, based on her furious expression in the light of the carriage lamps, not fast enough to keep her from shoving him out.

"You are wrong." He leaned across the compartment toward her, elbows on knees and hands clasped to keep from reaching for her. "About everything."

"Then deny it," she challenged. "Deny that you approached the War Office with the idea of turning the hospital into an academy."

"I can't," he snapped out, matching her rising anger. "Because I did go to Palmerston with the proposal."

"Because you wanted a promotion."

"Because I grew tired of watching good men die! Of hearing the cries of boys barely old enough to grow beards calling out for their mothers and sweethearts as they lay dying in the mud, coughing up blood with each gasping breath, missing arms and legs, faces blown off—" He let loose a curse he never should have uttered in front of a woman. "All of them terrified and in pain, frightened even more by the cries of others who were dying around them, the screams of horses, the artillery still firing in the distance." He looked down at his hands as they shook. In his mind, he could still see the face of every man whose hand he'd held while they died. "And you can do nothing but pray they die quickly, to put you out of the misery of their pain."

Even in the dim light, he saw her face pale. Yet her eyes remained just as disbelieving. "But you also did it for yourself, so you could be promoted. Which was why you picked *this* hospital, wasn't it? Because you told them that you had connections on the board that would make it easier to garner support."

"I do. Colonel Woodhouse, for one. We served together in Nassau. And the other men on the board who served in the military, who have connections to the War Office." His eyes fixed hard on hers. "But I did *not* mean you."

She gave a bitter laugh. "You knew I was still involved with the hospital. You had to know that I would be here."

"I didn't know for certain." Then he admitted, "But I'd hoped."

"So you could seduce me if your plans went awry?" She tore off her gloves and slapped them onto the bench beside her. "You *used* me, Maxwell. For the second time, you let me believe that you loved me only to advance your career."

That accusation was brutal, but not nearly as shattering as watching the tear slip down her cheek. His breath caught like fire in his chest at the sight of her pain.

"I came here so I could see with my own eyes that you've had a good life," he said quietly, in agony that he couldn't reach for her without making everything worse. "That the choice I made to let Collins have you wasn't for nothing."

"Let Collins have me?" she repeated, as if she'd misheard. As if begging to be told that she'd misunderstood.

But he didn't deny it, letting the true meaning behind that soft confession reveal itself.

She stammered in confusion, "But I—I never told you about George... You *couldn't* have known—not until after we—" Wretchedness marred her beautiful face, and she breathed out, "You knew. You knew when you wrote to break off that he'd offered marriage... How?"

Wordlessly, he reached into his breast pocket and removed the old letter. The one he'd carried with him every day for the past ten years, so he could read it whenever he doubted that he'd made the right decision to sacrifice his happiness for hers.

As he held it out to her, his hand shook. He'd sworn to himself to never show this letter to her. But now fate had given them the opportunity to rewrite their future, and *everything* needed to be revealed. If they had any chance at all of finding love again, there could be no more secrets.

She hesitated to take it, as if it were a snake ready to strike.

Then she snatched it from him. Her shaking hands held it up to the light of the carriage lamp. As she read, another tear slipped free. When she finished, she crushed it in her fist and pressed it against her breast. Her slender shoulders rose and fell with each gasping breath she took to steady herself.

"Damn you." Her eyes burned with a fire that stole his breath away. She cried out, raging at him, "Damn you both!"

"We wanted only the best for you, and the best I could do was let you go." He deserved every daggerlike accusation that she leveled at him for keeping this secret, but even now, while hating that he'd ever had to make that choice, he still couldn't regret his decision. "If I had told you about that letter, you would have tried to talk me out of it."

"Yes!" Frustration pulsed from her, and her fingers gripped the edge of the bench beneath her. As if needing to restrain herself from physically striking him. "Because I loved you! Because I needed you to... to..." Her words choked off, in proof that she realized what she was saying. That her need at the time went far beyond the help that he'd been able to give.

"You needed me to let you go so that you could marry Collins," he finished soberly, a great grief swirling inside him at all that fate had stolen from them. "I knew you'd have argued with me to reconsider if you'd known the truth. That you'd hate him for writing to me and would refuse to marry the man. So I had to let you think that I was a selfish bastard who had used you for his own gain, when it was the furthest thing from the truth."

"I deserved to know," she choked out, fighting back sobs. "You should have told me before now."

"And ruin your marriage by turning you against your husband? Or destroying your memory of him? Dear God, Belinda, that letter is bringing you pain even now. Think of the damage it could have done had you known before."

"I *deserved* to know," she repeated, and her pain clawed into his heart.

"For that, I am truly sorry. But I will never be sorry for wanting to make you happy, or for stepping out of the way so that Collins could give you the life you deserved. The one I never could." He reached for her hands then, unable to stop himself. He held tight, refusing to let go even as she attempted to yank her hands from his. "So you can hate me all you want to. God knows I certainly deserve it. But at least now you'll hate me for the truth."

She stopped trying to pull away. Instead, she hung her head as her tears came in a rush, no longer able to stop them.

"The truth is that I never used you. Not ten years ago, not tonight." He reached up to cup her face against his palm. "All I have ever done is love you."

An incoherent whisper of pure anguish escaped her, and his heart shattered.

Moving to sit beside her, he gently tugged her onto his lap and wrapped his arms around her. She shuddered and shook against him as she tried to come to terms with the past ten years and everything that had happened between them. But she didn't shove him away.

"I don't hate you," she whispered between sobs, her face buried against his neck. "Although you deserve it."

Relief swelled inside him, and he squeezed his eyes shut as he placed a kiss at her temple. "I know."

He prayed to God that she'd give him the chance to be chastised for that every remaining day of his life. Because it meant that every day would be spent with her.

"Deny it," he challenged gently, throwing her earlier words back at her. "Deny that you love me. Because that's what it will take to make me leave again." He reached up to caress his knuckles over her cheek. His voice cracked as he rasped out, "Because I sure as hell still love you."

She slowly pulled back. Anguish lingered in her watery gaze, along with a hesitancy to put her full faith in him, and that bothered him, enough that regret panged with each beat of his heart. But there were also the beginnings of forgiveness and understanding, and he clung desperately to those. Because he would never survive losing her a second time.

"Fate has given us another chance, and I'm not going to let it slip by without seizing it." He gently wiped away her last tear with his thumb. "I want a life with you, Belinda. I will do whatever it takes to have that."

Cupping his face between her hands, she brought her lips to his. In that kiss, he could taste her love. And her forgiveness.

She placed the crumpled letter in his hand. That letter had started all the pain and loss, and he never wanted to see it again. He turned to throw it out the window—

Flames lit the darkness. He could just see through the narrow streets that angled down toward the water the rush of people heading toward the fire and the smoke that billowed into the black sky. A sickening realization flashed through him.

"The hospital's on fire." He pounded his fist against the roof of the carriage as he shouted to the driver, "To the Royal Hospital—now!"

* * *

Belinda hurried to keep pace with Maxwell's long strides as they raced through the park and down Church Street, having left the carriage behind in the road that was jammed by traffic. They squeezed through the crowd gathering in front of the barracks, joined by the soldiers who filed out of the yard at the commotion to crane their necks to see for themselves what was happening. But the flames from one of the hospital's buildings shot up into the sky farther down the street and lit up this area of Brighton like a lamp.

They stopped in front of the hospital, and Belinda panted to catch her breath. Her chest tightened, both from the white-gray smoke filling the cobblestone street and from the terror that seized her. Her panicked eyes searched the growing crowd for the pensioners, to make certain each man was out of the building and safe. But it was impossible to find them all amid the commotion. Even in the light from the fire, she couldn't make out faces in the crowd, and the shouts that went up all around from the men and the piercing cries from the women only added to the unfolding confusion.

"Buckets!" someone shouted, and another cursed at every able-bodied man in the street to get in line to be part of the bucket brigade. "Buckets!"

Maxwell released her hand to join the effort.

"The pensioners!" Belinda grabbed his arm. "Some of them might still be inside."

He glanced over his shoulder at the building as the flames burned high into the night and blew out a determined breath. "Stay here."

He cupped her face in his hands to place a kiss to her lips, then he was gone, running toward the building. He tore off the sash of his dress uniform and dunked it into the trough to wet it through. Then he wrapped it around his head to cover his nose and mouth and raced into the burning building.

Her heart stopped. Oblivious to the commotion around her, she stared at the doorway where he'd disappeared and helplessly wrung her hands. *Dear God! Please…* She could see nothing through the windows but flickering red-orange flames. The roar of the fire and the shouts of the men were deafening, but her pounding pulse beat so hard that the rush of blood through her ears drowned out all of it. Each breath came labored, terrified… *Please God, save them. Save him… Please!*

A movement in the center upstairs window caught her attention. The outline of shoulders and a head silhouetted against the fire, hands grasping at the window casement to throw up the sash—

One of the pensioners was trapped inside.

She let out a fierce cry and pointed at the building, shouting as loudly as she could to get attention. *Anyone's* attention who could help. But amid the confusion of fighting the fire and the crowds now jamming the street no one heard her. No one else seemed to see the old man or hear his terrified cries for help.

Without thinking of her own safety, Belinda ran into the building to save him.

Heat engulfed her immediately and prickled at her skin, and she coughed as she breathed in the acrid smoke. Unable to see more than a few feet ahead, she staggered toward the main stairs in the center of the building. She'd been here so many times that she knew the place by heart. Thank God for that, because she needed to make her way up the stairs and down the hallway to the room where she'd seen the man, and in the smoke that stung her eyes and made each breath feel like an inhalation of fire, she was as good as blind.

Her fingers groped along the staircase banister as she tentatively made her way upstairs. She shook with fear, but determination surged through her veins. She didn't stop to think if what she was doing was foolish or even potentially deadly. Her concentration was on the pensioner and saving his life, the way the pensioners had saved her life all those years ago.

A spasm of coughing seized her lungs as she reached the top of the stairs, forcing her to her knees in an attempt to catch her breath. But she wouldn't stop. *Couldn't* stop. She would not let that man die!

She crawled forward on hands and knees. Her evening gown caught beneath her legs with each crawling stride until she had no choice but to yank it up to her thighs and crawl on. The cinders burned at her hands and her legs, and pain shot through her knees so badly that she cried out, only to be relieved when, a few moments later, the pain grew so intense that her knees turned numb.

"Help me!" the pensioner cried out, still clinging to the window. His voice trembled with terror and was little more than a breathy rasp, his throat raw from inhaling smoke and shouting. "Please—someone help me!"

"I'm here," she called out, then fell into another fit of coughing. Still making her way forward one determined inch at a time, she lifted her hand toward him, silently begging him to come to her, to let her lead him out of the building—

Until she saw the cane and the twisted leg and foot it supported. Her heart sank as tears of terror and grief blurred her vision.

She could barely move herself through the building. How would she ever be able to get him out, too?

But she would *not* leave him. Taking as deep a breath as she could without triggering another coughing fit, she held her breath and pushed herself up to her feet to rush across the room to him. Around them, the flames ate at the wooden beams overhead and at the walls, and the heat that had first prickled at her skin now burned. The building groaned and creaked as the fire devoured it.

She grabbed his arm and put it over her shoulder, then leaned him against her side. Slipping her arm around his waist, she held tightly to him as she began to walk toward the doorway, one agonizingly slow step after another. By the time they reached the hall, her lungs burned from holding her breath, and she fell to her knees to gasp at the air closer to the floor. The man stumbled and fell into her, but thankfully he didn't crash to the floor.

"Almost…there…" she assured him, but the distance between where they were now and the door leading out into the cool night seemed as far away as London.

Taking another deep breath, she held it as she rose to her feet and dragged the man along with her. So heavy! She staggered forward with such effort that her muscles screamed for mercy.

They reached the top of the stairs just as his damaged foot gave out, tumbling them both forward onto the floor. Exhausted and terrified, she cried out as tears streamed down her face. The helplessness overwhelmed her, and for the first time since she'd run into the building, she lost all hope of getting the man out alive.

"Belinda!" A shout broke through the roar of the fire.

"Maxwell," she choked out, unable to speak any louder. On her hands and knees, she reached a hand toward the dark form charging toward them through the black smoke.

"Here!" He shouted over his shoulder as he knelt beside her. The flames were closing in upon them, the thick layer of smoke lowering rapidly and threatening to poison what little good air hovered just above the floor. "Over here!"

His arms went around her, and she clung to him as he lifted her. With a cry, she reached back toward the old man, who lay on the floor, sobbing and coughing. But another dark form emerged from the fiery shadows. Oliver Graham grabbed up the pensioner and followed quickly after them as Maxwell ran down the stairs with her in his arms, then outside into the night.

The rush of coolness and the fresh air shocked her, and a shudder sped through her so intensely that a soft scream left her lips. The heat that had danced across her skin and burned at her lungs quenched instantly, leaving in its wake a coldness that was just as painful. Each gasping breath of cool night air that filled her lungs shivered into her, and she spasmed as she lost her breath, choking on the fresh air like a fish out of water.

She clung desperately to Maxwell as she struggled to catch back her breath, even as he carried her away from the building and eased her down onto the dew-dampened ground.

"I told you to stay put," he snapped out, but his anger was lost beneath the trembling of his hands as they smoothed over her face, then over her body… down one arm and up the other, then down her legs, checking for burns and wounds. "What the hell did you think you were doing? You could have been killed."

He pulled her to him, rocking her in his arms. He buried his face in her hair and crushed her against him so tightly that she was afraid she'd lose her breath again.

"Never again," he threatened, his voice rough with emotion. "Don't *ever* do anything like that again, do you hear me?"

Despite the fierce pounding of her heart at how close she'd come to being seriously hurt, or worse, she gave a soft laugh as she rubbed her cheek against his shoulder. Always the commanding officer, even now.

"I lost you once, Belinda. I *never* want to lose you again."

In that embrace, she felt all the love he carried for her, and she knew then that they could survive anything that fate threw at them. The fire had reminded her of what she'd known all along… that she needed Maxwell as much as she needed air to breathe.

She held tightly to him, her arms around his shoulders and her cheek pressed tightly against his. She watched over his shoulder as the building gave a loud groan, and the roof fell in, sending a shower of sparks and flames shooting into the black sky.

Yet the men who fought the fire didn't give up. She watched as the old pensioners organized the soldiers from the barracks into long lines of bucket brigades and showed them how to use shovels, pitchforks, and pickaxes to toss dirt onto the fire to keep the flames from spreading. Another group of soldiers had followed the lead of the more able-bodied pensioners and were beating at the flames with wet burlap sacks. They were working together, with the younger soldiers taking orders and learning from the pensioners.

"Maxwell," she breathed out as her heart began to pound hard and fast again, but this time with hope.

"What's wrong?" Concern thickened his voice as he turned her on his lap to cradle her in his arms. "Do you need a doctor?"

"I'm fine—better than fine. I think…" A tentative smile tugged at her lips, and she reached up to place her hand against his cheek. "I think I've found a way to save the hospital."

He grimaced. "There might not be a hospital left after this fire."

"Oh, there will be! And your academy, too." She threw her arms around his neck and hugged him with glee. "It will be perfect!"

Then she kissed him with all the love she held for him in her heart, all of her hopes and dreams for a future finally having its chance to be made real. Together.

Absolutely perfect.

CHAPTER EIGHT

"Gentlemen, thank you for waiting." Max escorted Belinda into the enlisted men's dining hall at the barracks.

In the sennight since the fire, the hospital's administrative offices had been moved to the barracks, so that the offices could be turned into temporary quarters for the pensioners. A move that Max now found fitting, given the changes that were about to occur.

The members of the hospital board climbed to their feet at Belinda's presence, but instead of sitting, she waved them all back into their places. "My apologies for our tardiness." She turned the force of her smile on Max, whose heart jumped. He prayed he never got used to this feeling. "We were waiting on a message from London with news that you might all find surprising."

That was an understatement. He was certain all the men present would be floored by the decision Palmerston had sent posthaste from the War Office, one Max had brought back himself, returning just in time for the meeting. So recently, in fact, that he still wore his dusty riding breeches and redingote, and his hair was mussed from the wind. Stopping only to change out horses, he'd made the trip in a handful of hours.

"What's going on, Thorpe?" Colonel Woodhouse called out, ignoring the duchess. He was the first to sink into his chair in front of Belinda, not bothering to hide his disdain for her.

Max bit back his anger at the man's disrespect. No matter. By tomorrow,

the colonel would be on his way out of Brighton and out of their lives…
to a new post in Africa. As General Mortimer's aide-de-camp.

He glanced at Belinda, who fought back a happy beaming. Cleaning
up after the fire and assessing the damage had kept her busy for the past
sennight while he'd been away in London, submitting a new proposal
regarding the academy. One that had her gliding through the world as if
on air.

"Plans for the academy have changed," he announced.

"I'll say they have," Pomperly interjected. Around the long table, the
men shook their heads at the damage the fire had done. "The place is
burned to the ground."

"Not burned to the ground, Your Grace," Belinda corrected. "Just one
building, one that the War Office has given us permission to rebuild as a
new dormitory for the cadets."

"You've had a change of heart, I see." Pomperly's gaze slid knowingly
to Max. As if he could see through his jacket to his breast pocket and the
special marriage license resting where the letter had once been. "Whatever
has changed your mind about the academy?"

"The fire," she answered. Joy lightened her voice. "More exactly, seeing
how the pensioners and the cadets worked together to fight it. I realized
that is what everyone needs—to be together."

Warmth grew inside Max's chest at the private meaning behind her
words, even as confused frowns greeted her from around the table.

"During the fire, the soldiers were taking orders from the pensioners,"
she continued, trying to explain the same rationale that he'd explained to
the War Office, "and the pensioners were sharing their knowledge and
experience with the soldiers. Both sides were calling upon their strengths
to work together to effectively fight the fire. Because of them, only one
building was damaged, and the main hospital was saved. If they can do
that to fight a fire, then surely they can work together to train better
soldiers."

The board members exchanged uncertain glances, then looked at Max
for further explanation.

"Therefore, instead of closing the hospital and relocating the
pensioners," he announced, "the buildings will be shared. The pensioners
and cadets will live together, so that the cadets can learn from the wealth
of experience held by the pensioners, and the pensioners—"

"Will feel needed," Belinda interjected, "and know that they haven't been forgotten by His Majesty's army."

Whispers went up from around the table as the men leaned together to share their thoughts.

"There will be separate training and sleeping areas, of course," Max clarified, "but they'll share the same common areas and take all their meals together."

"Not in separate facilities for enlisted men and officers either," Belinda added. That had been one of her stipulations for the War Office. "But all together, in one dining hall."

At that breach of tradition, the whispers turned into low grumblings.

"The officers will have enough time in encampments and forts to live separately from their men," Max put in. "When they're in training, they should learn everything they can about the men they'll be commanding, right down to how they think. What better way to do that than sharing meals and time together between duty shifts?"

That put an end to the grumblings. The men hesitated to express their thoughts about the changes, each waiting for another to speak first.

"It's for the best, for both the cadets and the pensioners," Belinda asserted. "Be assured that I would not support it if it wasn't."

The men nodded at that, knowing her reputation as a stalwart patroness of the hospital. Their resistance was softening.

"You should also know," Max announced, "that I've volunteered to remain here in Brighton to lead the establishment of this new joint facility." He didn't dare look at Belinda as he shared the news that he hadn't had time to tell her. "And to lead it into the future in my new post as its governor."

He heard her catch her breath. Her surprise crackled through the air between them like electricity.

"And I'll be serving as the liaison between the board and the governor," she added, her voice trembling from the news that he was staying right here in Brighton. With her. "To ensure that the pensioners will be treated as the heroes they are."

Max nodded. "Shall we put the new proposition to a vote, then? All those in favor of supporting a joint venture with the academy as part of the existing hospital say aye."

A round of agreement went up from the men, including Pomperly, who grudgingly voted in favor of the proposition. Then the duke stood, sketched a small bow to Belinda, and retreated from the room. Beaten.

The others stayed only long enough to congratulate Max on his new position and to wish Belinda good luck on hers.

"Governor?" Belinda repeated when they were finally alone.

"There wasn't time to tell you before the meeting. It came after I proposed our compromise to the secretary. I had nothing to do with it." He took her hand and raised it to his lips, placing an apologetic kiss to her fingertips. He wanted *no* misunderstanding between them about this. "Are you upset?"

"I'm thrilled for you." With love shining in her eyes, she laced her fingers through his. "We did it. We found a way to save both the academy and the hospital. It's over now."

"Not over." Max slipped his arms around her waist and drew her against him. "There's another compromise we need to make."

She stiffened warily. "Which is?"

"Since we'll both be working closely together to run this joint venture, I suggest another joint venture. Marriage." He caressed his thumb over her bottom lip when she stared at him, wide-eyed and openmouthed. "Seems to me the perfect way to make our jobs easier."

Her eyes sparkled as she returned his teasing. "Undoubtedly. It would save a lot of time waiting around for paperwork and messages if we could just pass them back and forth to each other across the breakfast table."

"Or just deliver them in person." He nuzzled his mouth against her ear. "In bed."

She laughed and hugged him tightly.

"Marry me, Belinda," he murmured, all teasing now gone. "Just as soon as we can."

"Yes." She threw her arms around his neck. "Oh yes!"

He grabbed her and twirled her in a circle, and she laughed with happiness. When he lowered her to the ground, he followed after with a kiss, one into which he tried to pour his heart and soul, all his love for her... all their hope for their new future.

"You should know, however," he warned when he finally shifted away, "that there is one thing about which I will never compromise."

When she imperiously arched a brow in quick challenge, he thrilled to think how wonderful his life was going to be with this fiery woman. "Oh?"

"How much I love you."

Then he lowered his head and kissed her again.

AUTHOR'S NOTE

Although the Royal Hospital Brighton and its conversion into an academy is a fictionalized event for this novel—and so is the fire that ultimately joins its two missions—it is based on real places and events.

The hospital itself is modeled on the Royal Hospital Greenwich, which served as a home for pensioners, beginning in 1692—taking its name from the original sense of hospital as a place for helping those in need, although it did have an infirmary on its grounds that helped the wounded and ill. Located in buildings designed by Christopher Wren, the hospital received oversight from a board of governors until 1873, when it changed from being a pensioners' home to the Royal Naval College. It trained men and women until it closed in 1998.

The fire is also based on real events at another royal hospital. On New Year's Day, 1872, the Royal Sussex County Hospital caught fire. It was saved when volunteer firemen and a detachment of the 19th Hussars worked together to save the building. The hospital has been expanded and renovated many times over the years, taking it from a 19th century hospital to a modern facility with cutting-edge technology and services. Its mission continues today.

Greetings! I hoped you enjoyed spending time with Belinda and Max. There's just something wonderful about a man who's dedicated to both his country and to his true love, isn't there? In my next novel, **HOW THE EARL ENTICES**, the hero Ross Carlisle (yes, one of *those* Carlisles!) isn't in uniform, but he's just as dedicated to serving England and just as blindsided by love. Find out what happens when treason, secret identities, and romance mix! Coming this September.

If you want more dashing heroes and strong women, then you should check out **AS THE DEVIL DARES**, which released in March. Robert Carlisle has met his match in the woman called the Hellion. When he's given a partnership in her father's company—*if* he can find her husband by season's end—it proves to be the biggest challenge of his life... because Mariah Winslow has ideas of her own about who should get the partnership. (Enjoy the special preview below!)

Haven't met the Carlisles yet? Then are you in for a treat! The three overly protective brothers from **HOW I MARRIED A MARQUESS** (a RITA Award finalist!) have gone from being the scourge of Mayfair to the heroes of the *ton*. When they meet three very special women, they've met their matches—in more ways than one. (A sneak glimpse into Book 1 in the series, **IF THE DUKE DEMANDS,** follows below).

If you want to stay in touch and keep up with my latest releases, best contests, exclusive content, and more (including all those pictures of the roses from my garden—I cannot help myself!), be sure to sign up for my **newsletter** by visiting http://bit.ly/2m7zWF0. You can also follow me on **Bookbub** (http://ow.ly/QznJ30c1qUn) where you'll receive news of all my releases and on my **social media sites.** Visit https://www.annaharringtonbooks.com/follow to learn more.

Happy reading!
Anna

* * *

Enjoy this special except of

AS THE DEVIL DARES

by Anna Harrington, Book #3 in the Capturing the Carlisles series:

Lord Robert Carlisle never backs down from a dare. But finding a husband for scandalous Mariah Winslow is one challenge he instantly regrets accepting. Robert will have to use every trick in the book to marry off the woman known as the Hellion, no matter how stunningly beautiful she is. Mariah Winslow has no intention of being a pawn in Lord Robert's game. She knows he only agreed to play matchmaker to secure a partnership in her father's shipping company, a partnership that's rightfully hers. Battle lines are drawn, and she won't surrender—no matter how tempting and irresistible she finds him.

"Mariah." Robert smiled against her cheek, and a stab of defeat pierced her. So Carlisle thought he'd won, did he?

Well, she'd prove to him that it would take more than a kiss to convince her to surrender.

When he stepped back, Mariah advanced.

She wrapped her arms around his shoulders and delved her fingertips through the golden curls at his nape, then pressed her body so tightly against his front that his heart slammed furiously against her chest. When she brushed her hips against his, a low

groan tore from the back of his throat.

Emboldened, she brazenly kissed him, and when he hesitated, stunned, she slipped her tongue between his lips the way he'd done to her.

That was enough to snap him out of his reverie.

He grabbed her shoulders and demanded in a raspy voice, "What the hell do you think you're doing?"

Despite the racing of her heart, she forced a shrug of her shoulders. As if it

were the most obvious thing in the world. "Kissing you."

Then she pressed against him again, her lips making fleeting contact with

his before he set her away. An angry scowl hardened his face.

"Don't you want me to?" she prompted as innocently as possible.

Something dark and heated flickered in his eyes, and she thrilled at gaining the upper hand. Hiding her own quaking she leaned toward him as far as his restraining hands would allow.

She purred huskily, "Surely the notorious Robert Carlisle knows what to do with a woman who wants to kiss him."

Despite gritting his teeth, his gaze fell longingly to her mouth, and for a moment, she thought he might just kiss her senseless again. And if he did, she wasn't certain that she could withstand it this time without falling completely apart in his arms.

"Don't tease me, Mariah," he warned in a murmur. "You're playing with fire."

"Am I?" Pretending that he hadn't affected her, even as that tingling heat still throbbed achingly, she sadly shook her head. "Well, I certainly hope the other gentlemen I'll meet this season are better at this than you."

She slipped away before he could reach for her again. Or she for him. "Or I'll be too bored to consider marrying any of them."

He stared at her coolly as he wiped his mouth with the back of his hand. "You *will* be married by season's end, I promise you."

He took her arm and pulled her toward the door. He flung it open and led her into the hall so quickly that she struggled to keep up with his determined strides. Anger radiated from him as he led her out to the carriage waiting in the street.

He placed her inside the carriage. But when she yanked her arm away, it wasn't relief she felt but an inexplicable sense of loss. For one maddening moment, she wanted to blurt out an apology, to beg him to crawl inside the compartment with her and keep kissing her just as he'd done before, all the way home to her doorstep.

But the devil inside her couldn't help one last parting jab, and she sniffed with mock disappointment, "If I'm going to be forced to give my first waltz to such a boorish man, I certainly hope you're far better at dancing."

He rose up onto the step and leaned inside, bringing himself close. "Don't

you worry, minx," he assured her in a husky voice that twined down her spine. "When it comes to having a woman in my arms, I do *everything* well."

Her breath strangled in her throat. Leaving her to gape at him in stunned mortification at her own heated reaction to the beastliness in him, he closed the door, then ordered the coachman to drive off.

The carriage rolled forward, and she slumped against the squabs. A curse left her lips at him, followed immediately by several more at herself.

They'd fought their second battle, yet for the life of her she couldn't have said which of them had emerged the victor.

* * *

A special glimpse of

IF THE DUKE DEMANDS

by Anna Harrington, Book #1 in the Capturing the Carlisles series:

Miranda Hodgkins has only ever wanted one thing: to marry Robert Carlisle. And she simply can't wait a moment longer. During a masquerade ball, Miranda boldly sneaks into his bedchamber with seduction on her mind. But when the masks come off, she's horrified to find herself face-to-face with Sebastian, Duke of Trent—Robert's formidable older brother. Sebastian offers her a deal to avoid scandal: he'll help her win his brother's heart if she'll find him the perfect wife. But their simple negotiation spirals out of control. For the longer Sebastian tries to make a match for Miranda, the more he wants to keep her all to himself.

Sebastian nuzzled his mouth against her ear.

Miranda gasped. That, oh, *that* was clearly not an accidental brush of whispering lips! He'd meant to caress her, and the warm longing it sent spiraling through her nearly undid her. Drawing a deep breath as she threw all caution and sense to the wind, she tilted her head to give him access to her neck, unable to deny the temptation of having his mouth on her.

With a pleased smile against her ear, he murmured, "What is it about my brother that draws you so?"

The tip of his tongue traced the outer curl of her ear. She shuddered at the delicious sensation, and his hand pressed tighter against her belly to keep her still in his arms.

The confusion inside her gave way to a tingling warmth that ached low in her belly. With one little lick, Sebastian had set her blood humming, making her body shiver and her thighs clench the way he had that night in his bedroom when she thought he was Robert. She knew who was kissing her this time, yet knowing he was the wrong Carlisle brother made no difference to the heat rising through her traitorous body. She should step away—this was *Sebastian*, for heaven's sake, and the most wrong man in the world for her, save for the king himself—but she simply couldn't make herself leave the circle of his strong arms.

"Robert is masculine," she breathed, her words barely audible above the aria swirling around them.

"Most men are," he answered, dancing kisses down the side of her neck.

When he placed his mouth against that patch of bare skin where her neck curved into her shoulder, a hot throbbing sprang up between her thighs. She bit her lip to keep back a soft whimper.

"He's handsome," she forced out, hoping he couldn't hear the nervous trembling that crept into her voice.

"Hmm." His hand on her hip drifted upward along the side of her body, lightly tracing across her ribs. She trembled achingly when his fingers grazed the side swell of her breast. "We're brothers. We look alike."

Oh, that was *definitely* jealousy! But her kiss-fogged brain couldn't sort through the confusion to discern why he'd be jealous of Robert. Especially when his hand caressed once more along the side of her breast.

"Not so much alike," she countered, although she'd always thought Sebastian would be more handsome if he wasn't always so serious and brooding. If he did more spontaneous and unexpected things…like licking a woman on her nape at an opera. *Oh my.* She shivered at the audacity of his mouth and at the heat it sent slithering down her spine.

"Very nearly identical," he murmured as his hand roamed up to trace his fingers along the neckline of her gown. Completely unexpected yet wantonly thrilling, the caress sent her heart somersaulting just inches from his fingertips.

"He's exciting…a risk-taker…" Her voice was a breathless hum despite knowing that in his rivalry with his brother he didn't want to touch her as much as he wanted to touch her before Robert did. At that moment, though, with his fingertips lightly brushing over the top swells of her breasts, she simply didn't care. At least not enough to make him stop. "He's thrilling."

When his fingertips traced slow circles against the inner curves of her breasts, she was powerless against the soft whimper that fell from her lips.

"Lots of men are thrilling." He smiled wickedly against her neck at the reaction his seeking fingers elicited from her. "I'm thrilling."

"*You?*" She gave a throaty laugh of surprise. "Sebastian, you're the most reserved, restrained man I—"

In one fluid motion, he turned her in his arms and pushed her back against the set wall, his mouth swooping down to swallow her words as he kissed her into silence. Her hands clenched into the hard muscles of his shoulders, and she stiffened beneath the startling onslaught of his lips, of his hips pushing into hers, all of him demanding possession of the kiss. And of her.

* * *

Also by Anna Harrington

How the Earl Entices
As the Devil Dares
When the Scoundrel Sins
If the Duke Demands
A Match Made in Heather
Once a Scoundrel
How I Married a Marquess
Along Came a Rogue
Dukes are Forever

Visit https://www.annaharringtonbooks.com/

Made in the USA
Middletown, DE
14 September 2018